DogPeople

Merry McInerney-Whiteford

A Tom Doherty **New York**

Associates Book

This is a work of fiction. All the characters and events portrayed in this novel are either fictitious or are used fictitiously.

DOG PEOPLE

Copyright © 1998 by Merry McInerney-Whiteford

"Rainy Day Women #12 & 35" by Bob Dylan.
Copyright © 1966 by Dwarf Music. All rights reserved.
International copyright secured.
Reprinted by permission.

Lines from *Are You My Mother?* by P. D. Eastman reprinted by permission.

This book is printed on acid-free paper.

A Forge Book
Published by Tom Doherty Associates, Inc.
175 Fifth Avenue
New York, NY 10010

Forge® is a registered trademark of Tom Doherty Associates, Inc.

Design by Judith Stagnitto Abbate

Library of Congress Cataloging-in-Publication Data

McInerney-Whiteford, Merry.
    Dog people / Merry McInerney-Whiteford.—1st ed.
        p.   cm.
    "A Tom Doherty Associates book."
    ISBN 0-312-85699-7 (alk. paper)
    I. Title.
    PS3563.C36945D64   1998
    813'.54—dc21   98-11955
                                                CIP

First Edition: June 1998

Printed in the United States of America

0   9   8   7   6   5   4   3   2   1

For Neil

Contents

With gratitude and abiding love for my childhood friends:
Suki Bullens, Jackie Kelly, April Metzger, Laura Stallard,
Paul Hyde, Joe Iarocci, Primo Lombardi, Curt Metzger,
and most especially Beth Pedicini

DogPeople

ChapterOne

Family Portrait: Dog People

When I was a child, I felt things moved in circles and held together in circles. Birth—the shape of an egg and my mother's belly when it was full with my sister Franny, the curve of a nipple, the tender spot on a baby's head—seemed crucially to involve circles. Death, too: "Ashes to ashes, dust to dust," they said at my grandmother's funeral, laid wreathes with black bows upon her grave. And everything that came in between seemed to come in circles. Arcs connected sunrise to sunset to sunrise. The hands of a clock, the dial on the phone, the knob on the television set—these all moved in circles. And all important holes like drains and spouts, pupils and nostrils and ear holes, were circular. Everything in motion—the wheels on my bike, the smoke from my mother's cigarette; everything at rest—the rings in the trunks of the trees around my house, the halo on a painted angel; everything essential—the golden bands on my parents' fingers—had to do with circles.

Like planets, Dad and Cat and Franny and I seemed to revolve around my mother, who was the eye, the center, the first and final cause of my family. We moved around her and somehow she drew us close and held us all together. She provided standards for truth. She determined rules of conduct. She set the mood. She called the tune. She made lists and schedules, told us what we had to do, what we couldn't do, what we had done wrong, what we should have done better. These she called the *Work Schedule,* the *Prohibited* list, the *Demerit* list, and the *Improvement Needed* list, and she taped them to the refrigerator door where they couldn't be missed. Each day, we were responsible for reading the lists. A neglected chore meant an entry on the Demerit list and five demerits meant a spanking. And my mother was serious about this.

Suki was my best friend and her mother always used to say, "Wait till your father gets home," but by that time everything would have cooled down and Suki would get a simple scolding or maybe no dessert—it was even possible that Mrs. Domandi would have completely forgotten to mention it to Mr. Domandi. But my mother always did things *now*—she couldn't have waited for my father to get home—and though I was almost too old for spankings and Cat really was, my mother was a spanker, but she only used her bare hand. My father was a spanker, too, but he used belts or Ping-Pong paddles or any other object that was ready to hand when the need arose: an extension cord, a hairbrush, a jump rope, a shoe, once even a loaf of French bread until my sister Cat's hair was full of crumbs and chunks of bread and the loaf had been beaten down to the size of a potato and my father tossed it in the sink where it became a leftover to be fed to the chickens. Even though I was becoming a woman and Cat really was one, my parents still made us drop our pants, and unless they couldn't wait, they'd holler for the other girls to come watch when one got a spanking so we would all learn something, they said—and they were right, we did learn something, though I'm not sure what we learned was what they wanted us to learn. Cat once put it to me in words, one night after I'd gotten smacked in the face with a hairbrush for saying Nixon was a dink.

"They don't mind hitting you," Cat said. "If you don't want to get hit, you have to get along with them, you have to agree with them."

"What if I think they're wrong?"

Cat looked at me like I was stupid. "It doesn't matter what *you* think."

She was right and it was good advice and it always worked, whenever I remembered it. Funny, Cat seemed to forget it a lot, too.

Once Cat and I were fighting over something—a book, snacks, a game. We were hitting each other and hollering and my mother ran in and started yelling at us and then my father tore into the room with his belt in his hand and he began whipping us with it, hollering, "How many times do I have to tell you two to keep your hands to yourselves?" The belt burned on my bare skin, on my forearms and face and neck. Suddenly, my mother pushed him aside—she was smiling and she repeated to him what he'd just said and he smiled, too. Then they laughed together and left the room and though I never saw the humor in this, I was glad, too.

My mother was very ordered, kept everything running smoothly, she said, and if it weren't for her, the family would fall apart. And because I couldn't yet conceive that my mother or father could be mistaken about important things, complicated mysterious grown-up things involving words and concepts I couldn't yet wrap my lips or mind around, I really believed this until the spring of the year I turned twelve.

This was the time I started getting hips and curly hair in dark places, when secrets were forced upon me and I first became aware of some of the many I had somehow already been sworn to keep. Franny was five then and Cat was fifteen, a real teenager, and she knew about rock and roll, drinking beer, and French kissing (which could not make you pregnant, she insisted, no matter what Danny Dawes said). Cat had already smoked cigarettes and played quarters and once even drove a car. She wore a bra and had had her period for two years and she was trusted to care for other people's kids until late at night, so I suppose my mother thought she was old enough to be left in charge of the house and me and Franny while she went to work three days a week in a cluttered and smelly antique store in Ipswich called *Old Stuff.*

This was my mother's first job, ever. None of the other mothers worked—except for Lydia and Perry Cohen's mother, Rachel, my mom's best friend, who was a waitress part-time in a coffee shop in Beverly called *The Daily Grind,* but that was only because Mr. Cohen had died and left them poorer than he'd kept them, which was poor *indeed,* my father said, so they needed the money. Billy Halliday's mom used to work and she would have been working now, too, they were *that* poor, but her husband wouldn't let her because of all their kids, I guessed, so they just lived in a crummy old shack down by the railroad tracks near the Catholic church, where my dad had grown up but where nobody else lived anymore.

Though my parents were always saying how poor we were, I didn't really believe it because we lived on twenty-five acres of meadows and woods in one of the largest houses in Salem with two staircases (not counting the ones to the attic and the cellar), a three-car garage, eight fireplaces, and more gables than that house downtown that people paid money to go inside, so I wasn't sure then why my mother had that job though she called it her *salvation* and said how happy she was to finally have something that really mattered to her.

At Old Stuff, Mom would sit on a rickety wooden stool and read books, watch television, do crossword puzzles, and talk on the telephone. Sometimes someone would want to buy something and she would write up a receipt and thank them. She made antique dealer friends. She went out with them at night. One friend called *Janie* had brown hair as short as Dad's, a voice that scratched like an old needle on a dusty record, and an eye that seemed to drift in its socket independently of the other—Cat called it a cheating eye— so that sometimes though Janie was facing Mom when you entered the room, she would also be looking at you. Often, Janie or another woman, an older woman with horn-rimmed glasses and long gray hair named *Tilly* would stop by the house to pick Mom up and I would crouch at the top of the front stairs and eavesdrop to try to find out why Mom preferred their company to ours, why she didn't want to take us out, to Reynold's for a frappe or maybe to a movie in Peabody, though Mom went out with Tilly or Janie or her other new friends every chance she got, whenever she wasn't busy with Rachel Cohen. Rachel Cohen was Mom's best friend but she was too poor to go out nights.

If my mother was busy with something when Janie arrived, I would go downstairs and say hi and Janie would say hi and look at me standing there and one corner of her mouth would twitch and she would say something like, "Isn't there somethin' you could go do for your mother? Some laundry or somethin'?" Then she would go into the kitchen and pour herself a drink and sit at the kitchen table and wait, flipping through a magazine and watching me standing in the doorway watching her. Mom's new friends were loud— they spoke loudly and laughed in loud bursts—and they even swore and all of this seemed to thrill my mother, it made her giggle and her face glow, though she'd have killed us for acting that way. Maybe my mother was so fond of her new friends because they liked to drink, too. My father didn't drink as much as my mother, only three or four cocktails and only at night; Rachel Cohen seemed too busy to come by and drink with her much these days; and, of course, we didn't drink at all, except for Cat who, as I said, had played quarters. Cat had also been to what she called *a kegger* and twice she had come home drunk but my mother and father didn't know any of this.

If we were awake when my mother got home, she would either yell at us—"What are *you* doing up?"—or she would take us in her arms, me and Cat and Franny at the same time, and she would kiss us all and say, "Oh, my babies! My *angel* babies!" and she would hurry us to her bed and tuck us under her arms and sing us songs about juicy lamb chops or the pronking goat and no matter how red her eyes, no matter how she talked or how strong and sharp the smell of her breath, you'd elbow and wriggle and strain to be closest to her body, to be closest to her heart where you would be safe.

At the dinner table, Mom started saying things like, "It's my turn to do my own thing," as if someone had said it wasn't, and she called her job a *career*. Before my mother began working at Old Stuff, Cat and I would get home from school and often find her there in the kitchen wearing her apron with the tiny violets on it, taking chocolate chip cookies right from the oven, pouring frosty glasses of milk, humming a song from a Broadway musical and the house would be warm and sweet. Cat might stop in the dining room, drop her book bag, close her eyes, and just listen and smell, so I would, too. Mom might sit with us at the kitchen table and listen to what we did in school and look at our papers and tests with shiny stars on them and maybe tape one on the fridge and hear about how nasty this teacher was and how this girl put gum in that boy's hair and so on. But now most often we would walk into a cold, dark, and silent house that didn't smell like anything and Cat and I would search it before snacks.

In the front hall, Cat would throw open the door to the closet and then we would step carefully into the dining room. We would check the basement, the downstairs bathrooms, the kitchen, the living room; upstairs, each bathroom, each closet, under each bed, the entire attic. We would open every door. We would turn on every light. All this time, Cat would talk loudly in what she thought of as a man's voice and I would try to respond in a woman's since there was no way to move about our house undetected, the stairs and door hinges and floor boards being so old, creaking peevishly when disturbed, like old people. By the time Mrs. Wyman brought Franny back from the kindergarten she ran in her home, Cat and I would be settled in and the house would be brightly lit and safe. These days if my mother happened to be home when we got off the bus, she was usually in the kitchen with Janie or Tilly or Rachel Cohen, drinking from a rocks glass or her blue cup, and we would have to stay out and there would be no snacks.

One night the previous winter, Dad said, "I want you *home,* where a wife should be."

When my mother said, "Goddamn it! I'm *entitled* to this goddamn time for myself!" my father pounded his fist on the dinner table and some of everybody's drink spilled onto the cloth, and the silverware and glasses jingled.

Cat and I stared at our plates and kept chewing but Franny slid under the table and began to whimper. Dad leaned forward with a furious face, his eyes too wide, his mouth tight, a vein sticking out at his temple like a small snake under his skin, the muscles in his neck bulging, his whole body trembling—and Mom took in a breath to speak and suddenly her eyes were huge and she looked as if she were screaming and she was clutching her throat and her mouth was open and her face was turning red. Then she sprang back from the table and ran out the front door and there was Dad, grabbing his steak knife, running after her and I thought, *He's going to kill her,* and Franny was crying and Cat was running to the door and I started screaming, *"No! No!"* Then everything was quiet except for Franny's sobbing. Finally, Cat came back to the dining room and said, "It's okay." And together, with their arms around each other, Mom and Dad were standing in the doorway and Dad was holding the knife with a chunk of meat on the end of it. Mom said, "It's okay, kids," and a little trickle of blood spilled over her lip. Franny screamed and Mom went to the bathroom to wipe it off. Then we all sat down and finished our dinners.

That's the way things were then and though it never happened, it was as if we had all agreed at some point that we would never talk about it, about the explosive fights and the dark things that hovered around us, waiting to swoop down and make every-

thing wrong—make my mother suddenly yell or run from the room
or drive off into the night, make my father grab for something—a
bottle, a knife, a fistful of my mother's hair—panicked, desperate to
take control somehow. Later, Dad would drop his head to his hands
and not speak for the longest time and much later, deep in the
night, he would creep into our rooms looking for something he said
he'd lost and he'd be weeping and everything would feel out of
place and disconnected and loose.

I never questioned that other families lived with the same private violence and by the same uneasy silence as mine and still I felt
there was something different about my family, something Cat and
I never talked about, something I couldn't even form a picture of,
that might have had to do with how far away we were from other
people. We had had Gramma Hattie, my mother's mother, and we
had seen her on Sunday afternoons and during vacations and holidays but now she was dead. We had no aunts or uncles, so we had
no cousins, and our few second and third cousins had either died or
moved away to New York or California. We lived at the dead end
of a dead end road which my mother called a *cul de sac,* though the
sign where you turned onto it simply said *No Outlet.* The road
stopped directly in front of our house at the top of the driveway but
a thin path cut into the woods so you could keep going if you were
walking or on your bike. Only once did Cat and I go down that
path—it led to Route 62, and Mom and Dad said it was dangerous,
said if they ever found out we had gone down it, they would blister our bottoms—but we never wanted to go back since there wasn't
really anything to do there, so exposed by the side of Route 62, and
we had meadows with tall grass and a deep woods and private places
to play.

We had more land than any other family in town, twenty-five
acres including the ten Dad had lost to Manny Thompkins in a
poker game in March of this year, the year I'm talking about now,
1968, the year I turned twelve. Dad said the ten acres was ours still,
really, it was just a matter of time till Manny put it up in a game and
Dad won it back. But Mom said Manny Thompkins was in no

hurry to give up the land—he didn't get to be owner of the Witch City Auto Body and Salem's chief of police by acting in haste, which probably helped to explain why, in his forties, he had no children, no wife, no fiancée. Manny was a man who played it safe, someone who liked to take risks, but the smallest risks possible, because more than anything, Manny Thompkins liked to win. Now he had a deal cooking with John Horton at Taylor & Sons Real Estate, who had already purchased much of the available wooded land in Salem. Horton was developing a thirty-acre plot by Suki's and he was looking to buy more. As a consolation to my father, or maybe to taunt him, Manny Thompkins said my dad could buy back the land anytime—anytime before the end of April, that is. For a thousand dollars an acre, that is.

From our property, you couldn't even see another house and we didn't know most of the people you would have called *neighbors,* the people whose properties were contiguous with the boundaries of our land. In fact, my parents didn't seem to know anyone much except the Cohens, Mom's antique dealer friends, Dad's poker buddies, and the people they had over for cocktail parties. Cat and I would usually have to stay upstairs then, so we never knew who most of these people were anyway. All I know is they sure weren't Suki's parents, because Suki's parents were Italian and my parents didn't like Italian.

Or maybe they didn't mind Italian as much as they minded the Catholic that went with it. My father seemed to find Italian all by itself comical and whenever we had spaghetti, he made fun of the accent, waved his arms, told Cat and Franny and me, "You eat-a you suppa." The Catholic part was another matter. My father seemed genuinely disgusted by Catholics, by holy communion, and by the Virgin Mary, and more than once I'd heard him say, *"Hail Mary, full of grace, She fell down and broke her face."*

This was 1968. This was the year of the Tet offensive and the beginning of the end of the illusion of American world hegemony; the year Martin Luther King and Robert Kennedy were murdered and with them the dreams of so many. This was the year of the frenzied, violent Democratic National Convention; a year of protests and love-ins and demonstrations, drugs and riots. It was a time of chaos and defiance and a yearning for sanity, a promiscuous unleashing of primal emotion and a longing to regain innocence lost. That's what I would read about it years later, but at the time, all of this belonged to Boston and other big cities, to the rest of the world. To us, these events were only headlines on quickly discarded newspapers or interruptions of our TV shows or reasons for a moment of silence during school. At most, they reverberated into our world only indirectly and then only briefly: Harold Lane's cousin from Portsmouth was killed in Vietnam and Harold got to miss two days' school to go to the funeral, got about two days' bragging out of it afterward, boasting about the huge American flag draped over the coffin, about the soldier in white gloves shooting a rifle at the sky, another blowing taps from a horn, about the casket's being closed because his cousin was "shot to shit," Harold said, "just a stinking pile of meat and teeth and bones," till kids wearied of the story because they ran out of questions Harold was able to answer.

In 1968, our fathers only wore jeans to do yard work and called them *dungarees*; they wore suit and tie to their offices and out to cocktail parties. They drove sedans, slapped cologne on their clean-shaves, went to the barber for their weekly trim. Our mothers baked cookies, bought groceries, cleaned house, played bridge, drove station wagons, wore lipstick and skirts to their knees, served their husbands, corrected their children, and swore to each other that this was how they liked it while they drank too much and popped Valium for their nerves. In school, girls couldn't wear pants and their skirts had to pass hem check, touching the floor when they kneeled, or mothers would be summoned; they took home ec, learned to measure Crisco in a cup of water, to bake a cake from a mix, to stitch a hand towel. Boys made small, useful objects like ashtrays and spice racks in shop; they were taken aside by teachers, given interesting books to read, permission to work on special science projects. By the end of junior high, the dangerous element began to emerge: bad boys slouched around in rumpled clothes, reeking of tobacco, their hair a frenzy of knots; bad girls used bleach, wore eyeliner and fishnets and Kleenex in their bras. Both smoked in the bathroom, skipped classes, took swigs from flasks filled with their parents' booze. They shoplifted; they got bad grades; they went all the way. Cat said that some even smoked marijuana, called it *pot*. They were the closest we ever came to the hippies but everyone called them *hoods*. My favorite hood was Billy Halliday.

Billy Halliday was one of thirteen or fourteen children who lived in a tiny house by the Salem depot. When we were younger, Billy Halliday was an absolute wiseass, jokey and snide and needlingly sadistic, never on the level, always in trouble and often in the principal's office. He stole all the toilet paper from the Boys' Room, pulled fire alarms, put tacks on teachers' chairs, and most teachers punished him for it but none as cruelly as Mr. Jones. One day in fourth grade, Billy Halliday put a whoopie cushion on Mr. Jones's chair and a puddle of vinyl vomit on his desk, and that combination seemed to send Mr. Jones right over the edge: he grew stiff and tall and his face turned red and he swore out loud, he said, "Goddamn it" without even moving his jaws. Then Mr. Jones walked over to Billy Halliday's desk and ordered him to stand. He told Billy Halliday he was a stupid little guttersnipe and slapped his face. When Billy Halliday began to weep, Mr. Jones called him a girl and he gathered Billy's bangs in a pony tail at the front of his head and he tied a red bow around it and made Billy wear it like that the entire day. No one laughed, none of us would even look at Billy Halliday, and we all hated Mr. Jones, who didn't understand what we all knew, that Billy Halliday had a terrible life, that, though he never said so, his black eyes and broken bones did not come from the honest impact of a schoolboy's fists in a fair fight, but were earned at home at the wrong end of his stepfather's temper. As we grew older, Billy Halliday became quiet and subdued and began to reek of cigarettes and liquor.

Billy Halliday always acted cool around other kids—tough, hard, and detached—but when I talked with him alone, he would tell me about the stories he said I must read: "The Tell-Tale Heart," "A Dog's Life," *Dr. Jekyll and Mr. Hyde.* And he'd recite funny little limericks and poems I'd never heard before, like this:

> There was a young man from Japan
> Whose limericks never would scan;
>> When they said it was so,
>> He replied, "Yes, I know,
> But I always try to get as many words into the last line as
> ever I possibly can."

And, one of his favorites,

> Billy, in one of his nice new sashes,
> Fell in the fire and was burned to ashes;
> Now, although the room grows chilly,
> I haven't the heart to poke poor Billy.

Billy Halliday knew serious poems, too, about love and death and war, poems by W. H. Auden and John Donne and W. B. Yeats. He'd learned them from his sister, who took a literature course at the community college, but none of the teachers and none of the kids knew this, except me—I'd seen the *Little Treasury of Modern Poetry* in his desk and he agreed to talk with me about it, about poetry, if I promised not to tell.

Nineteen sixty-eight was two years after Gramma Hattie died and the world had first changed shape for me. Unlike anyone I have known, my gramma had a world vision: she saw clean divisions between right and wrong, good and evil, truth and falsehood. She never told us what we should do or what sort of people we should be—she told us stories and myths that had the effect of making us want to choose a certain path, the path she wanted us to choose, I'm sure. My gramma was a wealthy woman who had never wanted for material things. When he died, my gramma's father left his large and sensible savings all to her, his only remaining child. Grampa Percy, my mother's father, had been a doctor and when he died, when Mom was just a little girl, he also left money for Gramma Hattie so she was able to stay in her house, now our house, on Wilde Road, and later, when Mom was grown, to move to the smaller, more elegant, federal house on Chestnut Street with hired help. When Gramma Hattie died in 1966, my mother had her house shut down—the cabinets and refrigerator cleared of food, the pipes emptied of water, the electricity turned off. We helped her cover Gramma's furniture with white sheets, roll up the rugs, secure the windows, and draw the drapes. Mom had the exterior of the house and outbuildings painted, the shrubbery trimmed and tidied, fresh gravel spread on the driveway. It was as if the house had also died and my mother was taking care of the embalming. In June of 1966, my mother locked the door and left Gramma Hattie's house and never went back. Once a week, my father stopped by to check up on the house and make sure there was no vandalism and last year, when the house finally sold, it was he who turned over the keys and did a final walk-through with the Realtor.

My mother said that Gramma Hattie was what you would call *a real lady.* Gramma didn't drink, except sometimes a glass of wine on holidays, and she would use words like *perhaps* instead of *maybe,* a lady's words; she said *wealthy* instead of *rich, portly* instead of *fat, simple* instead of *stupid.* Gramma Hattie thought smoking was for chimneys and drugs were for illness, and in her whole lifetime, my mother had never heard her mother swear. Though Gramma Hattie said she didn't like to cook or sew, she would bake cookies with Cat and me and knit us wool sweaters with reindeer and snowflakes and silver buttons. Gramma spent most of her time reading, visiting museums, and having tea with her friends, and my mother said these were the occupations and diversions of a true lady.

My gramma never wore pants—my mother couldn't even get

her to try pantyhose—and she kept her hair as she had always kept it, as she had worn it in the pictures of her as a young woman: in a soft flat knot on the top of her head poofed out at the sides. Sometimes when I went to Gramma Hattie's house, she would sit at her vanity and take the crooked pins from her hair and unroll the knot into a long silky tail and I would get to shake it out and smooth it, then stroke it with a silver brush that had her initial on it. A hand mirror, a comb, and a nail file also with *M*s engraved on them—for *Mehitabel,* which was my gramma's real name—lay on her vanity in a shiny row by a bottle of perfume that made rainbows on the walls of her room in the late afternoon. I would catch the rainbows on the backs of my hands and forearms and Gramma Hattie once told me if I caught one in my palm, I would be wealthy when I grew up. The bottle was made of crystal and it had deep cuts in the sides that made it sparkle. The perfume in the bottle was called *Joy* and sometimes Gramma let me slide the damp stopper behind my ears, on my neck, along my wrists, and in the crooks of my elbows, but it never smelled the same on me as it did on my gramma. Behind the perfume, a short wide crystal jar with a silver lid held a pink, satiny powder that Gramma Hattie let me puff on our necks; the powder had a sweet, soft smell which she told me was from tuberose and sandalwood and ginger. Sometimes, Gramma let me squeeze the pale blue bulb of her atomizer and mist her brush with eau de toilette before bringing it to her hair. Carefully, I would pull the brush from the pink crown of her head down her long back all the way to her bottom. Her hair was the whitest white and the softest thing I had ever touched. I might take a handful and bring it to my face, sniff it, and rub it against my cheek. As I brushed her hair, I would catch Gramma Hattie looking at me in the mirror, smiling. Her eyes were a clear blue and even I could see that she was beautiful, though she was very old.

Gramma Hattie told me she thought the world was divided into two kinds of people: cat people and dog people. While cat people were strong and independent, dog people were weak and needy. About dog people, Gramma said that none of their principles were held deeply, they would surrender one in a minute for self-interest; they had trouble taking responsibility for their actions, located the blame for their misdeeds in people and events outside themselves. On the other hand, a cat person had unshakable moral standards and she would regard herself with a cold, hard eye though she would judge others with charity. Cat said that though Mom had probably been a cat person, Gramma thought Dad was a dog person, which made the rest of us dog people, too.

Cat resented this because she said dog people were poor people, like the Cohens, who turned off all their lights on Hallowe'en and pretended they weren't home because they couldn't afford to give out candy; who never went to church on Christmas or Easter because they didn't have white gloves, crisp hats, or shiny shoes; and who were given coupons by the state to help with their school lunches and groceries. The Cohens were the closest we had to neighbors and though we were the same age, Lydia and I hadn't been friends since we were little, which made things somewhat awkward between Mrs. Cohen and Mom and me, since Rachel and Mom were best friends. Rachel Cohen's other child, her son, Perry, was big and slow and everyone knew he was retarded. Sometimes, Mrs. Cohen would bring Perry along with Lydia to our house when she came to visit, though Perry was a boy, a moron and much older than Cat and Lydia and me. If we tried to start a game of kickball, Perry would stoop down and grab the ball when it was pitched to him and start running circles around the well house with it, even though at the beginning of the game, he would promise he wouldn't do it. Perry couldn't ride a bike, so that was out. In tag, he would always push you down when he was It, although Lydia said he really didn't mean to. Perry couldn't stand still long enough to play statues, and he was too heavy to play leapfrog with us. When we tried to take our fingerprints, hypnotize each other, become blood brothers, or hold seances, Perry Cohen would always goof things up by spilling something or sobbing or farting loudly. Perry Cohen was enormous—taller and heavier than my father—and he had a huge pale face topped by a mat of jet black hair. And Perry

breathed funny like his nose and throat were too small and sometimes Cat called him *Snort,* but not to his face. The Cohens lived
about a half mile down the road near the sandpit and I had to pass
by there to get anywhere at all and I would see Perry out there
sometimes, raking leaves or hammering something. He would always wave and I would wave back but I would pedal faster until I
was past their place. Perry would keep waving and call after me,
"Hey, Little Strawberry!" and that gave me the creeps.

These days, in the spring of 1968, my mother
kept saying to my father, "We should have *savings.* What happened
to our *savings?*"

And my father would say, "*Savings?* With this place?" Or "Are
you *kidding?* With these kids, we're lucky if we break even."

When my mother would press, "David, what happened to the
money Mom gave us?" "What happened to our *this*-account?" or
"What happened to my *that*-bond?" my father would pound his fist
on the dining room table and say something hard and bitter and
small like, "I spent it all on myself, Molly," or "Haven't you noticed
my new sports car?" If my mother continued—and this was how I
saw it, my *mother* continuing the argument, my mother, like Cat, exposing wounds, pressing them, not letting go—if she kept asking
about the money, what happened to the money, my father would
storm to the back hall closet and grab the brown paper bag filled
with old bills and he'd empty it all onto the dinner table and say,
"Okay, Molly! You want to manage the finances, you go right ahead!
Help yourself! It's all yours, honey!" Then Mom's eyes would be full
of tears and she would apologize and we'd help her return the bills
to the paper bag while my father drove off somewhere to clear his
head.

Though we weren't really poor—poor people didn't live in
houses like ours—my parents kept saying, "We're not made of
money," "We're not the Rockefellers" and "We can't afford it." So
we never got to take a real family vacation (Mom said the times Dad

took us to Castle Bay, a gambling place full of casinos and hotels on the Jersey shore, didn't count) or to join Myopia Hunt Club or the Camelot Swim Club or to buy a snowmobile like the Taylors'. Cat wanted a canopy bed with a dust ruffle, a closet stuffed with party dresses and crinoline slips, and dolls so fine you don't even play with them. But Franny and I didn't care. I was what my mother called *cerebral* and Franny was the baby of the family, too young to really notice things.

I don't suppose our being dog people was particularly hard on my father because he had been raised that way. We had heard the story a thousand times—how Dad was an only child, the son of an actor and a housewife. His mother (Dad said Cat and I had called her *Gran* but I could never remember this, or her) had been one of five children, dirt poor. Dad's father's family was rich, owned a textile mill in Lynn, but Dad's father refused to go into business—he had a genuine artistic sensibility, Dad said, and lived a rich life of the imagination—so he was disowned as the black sheep. My great-grandfather told my grandfather, "You are dead to me," and then, for the rest of his life, treated my grandfather as if that were true. We had heard how when Dad was six, they moved from Salem to Hollywood, California, where my grandfather worked at Paramount Pictures as a stunt man. My dad got to visit the movie studios all the time and see the stars. Sometimes he'd list them for us: Gloria Swanson, Lawrence Olivier, Claudette Colbert—we didn't know their faces but their names were poetry to us. He remembered the studio parties—the Christmas parties, the Easter parties, the birthday parties—when all the celebrities would dress in their finest clothes and bring their adorable children and there would be ponies and games and piñatas filled with candy and polished coins and little presents for everyone. My grandfather was so handsome and talented that Paramount was about to give him a big contract and make him a star himself and give him a celebrity life and then my father would have been raised in luxury and so, too, would we, except that one day, my grandfather reached for something on a high shelf and accidentally dropped it on my grandmother and broke her jaw. It was some bizarre accident, a fluke. Then, for some reason my father couldn't fathom, really, it was beyond him, my grandmother divorced my grandfather—she must've thought he did it on purpose, that crazy old bat—and rather than giving him that big old contract, Paramount Pictures dismissed my grandfather and Dad never saw his father again as if my dad were dead to his father, too. After that, my grandmother moved my father back to Salem where she got a job as a short-order cook and they lived in a first-floor apartment near the Salem depot where the Catholic church now stood, "poor as peanuts." Bums would bang on their windows at night. They would eat the cheapest canned foods—soft, pureed vegetables that had turned funny colors and tasted of tin. They would take handouts by way of food and clothing from charities like Goodwill and the Salvation Army. And Gran would enter every sweepstakes, every contest, she learned of. If a canned hash company was holding a contest, they would be eating canned hash for weeks, Dad said. But my grandmother never won anything, except more canned hash— more of what she had already bought so much of to enter the contest in the first place. Somehow, Gran had put my father through college and now he was giving us better, more, than he had known. We had a lot to be thankful for, my father always said.

But my mother seemed to take it pretty badly, our having "definite financial limitations," as my father used to put it (which Cat said was just another way of saying we were poor). Like my father, Mom had no brothers or sisters (Gramma Hattie hadn't been able to conceive until her late thirties and my mother's coming-to-be was called a miracle) but my mother's parents had been wealthy. Grampa Percy came from a snobby old Salem family, originally ship captains and merchants, who'd held onto their money for generations, guarding it carefully, then passing it along to whoever came next. We never met Grampa Percy because he died when my mother was just seven years old and I think my mother always resented this, that her father had left her and never come back. Gramma Hattie's family had owned ships and she had money of her own, so when Grampa Percy died, as I said, my gramma was left a wealthy woman.

I think my gramma tried to compensate for my mother's not having a dad by giving her many lovely things when she was a child—a lot of fine clothes and leather-bound books and excellent toys. She had had frilly party dresses and shiny patent leathers in black and white; she had had her own set of the *World Book Encyclopedia,* a motorized car to drive around, a large doll house with electricity and running water, and wind-up toys that somersaulted, walked on their hands, hung by their knees, climbed ladders, drove cars, and played musical instruments.

Though Gramma Hattie never said it, I knew Cat was right in thinking Gramma believed Dad was a dog person, because whenever she came over, she would boss him around, asking him to get her a glass of juice or a cocktail napkin, asking him couldn't he help Molly out in the kitchen, didn't he think Molly deserved a nice vacation and wasn't it a pity Molly was wearing the same clothes year after year?

It seemed odd that my gramma was my mother's mother because they weren't at all alike. Gramma Hattie didn't drink or swear and she seemed to like spending time with Cat and Franny and me. When I was Franny's age, Gramma would let me sit in her lap and read books to her out loud, even though whenever I made a mistake, skipped or mispronounced or hesitated on a word, I would have to go back to the first page and start the book again. Gramma Hattie was very intelligent and she was the one who taught me how to read and play bridge, and when I was eight she even taught me about fractions and decimals and the negative numbers. Gramma Hattie had gone to Radcliffe and graduated a lifetime ago, she said. She had a soft voice, almost like a young girl's, and I never heard her raise it. Not once. Not even when she was angry.

There's so much to tell about Gramma Hattie, about Mom's family, about how they had been in Salem for a long, long time, just like Dad's family but without poverty or disgrace, about how we got to live in this house, the house my mother's family built hundreds of years ago, the house my gramma was born in. There's also much to tell about my parents, about how they met and courted and married, but I want to keep to the real story, the story of this spring of 1968.

This story begins the day after the shooting of Martin Luther King in Memphis, Tennessee, but that is not part of the story. They spoke about the murder on TV that night, the night before this story begins. They showed a picture of Reverend King with a thin moustache and a big shiny watch and his eyes downcast. They said lots of Negroes were rioting in the streets, shooting guns, setting fires, and throwing bricks at policemen. I asked my mother who the man was.

"King," Mom said. "Martin Luther King. A very fine Negro."

Franny jumped up from her place on the floor and pressed her palm onto the television screen. "That's a king?"

Cat called her stupid, told her she made a better door than a window, got up and changed the channel.

"Did you see his watch?" was all my father said.

The next day, the day this story begins, our principal, Mr. Pearson, did not ask that we observe a moment of silence in honor of this man; no flags were flown at half-mast for him in our town; and I didn't see one grown-up weep for the loss of him, so I had no way of knowing then that this was a tragic and historic moment, like when President Kennedy was killed. But then, in the spring of 1968, in my family, my school, my town, it wasn't a moment with any direct connection to the other moments of our lives, so it wasn't much of a moment at all. We didn't have any Negroes in Salem and some people had never spoken with one or even seen one in person.

I had known a Negro once, but only briefly and not well. A few summers before, when the Parkers packed up and moved to Connecticut for Mr. Parker's new job, a Negro family with three kids bought their house on Perkins Row, but the family didn't even stay till Christmas. They were the Redfords and Sally Redford was in my grade. She was the first Negro I had ever seen up close, the first Negro I had ever spoken with. On the opening day of school that fall, Sally's mother drove her, walked Sally to homeroom holding Sally's hand. Everyone stared when Mr. Jones opened the classroom door after Mrs. Redford's knock—no one knocked on classroom doors—and standing there in the hall were Sally and her mother. Kids who had already boasted that they had seen the Redfords during the summer sat quietly staring at the two dark figures until Mr. Jones regained himself, spoke softly to Mrs. Redford, smiled, put his hand on Sally's shoulder and steered her into the classroom, pushing the door closed behind him on Mrs. Redford's startled face.

Resting both hands on Sally's small shoulders as if she might otherwise make a run for it—*and who could have blamed her!*—Mr. Jones introduced Sally to us from the front of the classroom, a courtesy omitted in the case of all the other new kids that year and every other year as if Sally's difference weren't already shockingly clear. I felt as sorry for her as I had ever felt for anyone when Mr. Jones made Sally stand there at the front of the room and tell us all about herself.

"We've never had a Negro in our class," he explained.

While staring at the floor, in a soft, airy voice that seemed to want to stay in her mouth, Sally said her family had moved up from New York and she had two brothers and they lived on Perkins Row and her father worked for G.E. Aside from her being a Negro, she could have been any of us.

Sally Redford was even taller than I was, as dark as I was fair, and smart as a whip, maybe as smart as I was, maybe smarter, but no one seemed sure what to think of her or even how to judge her because she looked so different from the rest of us. Danny Dawes looked different from the rest of us, the skin between his small flat nose and upper lip was shiny and pink, bisected like a cat's by a thin, bright vein of red, and he breathed and spoke with a lot of air and liquid, but in the face of such overarching difference as presented by Sally Redford, Danny Dawes was suddenly one of us because Sally

Redford was not. To ensure her continued exclusion, and therefore his inclusion, Danny Dawes became Sally Redford's noisiest and harshest accuser, and he was probably the only person in Salem genuinely saddened by the Redfords' sudden departure in December. Danny Dawes threw spit balls and loagies at Sally Redford, called her *a nigger,* and got two other boys to join him in dry-gulching her after school one day and beat her so badly that her parents no longer permitted her to walk the streets of Salem alone. Some girls even joined Danny and his friends in tormenting Sally Redford, notably Lydia Cohen who, though she initially seemed to enjoy her new status, couldn't remain *in* for long because being *out* was what she knew, what she was used to, she had stood there for so long.

Mr. Jones's strange praise of Sally's work encouraged this view of her as fundamentally different from the rest of us: "That's very good," he said, nodding at her work on the blackboard, adding, "for a Negro."

Mr. Jones seated Sally and me next to each other, since we were far ahead of the rest of the class and had to be dealt with separately, and I examined everything about her. Sally's things were all different from mine—her shirts were made of silkier fabrics, I thought; her sweaters were cabled and had nicer buttons with interesting shapes like flowers and turtles. Sally wore red buckle-up shoes just like mine, but hers were much larger. Her book bag was purple and had long straps and exterior pockets and her initials monogrammed on it in red. But it was Sally's pencil case that got all my attention. Mine was a plain yellow hard plastic box with a sliding lid; inside, I had six yellow pencils with orange eraser tips and a white six-inch plastic ruler. But Sally Redford's pencil case was a hot-pink zippered pouch decorated with a Peter Max design of vivid yellow and purple and green flowers. Inside, she had bright pencils—red and purple and blue—but with regular lead so you could use them at school, a small pencil sharpener shaped like a man's head (you put the end of the pencil in his mouth) and, best of all, over a dozen erasers, the kind you fit on the end of the pencil after you've chewed or used up the original one. Sally's weren't the usual hat shapes in drab shades of orange and green; hers were cartoon colored and shaped like animals—cherry red cats and sky blue pigs and lime green owls! I wondered if they came from New York, too, if maybe that's where she got all her things, because I sure hadn't ever seen anything like them around here, either.

When Mr. Jones first seated us side by side at the table at the back of the room so we could do negative numbers together, I stared at Sally Redford all the time, at her rich hair twisted in three braids, thick and black as anchor chain, one gathered behind each ear, the third lying straight down the back of her neck. I marvelled at the tones of her brownness, deeper at her elbows and knuckles and knees, her palms fair by contrast, the color Cat would turn by summer's end. Though purples and hot pinks and greens made me look weak and pallid, *moribund,* my mother always said, no color could dilute the extraordinary vitality of Sally's skin. Crimson brought out the warmth in her face. Aquas made Sally's eyes seem brighter. Even white was purer, cleaner, whiter on Sally Redford. When we worked together at the back of the room, I would edge my bare arm across the table toward Sally's and I'd study the contrast between our skins: next to Sally's mine appeared to have a greyish pink hue, like one of the flowers pressed in our family Bible, like something old and dry and faded. In contrast, Sally's skin seemed to have a bluish purple tone, like a morning glory or a plum or a concord grape. Her skin and her size and her insistent hair and all the colors she could bear made Sally Redford seem so much more present and real and part of the world than I felt.

One day, Sally looked at me with narrowed eyes and said, "Quit it."

"Quit what?"

"Quit staring at me."

"I wasn't staring at you."

"Yes, you were. You were staring at me like I'm some kind of freak."

"I'm sorry. It's just that I've never seen a Negro before."

Sally said, "Yeah? Well I've seen too much of *you*," and I didn't know what to make of it but I felt small and guilty and pinched in on myself.

I didn't look at Sally Redford for a long time. First, I hated her for pushing me away and I did my math with hard strokes and thick, dark figures. At the bottom of the page, I wrote: *niggergirl*. Then, I felt heartbroken and I scribbled lightly in the margins of my paper. In my best penmanship, I wrote: *Sally, Sally Redford, Sally Ann Redford* (which was what the monogram on her book bag stood for, she said) and I sketched flowers and tear drops and hearts between the words.

I refused to look over at Sally, though, or to speak to her; she would have to come to me.

Before recess, Sally tapped my arm and when I looked at her, I saw she was offering me one of her pencils. It was purple as a crocus with a lemon-colored teddy bear eraser on top.

I laughed and took the pencil and thanked her and I went to kiss her face but suddenly Sally was stiff. When I pulled away, I saw her looking down at my paper; I saw her seeing the words I had written there. I saw her seeing *niggergirl*. I wanted to explain, but there was nothing to say. I wanted to apologize, I wanted to hurt myself for her, but I didn't want her taking that pencil back so I turned and hurried out to recess with it. After that, Sally kept her distance from me, sat at the other end of the table and before I could apologize or try to make it up to her, the Redfords had moved away.

Most kids gossiped about Sally Redford, looking for ways to explain her difference. For them, it was as if Sally's behavior or her being from New York or some other incidental fact about her had caused her to be a Negro and our acceptance of her as one of us would irrevocably compromise our whiteness—as if whiteness were some kind of good thing—and somehow, along with it, our well-being. Some kids said that Sally bit people and that her family ate cats and smelled bad. Some said the Redfords practiced voodoo and Danny Dawes insisted Mr. Redford had been in prison for murder. But I had spent time with Sally, worked side by side with her on mathematics too difficult for the other kids, and I knew that the difference between Sally and me wasn't the difference between evil and good but was precisely the difference between Suki and me—our ancestors came from different parts of the world. That was the difference.

And yet, somehow I knew it wasn't the whole difference. Being Negro (skin darker than my darkest freckle, hair like a fine grade of steel wool, pupils lost in dark irises, eyelashes curled tight as commas), dark so every pale part stood out like a bright moon in a night sky (the crescents of her fingernails, her teeth, the sclera of her eyes)—though I didn't want to think of it this way—being Negro was very different from being *us.*

I knew that the world was a different world for Sally Redford. I imagined that Salem was a difficult and dangerous town for her, with unwalkable streets and hostile people. I imagined Sally Redford was lonely. I imagined the ache in her stomach that must have come from knowing that she wasn't welcomed at Good Harbor Beach, that she wasn't invited to anybody's sleepover, that no boys around here would ever like her back. Sometimes I imagined showing her Salem, *my* Salem—*Here, this is the Citadel! Kirby's! Burying Point!*—but I could no more take Sally Redford to these places than she could bring me to the world she knew. I felt a hollowness and a kind of shame when I realized that though I could guess at what her life was like, Sally Redford lived it in a world I would never know. I would always be on the outside of that world, a pale, blank face peering in, unable to see anything but darkness.

Grown-ups talked about the Redfords, too, guessed at the Redfords' habits with regard to private matters not suitable for discussion when they themselves were the subjects, matters of religious practice, sexual appetite, and personal hygiene. Crazy beliefs and monstrous behaviors were ascribed to the Redfords and all sorts of accidents, mishaps, and petty crimes were blamed on them though there was never any evidence implicating any Redford. Still, some people said that, being Negroes, of course the Redfords knew voodoo. And of course, being Negroes, they had a different, defective conception of right and wrong. So when the Riggses' cat was set on fire on Hallowe'en and burned helplessly up at the Skeffington place, Mr. Riggs said the Redfords had done it—no one was seen running away and only Negroes are invisible in the dark. When someone broke into Kirby's Paper Store and cleaned out the register but didn't touch any of the merchandise, Manny Thompkins said it must have been the Redfords since a white person would have taken staples and cleaning supplies as well. And when, shortly after the Redfords moved in, real estate values in Salem fell, people understood that it had to do with interest rates and inflation, but they also said it had to do with the Redfords.

Nobody said much about why the Redfords moved away so suddenly, in the middle of the school year, just before Christmas, but I remember my mother and father's saying that it was probably a good thing and agreeing that the Redfords would be happier back in New York. Sally Redford never said good-bye and after she left, she never wrote me a letter or sent a note or a postcard with her address. Somehow I felt I'd done something to her, and when I thought about it I remembered I'd never returned that pencil with the teddy bear eraser. But then I realized it wasn't about my borrowing anything.

In 1968, my father was looking for ways to get rich quickly and without effort. I think he was trying to make up for being a dog person, for being a nobody who couldn't give my mother a life as gracious as her childhood. And I think he was trying to figure out how to buy back that land, my mother's land, the land he'd lost to Manny Thompkins in a poker game. My father believed in luck; he believed in long shots; he believed in complete change in the beat of a heart. My father believed there was a real probability that, if he took the proper actions right now, the *lucky* actions, his life would change completely, that maybe not tomorrow, but by this time next week he could really, actually be living in a mansion and driving a Rolls-Royce—he didn't just believe this was possible, he believed it was *closely* possible, metaphysically at hand, and he did everything he could to make it actual.

My father liked to enter lotteries and contests and sweepstakes. Once, he won a matched set of luggage at a raffle. When Cat and I were little, "B.F.," as Cat used to say (meaning Before Franny), Dad bought a metal detector that looked like an upright vacuum cleaner with a round disk on the end and sometimes he'd take us to Crane's Beach or Plum Island and while Mom and Cat and I would swim or play cards on the blanket or collect sand dollars and sea urchins and Neptune's toenails, Dad would wander way down the beach, out of sight, looking for treasures. He found a lot of tin cans and some broken, rusted tools and even some car keys, but never anything good. Then my father began to gamble. First, he just played poker with men from work every once in a while. Then Thursday night became poker night. And somewhere along the way, Friday night became poker night, too. One year Dad took the whole family to Castle Bay with his Christmas bonus. My mother was furious with him the entire time and she wouldn't leave the hotel room to go down to the casino with him though I would have given anything to go into that place that was lit up like a carnival, where people were laughing and smiling and carrying around buckets of nickels, and where you could hear a constant ringing of bells and the watery rush of coins. We never went to Castle Bay with Mom again but my father took us back twice when she was away. I liked Castle Bay because we got to get a suite and Cat and Franny and I could order room service and watch movies on TV all day. Dad never won much money, but he always said it was only a matter of time.

Lady luck, beating the house, down and dirty—these were phrases we learned from my father. It was strange: something about gambling distorted my father's thinking so that he would say things like, "I'm in for a big win—I've been losing all night," as if losing made winning more probable. When you were doing your math homework, you could find my father in the kitchen and ask him the odds of a fair penny's landing heads up on any random toss and he would tell you 1/2. But when we were strolling along the boardwalk at Castle Bay, Dad and Cat and Franny and I, Dad could bet a total stranger ten dollars that his own fair penny would land heads down after landing heads up four times in a row as if, even if the man *weren't* cheating, the probability of its doing so wasn't always exactly the same.

I don't know how much my father spent on poker games and trips to Castle Bay, but the rest of his money must have gone toward our home because it was a spacious, almost grand house, Gramma Hattie's old house, the house our family had built almost three centuries before, each generation adding on a room or updating the conveniences, making it more fashionable, shaping it to their needs and desires. Dad was always fixing it up, stripping off old paint and replacing rotten boards and tearing down whatever wasn't original, sanding, staining, shellacking, and generally restoring the house to the condition it might have been in a long time ago. Our house was built in 1673 and it was one of the oldest places in town. Everything about it was old: the tight, narrow staircase up the back hall and the tiny sloping closet underneath; the Indian shutters behind the homespun on the windows; the dirt-floored cellar where you could dig up pieces of coal; the musty outbuildings with potbellied stoves and rusted old signs on the walls. The house originally had four rooms but my gramma said that even then, it was considered grand as the rooms were large and the ceilings were high. Over the years, the house was expanded and when we moved in, my father put on his own addition: Cat's room, a family room, and a bathroom for Cat and me upstairs, and a foyer, a powder room, and the front staircase downstairs. Along the north wall of the kitchen, my father built a chimney and fireplace and along the back wall a picture window with a view of our buildings and gardens, our lawn sloping down to the main meadow and the woods rising thick and protective beyond. And every plank, every brick, every hinge my father used was from the period of the original house.

And all the furniture was old, though very little of it was handed down through our family. My mother didn't like the primitive pieces Gramma Hattie had passed on to her and, because Mom didn't have "sentimental attachments," she said, she was happy to sell them and use the money to buy what she liked from antique shops and estate sales: cedar chests and dark sea trunks with leather handles and heavy brass hinges, small pine and cherry tables, slatted Shaker chairs in the dining room, a high-backed settle in the foyer and, in the bedrooms, blanket chests, spool beds, bureaus, and desks. My mother used to say if anyone dropped a match in the house, it would go up like a haystack. The one piece of our family furniture that my mother retained when decorating the house was my many-greats-uncle Samuel Wilde's rocker; the rest, she said, was too dark or too rickety or too casual or just too ugly for her taste.

My mother loved all these old things, though they had no personal meaning for us, and she decorated around them with foot warmers and bed warmers, old crockery, glass bottles, iron tools, and trading signs. From time to time, she would remove an artifact from the wall and admire all its irregularities and imperfections: the dents from its forging, the welts from misuse, its lopsidedness, the overall homeliness of its appearance.

"See these scissors?" She caressed them, held them out to me as if she were showing me something very delicate and made of porcelain. "Can you imagine how long it must have taken to make these? Look—look at this blade, the sequence of hammer marks. Isn't that beautiful? And the rings, almost like enormous tears," she said, handing me the scissors.

I held them with two hands, looked intently, trying to pierce through the heavy ugliness of them and discover and be moved by whatever it was that stirred her so deeply, but all I could see was physical—a dirty, dull, useless tool. I knew she saw something else and I knew I had missed the point and I felt I had somehow failed her.

"Aren't they gorgeous?" When I said nothing, Mom offered again, "Well, aren't they?"

"I don't think they work," I said, and my mother looked at me like she had been slapped, gave a suck at the corner of her mouth, and snatched them from me. Then she carefully replaced them on the wall.

Something of my mother's that I fantasized would one day be mine was the collection of tea cups she kept on an old pine shelf in the kitchen. Sometimes, when I asked, she would take cups down for me, one by one, and let me hold them and admire their shapes and colors and take a pretend sip. There were cups with gilt rims and hand painted tulips and roses in warm reds and pinks; there were cups with wide bowls and mustache cups and cups that said things in flowery gold script—*September* or *For a Good Girl.* My favorite was a cup the color of pistachio ice cream with a pink handle shaped like an apple blossom and a saucer shaped like a leaf.

But still, for me, this old stuff was only so much old stuff—except for the few family things, I mean, our family Bible, Samuel Wilde's old rocker and, of course, our house itself. These things I could care about personally. After Gramma Hattie died, I didn't know what had become of our family Bible. My whole life up until then, the Bible had sat on a cedar chest at the end of my gramma's bed in her house on Chestnut Street and we would look through it together sometimes. The Bible was covered in dark leather and it was enormous, so heavy I couldn't lift it; Gramma Hattie had to carry it to her writing table and open it for us and I would kneel on a chair and she would guide me through it. She would tell me what she knew of the people whose names and birth dates and, sometimes, death dates, were entered in there; she would show me the pressed flowers, read me the poetry handwritten on stiff, crinkly paper, let me touch the silky locks of hair kept in those pages. There were facts in here, truths I didn't know about myself and other people. I knew this Bible might one day bring me some kind of understanding; I knew it might one day tell me something I needed to know about myself or about life.

The other old family thing we had was my many-greats-uncle's, Samuel Wilde's, rocker and I would rock in it and dust it and wax it from time to time. I would smooth its seat and arms and back with my palms and wonder at the man whose hands made this, whose body pressed against this wood, filling this space—my many-greats-uncle, who sat and rocked himself to death here. I would wonder what he looked like, how he spoke, and what he cared about most deeply, more than anything else in the world, aside from his daughter Sara, hung as a witch. The last old thing I loved was our house, but I loved it more for the space it left out, the land it claimed, than for the spaces it walled in.

Maybe because it was so old and imposing, windowed so that it seemed to have eyes on all sides, positioned so that no one could approach it unseen; maybe because, aside from its own little buildings, our house stood alone at the end of Wilde Road far from other people and houses and the traffic of everyday life in Salem; maybe because of the sad stories told about my many-greats-uncle who had built the house and had later died in it, after his daughter was hung as a witch; or maybe for another reason, because of something about my family, the fact that we were the kind of people who *would be* descended from a hung witch, our house seemed to harbor some dark secret and was widely thought to be haunted. Kids told stories of sneaking to our house late at night, creeping down through the woods and across our meadows, hearing moans and seeing gauzy headless forms dancing on our roof or galloping across the meadow on ghost horses or on our pony. I knew that was one reason some girls wouldn't come over to play after school. Some kids even called me *Witch Girl* for a while but it never really stuck because I wouldn't let it; I was good at acting as if they hadn't said it, hadn't said anything, and after a while, they'd let it drop.

I wondered about it, though; maybe it was true, maybe I was a witch girl. There were two strong pieces of evidence for this that would've gotten me hung right alongside my many-greats-aunt, Sara Wilde. First of all, the second toes on both my feet were far longer than the first. That was serious, Cat said; it was grave. But it was the second piece of evidence that was conclusive: on the right side of my chest, just beneath my ribs, was a small dark patch of skin with a pale bump in the middle. This was what my gramma said was called a *witch's tit*. Back then in the seventeenth century, people believed your blood carried your soul, so to give your soul to the devil, you had to give him your blood. A witch would give her soul to the devil by suckling his helpers, called *familiars* (who disguised themselves as small animals like cats or birds or snakes), from a "non-natural" nipple on her body, a witch's tit. So if you had a bump on your body—a wart, a pimple, a raised birthmark like mine—you were automatically suspected of being a witch. The test of whether a mark like mine was a true witch's tit was this: the accused person was blindfolded and then the bump was skewered with a needle; real witch's tits were cold and had no feeling (which Gramma said was how we got the expression *cold as a witch's tit*), so if the accused person felt nothing, the witch's tit was genuine and he or she was a witch. One story had it that Sara Wilde had just such a mark, like mine, and it was one of the reasons used to justify hanging her. Cat sometimes tried to talk me into letting her lance my mark with a needle but I never let her. In private though, I'd stuck it once myself and was glad to feel pain.

Gramma Hattie had told me all about Samuel Wilde. She said he had been a lonely man, a widower who left a son in England and whose wife died giving birth to his only other child, a daughter, my eight-greats-aunt who was hung for witchcraft in the summer of 1692. Gramma said that after his daughter's death, Samuel Wilde stopped living—he stopped sleeping, eating, tending to his farm, even going to church. Nights, he could be seen pacing the floor of his daughter's bedroom, now my bedroom. Days, he sat in the best room, our living room, in the rocking chair he had built himself, the chair that we still had and that still sat in that room, staring out the window, northward, toward Gallows Hill, just rocking and rocking. Before the year was through, Gramma Hattie said, Samuel Wilde died of a broken heart. You could think you heard him sometimes, rocking in that chair, crying for his lost daughter, but it was only regular night sounds made louder by the silence, my gramma said.

Still, there were nights when storms swept in off the coast and the winds howled down the chimneys scattering ashes through the house, when panes rattled in the window frames and floor-boards creaked as if finally releasing energy from the footsteps of my long-dead ancestors, nights when the front door shivered on its hinges, rain pelted the walls of the house like stones hurled by an angry mob, and I would lie in bed with the covers over my head and strain to separate all the sounds of the commotion and I swear I would hear the squeak and sigh of that old rocker. The one my many-greats-uncle Samuel Wilde had built. The one he had rocked himself to death in, still sitting in the living room right beneath me. And I would hear the lonely sobbing of someone with a broken heart.

I don't know whether I ever saw the ghost myself, but I saw some things. Once, in the bathroom, while studying my feet, wondering whether Africans really wore rings on their toes instead of their fingers like Cat had said, and whether long second toes really meant you were a witch, I heard a sound like a slippered foot dragging across carpet, a continuous, soft rasping sound, and I looked up to see the bath towel rising from the rack along the tiled wall. Keeping the very shape it had when it was simply draped over the rack, as if the bar were rising with it, which it wasn't, the towel slowly ascended the wall all the way to the ceiling as I watched, not in real time, neither believing nor skeptical but witness to an event I would never be able to narrate to myself or to another in any way that made it fit the world. Moments later, I was in Cat's room, in candlelight and a cloud of sweet smoke and a harmonica whining to a folk guitar. Cat was sitting Indian style on the floor, her pale hair parted neatly in the middle, tucked behind her ears, like a pair of curtains pulled back just enough to reveal startled eyes. I had thrown open the door to her room, rushed in without knocking.

"*What?*" she said.

Cat's hands had stopped in midair, strands of green and yellow and red tangled in her fingers. She had been weaving something with bright plastic ribbon. A cone of incense was smoking from a brass dish on her nightstand. A candle was spilling colors down the neck of a wine bottle. Someone was singing about fate and talking falsely and a wild cat.

I took in a breath.

"What!" she demanded.

"What're you doing?" was all I could think to say. How could I tell her what I had just seen when already it wasn't real—when, just as I was coming to put words to it, the experience faded and now seemed false?

"What am I doing? My *homework.* Geez, Einstein, what does it look like I'm doing?"

I asked if we could put on *Sergeant Pepper* and Cat said okay and I never told her or anyone else about the towel or about the many times while lying in bed in the dark staring into my room picking out my things which were only the darkest shadows in shadow, waiting for sleep to descend, I could see a filmy white head over my dresser or near my closet or by the door to the hall, or I could feel something fluttering near my face, tickling my cheek, and sometimes when I heard the train whistle high and hollow, I swear I'd hear a voice calling, a long, lonesome sepulchral wail echoing down from Gallows Hill. And I never told anyone of the times I heard Samuel Wilde in the living room beneath me, sobbing and rocking himself to death all over again.

Aside from the house, we had sweet feral meadows and a wood thick with sticky pines whose branches bent so low to the earth in winter under the weight of snow that if you parted them, you would find a circular space, like the inside of a teepee, dark and dry and fragrant with pine needles. Sometimes, Cat and I would make an Indian village in the woods, stamping out paths between teepees, sneaking blankets and pots and a thermos of cocoa up there. We had a Shetland pony called *Misty,* Maggie, our old cocker spaniel, sixteen chickens, and four barn cats—Lyndon, Ladybird, Eartha, and Pip. We had land, places to play, and safe, cool mossy spots in the woods where no one would find us.

During the time I'm talking about now, the spring of 1968, nights were often filled with red light and rage. You never knew for sure when it would come, but like a wild animal, you developed a special sensitivity to certain signs: the phone's ringing too often; someone's spilling milk; any mention of money; Mom's open hand slapping the table; the incessant tinkle of ice in glasses. Then suddenly my father would become angry. He would become someone else. We could be eating dinner.

My father might say to Cat: "If you and your sisters are going to eat like pigs, I'll feed you on the kitchen floor where you belong." Or he might tell my mother the dinner was repulsive—*pig slop*—he was going out to get some *real* food. He might yank the wedding band from his finger, slap it on the table, and say he never bargained for *this*. And he would slam the front door so hard, the door knocker would sound behind him after he'd left—*smack smack smack*—and you'd know it was nothing though it sounded like danger. Then my mother might leave the dining room and run upstairs and we would hear the bolt slam into place on her bedroom door and we wouldn't see her till morning. Or she might stay at the table with us, as stunned as we were, half-eaten dinners on the plates before us, surrounded by an awful silence none of us knew how to break. My mother might try to joke with us, then, but without confidence, so we would all end up feeling worse.

When Dad finally came home, I would listen to his heavy steps as he made his way to the guest room and sometimes I could hear him sob and I'd feel sorry for him. Much later, deep in the night, he might come to your room and you would wake, startled, and he might simply be standing there, solid and dark, and he would say something odd like, "Have you seen my nail clippers?" It was possible he would just leave when you said, "No," but it was also possible that you would wake very early and see him tiptoeing from your room.

Other times, it was Mom who would bolt from the table, dash out the front door, and drive away. Dad would have thrown something at her—his plate or his rocks glass—and she would scream,

"No!" and grab her purse and run. Sometimes she would stay out till late in the night and I would think she was gone for good. And I would hate her. And I would remember the way my father looked when he got angry—his eyes huge, his mouth flat, that vein sticking out at his temple like a little snake, his whole body shaking—and I would understand. Nights when Mom left, Dad would spring from the table, grab a bottle from the wet bar, and glare at us as he stormed through the dining room with it, as if he were daring us to go ahead and say something. He would pound up the stairs and then we would hear the door to the family room slam shut and we wouldn't see him till the next day. After tucking Franny into bed, Cat and I would say good night and go to our separate rooms. I would read deep into the night and later, I would sneak into Cat's room and crawl into bed with her.

In the day time, everything was always different. Dad would tap three times on the door to our rooms and say, "Boo-boo loo-boos? Up and at 'em!"

Cat and I would have cereal and toast and maybe fruit cocktail. Then we would brush our teeth and hair, take our lunch money from the blue candy tin on the window sill in the kitchen, and we would go out front and wait for the bus. The three rocks that marked the bus stop were like home base in tag—once we made it there, we were safe.

The rocks at the bus stop were enormous, tall as Franny and so heavy we couldn't move them. They weren't like the rocks that made up the stone walls lining the roads of Salem and the rest of the North Shore, rocks the size of Thanksgiving turkeys, hefted from the earth hundreds of years ago to make way for farming, stacked and fitted together to mark people's property. The rocks at the bus stop could have been among those flanking the shore all the way up to Maine—boulders tossed out of the sea as if to crush any creature daring to come too close, daring to live at the edge of the land. The rocks would be the set for whatever game we played as we waited for Mrs. Lindall to bring the number 7 here, to the dead end of

Wilde Road. The rocks might be tables or chairs, sometimes giant turtles, sometimes just rocks. We might play Mary Poppins or Batman and Cat would get to be the principal character since she had a long blue cape and was the oldest and I would have to be the villain. I always wanted to play that we were being swallowed by a whale, but Cat would rarely do it. Something about our being swallowed by a whale really bothered her and she would only agree to play it when she wanted to get something out of me like candy or money. To me, being swallowed by a whale seemed about the safest adventurous thing that could happen to you. It would be like finding yourself inside of an enormous, living artillery tank—nothing could hurt you—except no one would ever think to look for you there.

When we were on the bus, I felt proud of Cat, proud to have an older sister who was pretty and cool and had pierced ears. I knew the other kids saw me differently when I got on the bus with her: I wasn't just a pale little kid with a bandit's mask of freckles and curly red hair. I was the sister of Catherine Dalton. And the fact that Cat was somebody seemed to suggest that someday I might be somebody, too. Cat was the oldest and, everyone said, the prettiest, which only meant that she was prettier than me, since Franny wasn't really in the running. Cat was prettier than just about anybody: she had lips pointed on top, rounded and full on the bottom, just like my mother's lips and my Gramma Hattie's lips—*bow lips,* my mother called them—and blue eyes everyone was always making a fuss over, saying they were Elizabeth Taylor eyes. No one said I had Elizabeth Taylor eyes though I had blue eyes, too. Maybe everyone said Cat had Elizabeth Taylor eyes because she had such thick, black eyelashes, so she always looked like she was wearing makeup.

Sometimes, for no discernible reason, Cat would grow sullen and angry and when you asked her what was wrong she would say, "Nothing," and sulk and it was clear you were supposed to say more, but just what more I never knew. Though for years I didn't understand this blackness and I took it personally, as being about me, as being a rejection of me, a consequence of my not being enough for her, I finally came to know it from the inside, as dark storms began to form in me now, too, to rise from something black coiled deep inside me. These storms would grow and expand and finally fill me and then they would leak outside me, outside my dark heart, and hover about me and chase me sometimes, too. But while I tried to keep it all inside, Cat didn't seem to mind letting her blackness out sometimes—it almost seemed as if she *had* to let it out. I knew Cat better than I knew anyone, so seeing this dark side of her, angry and wild and out in the open but inaccessible even to me, made me feel a weighty loneliness.

Cat was a fine horsewoman, an excellent rider—everybody who knew anything about riding said so—and, until she'd settled down in her new home with us, our pony Misty would throw anyone but her. The first two times I had mounted Misty she'd bucked me off, both times into the snow, so I didn't get hurt. Misty was the prettiest Shetland pony I had ever seen, with a creamy mane and tail, a warm chocolate coat, and good bloodlines, my mother said. My father had won her from Manny Thompkins in a poker game the afternoon of Christmas Eve three years before—he said he had taken a long shot and split on a pair of sixes but none of us knew what that meant. When Dad lost the ten acres to Manny Thompkins, he offered to swap Misty for it but I heard him tell my mother that Manny Thompkins laughed in his face.

Since Cat had always wanted a horse, she got to have Misty for her own and though my mother didn't like my father's gambling and she generally punished him for it afterward by not smiling at him and hardly speaking to him for a day or two, this time, when he won Misty, she seemed pleased, said having Misty around reminded her of her childhood, a time when the barn was called "the stable" and it held two chestnut horses and a pony and for three seasons each year the gardens were bursting with flowers and the lawn was lush and finely trimmed and I think Cat liked that.

One warm afternoon in early March of this year, I realized that something was changing, something *had changed,* between Cat and me. I had just come back from Suki's house and Cat was out front grooming Misty. She would be showing her in an important competition in late May at the Topsfield Fairgrounds and now she had to practice making her beautiful. Cat was stroking Misty's front legs with the currycomb, smoothing her fur flat with the palm of her hand when I came running over.

"She looks great," I said, and Cat said, "Thanks," and stood and looked at Misty proudly, as if she had just created her and she were perfect. Then Cat pushed the hair from her face with the back of her hand and for the first time, I saw that she was a woman, no longer a kid like me. When had it happened?

We had come to the end of something, I suddenly knew that. Cat had crossed an imperceptible line—or a line you couldn't perceive until after you'd crossed it—a line I was approaching but hadn't yet reached, and there would be no going back. There would be no more steamy afternoons of running through the sprinkler in our underwear, not really boys or girls, just children. No more summer days on Singing Beach, where our feet played high, squeaky notes in the sand, filling waxed paper cups, building castles, or burying each other up to the neck in wet, sandy graves. There would be no more sitting together on the bus, making fun of Mrs. Lindall, our bus driver who had a pink bulbous nose, frog eyes, and a big red veiny spider under the skin of her cheek. No more taking baths together, making shampoo horns in each other's hair and bikinis with the Mr. Bubble bubbles. Soon, Cat would forget about Mrs. Lindall. Already, she was sharing her seat with Stuart Haskins whenever he took the bus. He would carry her books and I would sit alone at the back and watch them talk and laugh. And when it wasn't in pieces in the Haskins' driveway, Stuart would pick Cat up in his blue Rambler and drive her to school and I would have to ride the bus alone. Soon, Cat would say the sprinkler, sand castles, and sand graves were for babies, and Stuart Haskins would take her to Crane's Beach or Good Harbor, where all the teenagers went, and she would wear a real bikini and stare at her stomach and breasts the whole time and never once think of me back home, thinking of her. And, like the lady in the bath oil commercials on TV, Cat would soak in the tub by herself, cushioned in foam and shaving her legs. She would lock the door and she wouldn't let me in when I knocked.

I knew that no matter how old I was, I would never shut Cat out of my life, but I needed her more than she needed me. Cat wasn't afraid of Mom or Dad and I suppose she was right when she said she was the only cat child in the family. Sometimes, she said it was because she was a cat person that they named her *Cat*; other times, she said it was because they named her *Cat* that she was a cat person. I would always remind her that her name was really *Catherine*. When I was little, at the age when Cat's simply owning or enjoying something—a piece of jewelry, a book, a kind of candy— made it valuable, made me want it too, I would say "Me, too" when Cat said she was a cat person, but even then I knew it wasn't true.

Gramma Hattie once told me that cat people had power. "Power," she said, "is something people have to give you; it's not something you have on your own. It's a mark of a cat person that people give power to him—that it's nearly impossible not to." I guess my mother was a cat person then, and so, most certainly, was Cat.

As I said, Cat had a lot of nerve and wasn't afraid to let other people see her blackness, which was probably another thing that made her a cat person. Sometimes she would say things to my parents, things that must have risen from that dark place inside her— like "What's *wrong* with you?" or "I hate you"—things that might make her get hit, things I would never say but instead would lock deep inside me, inside the dark, tight coil of my true self. And sometimes Cat did things I would never think of doing, like skipping school or taking money from my mother's wallet or coming home drunk, twice. I was the opposite. I tried to make my parents laugh or smile, or if that was impossible, I would just try to stay out of their way, to be invisible to them. For instance, if my parents were fighting in the kitchen and it was very late and we had never gotten dinner, I might sneak by them, so quietly, and take a box of crackers or some doughnuts from the bread drawer and they would never even see me. But Cat would storm right in: "Sorry to interrupt, but what are we s'posed to do about dinner?" She might get slapped, and she knew that, she *had* to know that, but she would do it anyway. For Cat, a slap was just a slap and she could take it.

In school, I had always been good, a goody-goody was what kids called me because I was polite to the teachers and got all A's and was always asked to clean the erasers or to pass out jars of paste during Art. Being good was being safe, about the safest you could be, as far as I could tell, and I couldn't understand why anyone was bad. But still, Cat *was* bad. When she was a little kid, she gave the teachers trouble in the usual ways but when she got to high school, Cat began to get sneaky, stopped being bad for the teachers, and began being bad in bigger, more private ways. Sometimes, she did things that would've gotten her into big trouble if she weren't so clever, like sneaking Mom's stapler onto the bus and making her regular skirt a mini. The principal, Mr. Pearson, would see girls walking down the hall in their miniskirts and mostly, he'd let it go, but sometimes he'd be on the warpath and he'd make all the girls line up and drop to their knees. If a girl's skirt didn't touch the floor, Mr. Pearson would phone her mother who not only would not appreciate having to stop whatever she was doing to pick up her daughter or to bring her some decent clothes, but who would be furious about her child's having managed to sneak out into public virtually naked. But Mom would never find out about Cat's miniskirts—Cat would always excuse herself and rush off to the Girls' before getting on her knees for Mr. Pearson and there, in her own private stall, she would pry out the staples and let her skirt down.

In time, Cat began committing more serious wrongs, for reasons I wouldn't begin to understand until I grew. For example, one day, after Cat and I got back from downtown where we had had frappes at Reynold's Apothecary, Mom saw a jar of cold cream in Cat's room, a jar Mom hadn't bought. When she asked Cat where it came from, Cat said, "I stole it." Just like that. She didn't even try to lie. Mom hit her, like Cat must have known she would, then she put the jar in a bag and drove Cat back downtown and made her confess and apologize to the man who ran the place, the man my dad called *Bob*. That night, my mother and father spoke with Cat alone in the kitchen and I eavesdropped. They were talking about right and wrong. They were saying it was wrong to steal, could Cat see that? Cat said, "Of course." They said how disappointed and humiliated they were. They said how could they trust her now. They said she was selfish and immoral. I would have cried, but Cat simply said, "I'm sorry."

"Are you?" Mom said. "Are you *really?"*

Cat said she was.

"No, you're not," Mom said, and it made me want to scream, not out of anger, but because it made feel crazy that my mother always knew how we felt and we didn't. And it seemed that, whenever we really did know how we felt, when we were *sure* of it, she would never let us feel that way, especially if that way was sorry. "You're not sorry at all. You're just sorry you were caught."

"Of course, I'm sorry I was caught," Cat said. "But I'm sorry I stole, too." With that, I heard a slap, but still, Cat didn't cry or at least she didn't make any noise.

Later that night, I asked Cat why she stole the cold cream—it wasn't like she didn't have any.

"I don't know," Cat said. "Maybe for effect," but I didn't know what she meant.

Cat did other bad things like drinking—playing quarters and going to a kegger—but she didn't get caught. Still, it was like she *wanted* to get caught because when she came home drunk, she stumbled around her room, singing and laughing and knocking things over and I had to tell her to keep quiet and put her to bed before she woke Mom and Dad. It was funny that they never waited up for her. Suki's parents would stand in the front hall tapping on the face of a wristwatch when Laura finally, quietly, opened the front door. But my parents never even yelled at Cat for coming in late—maybe they didn't know—though that seemed to be just what she was waiting for, almost like what she had wanted.

Though Cat could be wild and unpredictable like this, most often, she was kind and generous and funny, and she sort of took care of Franny and me.

Franny was born when I was seven years old and I was glad that someone else would be called "the baby of the family" and that there was someone I could someday boss around. At the time I'm talking about now, Franny was five years old. She had light blonde hair, straight and silky like Cat's only short, plain brown eyes and a round, cheerful face with a tiny push-up nose. Though Cat and I played her games and read her books to her, tried to include and amuse her, I think Franny felt the years that separated her from Cat and me placing her by herself because she referred to us as *the sisters*. If Cat and I came back from riding bikes together, or when we left the bathroom after fooling around with Mom's makeup, Franny would greet us saying, "What are the sisters doing now?"

Franny had a bad habit. She wet the bed. Sometimes in the middle of the night, Cat and I would wake and hear her crying. Mom would be talking to Franny in short, deep syllables. Franny kept having a dream in which a little boy and girl brought her into a bathroom and helped her onto a light blue toilet and she would wake, horrified, on cooling sheets. My father might yell at Franny and a few times he even spanked her and made her sleep on the wet sheets, to teach her a lesson. He was always threatening to put Franny in plastic pants even though Franny was five and that would make Franny howl. Cat and I used to coach Franny about not drinking water before bed, about getting up in the night to go to the bathroom, but it didn't seem to help. Cat and I were very protective of Franny, though we would tickle her sometimes or hold her down and breathe in her face.

This is who my family was and how we were in 1968. For me, 1968 was when my life became divided in two, into my past, which was my childhood, the part I would look back on, like I'd heard people do, and have in mind when I used phrases like "when I was a girl," and the rest of my life, my life now and my future life. A line was drawn then, that spring, that split my world into those two parts, setting the first free, drifting away from the rest, from me, like an iceberg forever frozen, untouchable, safe. This was the time when I would realize that at some point unmarked by me, I had become divided in another way not just over time, but in time, at a moment: there was my outside self, easy and cheerful, which was for safety, and there was my inside self which I would just begin to notice now, though I think it took shape long before this. This was my true self, I knew it and it worried me because my true self was angry and sad and vengeful; my true self sometimes wished people harm; my true self sometimes wished people dead—not permanently dead, not dead forever, but dead in the sense that they would later get up, all sorry and apologetic, and they would try to make it up to me for whatever harm they'd done me.

When I thought about it, I was almost certain of the precise moment my inside self, my true self, came to be. It was three years before and I was the only child around that night—Cat was at Lisa Cutler's pajama party and Franny was a baby and had long been asleep on the other side of the house. It was Christmastime and my parents were having a cocktail party. The house was decorated with pine boughs and tiny white lights and it smelled of bayberry and cinnamon and spirits were high. Fires crackled in the fireplaces in the kitchen, the living room and the dining room. Wreaths with red velvet ribbons and gold and silver balls were hung on all the walls. Food was laid out on silver trays trimmed with cranberries and holly alongside stacks of white plates—my mother's Wedgwood Winter White. When the evening began, I got to open the front door and say, "Merry Christmas," take people's coats, and hang them in the front hall closet until it was filled; then coats got piled upstairs on Cat's bed. I spent most of the evening watching TV in the family room, wishing people would leave, hearing new arrivals stomping snow off their boots in the front hall, calling greetings and laughing. From time to time, I would sneak downstairs to the kitchen for snacks. I would try to duck around the women with tiny Christmas trees and Santas on their ears who would smack lipstick on my cheeks, engulf me in their perfume and boozy fumes, and tell me how tall I was getting. And I would try to avoid Mr. Winthrop who kept patting my bottom and saying how pretty I was, which was a joke because, first of all, I wasn't a baby, so having my bottom patted was an insult, and second, I was so far from pretty it was laugh-out-loudable, as Cat used to say.

By the time I climbed into bed that night, the party had reached a frantic pitch—voices were bellowing and screeching, laughter was thunderous and shrill and you could no longer hear the Christmas carols on the hi-fi. Some men were belching in the back hall, one after the other, deep resonant bullfroggy sounds punctuated by hysterical laughter, as if the men were taking turns, as if they were competing. I put on my earmuffs, which made everything far away, and I was just settling in to read when the door to my room opened.

"The bathroom's that way," I said, pointing toward my parents' room.

"What's that?" Mr. Winthrop stepped into my room, pushed the door closed behind him.

I slid the earmuffs back from one ear. "The bathroom," I said. "The closest one is through my parents' room."

Mr. Winthrop came right up to my bed and sat on it. "And what're you doing, little lady?" He had a smokey voice that made him seem damaged and dangerous.

"Reading," I said. I could smell his pungent liquor and smoke breath.

"Want me to read to you?" he said, as if I were a little kid.

"No, I was just going to sleep," I said. I thought it would make him leave, but Mr. Winthrop pulled my earmuffs from my head and then put a hand on me, on my arm.

"What're you wearing under there, Patty?" he said, and then he began to stroke my arm. "That's your name, right? *Patty?*"

I didn't say anything, but when I began to pull my covers

higher on my body, Mr. Winthrop grabbed them and pulled them back, pulled them down past my waist.

When I said, *"Don't,"* Mr. Winthrop clasped a huge hand over my mouth and slammed my head back against my wall.

"Now you just be quiet, Patty. I'm not hurting you, am I? I *won't* hurt you as long as you keep quiet."

Mr. Winthrop's face was close to mine and he was whispering at me. I could taste the bitter tang of his aftershave, his sour smoke and liquor breath. He was telling me that I was pretty; he was telling me I was enticing. *I* was making him do this, he said. He kept calling me *Patty* and I would have said, "My name's *Trisha*," but his hand was pressed tightly on my mouth and later, I would be glad for that, for not having given away that piece of me. I was breathing fast through my nose but it was like breathing through a straw. I didn't feel I could get enough air and Mr. Winthrop's face was so close to mine that all the air I got was poisoned with sour smokey liquor breath.

Mr. Winthrop told me to scoot down flat on my back. Then he pulled up my nightie with his free hand and began rubbing my stomach. When I struggled, he pressed harder on my mouth so my teeth hurt. "Now, you just stop it right now and be a good girl if you don't want to get hurt, Patty."

He put his fingers in my panties and said he would have to hurt me if I moved or if I ever told anyone—he was just doing what he had to do, what I was *making him* do. Besides, Mr. Winthrop said, what he was doing was good for me, it was an education. When he told me to open my eyes, I stared right past him at the ceiling and saw the hot air balloon cracked into the paint above him and I climbed into it. Then I was far away from Mr. Winthrop. I was looking down on us. I could hear him saying, "That's a good girl, Patty," but he couldn't say it to me. I was safe and untouchable up in the balloon. There was no way he could reach me. He didn't even know my name.

As he left my room, Mr. Winthrop said that if I ever told anyone, he would have to hurt me. It was important to learn not to squeal. That was part of a good education.

Mr. Winthrop had put something slimy on my belly but I couldn't feel it now. I couldn't feel anything—no soreness, no burning, no pain at all. I couldn't smell the stale smokey liquor smell he left in my room. I couldn't hear any more party sounds. I was coiled up now, far away, deep inside me.

The next day, I told my mother what had happened but she just said I had had a bad dream and took my temperature.

When I told her it wasn't a dream, it really happened, but thanks to the balloon on my ceiling I was safe, my mother told me it was time I learned to distinguish fantasy from reality and sent me to my room. I refused to go. I said, "But it's *true*," and my mother drew her arm back (I thought she was reaching for something behind her) and hit my face with her open hand and either the force of the slap or the shock of it sent me onto the floor. When I looked up at her, I saw my mother's eyebrows were raised, her eyes were opened to me and it was as if there was a rosebud in her mouth which she would give me—she wanted to, I could tell—but instead, her eyes closed and she swallowed and turned from me and something inside me moved.

Up in my room, I lay on my bed and looked at the hot air balloon on my ceiling and thought how I hated Mr. Winthrop—because of him, my mother didn't reach for something behind her but hit me to the floor; because of him, she had closed herself from me, swallowed the tenderness she wanted to give me. I thought of how I would drop a rock on Mr. Winthrop from that hot air balloon if he came near me again, and it was then that that thing inside me that had moved formed into something hard and coiled around a feeling I could hardly believe existed: a burning hatred for my mother. I would never have been able to bear this feeling myself, out loud, out in the open, but this hard private thing could and so it would—it would bear my rage and my sadness and it would protect me and be my true horrible self.

As thunder marks an approaching storm some-
times long before the lightning is visible, so, too, there were certain
facts, events, states of affairs that obtained or took place over the
months, even years, preceding this time, that I would later see as
signs of what was to come, what *did* come, the spring of 1968.

For example, there was the fact of our china. Until I was nine
years old, we had Wedgwood Winter White, a thousand pieces of
it—a dozen place settings and casserole dishes and platters—which
my mother cherished and seemed to want Cat and me to cherish,
too. Sometimes as she was returning clean dishes to the cabinet, she
would pause and examine a piece and show it to us.

"See how rich it is? Like it was poured from milk and dipped
in glass."

And her saying this would, for that moment, make me love the
china almost as much as she did, though china wasn't really something I cared much about one way or the other. But my mother did,
she loved that Wedgwood Winter White and we all knew it. For
years, it seemed that the surest way for my father to make up with
my mother after a fight was by bringing her more Wedgwood Winter White, which he would do, and he gave pieces to her from us
on her birthday, Christmas, and Mother's Day, which is how she got
so many of those milky plates and cups and bowls and platters.
Then, in the course of a single night in the winter of 1965, we lost
over half those dishes *like that* and my mother never replaced them
and she began collecting a brown Pfaltzgraff pattern instead. Here's
how it happened.

Cat and I were home on a weather day. It hadn't stopped
snowing since breakfast and by 3:00 P.M., we couldn't go anywhere.
Mom was supposed to bring groceries to Gramma Hattie who was
stuck in her house on Chestnut Street but we couldn't get out of the
driveway. My dad was still at work and the driveway was too long,
the snow too heavy and abundant, for Mom to shovel a path for the
station wagon—and even if she could have cleared the driveway,

Wilde Road itself had disappeared under the thick heavy snow. While Mom got busy on the phone looking for someone to help us, Cat and I put on long underwear and snowsuits and mittens and scarves and bounded out the back door.

The snow reached higher than the seats on the swing set, higher than the latch on the gate of the main meadow, higher than the bottom of the hole in the tire swing. It came up over my knees, embraced my legs to my thighs. Snow would never be as deep or as white or as beautiful as it was when I was this young. Within a few years, snow would be too cold and wet, a nuisance, and a reason to stay inside rather than a reason to go out. But now, we jumped and fell and pushed each other over and tumbled around in it as if we'd spent our whole lives on a tropical island. We rolled boulders for a snowman. We tried to shape snow bricks for an igloo but the work was too hard and so we ended up digging tunnels instead.

By the time Cat and I came back inside, cold and wet and breathless with raw faces and runny noses, Mom was sitting at the kitchen table with someone—with Mr. Nealy! Mr. Wally Nealy, the junk man, the town clerk, the supervisor of the cemetery, and the fattest man I had ever seen in person. Mr. Nealy lived with his fat sister Bettina in a tiny house at the edge of the cemetery but he spent a lot of time driving around in his green pickup truck, doing odd jobs for people, fixing, painting, hauling this or that, and in winter, he put a piece of metal on the front of his truck and scraped the snow from people's driveways for them. And now, he was here! Mr. Nealy at the kitchen table—*our* kitchen table—with our mother! They were blowing into mugs of cocoa when we came in and Mom rose and began helping us out of our snow clothes. She rubbed our faces with the kitchen towel and kissed our cheeks and nodded at the steamy mugs she'd set at our places at the table, like she'd been watching for us the whole time. She'd placed a bowl of miniature marshmallows between us, as if we could just help ourselves, as if she didn't mind how many we had. While she and Mr. Nealy spoke about boring things like garbage collection and the development on Meetinghouse Lane, Cat and I stuffed marshmallows into our cocoa and stirred and slurped the sweet, melty goop, then retopped our cups with more marshmallows until our cups and the bowl between us were empty.

Though it never seemed light that day, darkness came on early, and Cat suddenly said she wanted to go up and take a bath. Mom said we should both take baths, and Mr. Nealy said it was high time for him to get a move on, too.

We excused ourselves, said good-bye to Mr. Nealy, said it was nice to see him again, and just as I reached my room, I heard Cat call out—not a yell, absolutely not a scream or a shriek—just a high little laugh-call and before I could turn and head toward her room, I saw something lying across my bed and stopped. It was a white gown sprinkled with pink flowers, with ruffles at the cuffs and a pink satin ribbon laced through the ruffle at the neck. The fabric was as soft as Franny's diapers. The buttons down the back were pink and shaped like tiny roses. As I stroked the gown, I heard a sound and turned and there was Cat in my doorway, holding her gown to her shoulders, a stunned look on her face. We had never, ever had night gowns like these. I held mine up to me. The ruffle at the hem skimmed the tops of my feet.

"They're exquisite," Cat whispered. "Just *exquisite.*"

Without discussing it, we put on our gowns and hurried to our bathroom. We climbed onto the toilet together and looked at ourselves in the big mirror.

"Exquisite," I said, and Cat nodded at me in the mirror.

From where we stood, we could see out the bathroom window onto the driveway. The path from the breezeway, the road at the top; and the driveway itself had all been cleared—plowed and shoveled and edged with smooth, tidy white walls like in *The Cat in the Hat.*

Cat smiled at me in the mirror.

It had been a perfect day.

Later, my father would come home and we would hurry down to greet him in our nighties but when we reached the bottom of the stairs, Cat would stop and hold me back with her arm.

"What?"

She would say, "Shsh. *Listen,"* and I would.

"How much did it cost?" My father spoke in a flat voice.

"Nothing. He wouldn't take any money."

"He wouldn't take any money?"

"That's right."

"He didn't want to be paid?" My father said it loudly and sarcastically.

"Yes. That's right." My mother's voice was high now, almost shrill but hardly audible.

"Molly, *everyone* wants to be paid. Why wouldn't Wally Nealy want to be paid?"

"I guess he didn't need the money."

"Wally Nealy didn't need the money?"

"Oh, God. Can we not do this?" my mother said, pleading, almost in a whisper.

"I'm trying to get clear here, Molly. Did you say Wally Nealy didn't need the money? Is that what you said?"

"That's what I said." My mother's voice was soft and small, as if it were trying to hide.

"Are you fucking nuts? Why the hell wouldn't he need the money? The man can barely keep himself and that fat-ass sister of his in suet. Who the hell is Wally Nealy suddenly that he doesn't need the money—Wally Rockefeller?"

I'd never heard my father talk like this.

"David, he said it was no problem. He said he was out this way anyway. It only took him a few minutes. He said the cocoa was payment enough—"

We heard a crash, a china crash. Something big like a plate or a serving bowl.

"Please, David." Mom kept her voice calm and small as if it would keep her calm and small and therefore, somehow, a difficult target. Though it was after five o'clock, my mother hadn't had anything to drink. These were the days just before the liquor days, the drinking days, began.

"What I want to know is, what else did you serve him?"

We heard a chair scraping across the floor. My mother gasped and cried out at the same time, like she'd just been squeezed tightly. My father grunted.

"Hmm, Molly? What else? What else did you serve up to Fat Boy? *This?* Did you give him *this?*"

My mother screamed and then we heard another piece of china smash, then another, and my mother screamed again and Cat took off for the kitchen and I ran after her and before I even caught up with her, she had stopped at the threshold and was screaming, *"Stop, Daddy!"*

And there was Dad, his eyes wild, so big it seemed unlikely he could make out anything as small as Cat and me. And there was my mother, her eyes wide, too, her mouth wide, as she crouched in front of my father who had her hair in his fist, her throat in his other hand.

In a thin, rusty voice, she said, "Go upstairs." When Cat didn't move, she added, *"Now."* Her eyes were huge.

Cat grabbed me and we ran for the back stairs. As we began to run up them, there came a crash, screaming, then more crashing, china shattering. Then without pause, shattering, shattering, a stream of shattering china, and I made myself small, ducked my head low, and Cat curled herself over me, covering me. We stayed on the stairs like that until the breaking stopped.

I followed Cat to the family room, the farthest you could get from the kitchen without leaving the house.

Later, Mom came upstairs with cocoa in two plastic Yogi Bear mugs. Her eyes were red and her cheeks were flushed. There were dark marks on her throat, like three slugs. Cat and I were on the floor of the family room, close together. We had been listening. My mother set the cocoa on the floor, took a blanket from the closet and wrapped it around us, hugging us with it.

"Everything's okay," she whispered, as if saying it any louder might make it false. I looked at the marks on her neck and Cat reached out and touched one. My mother grabbed Cat's hand and kissed her fingertip. Then she kissed our cheeks and smiled thinly.

"Everything's okay," she said again. She turned and pulled the button on the television set. A man and woman took shape on the screen. They were strolling in a garden, singing.

"You want to watch this?" she said, like a really nice baby-sitter.

"Sure, fine," Cat said.

Mom nodded, then stood and moved toward the door. She paused at the threshold and turned and looked back at us. She seemed to want to say something, took in breath to speak, but finally she simply smiled a flat smile—not to express any kind of joy, but to keep anything further from being said, to close the episode—and then she nodded again and left the room.

As Cat and I drank the cocoa and looked at the TV screen, I swear I could hear my mother all the way down in the kitchen, collecting fragments of her Wedgwood Winter White, pieces of the small oval casserole she had promised one day soon would hold tapioca, the teacups and saucers she'd filled with hot cider and cinnamon sticks last Hallowe'en, the platter she'd covered with holly leaves and hot mushroom cap hors d'oeuvres on Christmas eve. The mugs we'd just had our cocoa in.

Suddenly I felt woozy. The hard playing in the heavy snow, like swimming in all your clothes, and all the sugar I'd consumed must have caused the great weariness I suddenly felt in my limbs, the emptiness in my chest, and the painful static in my head. And then I realized that the fabric on my nightie was too crisp, too stiff, as if someone had starched it, and I decided to change into my old red pajamas with the holes in the knees.

Later, all of the evidence I would have of this time, everything tangible I would ever own of this history, I would find in a Seagram's liquor box with "Trisha's Stuff" Magic-Markered on the side. My mother would hand it to me as I left for college. She'd decided to sell the house we lived in then (which would not be my family home, our home on Wilde Road) and she thought I might want this stuff. It was all she had of me in the new house, she said. When I opened the box, I would discover three photographs, two of Cat and me, B.F.: in one, we are smiling from the bare back of a chestnut horse. My arms are wrapped around Cat's waist and Cat holds the reins. We're barefooted and wearing tie-dyed T-shirts, cutoffs and long bright strands of love beads. Here, Cat stands beside me, her arm circling my shoulders. It is nighttime and my eyes are closed, probably anticipating the flash bulb. We are not smiling, but we are close together, touching at the sides. In the third photograph, Cat and Franny and I are in the barn, hay in our hair, holding baby chicks, laughing. We are all wearing Dad's old flannel shirts; we are all wearing sparkly earrings and red lipstick. And I would find some 45s: "Little Johnny Everything" and "Thumbellina" pressed in cherry red vinyl; "The Birds and the Bees" and "Please Please Me" pressed in black. Two report cards. A Silver Certificate. A red, white, and blue NIXON button. Two Steiff toys: a tiny terrier with a white muzzle whose name tag had been ripped off long ago and a tiger whom I called *Original* because his tag read: *Original Steiff Toy.* Slipped down the side of the box, I would find a folder and inside the folder, pressed between two sheets of translucent paper, a family portrait I drew that year, 1968, after the spring had ended.

In the middle of the drawing, tall and straight as a pillar, my mother stands, her long hair yellow and parted at the side concealing one eye, purple smeared across her mouth, a burning cigarette in one hand, in the other her blue plastic cup. My father, Cat, Franny, and I are placed equidistantly around her, tethered to her by ropes tied about our necks; my mother is bound completely from waist to knees. My mother is looking down at Cat, who is standing to the right in front of her. I drew Cat with long eyelashes, enormous blue eyes, with her hair in two long braids. I meant for her to have a crop in her hand, but what she holds is shorter, thick and yellow. Odd to look at it and see that I forgot Cat's mouth. Franny wears her purple tutu and she squeezes a Barbie like her own Fay Wray. My father stands behind my mother to the left and his eyes are open wide. A tiny bubble over his head has him thinking, "In actual fact . . ." I am skinny and my red hair is crazy in curls. We are in the kitchen of my childhood home and morning light streams in from the east. Shadows fall across the floor stubborn and black but there is motion here. We are a ride at the Topsfield Fair—we are a pinwheel. But the ropes are fraying, the ties are loosening. At any moment, one of us might fly off, hurtled into the abyss, throwing all into chaos, setting everyone free.

Chapter Two

Burying Point

      A week was a long time in those days, when I was twelve, and a school week right before vacation was as long as a week could get and just when it seemed it would never end, suddenly it was Friday afternoon, that thick, soft, slow time between the end of the school week and the start of the weekend, a time when the world wasn't the regular world, when the forests and meadows and roads of Salem might all seem open and full of possibility.

Everyone was happy on Friday afternoon. Cat could be going

on a date. Suki could be spending the night. Maybe my mother would cook a nice dinner. She and my father might both go out—maybe together, if he skipped his poker game—and then Suki and I would have the house to ourselves which would make it a different, bigger place, every room open to us, filled with stuff to explore. On Friday afternoon, it even seemed possible that David Hanson would call and I would spend hours in the comfy chair in the kitchen, twisting the telephone cord between my toes, talking in a hushed voice, laughing, looking imperious and annoyed when Franny came into the room, just like Cat did when Stuart Haskins phoned her. What happened on Friday afternoon could make a difference. And this Friday afternoon was fuller than most—a whole week, ten days, was held as a seed planted in it—because this Friday afternoon was the start of Easter vacation.

It was sunny and warm for early spring and school was out and I was at Burying Point waiting for Suki. After I had had a snack and changed into play clothes, Suki had called and asked if I wanted to ride bikes here, to Burying Point. Afterward, she would ride home and have dinner and get her things and then her dad would drop her off at my house so she could spend the night. Suki had to eat at her house because she had to have fish on Friday. Suki was Catholic and fish on Friday was a Catholic rule, one of the thousand rules Catholics had and, because I hated fish, fish on Friday was one of the many reasons I was glad I wasn't Catholic. My mother was working at Old Stuff but since Cat would be home all afternoon grooming Misty, who she'd be showing at the Topsfield Fair grounds next month, Franny was taken care of and I didn't have to ask anyone's permission to ride bikes, but because she couldn't help acting like the mom when Mom was gone, Cat had to grant it to me anyway. She said, "All right, you can ride bikes with Suki," as if I'd asked, as if I'd *had* to ask, which made me mad but she made it up to me by giving me fifty cents to spend at Kirby's.

Kirby's was Kirby's Paper Store and they sold newspapers from all over along with household odds and ends, cleaners and milk and butter, overpriced items your parents would only buy on Sunday morning when the supermarket was closed. But the reason Kirby's was legendary, the reason we went there, was the candy section, racks and racks of candy in bars, on sticks, as patties or powders or liquids in small wax bottles, little candy at two for a penny—hot balls and gum balls and strips of paper with bright sugar dots. At five cents a piece or six for a quarter, you could get a pack of Bazooka, a candy bead necklace, or bundles of fat chewy licorice sticks. Kirby's smelled like my attic, a warm, dusty, sweet smell of old paper and cardboard and dried glue and it had wide floor boards that creaked.

Next to the register by the door, a tall, balding old man was always bent over a newspaper spread on the counter, pretending to read it while he spied on us from behind thick glasses that made his eyes huge like he could see everything. It seemed the man expected us to steal something and though we never did, not once, he always made me feel guilty like Suki said she felt with her priest, Father Giuffrida, because, she said, he could see her sinful mind with his holy heart. I supposed this man's name was Mr. Kirby though he never said so and we never asked.

After loading up on candy, tonic, and Twinkies, Suki and I would ride our bikes here to Burying Point. We would hide behind the large tombstone of a girl called *Martha Anne* who had died in 1741 when she was almost our age, twelve, and we would devour all that stuff in one sitting.

The first time I came to Burying Point without parents was with Cat, who knew the paths of the cemetery since she had marched along them when she was in Mrs. Raymond's Brownie Troop 62. All the girls were in uniform—itchy light chocolate dresses with stretchy belts, orange ties, and dark brown beanies—and they had stood solemnly at the summit of Burying Point with their hands on their hearts while someone played taps and someone else lowered a flag. Afterward, they got to eat strawberry ice cream from Dixie cups and make rubbings of the gravestones, but my mother threw Cat's away because, she said, they were morbid. Later, Cat took me back here, with crayons and sheets of blank newsprint and masking tape and showed me how to make rubbings. This was after Mr. Nealy had put up the "Grave Rubbing Prohibited" sign but Cat didn't care; she said the sign was for tourists and didn't apply to us. After smoothing the paper across the front of the stone and taping it to the back, she peeled the label from a purple crayon and began to rub the length of it across the paper covering the stone. At first, it looked like she was making scribbles but then white letters and numbers began to come clear. We each made three rubbings before Mr. Nealy came along and chased us out. My mother said the rubbings were gruesome and began to crumple them when Cat grabbed the one I had made for her, one of John Hathorne's stone, and said, "Not this one, Mom. This is history," which I thought was pretty smart since it made the rubbing seem educational, and my mother let her keep it and even helped her tape it to her wall.

After our mothers had finally agreed Suki and I were old enough to ride our bikes alone, we came here to Burying Point. The first time, we didn't even get off our bikes—we just held our breath and stared into the cemetery as we rode past. The next time, we stopped, leaned our bikes against the stone wall, and peered in from beneath the sign at the entrance that said:

Burying Point
Est. 1642
GRAVE RUBBING PROHIBITED

except someone made the u in *"RUBBING"* into an o. But we didn't dare go in, not until our fourth trip. Truth was, we were scared of dead people. When we were little, Suki would hold her breath for at least a minute whenever anyone said the name of a dead person—her sister Laura had told her that saying a dead person's name was like conjuring him and then the dead person would come and steal your breath unless you held it.

"There's nothing to be scared of," I said. "Dead people don't even have skin or bones—they've been eaten up by worms. They're not *real*. What's to be scared of? It's like being scared of zombies."

"I *am* scared of zombies," Suki said, and so was I.

Until we'd actually gone in ourselves, on our own, whenever we passed Burying Point with one of our mothers, Suki and I would both hold our breath and duck down in the backseat so the dead wouldn't see us and steal our breath later on—at night, say, maybe when we were sleeping. Once we'd sneaked in here together, however, once we'd trespassed and grave-rubbed and loitered, spent hours eating candy, smoking cigarettes, and climbing around on gravestones, we figured it wouldn't make any difference if we held our breaths or not; we figured we were too far gone now; we figured we'd already given ourselves over to the dead. Still, Suki taught me the Hail Mary prayer and we'd always say it before we left, just in case it helped.

I checked my Cinderella watch again: 3:05. As usual, Suki was late. I turned the little paper bag upside down, spilling its contents onto the grass. Things had to be piled alphabetically—first, there was the stack of four Bazookas, then the two Bonimo Turkish Taffies, then the Milky Ways, then the package of Twinkies and finally, the wax lips. The candy sat around me in a semicircle, the wax lips in the middle. The lips were large and swollen-looking. The red pair faced me; the blue pair was turned to the side, toward the eskar. The lips softened, then bent into smiles. Like in the movies, the red ones said, "Kiss me, you fool." But the blue ones said, "Forget me not." That was the inscription on the silver cup Gramma Hattie gave me two years earlier, the year I turned ten, four months before she died. She gave it to me at Christmas and she died just after Easter. The cup was inscribed:

Mehitabel Warwick Pope

August 17, 1887

Forget me not

"I won't forget you." I said it out loud, even though my gramma was buried on the other side of the cemetery.

Then the stuff went back into the bag, again in alphabetical order, and I placed it in front of the tombstone. I knew it by heart, but I read the inscription again:

> She looked into this world to see,
> A sample of our misery.
> Then turned away a languid eye,
> To drop a tear or two and die.

Above the inscription was the child's name, Martha Anne, and above that, the head of an angel with wings instead of shoulders. The angel's eyes were as big as dimes though her head was smaller than my fist, as if she were very young and frightened.

A languid eye. Languid, I thought, must mean sick or blind. The inscription backward went: "die and two or tear a drop to . . ." and then it was 3:07.

Though we had agreed to meet at Martha Anne, it was just a couple of steps to John Hathorne. A small rectangle tilting out of the ground at a funny angle and all it said was:

> HERE LYES INTERD
> Ye BODY OF COLO JOHN
> HATHORNE ESQR
> AGED 76 YEARS
> WHO DIED MAY Ye 10th
> 1 7 1 7

except the J in John looked like a capital I and some of the letters were strangely connected or raised up and shoved in place with the tip of an arrow. At the top was a skull with shoulder wings. The skull was shaped like a light bulb with a triangular nose and teeth straight and close as a zipper. I must have seen the image of this stone every-day, in Cat's room, above her bed, but maybe because it had become

ordinary, and ordinary, everyday things have a way of fading and becoming invisible, whenever I saw it here, it seemed unfamiliar and
gruesome.

The stone didn't say that John Hathorne was a magistrate, a
kind of judge, at the witchcraft examinations, but I knew this. When
you're from Salem, and your parents are from Salem, and their parents, and their parents, too, all the way back to your great-great-
great-great-great-great-great-great—many-greats—uncle, chances
are you know about John Hathorne.

Onion-colored crocuses, purple and white, had sprouted up at
the base of John Hathorne's stone. No smell, but the kind of flower
that would come back, every spring, year after year. I picked one of
the white crocuses and put it in my jacket pocket. There weren't any
flowers on Martha Anne's grave but here, just a few feet away, a little garden bloomed over the head of John Hathorne. I picked another flower, then another, then all the flowers, with both hands,
stuffing them in my pockets, petals falling onto my sneakers and the
grass at the base of the stone. Pockets and fists filled with crocuses
and a vein drumming in my neck as I stared hard at that name, *John
Hathorne*, then spit at the tombstone. Kicking the stone with the toe
of my sneaker, I went, "Burn in hell. Burn in hell."

Back at Martha Anne, the little paper bag moved to one side,
I ordered the crocuses around the base of the tombstone: purple,
white, purple, white. Three-fifteen. Closing my eyes, I lay straight,
rigid on top of the grave, flowers at my head.

My eight-greats-aunt, Sara Wilde, never got flowers on her
grave. Because she never got a real grave. Her body, like the bodies
of the other witches, was committed to the earth in an unhallowed
grave somewhere in the Village of Salem. That's what the books in
the library said. "An unhallowed grave." But Gramma Hattie said
differently: she said Sara Wilde was dumped in a hole up on Gallows
Hill with the seven other people hung with her that morning. Sara
Wilde didn't have any clothes on—they were stolen by the people
who came to watch, her friends, her neighbors—and her hand and

a foot and someone's chin were left sticking out of the dirt when the diggers were through and everyone went home to eat. I don't know much more than this about John Hathorne and Sara Wilde, and neither does anyone else. But there are stories.

As I lay on the grave, my eyes closed, I felt a warm breeze pass over me and my hair blew across my eyes. When I smoothed it back in place, I sighed and then I thought of my mother, making this same gesture with her hand, stroking her hair from her eyes with the backs of her fingers in just this way, and sighing just as I had but her eyes were open and she was in the living room at home and I was watching from the wall cupboard, watching something I had never seen before and I would never tell anyone about, though I would remember it my whole life. It happened two weeks earlier.

At dinner that night, my parents had both been in high spirits: my mother began humming while she helped me set the table; my father uncorked two bottles of wine and poured it in their good crystal goblets. During dinner, Cat and I did most of the talking and on this occasion, we amused our parents, made them smile and laugh as we told stories about school and our teachers and Cat did her imitation of Mademoiselle Marsh, the twangy, Southern, sway-backed old French teacher who waddled like a duck. My father laughed so hard you couldn't see his eyes and my mother clapped her hands when Cat jumped up from the table and began waddling around it, doing her "Marsh Marche" while chattering on in a Southern American–French accent: "Moi, je ne peux pas parler dans un accent français parce que je suis de Virginie . . ." At dinner's end, my mother didn't notice or care that none of us had eaten the zucchini or that Franny was now holding her fork with her left hand; she simply excused us all, told us we could grab some cookies and go upstairs and watch television or read but I sneaked into the living room by myself.

From there, I could monitor their voices and I could tell they didn't hear me drag the chair to the wall by the fireplace and climb up on it and into the wall cupboard where we weren't allowed to be. The wall cupboard was a space about the size of my bureau with three shelves in the way back but no drawers and no light and nothing in it but old wooden beams and a brick wall which was the side of the chimney and Gramma Hattie's old books with their dry, sweet smell. The cupboard was way out of reach, high up on the wall and even on tiptoes, I couldn't unlatch it. To get in, you had to pull a chair close into the wall, unlatch it from your tiptoes, then climb the back splats quickly pushing off the top so the chair wouldn't slip out from under you. Once you crawled in, you had to slide the chair away, easing it across the floor with your foot, so you wouldn't get caught up there where we weren't supposed to be, reading books we weren't allowed to touch.

I never knew what the cupboard was really for. A couple of years earlier, after I'd first read about Harriet Tubman and the Underground Railroad, I wanted it to have been built for hiding slaves but my mother insisted that no slaves needed to be hidden this far north—we had never had slavery, so Negroes have always been safe and welcomed on the North Shore of Massachusetts. I didn't ask her why, in that case, none lived here. I didn't mention the fact that the only Negroes I'd known, the only Negroes I'd seen in person, the only Negroes who, as far as I knew, had *ever* lived here—the Redfords—didn't feel so safe and welcomed that they could stay for even half a year.

My parents didn't know what the cupboard was originally intended for either: my mother said it was for storing cookware which would then have been handy to the fireplace but my dad pointed out that all the food was prepared in the great room, now the dining room, and such a high shelf would have kept everything too far out of reach to be convenient. When I was little, the cupboard held their record albums—Alan Sherman, Burl Ives, Harry Belafonte—but the heat of the chimney eventually caused the records to buckle and warp and though they were still playable they looked pretty funny spinning on the turntable, like some kind of ride at the Topsfield Fair. My parents moved the albums to the back of the back hall closet and now they used the cupboard to store these old books, which they kept on the shelves in the very back.

The books had been Gramma Hattie's—she had had a large collection of old soft leather covered books—and Mom and Dad moved them all here when she died. The books weren't old enough to be worth the trouble of selling so we got to keep them, at least for now. As a child, whenever I visited my gramma, I would admire the books as they sat on her shelves, run my fingers down their gilded spines. I'd read their titles and savor their grown-up colors and Gramma would tell me to pick one and bring it to her—books were for reading—and I would get to choose from among the world's great stories dressed up in supple leather with bright golden lettering; I would get to stroke the smooth cool covers and to hold them, small and light and easy in my hands. Some of the books came in sets (Charles Dickens in crimson, Robert Louis Stevenson in olive, Edgar Allan Poe in black) and some were singletons, including a dry brown flaking volume called *Self-Reliance*, a warm ivory and caramel marbled book titled *Un Amour de Swann* and a copy of *Huckleberry Finn* with a faded picture on the cover of a boy in a straw hat with a jack-o'-lantern smile holding a shotgun and a dead rabbit by the feet.

For one of my parents' wedding anniversaries, Gramma Hattie had wrapped up the set of Mark Twain and the copy of *Huckleberry Finn* with the boy on it and given them to my parents in two boxes with shiny gold bows. I couldn't wait to get my hands on them, but after they drove Gramma home that night, my parents unpacked the books and shoved them onto the shelves in the back of the wall cupboard and told me to keep my grubby little hands *off.* If I needed to read Mark Twain so badly, I could go to the library. I heard my parents agreeing that they needed a bunch of old books like a hole in the head. They'd been expecting a check. After they'd settled the books on the shelf, my parents slammed the door to the cupboard, latched it, and grumbled off to the kitchen to drink. Later, after everyone had gone to bed, I tiptoed in with my flashlight. That was the first time I sneaked up into the wall cupboard. And now, all of Gramma Hattie's books were hidden in the back of that closet, which I liked, because it kept them safe, and which I didn't like, because I worried they would warp and buckle like those records.

Though my parents never looked at the books, never took them out to admire or read them, they insisted they were off limits for us—one day they might be worth something—but sometimes when my parents weren't around, I would sneak into the living room with a flashlight and a blanket and climb up into the cupboard and read those wonderful tales of Jim Hawkins and Pip and Pud-d'nhead Wilson. If the fireplace had been used, the cupboard would be cozy and warm and I'd read myself to sleep in the small darkness. Because they had no interest in the books and so never opened the cupboard, and because I was careful to slide the chair away with my foot once I made it up into the wall, I never really worried about being caught reading up there.

On the evening I'm talking about now, an evening two weeks before I found myself alone at Burying Point lying on Martha Anne's grave, waiting for Suki, I didn't even bother with the flash-light but read with the cupboard door open feeling especially safe since I'd heard my parents' chairs scrape against the dining room floor, then heard my parents' voices grow small as they moved into the kitchen and began making cocktails. It would be hours before they even remembered they had children. I'd just begun *The Ad-ventures of Tom Sawyer* and already I was wondering whether I was going to be able to put up with him—Tom Sawyer, I mean—long enough to finish the book. Here he was on page twenty-six, de-lighting in the knowledge that he had brought his aunt to her knees in her heart. He was the kind of boy who liked pulling wings off flies and putting firecrackers in frogs' mouths and cutting earth-worms in two. I was thinking maybe I should read *A Connecticut Yan-kee in King Arthur's Court* instead when I suddenly heard voices and footsteps coming from the dining room. I pulled the cabinet door almost completely closed, leaving a thin crack through which I could see my parents enter the room and hurry toward a side table that held a tall vase filled with dried field flowers. My mother nodded at the vase.

"Blue," she said decisively.

"You're right," Dad said.

"How could you've ever thought it was *purple?*"

"I don't know."

My mother tapped a pane of glass in the window beside her. "This is purple." She nodded at the vase again. "This is blue."

"Blue it is," Dad said. Then he moved very close to my mother, put his arms around her. "Like your eyes."

"My eyes are brown."

"Let's see."

My mother raised her face to my father's and he looked intently into her eyes. Then he kissed her. My mother kissed him back and then they were kissing together and they stayed like that, kissing, slowly moving their heads, taking in airy breaths through the nose, making sounds like rustling petticoats. A movie star kiss.

I wanted to say something to let them know I was here, I wanted at least to sigh or cough, but I couldn't feel my throat or the place inside where your voice comes from and so I was silent. I couldn't even move to make a sound.

My father leaned back, pushed my mother's hair over her shoulder with the back of his hand, leaned down to her neck and began to kiss it. Then his hand was lost in her hair and my mother turned her head to the side, like a cat trying to make you stroke her *there,* and she made a soft moaning sound. When my father pulled back from her, drew his hand from her hair, some strands fell across my mother's face and she smoothed them from her eyes with the backs of her fingers and sighed softly and I thought to myself, *she is in love* and a shiver passed down my spine, as if a handful of snow had been slipped in my collar. With his free hand, my father began to unbutton my mother's dress, still kissing her neck. When her dress was opened to the waist—I could see the lace of her slip, the straps of her bra—my father eased his arms around her again and started rocking my mother from side to side, kissing her face, her ear, her neck, and my mother sighed again and laughed softly as he moved her back toward the fireplace, toward me, then—*boom*—he pressed her head against the cupboard door shutting it completely, leaving me in a warm darkness filled with the strange sounds of my parents' voices, not talking voices but soft, throaty voices, like little animals. Like little engines.

A couple of years before, when Suki first told me that the only way a woman could have a baby was for a man to put his penis in her, I thought she was lying, simply trying to shock me. But when I said, "No, sir," Suki said her sister Laura had told her.

I thought about it. "You mean your father put his penis in your mother?" I tried to picture Mr. Domandi doing that to Mrs. Domandi, but I couldn't. Mr. Domandi was too nice to do something so horrible. And you would have to be really rotten to do something like that to someone as sweet as Mrs. Domandi. Besides, I couldn't figure out how he or any man could have done that. From what I understood of it, a penis was just a little worm of flesh, a little hose, not something you could just *put inside* someone. Not that I'd ever seen one.

"Yeah," she said. "Your dad did it to your mom, too."

I didn't have to think about this. "My parents would never do that."

When Suki said they had to, to have babies, I told her that I knew for a fact there was another way and that that was how my parents did it—the *other* way. But when she told me to tell her about this other way, I couldn't say anything and when she said, "There *isn't* any *other* way," I wanted to hit her.

Later, when I asked my mother about it, she said Suki had been telling the truth.

"You mean you let Dad do that to you?"

"Yes," she said.

"Why?" I thought she might say something about wanting to have children, but she said, "If you love your husband, you'll do that for him," which made me realize that Dad must *want* to do that, not just for children, which made me realize that men and women weren't at all alike.

Suki told me that the only married women who didn't have to do it were nuns, who were married to God, and I couldn't understand why all women weren't nuns. We decided then that when we grew up, we would be nuns together and we swore it in a blood oath over pricked fingers. But in a faraway place in my heart, I still held out hope that there was another way to have children. It wasn't until sixth-grade health class that I gave up on this altogether.

And now it looked like I'd been wrong about the other part of this—that men and women weren't at all alike. Now it seemed clear that, for some reason, my mother had misrepresented things when she implied that men liked intercourse and women didn't. Just now, my mother had been smiling, sighing, laughing softly—it didn't seem she was doing something *for* my father at all, that she was putting up with something or *letting* my father do something to her. I could hear them now, only inches from me on the other side of the cupboard door, both moaning and sighing. I could hear clothes rustling, unzipping. I could hear breathing, murmuring, my mother giggling. And they were so close.

I brought my fists to my ears and rocked back and forth but still my parents made so much noise, there on the other side of the cupboard door, and just when I thought I couldn't take it anymore, just when I thought that, like the man in "The Tell-Tale Heart," I would have to scream out my guilt or die, I suddenly remembered the look on my mother's face as she smoothed the hair from her eyes with the backs of her fingers and sighed softly. And I remembered my mother's saying, "You'll do it for your husband if you love him." And here she was, here they were, and that meant that what I had hoped was true: *she loved him.* In spite of everything she said, in spite of everything he did, my mother loved my father. And I supposed the reasoning went the other way, too, and that my father must also love *her.* When I thought of all this, a warm feeling came over me and my breathing moved up high in my body and my eyes grew hot and I felt I might sneeze. It never occurred to me then that there was any difference between *you'll do it if you love him* and *you'll do it only if you love him.* My mother had never offered the second of these, but it was this that now made me smile and feel lighter and secure.

For a long while, I rocked and put other pictures and sounds in my head: playing kidnap and pony express with Suki; riding bikes along the dirt path through the woods toward Devil's Rocks; climbing the cedar tree out front with my cat Pip. And then I tried to imagine kissing David Hanson but when the picture took shape, it was Billy Halliday I was kissing. *Billy Halliday!* The only hood I knew by name, the only hood I was sort of friends with. And though in real life, he was bad, in the picture in my head, Billy Halliday was good and his kisses were warm and sweet. Suddenly, a ribbon of light fell across my thigh and stretched all the way to the back shelves, to my gramma's books. The cupboard door was ajar now, free, and after a few moments, I peeked through the opening and into the living room where I saw my parents lying together on the couch, a tangle of limbs and hair and rumpled clothing. My father's head was tilted upward from his neck; my mother's was tucked under his chin. Their eyes were closed and soon I could hear them breathing deeply, rhythmically, together. I would never tell.

"Boo!" and now here was Suki, hands behind her back, smiling wisely, almost laughing. As always, her short brown hair was sticking almost straight up on the top of her head, like a little crown. Suki had a big, round face, even bigger and rounder than mine, and the lips on her big mouth were almost always stretched into a grin. Suki probably had the biggest mouth in Salem. She could fit her whole fist inside.

"What're you doing?" Suki said.

"Just lying here."

"Did I scare you? Were you scared?"

"Not scared," I said. "I wasn't scared. I was thinking about something."

"Oh yeah?" Suki said. "Like what?"

"Like where you were."

"Where'd you get the flowers?" Suki asked.

"John Hathorne."

"What's in the bag?"

I got to my knees and emptied the bag on the grass and there was the pile of candy, the lips on the bottom. I started to set everything in order, but Suki grabbed the red lips and put them on. She looked like Daisy Duck.

I put on the blue lips and moved toward Suki. We were both kneeling.

Suki took the lips from her mouth. "I'm gonna pretend it's Curt Metzger," she said. "How 'bout you?"

I said I'd pretend it was David Hanson. We leaned our faces together and put our arms around each other. Our wax lips touched. We stayed like that.

When we didn't have wax lips, which was most of the time, Suki and I might play that we were kissing boys by rolling our lips into our mouths and pressing our faces together where our lips weren't, kissing without lips, you might say. It wasn't very comfortable and the skin around our mouths might get sore and red but we'd do it anyway.

Now Suki's breath was hot on my face and I could smell milk. My eyes were closed and I was trying to make Suki be David Hanson. But in my head I didn't see David Hanson at all; I saw Billy Halliday.

Suddenly the staticky sound of tires on the path cut through the cemetery and we both jumped up and turned to see Mr. Nealy drive by in his green truck, an ordinary sight in Salem, especially here at Burying Point which was practically his home.

Mr. Nealy lived in a tiny old tumbledown house right next to Burying Point, almost *in* Burying Point, with his fat sister Bettina who all the kids said was missing some body parts—the tip of her little finger and three toes on one of her feet—who kept mainly to her house and whom hardly anyone ever saw but all the kids talked about and called *Butt-ina.* When I was little and I first heard about those missing toes of Bettina Nealy's, I thought of those stepsisters in Cinderella who mangled their feet to get them into that glass slipper and I wondered if maybe Bettina Nealy had whacked off her own toes.

"That's stupid," Cat had said. "Why would she do *that?*"

"Maybe so she could wear regular shoes," I said.

Cat didn't think so. "Why would she want to wear regular shoes when they make perfectly good fat people shoes?"

I didn't say anything but after I thought about it, it occurred to me that maybe it was worth it to her just to feel like everyone else, just to feel *normal,* even if it was only on her feet.

While Bettina Nealy never went anywhere and didn't have a job, Mr. Nealy seemed to have more occupations than anyone else in Salem. He was the town clerk in charge of all the records concerning marriages and deaths and births and land sales, the person who had to squeeze an official seal onto your papers for them to count legally. He was the junk man, the person your parents would call when they had something that they needed to get rid of that was just a little too good or a little too big to be garbage. He'd taken away all kinds of things for us—a rusty old potbelly stove, three barrels, a broken lawn mower, stuff that my mother said wasn't junk but would be antiques one day, and my father said *everything* would be antiques one day but she ignored him. Mr. Nealy didn't just fill the back of his truck with our things, of course—he took *everybody's* unwanted stuff: the Stallards' deep freezer, the Sheehans' busted wheel barrow, the Domandis' old tires. But what Mr. Nealy did with it all I couldn't have guessed; he didn't have a barn or a shed and it simply wouldn't have fit in that tiny house with him and his sister.

As far as Suki and I were concerned, Mr. Nealy's most thrilling job was being supervisor in charge of cemetery maintenance and re-

pair which meant he buried all the dead people. Suki and I figured
he probably had to touch dead bodies from time to time, like when
a coffin fell open or when he needed to make sure that he was
burying the right person in the right hole. Suki said she bet that Mr.
Nealy had to check each body before he buried it to make sure the
person was really dead. She said he'd have to squeeze the corpse's
wrist to feel for a pulse; he'd have to peel back the eyelids to see if
the pupil got small; he'd have to put a mirror in front of the mouth
to see if it steamed up. Otherwise someone might be buried alive.
I told Suki she read too much Edgar Allan Poe.

In his free time, Mr. Nealy often seemed to be cruising around
Salem in his pickup truck. Suki and I figured he wanted to avoid
going home and bumping around that tiny house with his fat sister, though Mr. Nealy told everyone he was patrolling the neigh-
borhoods of Salem looking for troublemakers, hoodlums, and
housebreakers, so he was well liked by all the grown-ups but not by
Suki and me. Mr. Nealy was always chasing us out of the cemetery,
yelling at us: "You girls stay outta here. This ain't no place for girls."

A couple of weeks before, Suki and I were smoking cigarettes
on a memorial bench in the newer part of the cemetery when Mr.
Nealy pulled up in his green truck.

We smushed out our cigarettes as Mr. Nealy lumbered toward
us in his dirty yellow jumpsuit, a big fat fatso. Suki said the jumpsuit made him look like an enormous baby chick, or maybe Baby
Huey, who was a duck.

"Just what do you think you're doin'?" Mr. Nealy stood with
his feet wide apart, probably because his legs were so fat, and crossed
his arms.

My heart was beating at the bottom of my throat and my
stomach was high in my body and I couldn't have spoken if someone had paid me.

But Suki stood up. She stood with her feet wide apart, too, and
said, "Nothing."

Mr. Nealy set his puffy hands on his hips. "Well, you girls'd
better go do nothin' somewheres else."

Suki put her hands on her hips, too, and said, "This is public property."

"Yeah? So?"

"That means we can be here if we want to." Suki was speaking snidely, making this smug face, the kind of face that made my mother call me "obstinate," then hit me and send me to my room.

Mr. Nealy squinted and started chewing on his cheeks and didn't say anything for a few moments, so I thought Suki had him until he took a deep breath, and said, "Let me explain something to you girls. This is *my* cemetery. I run it, see? I take care of it. I bury these dead folks, I mow the lawns and keep up the flowers. Your folks and the rest of the folks in town trust me to keep it safe and nice and clean, see? That means I have to keep out the riffraff, the scum, the bums, the *juvenile delinquents* come in here to smoke cigarettes and deface public property and do God knows what else."

"Yeah? So?" Suki said.

"That means *you*," Mr. Nealy yelled.

"We're not scum," Suki said. "We don't have to leave."

"This ain't no playground! *Out!* Or I'll have to call your parents, let them know their little girls hangin' around Buryin' Point, smokin' cigarettes, doin' God knows what else."

Mr. Nealy was always threatening to tell on us but he never did. In fact, he never did anything mean to us except for chasing us out of Burying Point, which wasn't really mean because we knew we didn't belong there anyway. Whenever I would come here with my parents, Mr. Nealy would always be friendly and say, "How do you do?" and use my name, like he was a nice man who thought I was a nice little girl. Things were always different in private.

The moment froze into a minute, no one saying anything until Mr. Nealy started flapping his arms like he was actually trying to raise his enormous yellow body into the air: *"Out! Now! God-damn it, now!"*

We took off and ran out of the cemetery to where we had left our bikes. And we hadn't come back here till now.

Suki and I fell down on top of Martha Anne, but Mr. Nealy was staring straight ahead, both fat hands on the steering wheel.

Suki pushed her wax lips against mine and my front teeth cut into my lip.

There were bones beneath us, the bones of a little girl who had a Christian burial: people shrouded in yards of black sackcloth, dabbing at their eyes with lowered heads and heavy hearts; a few men blowing thin, doleful notes out the bells of trumpets while a sour old preacher spoke about how everyone else will die and how they might join this lucky little girl, now disencumbered, now free of the burdens of the flesh. That's what Reverend Pinkham had said at my gramma's funeral—that she was *lucky*—but I don't think getting stomach cancer, then falling down the back stairs and breaking your neck is any kind of luck except bad.

And so close, just a few feet away, lay the body of John Hathorne.

I imagined John Hathorne pressing his mouth hard against the mouth of my eight-greats-aunt, Sara Wilde. In the winter of 1691.

Bits of different versions of what happened filtered down through the many years that came and went since then and this is the version I know, though I can no more say what parts are true than I can say just what was contributed by my gramma, what came from books, and what of this story comes from me, from my imagination or from a place inside me I can't even see, a place of unspoken memory transmitted through the generations—*this is who we are*—along with more outward traits like crazy red hair or enormous hands. Still, this is what I know of this time and it is truer to me than any history I might read in a book. And the story goes like this:

In 1691, Sara Wilde was eighteen years old and John Hathorne wanted to marry her. He told her so. Sara's father Samuel Wilde had promised her to Hathorne in exchange for an important tract of land by the Frost Fish River. But Sara Wilde said she wouldn't marry him, it didn't matter what kind of deal they'd made, what sort of promises were exchanged. After that, my gramma told me, there had been an incident.

Samuel Wilde was a widower and though he had a grown son in England, Sara was like his only child. Sara Wilde had the two qualities every man then desired in a woman: first, she was beautiful, like my mother, Gramma said, with fair, silky hair and pale eyes and all the men were dazzled by her. And second, and maybe more importantly, though she was a girl, Sara Wilde was strong and worked as hard as any man, sanding floors and chopping wood, dressing animals and toting water. With her, Samuel Wilde ran a good farm and never had to rely on the charity of his neighbors. At the end of each day, Samuel Wilde would go to the ordinary, which was like an inn and a pub and a meeting place, and he would settle in a corner with a tankard of ale and scowl into it most of the night. That's the kind of man he was, Gramma Hattie said: hard working, hard drinking, solitary, and sour. So usually, Sara Wilde was home alone come early evening. Everybody knew that. John Hathorne knew that. That was why he went out to the Wildes' that winter night.

It was cold and dark then, the sun having set in a clear sky, and Sara Wilde was down at the barn—*our* barn, this was *our* same land—tending to the newborns when John Hathorne walked in, pretending to be looking for Samuel Wilde. He smiled at Sara and he moved close to her. He told her he was going to marry her. He told her she was practically his already and moved even closer to her. Sara Wilde grabbed a shovel, she knew he had evil intentions, and when John Hathorne reached for her, she hit him with it. John Hathorne doubled over, cursed at her, then left and never bothered her again in that manner.

Even though she had so many relatives here—her sister Isabelle, her brother William, Grampa Percy—Gramma Hattie would never come with us to Burying Point. On Memorial Day, Cat and I would pick lilacs to put on graves, but Gramma wouldn't leave our kitchen. She would sit at the table with her hands folded and she would frown. When the lilacs were all bundled and tied with white ribbon and we were all zipped and buckled and ready to go, my mother would ask for the last time, "Are you sure you won't join us, Mom?" and Gramma Hattie wouldn't say anything. For a long time, I thought Gramma was angry at us kids maybe because while my mother prayed at Grampa Percy, Cat and I would laugh and run around the graveyard and climb on tombstones and make fun of people's names when the cemetery was supposed to be a sad, solemn place. And then one year, the year I turned nine, my gramma told me it was John Hathorne she hated. She said she was a good Christian woman, about as good as the next, but there was no room for doing what my mother insisted we do each year, there was no room for decorating the grave of a murderer. Then Gramma Hattie leaned her soft old face close to mine and looked at me with bright blue eyes, as bright as Franny's when she was born, and said, "They say it was Eve who corrupted Adam, you know, but think about it. Eve wasn't corrupt on her own. She listened to the snake. It was the snake that corrupted *her*. And who was that snake? Why, it was the devil himself! A *male*. Men are the source of sin, and don't you ever forget it."

My mother never spoke about the stories passed down through the generations from Sara Wilde's aunts and uncles, from her English brother and his children, to their children and their children and so forth, even though everyone knew Sara Wilde had no grave and they knew why. My mother only said that it wasn't exactly John Hathorne's fault that Sara Wilde was killed. People believed in witchcraft and witches in those days and they meant to do good, not evil.

But my gramma said: "The road to hell is paved with good intentions."

Even though she wasn't very involved in church anymore, and she no longer taught Sunday school or worked at the Christmas-in-July Bazaar or ran the First Church supper booth at the Topsfield Fair, my mother talked a lot about God and sin and said the family must show Christian understanding toward John Hathorne.

"He was a child of his time," she said.

So when we visited our relatives at Burying Point, we visited John Hathorne, too. And on Memorial Day, John Hathorne also got a bouquet of lilacs tied with white ribbon. For the sake of Sara Wilde. For our name's sake.

I could feel the crocuses on the side of my face. The ground pressed up on me. I pushed Suki away and the lips fell from her mouth.

"What's wrong?" Suki said.

"I wonder what Mr. Nealy's doing."

Suki looked up at the eskar, then at me.

"Do you wanna go?" Suki asked. She smiled. "Let's go!" she said, and got up and started running toward the wooded eskar, dodging tombstones and ornamental bushes, grabbing onto shrubs and clumps of grass and skinny young pines as she scrambled up the side of the eskar, looking back at me, at once whispering and yelling, "Come on!"

I left the pile of candy and ran after her.

When I reached the top of the eskar, music was playing. A rock-and-roll song. Suki was lying on her belly, arms folded under her.

"What's going on?"

Suki turned quickly: "Shsh! I don't *know.*"

I crawled across the dirt and pine needles and then I was lying next to Suki. We were trying to hold our breath.

On the other side of the eskar, Mr. Nealy was leaning against his truck on both elbows. He had parked in the small gravel circle at the end of the paved path. The driver's door was opened. A song about a little beauty named Trudy was playing. Mr. Nealy's feet were spread wide and his belly stuck way out. He looked like he was trying to stick it out as far as he could. It was one of those round droop bellies, like a basketball in a hammock, as opposed to a high pregnant-woman belly. His eyes were closed, but his head was turning back and forth, maybe to the music.

This was the quietest part of the cemetery. No one buried here was old enough to be history or young enough to still have family visiting. This was the part with obelisks—little Bunker Hill monuments—and memorial benches and vaults. From where we were lying, it looked like a granite spike was growing right out of the top of Mr. Nealy's head. His head was turning slowly from side to side but the spike stayed put. Mr. Nealy at the stake. And he was smiling.

I whispered this to Suki, about the spike coming out of Mr. Nealy's head, and she laughed and Mr. Nealy's face went blank and his eyes opened. He looked up at the eskar. He stood up straight. Then Mr. Nealy took a step toward the eskar, toward us. There was a loud crunching sound. Suki and I were stone, not breathing at all. And then another truck appeared, circled around Mr. Nealy on the grass along the edge of the clearing and pulled up along side his truck. Mr. Nealy was looking at the other truck now and smiling.

"Ray!" Mr. Nealy said.

A man in blue jeans climbed out of the truck. He was wearing a red-and-black checkered shirt and he had a very red face and a flat nose and right away I thought he was from Maine. The man was my father's age. He looked like someone my father might play poker with. When he turned toward Mr. Nealy, a strip of white as long as a pencil and wide as a ruler gleamed from the man's dark hair. The man hurried over to Mr. Nealy and patted him on the arm. They shook hands and they both laughed. They put their arms around each other, slapped backs. The red-faced man laughed, a funny kind of laugh through the nose, like, "Haw, haw, haw." Mr. Nealy took a flat silver bottle from the back pocket of his jumpsuit, unscrewed the cap, and offered it to the man. The man took a long gulp, squinted his eyes, and gave his head a quick shake, like he was forcing down medicine, and handed the bottle back to Mr. Nealy. Mr. Nealy laughed again and took a long gulp, too. Mr. Nealy had a loud, abrupt Santa Claus laugh, so I wondered if he really thought something was funny. The men looked at the ground and the red-faced man made noise like air coming out of a tire.

And then the men weren't laughing. They weren't smiling. They were quiet and they leaned together against the truck, passed the silver bottle back and forth. They didn't look at each other, but they leaned together. Though the man's head was blocking most of Mr. Nealy's face, I could still see the curve of Mr. Nealy's belly. If I squinted, I could make the belly belong to the red-faced man.

Suki and I weren't saying anything, we were just waiting.

The men seemed to be waiting too. They were still not talking. They were still not looking at each other. But they were close. They were standing so close together, as close together as Suki and I were lying. And they weren't talking and we weren't talking. Mr. Nealy let the silver bottle drop from his hand. Then it was like time slowed down and down and Mr. Nealy's arm reached behind the man, reached back around the bed of the truck. I didn't see his arm and I wondered if he was going to take something from the back of the truck—a shovel, maybe—and smash the man with it. But then his arm kept coming and circled the man's shoulders. Mr. Nealy's arm stopped and his hand rested cupped in this empty space before the man's chest where a breast would have been if the man had been a woman. Still, they weren't looking at each other. And it was taking so long.

I looked at Suki, I wanted to leave, but Suki was staring at the men. I tapped her arm and it made a little jerk in my direction but she kept staring. And then, like a toy wound too tightly, everything suddenly stopped. There was no music. No one was breathing. But everything—the trees around us, the tombstones and monuments, the men by the truck, the truck itself—everything shivered with possibility. I saw myself running but I couldn't move.

I jumped when the high, hollow whistle of the evening train echoed off the stones in the little glen and with a jolt it all started up again—*lips together!* But then slowly: Mr. Nealy's hand on that man's red cheek, the man's hand in Mr. Nealy's hair. And time began to uncoil. Things started to happen. Mr. Nealy and the man were holding each other. They weren't fighting, but they were holding each other. I thought: They're wrestling. Not wrestling, but like wrestling. They were rubbing against each other, rubbing together. Then the other man, the red-faced man, pushed away from Mr.

Nealy. I waited for him to scream but instead, he raised his head and made this sputtering horse noise with his lips. Then he pulled down his pants. He unzipped his pants and bent over and pulled them down, and with them, his underwear.

I had never seen it before, but I had heard about it. Suki had talked about her brother's, Kenny. A snake. And I had read those *Playboy*s with Suki, the ones Kenny hid under his bed. About a man's penis growing and moving and all. So I had this idea that it was an animal, unpredictable, something with a mind of its own. My father was very private about his. I had walked in on him in the bathroom but he had always been sitting, always hiding it between his legs.

But suddenly I saw the red faced man's and it was so small and pink. And it had this hat on the end of it. I could see it from here. It didn't look like any snakes I had seen. It was tiny. With a hat.

Once, when Suki and I were little, we examined each other between the legs. This was when we were both in what we called *the disgusting stage,* when we thought a lot about nakedness and going to the bathroom. It wasn't really that we liked boys, then; it wasn't like now. We were just curious. Well, we knew what ours looked like, we had seen each other's, and our own with a mirror, but we didn't know what to call it. It seemed funny there were so many names for penises: *dick* and *willy* and *prick* and *weenie* and *cock.* But neither of us knew any word for what we had. Suki's mom called it her *privates* and my mom didn't call it anything. If you had a problem there, like when Cat got her period, you had "a female problem."

Suddenly I remembered the magazines. I remembered that there would be a moment when that thing would explode. That was the word they had used in the magazines—*explode.* And *erupt.* And then I really wanted to get out of there, but I couldn't get Suki to move. Suki even told me to shut up. She kept staring and I kept staring too. And it was like everything had stopped again, like there was no motion, like the whole world was still.

And then Mr. Nealy was kneeling—"Nealy kneeling" but it

wasn't funny—and the man, still standing, turned his red face to the sky. His mouth was opened, like a chicken in the rain, but he wasn't making a sound.

I could see the silver bottle on the gravel near the back of the truck.

And then Mr. Nealy—the junk man! our Mr. Nealy!—leaned forward and grabbed that man's penis with both hands. I gasped and Suki yelled out, *"Oh my Lord!"* and suddenly the two men were looking up toward the top of the eskar, toward us, and I said, or thought, *They see us,* and Suki hollered, *"Run!"* and I took off.

I slipped down the side of the eskar, grabbing onto little bushes, and then picked up speed and started running on the grass. Even when I closed my eyes, I could still see Mr. Nealy holding it. *A snake.* I could still see the man's red face turned up to the sky. I kept running, past the gravestones—1852, 1821, 1797—toward Martha Anne.

I could hear Suki behind me. Both of her hands pressed on my back and I let her push me over. We fell on top of John Hathorne. We rolled onto our backs. I could feel a pack of Bazooka under my shoulder. I wondered about putting the candy in order, but I realized we weren't going to eat it now.

Then Suki leaned over and kissed me. I had never been kissed before, on the mouth, with real lips. I listened for the sound of Mr. Nealy's truck but it didn't come.

We were kissing but we weren't moving. Suki's breath was hot on my face. I closed my eyes and felt Suki's weight. My first kiss. And Suki's mouth was hard on my mouth. Like a fist. I wouldn't forget.

Chapter Three

*Fat People, Poor People, and
Dead People*

Tall oak trees sprouting pale green and yellow
leaves lined the streets that twisted from Burying Point all the way
back to my house at the end of Wilde Road. Winter had receded
from Salem like a boulder rolled off the earth revealing a new, quietly burgeoning world underneath and everything was still damp
and pale and tender, like skin that's been under a bandage for a long
time. You could smell the earth releasing a thousand exotic odors,

rich smells of fertility and ripening and it filled your head and made you feel new, too.

Suki had taken a shortcut back to her house that afternoon up Osgood to Meetinghouse Lane because Mrs. Domandi said she had to be home by five *or else.* The Domandis were like that—they always had to know where their children were and where they were headed and what they would do when they got where they were going. After dinner, Mr. Domandi would drive Suki over to my house so she could spend the night. We would make root beer floats and stay in the guest room and keep sneaking downstairs for snacks and watch old movies and strain to keep our eyes open so the night wouldn't end.

Suki and I had bolted out of Burying Point, hollering and shrieking, a little crazy with what we'd just seen. We'd sneaked back up the eskar before leaving but all we saw then was the two men lying on the ground, on their backs, and they were quiet and no one was moving. It was like they were waiting to be buried there, or like they had already been buried and had somehow risen up through the dirt and were now floating on top of it, floating on the earth like fat men float on the ocean. I could see the silver bottle on the gravel near the back of the truck. Though earlier we'd both had a good view, somehow, we didn't know what to make of it, these two men being about as crazy as we'd seen anyone be. We hurried back down the eskar. As we ran toward our bikes, we laughed and stumbled around and acted like we were drunk. And after we began to ride off in opposite directions, Suki hollered back to me to say a Hail Mary, something we usually did together before we left Burying Point. She began yelling it out and I joined her, hollering across the tombstones: "Hail Mary, full of grace, the Lord is with thee. Blessed art thou among women, blessed is the fruit of thy womb, Jesus . . ."

It was 2.2 miles from Burying Point to my mailbox—Cat had measured it with her odometer—and those miles stretched out long and full of possibility like the vacation days ahead.

When I passed David Hanson's house, I might see David in his front yard, playing catch with his little brother. He might call my name and I would stop and we would talk. My knees would be loose. My hands would be clumsy and in the way and I wouldn't know what to do with them, and they would worry me. David Hanson might talk with me about Russia and Johnson and the war; he might ask me to go shoot baskets with him.

But when I passed David Hanson's house, David's little brother was sitting by himself at the end of the driveway, guiding a toy ambulance into a rock, going, "Zzzooom. *Crash!*" Like all the little boys, David's brother had a whiffle haircut, short and stiff like the bristles on a nail brush, like a soldier's hair, so short you couldn't tell what color it was. David Hanson wasn't around.

I studied the bag of candy in my basket, the way it hopped when I hit a bump in the road, banging against the wire jingles of my basket, jumping and trembling. I rode one hand. I rode no-hands. I counted mailboxes between streets.

As I neared the Cohens' house, I whispered, "Please don't let Perry be outside." As I've said, Perry Cohen was big and scary and mental and he was often out working in the Cohens' yard trying to repair something but he didn't have the tools or the knowledge to stop their house from being the dump that it had become. The Cohens were our only personal poor people and *poor* was one of the three things Suki and I had decided long ago that we never wanted to be, the other two being *fat* and *dead*. These qualities seemed bad in themselves but they also seemed to bring along other bad things. For example, fat people never seemed to be just fat—they seemed to be poor and unhealthy and sad, too.

The only really fat people I knew were the Nealys, who were probably the fattest people in town. All the kids made fun of them—not to their faces, of course, but even behind their backs, it was mean. Kids called them all kinds of fat names—*the Lardos, the Fatties, the Hippos*—but mostly kids just referred to them as Crisco Mealy and his sister Butt-ina, who, as I've said, was really named *Bettina*, which was a funny name even if you weren't fat, maybe *espe-*

cially if you weren't fat. It was a fat name, I thought, like *Elsie* and *Bertha* and *Beulah*. I'd seen Bettina Nealy once before she had grown really huge and took to staying indoors all the time. She was out in her little vegetable garden when I rode by on my way downtown one afternoon a few summers earlier. I was so surprised to see her, to see someone other than Mr. Nealy in the Nealy yard, and I slowed and stared as I rode past. Bettina Nealy's hair was long and light brown and smooth and trimmed in a straight line across her back and I remember admiring how shiny and thick it was, how rich and warm, like caramel, and I remember thinking how I'd have given quite a lot to have that long, straight, gleaming hair. When I rode over a piece of metal on the sidewalk, it clanked and Bettina Nealy started and turned toward me and saw me staring at her. Her mouth was open and her eyes were wide and they were the most extraordinary eyes I had ever seen, the palest but the brightest blue, like stars in her face—luminous, dazzling; you could've seen them miles away—and when I saw them, I gasped. Bettina Nealy must have seen the surprise on my face but I knew she had taken it for something else, something unkind that I did *not* feel, when she dropped her trowel and began blinking quickly, wiping her hands on her shift and gasping, "Oh! Oh!"

I called, "Hi, there!" to her, but Bettina Nealy was hurrying to her back door by then, panting and puffing a little, with a pained expression on her face that made me want to cry because I knew I'd caused it. I never saw Bettina Nealy again after that and before the year's end, my mother would hear that she had grown much fatter and was now housebound and I always felt personally responsible, as if just when she had dared to come out, I had scared Bettina Nealy back into her house for good.

Later, in school, I would read about a sculptor who believed his beautiful statues were already fully formed, waiting within the marble which would constitute them, and he would regard himself as somehow freeing them from their stony tombs. When I read that, I thought of Bettina Nealy, of her glorious hair, of her heavenly eyes, and I wondered if within her a beautiful form waited to be freed from its flesh-and-blood tomb. By that time, Bettina Nealy would have become so fat that people said they had to make special furniture for her, widen the doorways, put steel supports through the floors; so fat she couldn't buy clothes from the store anymore, even from Sizes Unlimited in Lynn, or fit in a car or a regular dentist's chair if she'd been able to get there at all. But as it was, Bettina Nealy couldn't get anywhere because she couldn't leave her house and she couldn't leave her house because she didn't have any shoes—even without all her toes, her feet were too fat for them—and even if she'd *had* shoes, Bettina Nealy didn't have *time* to go anywhere: she had to eat constantly to stay so fat. At least, this was what Danny Dawes had said. Danny Dawes said his mother told him that each meal, Bettina Nealy ate what the entire Dawes family—two parents and two growing boys—ate in one day, *more,* even, and to keep from losing weight, she had to get up to eat twice during the night. Danny Dawes said his mother should know; she was a nurse and sometimes took care of Bettina Nealy at her house when she had the flu or a fever.

When I asked Danny Dawes what was so wrong about Bettina Nealy's being fat, he said it was simply the fact that she was fat that was wrong.

"Why?"

He looked at me like I was insane. "If a person's fat, it means they're *greedy,*" Danny Dawes said. "Fat people take more than they should. Fat people want it all."

I didn't agree with him—I didn't think fat people ate too much because they were greedy or because they wanted it all; I thought of that statue within the marble and I thought of Bettina Nealy hurrying back into her house when she saw me and I felt sure that *that* was what it was about, wanting to disappear, wanting to *hide.*

After she'd retreated into her home, the only times Bettina Nealy had left that little Nealy house was when the doctor couldn't come to her—like when she had to have her appendix out—and then, Mr. Nealy needed the help of three men to load her into the back of his green truck and haul her off, that's how big she'd gotten.

I'd read about a fat man once, a man so huge, the book had said, that when he died he had to be buried in a piano case. I remember wanting to be amazed by that, but I couldn't understand it. What was a piano case? The part with the strings and hammers? It seemed to me that that part was wide, but not deep. I couldn't get a fix on this image, a fat man in a piano case—how would they close the lid?—but it did make me wonder who would build the coffin that Bettina Nealy would one day be buried in and that was the first time it struck me: Bettina Nealy was living her whole life only feet away from where she would spend her death.

Sometimes I wondered about that, about the Nealys' living so close to the cemetery. I wondered if there was something peculiar about the vegetables Bettina and Wally Nealy ate that made them so fat. After all, these vegetables were grown right next to the cemetery, practically *in* the cemetery since there was in fact no wall separating the Nealy property from Burying Point, no wall marking off the vegetable garden from the burial ground. Without the walls which around here, throughout Salem and the rest of the North Shore, defined things, *made* things what they were, told you what was what and who owned it—*this* was the start of the Proctor estate, *that yard* belonged to the First Church, *this here* was the Cabots' meadow—without those walls, who could really say what something was? In this case, who could really say where *graveyard* stopped and *garden* began? It scared me to think that those two Nealys were eating stuff harvested from among corpses, but I kept it to myself. I thought Bettina and Wally Nealy suffered enough without my adding to it anymore than I already did, which was plenty. After all, I was the one who scared Bettina Nealy back inside.

But Suki and I didn't think about being fat much since being fat was something we never worried about personally: we were both skinny, in spite of eating constantly, as much as Bettina Nealy, I was sure, and neither of us had any fatties in our families or among our personal friends. Being poor was a different story, however. Not for the Domandis—they didn't seem to think about being poor or not being poor, at least, they never talked about it and they all seemed to have what they needed and enough of everything else so that no one in the Domandis' household ever complained, at least not in front of me. In my family, though, as I've said, my parents were always implying we were poor and somehow there never seemed to be enough, especially these days.

It used to be that my mother kept reserves of everything, like she was preparing to open a little grocery store or like she was expecting a disaster—maybe a hurricane or war. We wouldn't have one extra box of cereal, we would have five. Cabinets would be filled with cans of fruit and soup, stacked neatly in rows and columns, boxes of crackers, bags of sugar and flour. Sometimes the cabinets were so full you couldn't shut the doors. Our freezer was as big and deep as the one in Kirby's, packed with beef and chicken, clear plastic bags of peas and beans from our garden, tubs of ice cream, loaves of bread. Behind the stairs in the cellar, Dad had built shelves that Mom used to keep stocked with jars of jams and pickles and relishes that had simmered for hours in kettles on the stove, filling the house with a bitter, sweet, inescapable smell that made you unpleasantly conscious of your stomach. The bottom two shelves held extra cleaning supplies, bath soaps, paper goods, and giant glass jugs of water. When I asked her why she kept so much stuff around, Mom said it was probably because she grew up during the depression and saw people starving. A good supply of necessities, she said, was like money in the bank.

But around the time she started working at Old Stuff, we began using up the reserves so that now, the freezer had been emptied of bread and juice and meat and all that remained were a couple of bags of vegetables and a few Popsicles and some tubs of ice cream, dry and streaked with crystals. The shelves of the kitchen cabinets were often so bare you could see clear to the wall behind them, feel grains of rice and sugar granules spilled on them so long ago they no longer attracted ants. Only the water and a few jars of green tomato relish were left in the cellar. These days, we ran out of things like toilet paper all the time and had to use napkins or paper towels. So these days when my parents said we were poor, sometimes I would wonder.

Now, as I passed the Cohens' empty yard, I looked up at the house and glimpsed a shadowed head in Lydia Cohen's window and I felt glad I wasn't her and that I didn't live in her poor, falling-down house with her bland mother and her re-tarded brother. I knew exactly where Lydia was sitting in her dark little room—at the foot of her bed, with her knees almost touch-ing her wobbly old side table. I knew that she was staring at her bul-letin board probably at the photograph of her father and a shiver went down my spine and I thought, *Somebody's dancing on my grave,* which is what Cat always said when she felt a shiver but it wasn't cold out. The curtains in Lydia Cohen's room were the same grey lacy ones she'd had up since before we'd started school seven years ago. They looked like they'd come from someone's dining room. Her walls were papered with a dark grey green and on her floor was a blue spiral carpet, threadbare in places so you could see the floor-boards dry and pale underneath. The Cohens were very poor. I knew all this personally because Lydia Cohen had been my first best friend, my best friend for years when I was very small. Our moth-ers were best friends and, when Lydia's father was still alive, our par-ents were best friend couples.

Mr. Cohen had died when Lydia and Perry were very young, so long ago now that neither of them remembered much about him, though Lydia remembered the story of how he had died and she told it to me when we were small. One Thanksgiving, Mr. Cohen had driven to New Hampshire to pick up his mother and bring her back to Salem for the holiday, like he did every year. Only this year, coming home through Rowley, Mr. Cohen took a corner too fast and ran the car off the road into the Ipswich River and Mr. Cohen and his mother drowned. When she first told me this, Lydia seemed not despondent but baffled and I felt baffled, too. I knew from Cat that Mr. Cohen hadn't drowned at all. Cat said she and I had been coloring at the kitchen table while Mom was baking when the telephone rang. Mom held the receiver with both hands and she kept saying, *"Oh no. Oh no. Oh no."* After she hung up, Mom told Cat to keep an eye on me and left. Later, Cat heard her talking on the phone, saying, "They found his head twenty feet away, on the riverbank." Cat swore this was the absolute truth, but I didn't say anything about it to Lydia.

The first time I slept over Lydia's house, when we were only in first grade, she showed me the old black-and-white photograph she kept tacked to her bulletin board, a photograph of her father, a pumpkin-faced man with slicked-back hair—a teenager, it seemed, too young to be anyone's dad—dressed in a dark suit, hands on his hips, smiling broadly at the camera. It was the closest I had come to a dead person—not a grandparent or some kid's great-uncle from another state, but my friend's father—and even though I didn't remember Mr. Cohen myself and I was only looking at a photograph and Mr. Cohen was very young and alive in it, seeing it made my stomach feel empty and tickled and tight. I felt as I had when Cat showed Suki and me a dead fox in the woods behind our house. The fox was filled with maggots, Cat said, small worms that get under your skin when you die and eat you from the inside out. The fox was dead, but the maggots inside made its skin move, or so I imagined when Cat said it. I had wondered if Lydia knew that by then her father had been completely devoured by little worms, that all that remained in his coffin was worm poop, like Cat had told me, but I didn't ask.

Lydia said the photograph had been taken two months before her father died. *But he looks young,* I wanted to say. Until that moment, I had thought that only old people died.

Lydia had also showed me some of her father's things, things Mrs. Cohen kept at the far end of her closet where thin light from the bare bulb hardly reached. In a shoe box tied with a purple hair ribbon, a silver cigarette lighter with the initials WJC—for William Jonathan Cohen, Lydia said—a Hohner Marine Band harmonica, and a tortoiseshell comb rested on top of a stack of letters secured with a green elastic. Lydia said they were love letters her father had written to her mother long ago, before they were married, but Lydia wouldn't let me read them. The shoe box sat on a shelf above two pin-striped suits and beneath the cuffs of one of the suit's pants stood a pair of black shoes just where feet would be. Mr. Cohen must have worn those suits; maybe one of them was the one he had on in the photograph. He must have smoothed his hair with the tortoiseshell comb, put these clothes on, and made them warm and rich with a grown man's scent. He laughed in them and sweated in them. He lit cigarettes with that lighter and slipped it in the pocket of his jacket. And in the evenings, lazy summer evenings, Mr. Cohen would take the harmonica onto the front porch and blow some happy little tune. His lips were once there, pressed against these holes warming them as the harmonica sang with his breath. The comb ran through his hair; its teeth glistened with sweet pomade. He walked in these shoes. You could still see the humps of his small toes at the shoes' edges. His body had filled these clothes, given them shape, smell, warmth, life. Seeing and touching these things made me woozy and I didn't understand why Mrs. Cohen would want to keep them and I wasn't even sure it wasn't wrong for us to be looking at them.

The Cohens' house was old like ours, with a steep, narrow staircase and low ceilings and four fireplaces, but since Mr. Cohen died, things were falling apart. Outdoor shutters missing slats dangled precariously from rusty hinges. The chimney was crumbling and the flues were full of squirrels' nests, so the fireplaces were stuffed with rat poison and burlap sacks and couldn't be used. Floorboards were so dry and in need of sanding you couldn't walk barefoot in the Cohens' house without having to dig thick slivers of wood from your feet afterward. Paint curled from the clapboard in wide strips that Lydia and I would pull and drop on the ground around the foundation making Mrs. Cohen scream at us about lead poisoning. On the front porch, the floor had busted through and no one was allowed there anymore. While my father was breathing life into our old house and despite Perry Cohen's attempts with glue and nails and tacks, the Cohens' house was dying.

After Mr. Cohen was killed, little by little, Rachel began losing the few things he'd left behind. First, small ads appeared in the Classified section of the *Salem Evening News* offering the contents of the Cohens' basement and garage—tools and car parts and a bench saw. My mother would spot the ads and read them to my father. Soon, my mother saw Rachel Cohen's best clothes laundered, pressed, and tagged, hanging on racks in New to You, the women's consignment clothing shop in Danvers. And one day, Rachel Cohen arrived at our house in tears, having just sold her grandmother's jewelry at Bunky's Pawn Shop in Lynn to cover three months' of electric bills. Two springs after Mr. Cohen's death, a water pipe burst in the Cohens' cellar and Rachel had to sell the station wagon to pay for the cleanup and repair. She wept all weekend, saying it was probably the last car she would ever own. As time passed and there was nothing left to sell to pay for repairs, what broke was discarded or ignored, if irreparable by Rachel or Perry, and the Cohens' house began to take on its current forlorn aspect of decay and neglect. Without a man's money and a man's hands, their property, their house, their clothes, their dishes, the Cohens themselves and the artifacts of their lives looked as unloved and abandoned as Rachel Cohen felt and this was the sorrow of her life—not its lacking material comfort, but the absence in it of a husband to love her and for her to love and care for because Rachel Cohen felt most truly alive, most truly herself, when wrapped around the life and soul of a man who loved her back. I heard her tell my mother this one afternoon. "Without someone to love who loved me," she said, "I would be dead."

Three months after Rachel Cohen sold her station wagon, she got the job at the Daily Grind in Beverly, brewing coffee and waiting on tables Monday through Thursday, sunrise till midafternoon. Since my father left early for work each day and had to pass by her place anyway, he drove Rachel Cohen to work four days each week. Cat and Mom and I teased him about this, since Rachel had a big crush on my father. Every body knew that. Though she was too poor, she said, to exchange gifts with our family on birthdays or holidays, Rachel Cohen was always making things for my father: a matching scarf and cap at Christmas; a lemon chiffon cake on his birthday; a casserole or baked beans and brown bread if Mom was sick. Once she even sewed my father a bathrobe from thick white terry and embroidered DAVID in red on the left breast, "close to his heart," Cat said. Whenever Rachel Cohen saw my father she would blush and ask if he might come over and help Perry with a plumbing or roofing or window problem. Dad always said yes and later Mom would kiss him for it. When Cat asked Mom if it bothered her, Rachel Cohen's crush on Dad, Mom laughed and said she thought it was sweet and touching and pathetic. Mom never doubted that Dad would always be faithful to her, so she felt safe joking that if Rachel wanted him so badly, she could have him— Mom would give him to her with her blessings. Mom said that like a loyal dog, Dad would never leave. He didn't even *look* at other women, she knew that. He was completely devoted to her.

Since Mrs. Cohen left for work so early, Lydia had to feed and dress herself and Perry, collect her books, and get out to the bus stop each morning, and she always showed up at school in wrinkled clothes with a shiny face and a smell of old pillowcases. Sometimes, the other kids would tease Lydia, trip her in the hall, knock her books from her arms, and ask if she would be going to the father-daughter dance: it was as if nobody could quite forgive her for having a dead father, or as if it were something about her that made her father die, as if she were just the kind of person who *would* have a dead father.

It had been a long time since Lydia Cohen and I were best friends—or even friends at all—though from time to time, I would see her alone at a long table at the far end of the cafeteria and I would carry my tray over and sit with her and be her friend. But before lunch was through, I would be reminded all over again that Lydia was a cold, sour, and angry girl, and I would only be her friend for that one lunch and I would end up feeling worse.

The Cohens were our only personal poor people, so I suppose I thought being poor meant being friendless and sour and dismal, dirty and rumpled and alone, and I suppose I even felt it had something to do with death and maggots.

The Cohens weren't the poorest people in town, though; this distinction belonged to the Hallidays, who lived down by the depot in a rickety house almost as small as the Nealys' with a couple of skinny dogs scratching around in a scrubby dirt yard. There were twelve or thirteen Halliday kids total, only the last four or five of whom actually belonged to Mr. Halliday. The first bunch of Hallidays, including Billy Halliday, were born *Burtons,* but Mr. Burton died a long time ago, before anyone I knew could even remember.

For years, Mrs. Burton struggled to care for herself and her eight or nine kids—she cleaned people's houses, baby-sat, baked cakes, took in people's wash—until she met and married this Halliday man who adopted her kids and gave them his name and people said she was lucky to find someone who'd put up with another man's leavings like that. They said it as if Mrs. Burton wasn't kind and beautiful *(but she was!)* and as if the Burton kids were Mr. Burton's droppings or something. As it was, I felt sorry for Mrs. Burton's having Mr. Halliday for a husband; I thought anyone would be better off poor and alone than with someone like him. Mr. Halliday was not a handsome man—he was tall and thick, with snarly black hair, a red face, bloodshot eyes above a purple nose, and arms inscribed with smudgy green tatoos of anchors and eagles and the name of a girl who was not his wife—and everyone said he was mean as a snake. Mr. Halliday smoked cigars and opened beer bottles with his teeth and drank a bottle of whisky by himself every night. Jimmy Hartfield said that before Mr. Halliday met Mrs. Burton, he was a bum living in a cardboard box up in the woods behind Burying Point; he ate wild animals that he killed with his bare hands—squirrels and chipmunks and groundhogs—and when it snowed, he slept in people's outhouses or sheds or unlocked cars. After he married Mrs. Burton, made her Mrs. Halliday and her kids Halliday kids, he gave her four or five more babies to take care of, as if all Mrs. Burton—Mrs. *Halliday*—wanted in the whole world to make her happy was children. I didn't imagine anybody was like that.

Cat said Mrs. Halliday had so many babies because she was a Catholic and that's how it was with them—Catholics had to have a lot of children; it was one of those Catholic rules. I guessed that meant Suki could expect some younger brothers or sisters to come along and save her from being the baby of the family, but when I told her so, she said her mother couldn't have any more babies but she didn't know why. It seemed mysterious to both of us, Mrs. Domandi's not being able to have more children, one of those things we'd be told we'd understand later, if we asked, though we knew that by the time later came, we wouldn't take special notice because we'd have forgotten we ever specially wanted to know. Privately, I wondered if Mrs. Domandi didn't just decide she wasn't going to put up with any more of Mr. Domandi's penis in her.

Billy Halliday was my age and he was the only boy I sometimes liked better than David Hanson. But I couldn't look at Billy Halliday or think about him and, at the same time, think about Russia or Johnson or shooting baskets or the war; when I looked at Billy Halliday, my head filled with Billy Halliday and everything inside me—my stomach, my heart, my breath—rose up and I felt I was standing at the edge of a very high place.

Billy Halliday was not exactly handsome—his blonde hair was coarse and snarly and dull and it never lay smooth on his head and he had a scar like a crescent moon on the cheekbone under one eye—but Billy Halliday had a way about him. He had a gentle, soothing voice, sleepy brown eyes, and a pleasant mouth that it was hard not to watch when he spoke.

Billy Halliday was the boy I shouldn't have liked but did—at least my wicked self, my private inside self did. When he came into my head, my wicked self would kiss him and my good self would try to push him out with images of David Hanson, but my wicked self always won because, although he was rumpled and dirty and smokey, although he cut classes and skipped school, although he had liquor on his breath sometimes, even showed up at home room drunk, and although I knew I really shouldn't have liked him, there was an emptiness inside me exactly Billy Halliday's shape, an absence that had been there all my life, it seemed, that Billy Halliday—*only* Billy Halliday—could possibly fill. And when Billy Halliday came into my head and filled that space, my head emptied of everything else. So when I thought of Billy Halliday, I could think of nothing but Billy Halliday.

And somehow, though we never sat next to each other and only spoke when no one else was around, and though we had no friends in common, Billy Halliday knew I liked him and he didn't hate me for it, but began slipping notes into my book bag and through the vents at the top of my locker, little greetings in Spanish or French or both—*¡Hola, cherie! ¿Qu'est-ce que tú haces?*—or sometimes lyrics to a song or a poem like nothing I'd ever heard before, like this one:

> If I were only dafter
>   I might be making hymns
> To the liquor of your laughter
>   And the lacquer of your limbs.

It made me shiver to get notes from Billy Halliday.

Like Lydia Cohen, Billy Halliday had a dead father and like the Cohen family, the Halliday family was poor, even poorer than the Cohens, though there was a dad, a replacement dad, that red-faced, cigar-smoking Mr. Halliday who everyone knew gave Billy his black eyes and broken bones, though Billy never said so. It was having all those kids that kept the Hallidays so poor and Jimmy Hartfield said there would have been even more Halliday children if two hadn't died when they were very little. Dead children were a real rarity in that place in those days; the only ones we knew of for sure were the two Hallidays, though Danny Dawes said the Weavers, a wealthy couple who had a little girl named Patty, had had another daughter, Emma, who died long ago. Once, when Suki and I rode by the Weavers' place, we saw Danny leaning over their fence, calling to

Patty Weaver, who was playing in her sandbox: "Hey, Patty! Where's Emma? Huh? Where'd she go?"

Patty Weaver just sat there in the middle of her sandbox with a puzzled look on her face. Suki threw a rock at Danny Dawes and he rubbed the back of his head and cursed at her, called her *a doggie dick,* and rode off in the other direction. But Suki and I didn't really believe in the Weavers' dead baby because we figured the Hallidays' being poor had something to do with their losing children—*that* was the connection, it seemed. Unless you were poor, you died old, like grandparents. If you were poor, you could die anytime—as a child like those little Hallidays or as a grown-up like Mr. Cohen and Mr. Burton, Billy's real father. It would've been hard not to notice the connection between being poor and being dead—these poorest families in Salem were the only ones who had dead people in them who weren't also old people—though just how that connection worked, I couldn't have said. Still, it seemed that being poor was a dangerous way to be and it made me worry for Billy Halliday.

Billy Halliday was the only kid I knew who drank liquor. The first time I smelled it on him was in fourth grade during a penmanship lesson. I had had to pass out the pencils and when I gave Billy his, I smelled it. Afterward, I told Suki he had my mother's night breath.

"He's drunk," she said, and I felt I'd run smack into a wall I somehow hadn't seen in front of me though it'd been there all along.

The last time I smelled liquor on Billy Halliday was a couple of weeks before when I was walking around downtown by myself waiting for Suki. We were supposed to meet at three o'clock at Reynold's Apothecary and I'd arrived early. I didn't want to go in by myself and be a lone shoplifting suspect, so I decided to walk down to the depot and look around. Wherever there were trains, there were possibilities, chances for tremendous changes in a moment's time. You could do what they did in the 1930s and jump on a train and hide yourself in whatever they were carrying—hay or coal or farm animals—and you could take that train all the way across the country or down to Mexico or up to Canada and you could start a whole new life. After I passed Billy Halliday's house, sneaking peeks at the windows to try to glimpse Billy Halliday, I heard a rusty sound and a *smack-smack* and I turned to see Billy Halliday striding across his yard, the storm door of his house banging behind him.

Billy Halliday walked right up to me and bowed his head a little, like an old-fashioned gentleman, like if he'd had a hat, he'd have tipped it. "Good afternoon."

I felt trembly and loose in my joints but I said, "Good afternoon."

"And where are you headed this fine day?"

"Just walking around."

Billy Halliday lowered his eyebrows as if he were thinking that walking around was a strange thing to be doing in his part of town when you're from my part of town.

"Like train tracks, do you?" he said, nodding toward the depot.

"I like trains," I said.

Billy Halliday smiled and a dreamy look came over his face and he squinted a little as if he were looking at something far away, trying to see it more clearly. "One day, I'm getting on that train and I'm gonna take it far away from here."

"Oh, yeah?"

"Yeah," he said. "I'll take it to Mexico and I'll get a donkey and mine for silver and have myself an adventure."

I could smell the liquor on his breath. "This train doesn't go to Mexico."

"It doesn't matter where I go, really, as long as I'm gone." Then Billy cleared his throat and said, "So, you're just having yourself a little stroll here on the scenic side of town, huh?"

I nodded.

"Me, I've been sucking liquor from my stepfather's stash all afternoon and now I need a smoke. Mom doesn't let anyone smoke in the house." Billy Halliday poked his fingers into the breast pocket of his denim jacket and pinched a cigarette from the pack wedged in there. Then he said, softly, confidentially, "Don't tell anyone but I was suspended today." He made an exaggerated wincing face. "Now I'm arming myself for my stepfather's return from work. Bracing myself." Billy nodded at me then whispered, "He won't be happy at the news." Billy Halliday paused to light his cigarette, and said, "Want one?"

I'd never smoked with anyone but Suki but I nodded and Billy Halliday gave me a cigarette and lit it for me.

We began walking again.

Billy exhaled a long stream of smoke and said, "Yeah, the son of a bitch is really going to nail me."

"Who?"

"The man I'm supposed to call *Daddy.*"

"You don't like him?" I said. I couldn't believe I was walking with Billy Halliday, smoking with Billy Halliday. Just Billy Halliday and me.

"Ivan? He's okay." Billy laughed and took a long pull on his cigarette. "If you like rat poison."

"His name's *Ivan?*"

"That's what Rosie calls him—Rosie's my oldest sister. You know, like Ivan the Terrible. His real name's *Robert. Robert Stockwell Halliday.* What an asshole. And now I'm *Billy* Halliday, as if he's my damn father." Billy took a long pull on his cigarette, squinting his eyes like he was considering. Then he said, "My mother thought he was so wonderful to adopt us but it wasn't what she thought. He didn't *like* us or anything; he didn't even do it to make her happy. He just wanted rights to us; he just wanted to make sure he could keep my mother in that choke hold he got her in when they first met. See, we all belong to him now, or that's what he says. All the little Halliday children." Billy shook his head. "Oh, man, when I first found out that there was a black singer named *Billie Holiday* and it was a *lady,* I was ready to shoot somebody. But then Rosie played me one of her records. Ever heard her?"

I shook my head.

"Oh, man, she's incredible. It isn't that she has this beautiful voice or anything, but there's something about the way she uses it. It's like she gets inside your soul and tells you what it's like." Billy was looking off when he spoke as if he could hear her singing now from far away. "I tell you what—it made me like black people a whole lot more."

Billy didn't say *Negroes* or even *colored people,* which was what everyone else said unless they were being vulgar. Billy said *black people* and I wondered about that, how he ever thought to say that and why.

We reached Front Street and turned left onto it, toward the center of town.

"So I guess I've got a head start on vacation," Billy said. "And I get this week, next week, plus Easter vacation. I should take a trip or something." Billy said it as if he'd never gone anywhere and he had no intention of doing so now.

"Know why I got suspended?" Billy leaned toward me and whispered, "Three D's and two F's." Then he dropped his cigarette into a sewer grate and I did the same.

"That's *awful.*"

"Which? Getting kicked out or getting those grades?"

I'd meant getting kicked out but I said, "Both."

"No kidding. A guy like me getting those kind of grades? Shows you the sorry state of our academic institutions. And what a solution they've come up with—*Son, you're taking the next two weeks off.* Like *I* can afford to miss school. I mean, *you* can afford to miss school, Miss A-plus, they should suspend *you*—you work too hard; you need a break. But me? I can hardly read—not that I care, but, Jesus! They must be mental." Billy screwed up his mouth and crossed his eyes and began speaking like a dope: "Jeeperthz! Thith William Halliday ithz doing *terrible,* jutht *terrible.* He hardly ever comethz to clath. We'll show *him*! We won't *let* him come to clath! Duh."

"But you're smart. You know all those stories and poems. You shouldn't be getting those grades. You should be on the Honor Roll."

"*The Honor Roll?* No, *you* should be on the Honor Roll—the Honor Roll was meant for kids like you. Me, I don't need the Honor Roll. But I'll tell you what: I wouldn't mind an English class where we read something other than *Lord of the Flies* or *Death Be Not Proud.*"

"Like what?"

"*Like what?* Like *Daniel Martin,* ever read that?"

I shook my head.

"Yeah, me neither but I started it once. Belonged to Rosie—she had to read it for class at the community college. It was hard, it was really hard, but it was great. This guy, Daniel Martin, he's an adventurer and he sails around and he's not very polished but he sees things and he knows things and he's cool. I didn't get very far into it but I just know that Daniel Martin gets to have some fine adventures and fuck some sweet ladies."

"Jesus!" I'd never heard anybody say something like that.

"What?"

"You're disgusting."

"Sorry," he said, but he didn't sound it. After a moment Billy added, "I can't afford manners—at least not very good ones."

"What d'you mean?"

"Figure it out yourself, Honor Roll."

I felt wounded. I wanted to hurt Billy Halliday, but then he touched my arm and said, "I'm sorry."

He reached his arm around me and pulled me to him and all the breath emptied from my lungs and I smelled liquor and it felt safe and soothing, though I knew it shouldn't have, and my whole body was electric and I realized that Billy Halliday was going to kiss me. Suddenly, there was a loud honking and I was looking at Billy Halliday's ear because he had turned to see the dull grey car filled with teenage boys that had pulled up along side us. The windows were down and I could see the boys were all hoods in leather jackets and long hair and they were laughing with Billy who was saying their names and laughing, too. No one was looking at me and I stepped back while they talked about getting liquor and I said a little prayer that they wouldn't take Billy away with them. Then Billy was nodding, saying, "Yeah, yeah. Okay," and he turned and called back to me, "We're going driving. Wanna come?"

I did, I did want to go with Billy Halliday even if it meant being with those hoods in that dull grey car but then I heard my name and I heard it again and I looked up and there, across the street, was Suki, small and stupid, waving at me.

I'd forgotten all about her.

I shook my head at Billy Halliday and he winked and said, "Later," and ducked into the car and it screeched as it took off, leaving a smear of black on the pavement.

Now, as I passed Camp Meeting Road on my way back from Burying Point, a cloud slid in front of the sun and the shadow before my bike grew longer and thinner, fading to a pale grey needle until it was hardly there at all.

When I was alone out in the world, like now, riding my bike or walking, without meaning to, I kept looking for Billy Halliday blasting around in that dull grey Chevy full of teenage boys. I would imagine them slowing, pulling up along side me and calling out "hello" to me. I would stop and we would talk and then they would ask me if I wanted to go for a ride. I'd done the scene in my head a hundred times and now, when I heard a horn sound and I turned and saw behind me, coming toward me, that same dull grey car, I knew just how it would go.

I pulled over and stopped and held my breath and waited. If Billy was in the car, of course he'd ask me to ride with them and I would bring my bike into the bushes beside one of those elm trees. I waited. *God, please let Billy Halliday be in that car.*

Then there was a great roar, a horn sounding and I could see Billy Halliday's face in the passenger's window of the car and I smiled and began to wave. Then Billy was leaning out the window; his eyes were huge, too big to see something as small as me here by the side of the road, and he was barking. *Barking!* And there was howling, like coyotes howling, a thousand high voices shrieking, and then there was a rain coming down on me, cold liquid, paper, metal, cans. I crossed my arms over my head, in front of my face. Honking! *Barking!* Things coming down on me. Then a smashing of glass and I staggered from my bicycle and it fell onto the pavement. I saw the car disappearing up ahead, heard the horn stretching around the bend behind it. Something cool slid down the side of my face.

Then I was standing by myself on the road. Empty cigarette packs and candy bar wrappers and soda cans were scattered all around. My face, my hair, my clothes were cold and wet and sticky. As I walked back toward my bike, I saw the bubble gum and bars of candy on the road by the torn paper bag and, beside it, like a wad of gum or a nickel left on the train tracks, a bright red and blue smear, the wax lips flattened to garbage on the pavement.

I grabbed my bike and straddled it and as I went to push off I stepped on a chunk of glass and felt it crunch into pieces under my foot. It was part of a bottle they'd thrown from the car. I'd heard it shatter on the pavement. The label was red and white and black but I didn't have to read it. I knew what it was by the smell. My mother's night breath.

ChapterFour

Thunder

At dinner this night, the first night of our Easter vacation, Mom kept trying to discuss the party she had planned for the following weekend: next Friday night, my parents would be having a barbecue, the first one we'd ever had, as far as I could remember. Every time Mom brought it up, Dad would say it was too goddamn early to have an outdoor party and my mother would say he was too goddamn antisocial to have any kind of party and then they would drop it for a while. It seemed that for weeks, all we had been talking about, all *Mom* had been talking about, was that barbeque; Cat and I had Easter on our minds. Next Sunday, we would wake to baskets filled with jelly beans and chocolates and marshmallow chicks; we would rev ourselves up on sugar, dress in our fresh new Easter outfits—new dresses, new patent leathers, new hats, gloves, and coats—and we would all go down to the First Church where everyone else would be dressed up, too, and they would smile at us and say how nice we all looked. Early in the afternoon, there would be an Easter egg hunt in the churchyard behind the parish house; later, people Mom had invited would join us for an Easter dinner of lamb and mashed potatoes and minted peas.

But now, it was Friday night and no one but Mom wanted to discuss next weekend and how much fun we would have then; everyone was in a hurry to be excused from the table and go have fun now. Cat wanted to get ready for her date with Stuart Haskins— he'd be picking her up any minute, honking his horn from the driveway, setting my father's teeth on edge. Dad was already late for his poker game, seeing as how my mother couldn't get dinner on the table at a decent hour like a normal wife. Janie would be picking Mom up and they would go out for a few hours to places unknown where they would drink. Me, I had to baby-sit Franny, put her to bed by eight, but in exchange, I got to have Suki over. We would have snacks and call boys on the phone and watch movies in the guest room late into the night and strain to keep our eyes open as long as we could. This was Friday night. What could be more fun than that?

In the middle of the night, Suki and I woke and heard the storm approaching. We stayed huddled on the guest room bed until it passed; moving around in thunder and lightning somehow seemed more dangerous than being quiet and small in one place. When the thunder sounded from some distance—we counted twenty between the flash and rumble—we headed for the kitchen to go get snacks. At the top of the stairs we both heard the sound and stopped.

At first, I thought it was the dog but then Suki said it: "Someone's spitting."

A loud crash interrupted the spitting sound.

My dad yelled, "Christ almighty!"

Then the spitting started again. I kept thinking it was Maggie, our cocker spaniel, who was old and had heartworm and coughed all the time—I didn't know why since the picture in the vet's office showed the worms twisted up inside the heart, not in the throat or the lungs. Still, Maggie hacked and gagged and spit up nothing like an old man. My father would say he should put her out of her misery and he'd make his hand a gun and point it at her. Then his hand would buck and he'd make a sound with his tongue, a sound like a small stone hitting water.

My mother shrieked and there was another crash.

"Come on," I said, and Suki ran after me to my room.

We got under the covers.

"I don't like Billy Halliday anymore," I said.

More smashing from downstairs—dishes, glasses, coffee cups—loud bangs and booms—furniture being overturned—dull thuds—someone slamming against a wall.

Suki looked at me with big eyes but she said, "So who do you like?"

Cabinets slapping shut. Plates, bowls, a canister shattering on the floor.

"No one."

"Not even David Hanson?" Suki said.

"He's a retard. When we were dissecting pregnant sharks in science club, David started throwing the babies around going, 'Flying Fish!' "

The back door slammed and all was quiet. I stared at the floor and listened hard.

"Hey!" Suki pinched my arm and now I shoved her back on the bed.

"How 'bout Perry Cohen—like *him*?" Suki rolled onto her side cracking up because Perry Cohen was a moron, big and slow with a large head and a big dopey face under a mop of inky black hair. Though he was eighteen, Perry Cohen was still in junior high and he only took shop classes and some kids said he still couldn't read or write.

Then there were voices from outside. My parents were beneath my window now.

"I hate you!" my mother yelled. You could hear her through the walls and windows of the house; you could hear her clear into my room.

I heard skin slap on skin and I ducked and my mother screamed. There was grunting and another smack and I grabbed Suki and held onto her tight and my mother screamed again. She was yelling something I couldn't make out and then it was as if my mother were hollering from far away.

Suki and I were stiff, holding each other hard, and I wanted to ask her whether I should call someone but I didn't. I'd heard my parents argue plenty—I usually hid at the back of my closet with Maggie or in Cat's room or up in the attic—but I'd never heard this before. And then I thought of Maggie and I took off toward the guest room but there she was lying in the hall at the top of the back stairs. I picked her up like a lamb. Suki was beside me.

"She okay?" Suki said, then stroked Maggie's face and leaned in close and talked to her with a puckered mouth: "You okay, munchkin?"

I put Maggie on my bed and Suki and I lay on either side of her. We didn't say anything but we put our arms around each other. I could feel Maggie's breath on my neck, her heartbeat on my arm.

In the middle of the night, Suki asked if I was hungry. I hadn't even known I was awake.

We crept down the back stairs to the kitchen.

"Watch it!" Suki said. The lights were all on and shards of glass glittered from the floor.

On the counter, broken dishes with jagged edges looked like dangerous weapons. Cabinet doors were opened. Boxes of cereal and macaroni were on the floor, spilling their stuff. On the wet bar, a liquor bottle was on its side, liquor pooled around the neck, liquor dripping onto the floor. At the threshold of the kitchen, a can of cleanser lay in a mound of green powder. It was just powder, just cleanser, but it was all over: on Mom's cookbooks, the kitchen table, the backs of overturned chairs, even the little TV Mom watched while she was baking.

And then in the mess, by the stove, broken stuff was heaped in a pile.

When I stepped onto the kitchen floor, Suki grabbed my arm and said, "We'd better not."

"Wait here," I said, and as I moved into the kitchen, across the floor, feeling the pieces of glass and gritty powder and cold linoleum under my feet, things in the pile of stuff by the stove began to take shape. I could see a small, hot-pink flower. I could see a purple saucer with gold trim. And there were daggers, many daggers, bright daggers of green and yellow and pink. Daggers covered with hand painted flowers. Daggers streaked with gilt. A pale blue dagger emblazoned with the words *Good Girl* in gold.

I didn't realize I was staring, not moving, until Suki said, "What're you doing?"

From the freezer I got two Popsicles and tiptoed back to where Suki was waiting. I didn't get any cuts—Mom always said the soles of my feet were like leather—and Suki looked at me like I'd done something special. I glanced at the empty pine shelves still nailed to the wall.

Up in the guest room, Suki flipped on the TV and an old gangster film was on. We got on the bed and sat under the quilt so we made mountains with our knees. A guy in a dark suit with big shoulders and a hat pulled low on his forehead was talking out of the side of his mouth to another guy dressed the same way. The first guy said, "Hey, Ralphie. I've got a couple of dicks on my back," and Suki and I cracked up. I watched Suki laugh. I took her hand and held it tight. Tomorrow she would go to her home which I suddenly knew wasn't anything like this home: the Domandis' world did not include liquor and then I realized it probably therefore did not involve spitting and screaming and smashing things either. I wished Suki could stay with me or I could go and live with her at her house. I knew nothing really bad could happen as long as she was around.

I woke deeper in the night, uncomfortable, vaguely in pain, with a murkiness about me, as if I'd wet the bed but I hadn't. I sneaked out from between the sheets, out of the guest room, careful not to wake Suki, and I found I'd gotten my period while I slept. It amazed me that something like that could happen to you without your being aware of it. Having your period was such a monumental event it seemed only reasonable you should know about it in advance, just as you get that dry nose tingle and that feeling of being on the brink before a sneeze. Or the rumble of thunder before the storm. At the very least, it seemed you should waken when that switch was thrown and you went from not having your period to having your period.

I first learned about periods the year before in sixth-grade health class. Apparently, my mother never saw any reason to tell me about menstruation—probably because she'd survived Gramma Hattie's not telling her—and later, Cat said she'd have told me herself but she'd assumed I knew. Cat couldn't remember when she'd first found out about periods or who told her, she'd known for that long.

Sixth-grade health class was very controversial and an extremely big deal; you had to get your parents' written permission to take it. Whispered about by sixth-graders, anxiously anticipated by fifth-graders, sixth-grade health class was the only titillating subject before high school and it wasn't even a real course, but only lasted a few short weeks.

During the final week, you learned about hygiene—brushing your teeth, washing your hands, bathing regularly. The middle week of health class, you watched a two-part film strip about drugs. In the film strip, teenagers with long hair and tie-dyed T-shirts smoked greasy brown drug cigarettes to a rollicking song with a happy tambourine and a steady drum beat. The song went:

Well, they'll stone ya when you're tryin' to be so good
They'll stone ya just a-like they said they would
They'll stone ya when you're tryin' to go home
Then they'll stone ya when you're there all alone

The song made me think of that Shirley Jackson story we had read, but it was accompanied by pictures of those same teenagers sticking needles in their arms and the whole thing—the song, the pictures of the ugly, dirty teenagers, the needles, the drugs—made me feel sick and scared to the bone. Grown-ups said once you tried a drug, you were an addict and if you tried marijuana, you'd become addicted to heroin. They said that if you were an addict you couldn't think anymore and you would do crazy things like drink turpentine and walk down the street naked and your children would be mutants with no arms or three eyes and maybe no brain at all.

The first part of health class was the most exciting: here, we learned the details of human reproduction, the so-called *facts of life* everyone cryptically alluded to, talked around all our lives.

For health class, as with shop and home ec, the grade was split into two classes, divided by sex. Girls were instructed by a woman, boys by a man. It was Mrs. Rider who would pass along all the bizarre information to us. Unlike Miss Driscoll, the cooking teacher who was practically still a teenager, Mrs. Rider was a real grown-up with grey hair but she was lovely and sweet, safe and small as we were with a face like Honey West. She would be the one who told

us the names for male and female body parts—some of whose existence we had no knowledge of—along with their functions. Mrs.
Rider would be the one to break it to us about human reproduction. In plain simple words she would tell us about ovulation, menstruation, erections, ejaculation, and intercourse. Even Mrs. Rider's
gentle, calm voice and the fact that she'd lived through all of this,
even had three grown children, couldn't soften the hard ugly facts
she was letting us in on, including the unspoken truth we each had
to acknowledge about our own coming-to-be and the disgusting
behavior of our own parents.

This was when I finally, absolutely had to give up on my
"other way" theory about conception, the one that applied to myself and my sisters, that explained how we got to be here without
our parents' having done something so horrible. Even though my
mother had said Suki's story about conception had been essentially
correct, she and Dad did it, for a long while I refused to believe her.
I told myself she was just trying to cover for all the other parents
who did do it—for the Domandis, for example—so they wouldn't
look so bad. But now I knew that it was all true. And it made me
hate my mother.

Mrs. Rider would tell us about the changes we were going
through and the changes we could anticipate, though about half the
girls seem to have some idea about this already. The second day of
health class we watched a film strip called *Beautiful Changes.* In the
first frame, against a satiny hot-pink background, the title was put
to us in swirly letters so you'd really believe it, I guess:

Beautiful Changes

I remember most particularly the frames showing a line drawing of a woman sitting at a vanity in a robe and high-heeled slippers with a big puff on each toe. In the first of these frames, the
woman's head was held high and she was smiling into the mirror.
And there was a lot in the mirror for her to smile about! Her hair
swirled down from a high ponytail, her lips were shapely and dark,

and her eyelashes were represented as lush by a thick line on each lid. The man's voice on the accompanying record said that now was a time of beautiful changes. But in the next frame, the woman was no longer smiling and a tear seemed to have popped from her eye; small arced lines under the tear seemed to indicate that it was in motion.

In the final frame, the woman had dropped her head onto her arms which were folded on the vanity and it wasn't hard to imagine she was sobbing. The man's voice told us to expect sudden and inexplicable changes of mood—sudden sadness, sudden tears. After the film strip, all I could think about was that vanity and those slippers. How could I have a time of beautiful changes, something I was desperately in need of, without them? The man hadn't said. But without those beautiful changes, how would I be able to bear the sudden sadness and sudden tears? I wanted to ask Cat about it but she was already invested in some pretty hard teasing, telling me Mom should take me to the doctor, it looked like my case of the Uglies might be terminal.

When I asked my mother whether I could have a vanity, she laughed and said, "Certainly."

"When?"

"Right after I get mine," she said, and tossed her silky hair and I knew she was kidding, it was a joke to her, just a lot of silliness, and I hated her for it. I hated her for being so pretty that she didn't need a vanity or high-heeled slippers with puffs on the toes and for finding it a lot of silliness that I did.

Though my mother didn't have a vanity, she had many wonderful things, some of which she kept in small boxes in the second drawer of her bureau with her scarves—jewelry and photographs and old rare coins—stuff she would take out and show us on slow rainy Sundays. Under her bed, in a grey metal box with a combination lock with numbers that slid around like on an odometer, my mother kept important documents and certificates printed with black ink, some embossed and some with seals, concerning matters that did not concern *us*—meaning Cat and me—she said. She kept other fine things on the shelves of a cabinet outside her bathroom: on the top shelf, perfumes in short glass bottles; then a shelf for her curlers, her heating pad, and her hair dryer, and a shoe box full of products with strange names like "cuticle remover" and "depilatory." The next shelf was filled with paper products, toilet tissue and Kleenex and boxes of tampons and sanitary napkins.

When we were little, Cat and I would go through these things, which were all special simply in virtue of being our mother's though almost nothing on the paper shelf made sense to us. We didn't know why she had these strange things and why, though the boxes were half empty, we'd never seen her use them. Still, we supposed these things must have purposes and sometimes we would try to figure them out. One afternoon, Cat pulled the box of sanitary napkins down from the shelf and spilled it onto the floor. We picked the napkins up and began examining them, tying them around our waists with the long, ribbony ends, then around our necks, eventually putting them on our heads and tying them under our chins, deciding that they must be hats. We began laughing at each other in our funny hats, tossing the napkins around, screeching and laughing, when suddenly we heard our mother's voice: "What do you girls think you're doing?"

I knew we were in big trouble but when Cat said, "I'm sorry we were playing with your little hats," Mom cracked up and bent down to us and scooped us into her arms. Then she hugged us both together and kissed our faces and told us to go get a snack.

Still, she never told us what these things were for. I had to find out from sixth-grade health class and from my mother's *Redbook* and her *Ladies' Home Journal*. But nothing in her magazines provided any clue as to how I was going to get through this time and have those beautiful changes. I remember all the cryptic advertisements in them which never mentioned menstruation but commanded things like, "Have FUN wherever you go! Be Vibrant! Be Happy!" or "ENJOY THE NEW LOOK OF CONFIDENCE" or "Change to cool comfort, poise and freedom!" but I couldn't see how buying Kotex or Modess or Tampax would really help you accomplish these things. I remember an ad comprised of two photographs of a young woman with short bangs: the photo at the top of the ad showed the woman touching a hand to her wrinkled brow, looking cranky; immediately above her were the words, "Peggy's DISMAL" and immediately below her, "PERIODIC PAIN" with some text underneath. At the bottom of the ad was another picture of the same woman, smiling into the camera with a calm face now under the words, "Peggy's BRIGHT with **MIDOL**." Lines seemed to radiate from her head, to indicate the brightness, I guessed.

This was sort of how I felt these days, and how I thought of myself, like I was two people sometimes: Trisha Dismal/Trisha Bright. Suddenly a darkness would come over me, out of nowhere, like a storm, but I wouldn't sob onto my folded arms; I'd stomp my feet around my room or charge out the back door of the house and run down the hill across the lawn into the meadow, run and run until I ran out all the black and grey that had washed down onto me or risen from inside me, from that coiled thing, filling me up so I was drowning. Moments before, moments later, I might be smiling, laughing, carefree Trisha Bright—as if Trisha Dismal had never been, as if she didn't exist.

My mother seemed to see me this way, too. "Trisha, you're a yo-yo," she'd say, and I'd grit my teeth and say, "I am not," just because I couldn't bear her knowing every bad thing about me.

Sometimes I hated my mother even though I felt I'd be nothing without her—not that I'd *die,* but that I would disappear, crumble into a thousand tiny pieces and blow away in the wind and it would be as if I'd never lived at all.

After I cleaned up, changed my nightie, got a dry towel to put on top of the wet spot in the bed, I tiptoed back into the guest room, slid under the covers, arranged the towel, and lay still for the longest time. The next morning, while Suki would be showering, I would change into my clothes, strip the guest bed, and pull the coverlet back over the mattress so she wouldn't find out I'd gotten my period in the night. I still hadn't told Suki I'd started menstruating. I knew it would come between us if I had my period—she would be a girl, I would be almost a woman, a girl-woman—so I couldn't let it be real. Now I listened to the soft rhythm of Suki's breathing, the easy creaking of the house, and finally I heard people downstairs, moving dishes and pots and pans and furniture in a calm, normal way. By the time Suki and I came down, everything had been cleaned up and it seemed like a regular morning.

When we entered the kitchen, I saw my mother's pine shelves, still nailed to the wall, empty. There were no more teacups. Like *that*. My mother was busy in the sink and she kept her back to us when she asked us how we slept. As she turned to take something from the oven, I saw that she was wearing sunglasses and my mother saw me see and she bowed her head a little and smiled weakly and I saw more: one side of her mouth was goofy, swollen like she'd just been to the dentist.

"Have a seat," she said, and Suki and I looked at each other as we settled into chairs at the kitchen table.

When she bent over the table to set the basket of popovers on the lazy Susan, I could see behind her glasses, the purple on the cheekbone beneath her eye, the scabbed-over wound like a long thin paisley, like a tear running down her face. My mother was ashamed and she stroked my hair and didn't move for a moment and it was as if she were thinking of the right thing to say but when she finally spoke it was only to ask would Suki and I like juice.

After we had breakfast, Suki had to go home to clean her room. I walked her out to the top of the driveway where we sat on the biggest rock and waited for her mother. We held hands but we didn't say anything; we just waited. When Mrs. Domandi's blue station wagon appeared from around the bend coasting down the hill, Suki smiled at me and squeezed my hand. "See ya," she said, and ducked into the station wagon. The top of my throat was too tight and small for any words to come out but I nodded and my eyes burned as I ran back down the driveway to my house.

The rest of the morning, Franny and I stayed in the kitchen, watching cartoons and eating doughnuts. Cat finally shuffled downstairs around noon, groaning that she was beat because she didn't get in till two. I knew it was really three—I'd heard her come in. Three A.M.: a time I only knew as *the middle of the night,* a time when TV stations were all off the air and everyone who wasn't getting a glass of water or going to the bathroom was asleep. Dad still wasn't around and Mom had gone back up to her room, so Franny and I were the only ones available to give Cat grief about getting in so late, about sleeping so late, but what could we say? It was almost like we needed a sense of the rightness of things to point out the wrongness of other things, like staying out till the middle of the night; as it was, staying out till the middle of the night seemed reasonable. Before last night, I'd have stayed away as long as possible, too. But now, I thought of the bruises on my mother's face, that scabbed tear on her cheekbone. And all the damage that had been done.

As Cat sat down at the kitchen table with a bowl of sugar cereal, she glanced toward the empty shelves on the wall and said, "Mom cleaning the teacups?"

"Dad and Mom had a bad fight last night."

Franny was sitting in the comfy chair by the picture window, wearing a pink polka-dot playsuit, trying to press an arm back on a Barbie.

Cat looked up from her bowl and spoke with her mouth full: "Bad? What d'you mean 'bad'?"

"She was wearing sunglasses this morning."

Cat swallowed and said, "So?"

"In the house."

"Sunglasses?"

"She has a black eye."

Cat dropped her spoon in her cereal bowl. "Jesus, God," she said. She whispered it. "Where is she?"

"In her room. I don't know where Dad is. I haven't seen him since last night."

"Jesus. He hit her?"

"Yeah. What're we going to do?"

Cat rubbed her eyes with her finger tips, raked her open hands into her hair, and held her head for a moment. Then she said, "I'm going to finish my breakfast and then I'm going to take care of Misty and the chickens. You're going to go tidy Franny's room and then you're going to clean your room. That's what we're going to do."

"But what about Mom and Dad?"

"They can take care of themselves."

After I finished straightening Franny's room, then my room, I ran down to the barn, and in the cupboard by the barn door, I rooted through a box of old pieces of metal, hammer heads and bits and stirrups and hinges, until I found a horseshoe. I shook it loose from the other stuff and headed out of the barn. Back up at the house, I got a hammer and two thick nails from the garage and I tacked the horseshoe up on the wall above my bed.

By two o'clock, there was still no sign of my father and my mother remained in her room when Suki phoned and said to come over. As I was heading toward the garage for my bike, Cat said, "You've got it wrong."

"Got what wrong?"

"The horseshoe. It's upside-down. It has to hang like a U, to hold the luck. You'd better turn it over or all the luck will run out."

Suki's house was clean and modern, tucked in the woods with a small, swampy apron of yard covered with soft grass and bordered by a tiny creek. In summers, the Domandis' lawn would be warm and squashy between your toes and it made me think of what I'd read about the South—a murky place where the air is thick and full of steam and the ground isn't really *earth* but more like clay, soft and spongy under your feet so you couldn't be sure you didn't step in something unless you weren't wearing shoes. Though it was only a creek and not a river, nothing you could swim in or canoe on, Suki and I loved it, that constant bubbling of water full of little fish and tadpoles and turtles and toads, a ribbon stretching to and from water far away, somehow connected with all the other water, I was sure, with the Atlantic Ocean, yes, but also with the Ipswich River, the Merrimack, the Hudson, the Mississippi, even the Pacific Ocean—*all* of the water. Sometimes, I thought of the creek as a telephone cable or a string between tin can telephones because it connected and made close remote places, bringing *that* fish *here*; *this* plant, *this* pebble, *this* silt, *there*. Other times, I couldn't help but think of the creek as a capillary or a vein or an artery just as the land sometimes seemed like a body, like a living being, to me.

On three separate occasions, Suki and I rolled up notes and slipped them into old spice bottles and launched them down the river. Each time, the message became more desperate—first, we just wrote, "Help!" Then we added, "We're being held captive by a cruel man and woman!" Finally, we mentioned the fact that we were heiresses and promised a reward. And each time we put Suki's phone number at the bottom so we might find out how far our missives had gone. While we waited to hear from our rescuers, Suki and I told each other improbable tales of where they'd ended up and who'd found them—a riverboat captain in Louisiana was on his way to the phone *right now*—until Suki's brother Kenny brought the second bottle home with him one afternoon. He said he'd found it by a storm pipe at the foot of the hill on Meetinghouse Lane, just sitting there like a piece of garbage. He read the little note out loud to us in a ridiculous falsetto voice—*Help! We're being held captive by a cruel man and woman!*—though we knew what it said and he laughed in a wise-guy, know-it-all, smarty-pants way and called us *lamebrains*. The next day, Suki and I began a hunt along the creek and we found the other two bottles stuck in rocks and branches, not even a hundred yards from where they'd set sail. We threw them in the garbage without even examining them. Now they were simply an embarrassment.

After that, we lost interest in the creek and the next summer, when we were ten, Suki and I built a bridge over it with scraps of wood Mr. Domandi gave us, bits left over from something he was building in the basement. Just before the bridge, we dug a hole in the muddy earth and inserted a green plastic bucket for tolls, which nobody ever paid, since we were the only ones who crossed the bridge and we were exempt. Deep in the woods, we made a tree fort, hammered four slats of wood the size of chalkboard erasers up the trunk to the lowest branch, then tacked boards onto adjacent branches where we could sit and pretend we were hiding from Indians, though we knew the Indians living in Massachusetts had been friendly before the whites came and stole everything from them and chased them off or killed them. In a hollow just above our seats we stashed a tin the size of a jewelry box with a lady drinking a bottle of Coca-Cola painted on the lid. Inside the tin we kept our Super Balls, our marbles, our matching blue-haired trolls, and the multitude of tiny lipstick samples Suki's mom gave us.

As we grew, the tree fort became small and flimsy and low to the ground and we became interested in playing games more closely related to who we might be or become—*prehearsing,* Suki called it— which didn't involve fighting Indians or sitting in tree forts or building bridges over creeks, though just what it did involve aside from kissing boys was unclear to us. Nancy Drew, Honey West, and Emma Peel could fight crime and right wrongs if they wanted, but real women only seemed to be able to be cheerleaders or nerds, then maybe college students, then wives and mothers. That was the ultimate goal, that was what everything was about—getting married and having children—and it made me feel crazy and scared that this wasn't anything I wanted. But if you didn't have a husband and babies, you would be a schoolteacher, a nurse, a librarian, or a switchboard operator, and you would be alone and lonely. And you would be called an *old maid* which was also the name given to the unpopped, unpoppable kernels of corn left over at the bottom of the bowl—hard, unwanted failures. Unless, of course, you were a nun, in which case you weren't really an old maid at all—you were married to God, Suki said—and you wouldn't be lonely because you'd be around all the other nuns all the time, singing and having a lot of fun, it seemed, like Debbie Reynolds and Julie Andrews and Sally Field. Once again, it seemed being a nun was the best deal for a woman and I couldn't understand why more women weren't nuns. We knew some women had done great things—Joan of Arc, Elizabeth Taylor, Helen Keller—but we didn't have any idea of how to go about being like them.

These days when we were at the Domandis', mostly we hung around in Suki's room, or in the family room in the basement, which was quiet and private and far away from the goings-on in the rest of the Domandis' house. We would phone boys, make crank calls— *"Is your refrigerator running? Well, you'd better go catch it."*—listen to 45s and read teen magazines. Sometimes at night, we turned off the lights in the basement and with a flashlight we'd take turns reading out loud from her book of Edgar Allan Poe stories: *"Was it possible they heard not? Almighty God! no, no! They heard! they suspected! they knew! they were making a mockery of my horror!"* We would scare ourselves stupid until one of us howled and sent us both screaming up out of the basement and into the Domandis' calm, bright, warm kitchen where all was clear and sensible and safe and nobody had murder on their mind. Sometimes we smeared the lipstick from Mrs. Domandi's little samples thick over our mouths and got busy fending off all the boys who tried to kiss us. There were pillars in the basement, for support, I supposed, and those pillars would be the boys who grabbed us and tried to take advantage of us as we casually strolled around—we were *that* desirable, *that* irresistible. After we escaped them, before we got involved with something else, Suki and I would check out our kisses on the pillars—pink, red, crimson, mauve kisses—and we would feel a kind of pleasure or pride, like those kisses were promises of good things to come, wonderful things we would do or be.

While our house and all the stuff in it was old and musty and worn, it seemed everything in Suki's house was fresh and new. The furniture all came in sets like the kind they gave away on game shows; the individual pieces all belonged together. In the living room, the armchairs matched the sofa and love seat, and the coffee table looked like a little version of the stereo console. The den had a red–and–blue plaid sofa and two matching chairs. While our furniture was all bare wood or modestly upholstered, straight-backed and stiff, the sofas and chairs at Suki's were overstuffed, soft and clean and so comfortable we fell asleep on them watching the late show on Saturday nights. Instead of Indian shutters and coarse homespun curtains like we had, the Domandis' windows were all covered with venetian blinds, crisp, smooth drapes and soft, easy swags. And except for the kitchen and bathrooms, the whole of the Domandis' house had wall-to-wall carpeting, rich on your bare feet, delicious in between your toes.

The walls in our house were all painted white and covered with old artifacts—Mom's iron tool collection, old maps of places we didn't know in languages we couldn't read (like the map of Angleterre hanging in the living room, a place I'd never even heard of, next to a sea called La Manche), antique paintings of strangers, people unrelated to us or to anyone we knew (like the long-nosed old gramma hanging in the back hall who had a face round and slightly dimpled like an old grapefruit and who looked like no one I'd ever met)—orphaned old things my mother and father took such a liking to they abandoned their own old stuff in favor of them for reasons I could never fathom.

The Domandis' walls, on the other hand, were covered with paintings of Laura, Kenny, and Suki as tiny babies, then as young children, posing singly and as a group. There were photographs of the whole family, photographs of Mr. and Mrs. Domandi together, of each child singly and of the three children collectively at various stages of their childhood. And another nice thing about the Domandis was that they all resembled each other; just like their furniture, they looked well cared for and like they belonged together, like they'd all come from the same artful maker. In the den, Mr. and Mrs. Domandi's diplomas hung side by side above prints of buildings at Boston College. A photograph Mr. Domandi had taken years before of Bass Rocks in Gloucester, a place of Mr. and Mrs. Domandi's courtship, had been enlarged and now hung, framed, over the fireplace in the living room. Everything on the walls of the Domandis' house seemed to relate to them, to speak of them, in a personal way. Everything except the bleeding Jesuses, that is. Little Jesuses nailed to the cross, bleeding from their hands and feet, bleeding from their foreheads crowned with thorns, hung on the walls of every room in Suki's house, even in her bedroom, and a tiny gold one dangled from a dainty chain around Mrs. Domandi's neck.

The first time I went to Suki's and spotted the Jesus suffering on her living room wall, I screamed. Suki said to shut up, it was no big deal, it was a crucifix and they had to have them on the walls because they were Catholics. I thought the Catholics had to be some kind of crazy people to make the Domandis have these bloody, dying Jesuses on the walls. I didn't notice the one hanging above Suki's bed until I accidentally knocked it down when I was doing a somersault. Suki laughed and said she didn't like them either, and then she picked it up and made the Jesus sing "Hound Dog" just like Elvis Presley. I laughed and we let it go and we never talked about the Jesuses again, but I understood that the Catholics were very different and I was glad my family was Protestant. As far as I knew, Protestants didn't have to look at anything horrible or repulsive if they didn't want to.

For the past year, they'd been building houses near Suki's, cutting down trees and raking the soil with bulldozers. Sometimes I would steal cigarettes from my mother and Suki and I would go down to watch the men work. In the summer, they worked without shirts and the tools on their belts made their pants hang low on their hips. They drank cans of beer and hammered up doorways and floors. Though we would hide in the woods, sometimes a man might see us and whistle and call to us, "Hey, girls!" and we would run away. At first, we didn't know what they were up to. When we saw the concrete foundation sunk in the earth, we imagined they were building a swimming pool or a bomb shelter until they put up the frame and it was clear they were making a house.

After the workmen left for the day it would still be light out. I would be staying at Suki's for the night. We would eat dinner with her family, then we would tell her mom we were going out to ride bikes. But we would only go down the hill, as far as the building site. We would drag our bikes into the woods, then drop them. Carefully, we would climb into the house—before they had made the stairs, I would link my fingers and Suki would step up from my hands, then pull me up after her—and we would each choose a room for our own and tell how it would be decorated. We might pretend we were twenty years old and roommates and we had boyfriends visiting us. Afterward, we would sit behind the frame of the house and smoke cigarettes. We would try to smoke like my mother, making the smoke come out of our mouths for a long time while we talked, but we couldn't do it.

Once two houses were completed, enormous pristine doll-houses awaiting only the furniture of a family, we began to feel uneasy about them. At first, the new houses were simply different, interesting carvings up of spaces that were ours, structures we might have erected ourselves had we the materials and know-how. But the addition of paint and shutters and locks on the doors and windows made clear the fact that these places had been seized, cut off from us, and we were not welcome inside. I suppose it was then that we understood that the more trees they felled, the more houses would be built, and the more our space, our privacy and our freedom would be diminished. Sometimes, Suki and I talked about setting the woods on fire and taking back that land, but I guess we both knew we'd never do it because we weren't bad kids and because in our heart of hearts we knew that the land had never really belonged to us, we'd never *owned* it, at all. I began to think about the people who would live in these houses, the new families with new kids who would play on this land, dig holes in the ground, build forts. Suki and I had known these woods since we were small. We had climbed these trees and buried half dollars at the bases of our favorites, long forgotten now. When we were ten, we played spin the bottle here with David Hanson and Bruce Hartman, though no one had actually kissed. And this was where we had shared secrets and our first cigarettes. It had never occurred to me that the woods wouldn't always be there, that someone else, some new kids, would take our place there, in this space, telling their secrets, playing their games, and that then we would be like nothing to the land, just ghosts.

That afternoon, when I rang Suki's doorbell Mrs. Domandi answered.

"Hi, sweetie," she said. Mrs. Domandi wore funny cat's-eyes glasses with tortoiseshell frames and bright red lipstick on her mouth. She had long dark hair she wove in a thick braid that hung over her shoulder and she had a high, happy voice. Mrs. Domandi always wore skirts.

"Come on in. Suki will be down in a minute."

I followed her along the hall to the kitchen in the wake of the familiar Domandi family scents of cloves and bay leaves, but I also smelled fruit. Long before this, Suki and I had noted how each family has a distinctive smell (for example, the Cohens exuded a pungent bitter odor like old tomatoes and cigarette smoke) as it has its own unique vocabulary for bodily functions and other private matters (our family called them "stinkies"; Suki's family called them "boompses"; the Cohens just called them "farts"). The Domandis and their house always had a pleasant aroma of cleanliness and nourishment and good care.

Kenny was sitting on a stool at the kitchen table reading the funnies when we walked in. The kitchen table was covered with photographs, stacked and spread out.

"Forgive the mess," Mrs. Domandi said. "I'm trying to catch up on the scrapbooks." She took a photo from atop a pile and handed it to me. Suki and I were wearing our matching orange bikinis, arms around each other's shoulders, squinting in the sun and smiling.

"At Good Harbor last summer, remember?" Mrs. Domandi said, smiling and returning the picture to its pile.

I nodded. "That was fun."

"It *was* fun, wasn't it? Kenny, Trisha's here." Mrs. Domandi moved toward the stove.

"Hey, Trisha," Kenny said, not looking up.

"Hi, Kenny," I said.

Kenny Domandi was cool; everybody thought so. He had been a star in Little League and he played trombone in the high school band. Aside from that, he was the only teenage boy who would say hi to me, so I had something of a crush on Kenny.

"How's your family, sweetie?" Mrs. Domandi asked, stirring something on the stove with a wooden spoon. Though our families weren't friends, Mrs. Domandi was always concerned and solicitous about my family. The Domandis had invited my parents to dinner twice and both times my parents had said thank you, but they couldn't make it.

A strange thing about Mr. and Mrs. Domandi: they didn't drink liquor. I wondered if maybe my parents knew that and maybe this was the reason they never asked the Domandis over to our house. It seemed that, for my parents, the point of having people over was to drink—no one who came to our house didn't drink. Even when people came for dinner, cocktails were the big focus of the night and sometimes everybody would be so excited and distracted with the cocktails, they'd forget about dinner and it would burn or get cold. My parents never asked whether someone wanted a drink; they asked *what* they wanted to drink. "Name your poison," they'd say. And it was odd that that was how my parents talked about it—lightly, jokingly, calling it *poison*—when really they acted as if alcohol were about the most valuable thing on earth, or at least the most important thing in their lives.

I remember a day a few months before when my parents had decided not to drink for an entire twenty-four hours. Not a glass of wine, not a beer, *nothing*, they had agreed. All evening they sat in the kitchen with their backs to the wet bar, reading the newspaper, then their magazines, then their own reading books. Whenever I came in the room for juice or a snack, they would look up brightly, almost hopefully, as if they'd thought I might be there to pour them drinks and to rescue them from their misery. That night my parents stayed up much later than usual, as if they were waiting for something, and when they finally went to bed, they came upstairs together, almost as if neither trusted the other alone in the kitchen with the wet bar all stocked with liquor as it was, unlocked and unlockable, as if the other might drink up all the liquor once and for all, leaving nothing. About an hour and a half after they'd gone to bed, I heard the old metal latch on their bedroom door clatter like a couple of knives—*clack-clack*—then their quick steps in the back hall, then pounding down the stairs, and I knew they couldn't take it anymore. I tiptoed down the back stairs and from the dining room, I heard nothing though I could see the kitchen lights were on. When I peered around the door frame, suddenly I saw them standing before the wet bar, each with a glass raised to the lips, gulping. They both had their eyes opened and though there was nothing sinister about them, I don't think they saw anything at all, as if they were blind with purpose. They reminded me of the kittens our cat Eartha had had last winter, staring nowhere while they fed at her side. Then they set their glasses on the wet bar and my mother got the ice and a lime, my father got an additional bottle from inside the bar and without speaking, they made drinks and drank them up quickly. When they sat down at the kitchen table with more drinks, I decided I'd better go back up to bed before I was discovered. Almost an hour passed before I heard their slow, stumbly steps on the back stairs—as if their feet were stuttering, their walk were slurred—and in no time, they were asleep.

That was the only time I remember my parents not drinking. When my mother had her appendix out, she made my father sneak liquor into the hospital for her. He put it in an old bottle of witch hazel and they laughed about it for a long time afterward:

"How 'bout some witch hazel, honey?"

"On the rocks with a twist? Sure!"

Even when my mother was taking pills that came in bottles with warning labels saying not to drink alcoholic beverages while taking them, she would call to me to make her a drink. She might be in the living room, or the guest room, resting. When I reminded her she wasn't supposed to drink alcoholic beverages while she was taking those pills, my mother would grunt and sputter air while she got to her feet—"Fine, I'll just fix it myself"—and then she'd moan and grab at some part of her body and wince. I'd apologize and say, "Okay," and my mother would ease back onto the couch and recite the recipe for me: "Three little glasses from the Smirnoff's bottle, two ice cubes, a chunk of lime *this* big."

But in the Domandis' house, there was no bar stocked with cocktail glasses and jiggers and ice buckets, long silver spoons and shiny metal shakers and tall bottles of liquor. They didn't have cocktail time when the kids had to get lost and though Mr. Domandi would watch football and baseball on TV like my dad, he never had a beer can in his hand, a row of empty beer cans on the coffee table in front of him. After dinner, Mrs. Domandi would bring Mr. Domandi a tiny cup of espresso coffee instead of a cocktail, as if that were a normal thing to do. Before I noticed this about the Domandis, I had always assumed that all adults drank liquor, that drinking liquor was part of what it was to be a grown-up like playing was part of what it was to be a kid. If you were very old, like Gramma Hattie, then you might only drink a glass of wine on holidays, but if you were my parents' age, there was no question but that you drank. For a long time, I wondered what was wrong with the Domandis.

"They're fine, thanks," I said.

"Good," Mrs. Domandi said.

Suki came in the kitchen, her hair smooth and shiny on her head, the shoulders of her T-shirt dark with water.

"Come on," she said, and I followed her back up to her room.

Suki put Herman's Hermits on the stereo and we sat on the floor Indian style.

I sang, "Missus Brown, you've got a lovely daughter," and while she pulled the blue suitcase out from under her bed, Suki sang the harmony: "Love-ly daugh-ter."

Then she unzipped the suitcase and retrieved the red, white, and blue notebook we kept hidden there. It was like our journal, a log of what we did and what we thought about and what we wanted, along with our list at the back of our favorite words. When we first started the notebook, two years before, we wrote down words we didn't know the meanings of and then their dictionary definitions—*precocious, ostensible,* and *confabulate* were the first. Later, we wrote down words whose sounds we liked in columns underneath our names, like this:

TRISHA	SUKI
tabernacle	pentecostal
Timbuktoo	prima ballerina
prestidigitate	décolleté

I didn't think *prima ballerina* was a word but I gave it to Suki since she gave me *Timbuktoo.*

Suki said, "Okay, what'll we say?"

I shrugged my shoulders.

Suki spoke out loud while she wrote: " 'Suki still likes Bruce Hartman. Trisha still likes David Hanson and Billy Halliday though she says she doesn't.' " I shoved her and Suki laughed and said, "What else? Oh, I know. 'We went to Burying Point yesterday and saw Mr. Nealy and another guy.' "

"You're going to write about that?"

"Of course."

"What are you going to say?"

Suki burst out laughing. Then she began writing again. " 'We saw the guy's wiener.' What else should I write?"

I couldn't say anything.

" 'Mr. Nealy touched the guy's wiener'?" Suki laughed. Then she wrote again as she said, " 'Mr. Nealy touched the other guy's wiener.' What else?"

I shrugged my shoulders. "Say we'll walk downtown this afternoon."

"Walk? You wanna?"

"Yeah," I said. "I have a dollar."

Suki thought about it for a minute and then she said and wrote: " 'Today, we'll walk downtown. We have a dollar.' "

Suki's house was on a crabbed and twisty old road, once an Indian foot trail, called Meetinghouse Lane, that crooked all the way to the First Church past the parish house to Osgood Street. About half a mile from Suki's, on the way downtown, Meetinghouse curled in a tight S shape down an enormous hill. There were no houses on this part of the road and few cars travelled Meetinghouse Lane so if we were on foot, we could yell and link arms and run in the middle of the road and be escaped convicts. We would duck the pretend bullets whizzing toward us; sometimes if we heard a car coming we would hide behind thick old trees until everything was safe. We might shoot at passing cars with finger guns.

Meetinghouse Lane curved through a thick wood and this day, as we walked toward town, I realized that people had been walking this same road, this same path, for hundreds and hundreds of years—Indians first, then Colonial people in black and white—and I imagined them walking along with us now, all of us headed toward lower ground where the land flattened out then sunk into the sea. I imagined all the people who headed toward the First Church on foot, or on horseback, or driving carts, to see John Hathorne examine the witches, to see the bewitched suffer, to see actual, living, flesh-and-blood devils.

We didn't hear the light blue convertible until it stopped behind us. A lady wearing dark sunglasses and a filmy pink head scarf was behind the wheel; two clean, silky-looking sheep dogs were smiling and panting in the backseat.

"Would you girls like a ride?" the lady said, tilting her head down and peering at us from behind her sunglasses. The lady had hair like mine only tamer and more gingerbread than carrot and her eyes were a startling green.

It was too good to be true, this lady offering to drive us in her convertible. Franny and I had a thing for convertibles, always picked them out when we were driving with Mom, though Franny called them *reversibles.* I had never been in one before.

Suki said, "Sure," and the lady said, "Hop in."

We sat in front with the lady and, normally, with a grown-up we didn't know, we would have behaved ourselves but here we were in a *convertible* so there wasn't any normal about it! As soon as we began to move, the wind rushed at us, all around us, and Suki squealed and I squealed and the lady laughed loudly but the wind was even louder. Suki and I hollered and laughed at each other, our hair shifting and parting quickly, wildly in the crazy currents of air. The lady kept smiling at us, the tails of her pink scarf, strands of her gingery hair streaming in the fast air. We laughed and screaked at each other, the trees, the stone walls, the road, the air zipping by us as if we were flying downhill on bikes but we were sitting still, so to speak, we were in a car. *We were in a convertible!* Like the characters on TV shows like *Route 66, 77 Sunset Strip,* and *Hawaiian Eye.* The lady drove us all the way to the center of town and I kept imagining that she would want to bring us home, that she would want to adopt us. But when the lady stopped her car at the town square, everything else stopped, too.

The lady said, "Here we are," and Suki pushed open the passenger's door in the thick still air and climbed out and I followed her and suddenly we were outside the car and far away from the lady and her silky clean sheep dogs in the backseat. The lady smiled and waved as she drove off.

Downtown, there were five stores: Buster's Market, Reynold's Apothecary, Carlotta's Salon de Paris, Dawson's Hardware, and Kirby's Paper Store. The only ones we were really interested in were Kirby's, of course, because it was really a candy store, and Reynold's, because of the soda fountain.

As we walked around, it occurred to me that there was something funny about downtown Salem. To look at it, you'd never guess that twenty people and two dogs had been put to death here because of witchcraft. You'd never imagine there was once a prison here crammed full of people from age three to more than ninety years old, all accused of being witches. Now you'd find almost no trace of this time and these events except for one or two little tourist attractions where the focus was more on seventeenth-century architecture and craft than on what people who didn't live here called *the witchcraft hysteria*. For example, Giles Corey was pressed to death outside the old courthouse when they were trying to get a plea out of him. If he didn't plead one way or the other, he couldn't be put on trial, that was the law then. So they put a board over Giles's body and covered it with rocks to try to force out his plea, as if it were something stuck inside him and they could squeeze it out. Some people said that when the board was loaded with rocks and Giles was nearly dead, the sheriff asked him, "What is your plea?" and Giles only said, "More weight." They also said that he died because he choked on his own tongue. Everybody knew this, the kids all knew this, but no spot commemorated this—not a statue, not a rock, not a plaque. You could read all you wanted about the witchcraft hysteria in New England in 1692 but if you didn't know our town's name you'd never know it happened here.

Even Gallows Hill where all the witches were hung, where my many-greats-aunt Sara Wilde was hung, was unmarked, just a scrubby old incline hidden now by twisty knotty old trees and thorny underbrush, abruptly slipping down from a small flat field, Gallows Hill Park, the highest point in Salem. A visitor who drove up Prospect Street all the way to Gallows Hill would see children playing, an empty flag pole, a grey caretaker's house. In winter, he would see children sliding down the hill on the toboggan chute; in autumn, he might see a bonfire, thirty or forty barrels high, visible for miles around. But at no time would he see anything to tell him that this was the site of the witches' executions, the place where everybody came together to watch their friends and neighbors hang from the neck till dead. Most tourists think the witches were burned. If you weren't from Salem, you wouldn't be able to find Gallows Hill without someone's help, but most people here would say they didn't know where it was or they might tell you it was actually in Danvers. In school, we learned no more about witchcraft in Salem than Suki's cousins in Akron or kids anywhere else, but still, we all knew things.

First, Suki and I decided to go to Reynold's for root beer floats. Reynold's had the bright lighting and chrome edges of the school cafeteria and it always smelled like vanilla. Five stools were anchored to the floor along the counter, the two by the back room now occupied by Manny Thompkins and a big fat guy in a yellow shirt staring into his coffee cup. As Suki and I climbed onto the stools farthest from them next to the cigar case and the sunglasses display, Manny looked up and glared resentfully, as if we were taking something of theirs, which was funny because really Manny Thompkins was taking something of mine—ten acres of our land, land my family had owned for hundreds of years—unless Dad could find some magical way of buying it back from him before the end of the month. Suki kicked me hard in the calf bone and I hollered, "Quit it!" and the other man, the fat guy, looked over at us, too, and I saw that it was Mr. Nealy! *Mister Nealy!*

As if they could read our minds and didn't like what they saw there, Mr. Nealy and Manny Thompkins were glaring at us, not smiling, until the man who ran the place, who filled the prescriptions and made the sodas and frappes, a man with a tidy beard and a red pocked nose whom my father called *Bob* but we didn't call anything, emerged from the back room and asked if they would like a refill and the men settled back into wherever they were before we arrived. This was only the second time I'd been here since Cat stole the face cream; the last time, the man called *Bob* wasn't here. I wondered if Bob remembered Cat and whether he knew I was Cat's sister and remembered I was with her that day and thought I'd steal something now. I wanted to tell him I didn't know Cat was stealing it, she didn't tell me, I didn't take it, but these thoughts seemed disloyal and, anyway, I'd never have put them in words.

Suki tapped my arm and I jumped. "Look," she said.

I turned to shush her and saw that she had put on a pair of cat's-eyes sunglasses, just like her mom's only black.

"Dahling, vat do you think?" she said, like Zsa Zsa Gabor.

"I think you look shtupid," I said, and we laughed.

Then Bob replaced the coffee pot on the burner and moved toward us, wiping his hands on his smock.

"What'll it be today?" he asked, and Suki said we would like the usual and laughed but Bob ruined it when he said, "Root beer floats?" as if he didn't know.

While Bob went to make our floats, Manny Thompkins rose and clutched the waist of his pants with one hand and I imagined he was going to unzip them but he thrust the other hand deep into a pocket and yanked out a fistful of change which he slapped on the counter.

As the man set Suki's float before her, a paper cone in a metal stand like an angular hourglass with a ball of ice cream on top, Mr. Nealy stood up and adjusted his pants at the waist and Suki gasped but nobody turned to look at her and Manny Thompkins said, "Be seein' ya."

"Take it easy, fellas," Bob said, offering Suki a long spoon and a straw.

Suki said, "Thank you."

The bell at the front door jangled and Bob turned away to finish making my float.

Suki kicked me again and whispered, "Wonder if they're going to Burying Point," and we laughed.

I elbowed Suki and pointed to the cigar case. "I'll get two of these," I whispered.

Suki made a funny face, like she hadn't heard what I said, but just then Bob brought me my float.

"Will that be all?"

I stared at the round puncture marks in the skin of his nose. "My dad asked me to pick up a couple of cigars for him." I felt my face start to burn. "But I forget which kind. Which is the cheapest?"

Bob made his mouth tight and lowered his eyebrows so tiny holes appeared between them, and he said, "That'll be the White Owls." He got the cigars from the case, set the box on the counter before me, and said, "Your dad wants *these*?"

I said, "Yeah."

"How many?"

"Two," I said.

Bob paused for a moment as if he knew I was lying, but he slid the cigars into a little paper bag anyway, as if he couldn't really believe we were going to smoke them. That was the beauty of it. "That everything, then?"

"Matches," Suki said, and Bob and I both looked at her.

Then Bob reached down beneath the counter, got a book of matches and dropped it into the paper bag. "Let's see . . . that'll be seventy cents, all in all."

I handed him our dollar and he brought back a quarter and a nickel. We could still get seven candy bars at Kirby's.

Usually we sipped our floats, savored them, poked at the ice-cream blobs with our straws, but I'd just lied, practically stolen from the man myself, so I was in something of a hurry to get out of there. Suki seemed to feel the same way about things because in a moment her straw was making that loud, wet, end-of-the-drink sound and she bounced down from her stool and said, "Let's go."

As we approached Dawson's Hardware, we walked carefully to avoid knocking over the small stacks of bricks sitting on the sidewalk. Last week, some old man had mistaken his accelerator for his brake and plowed straight into the side of Dawson's, knocking out a window and part of the wall. They'd replaced the window but still had to brick up some of the wall and trim.

Suki suddenly stopped, put her arm around my shoulders, and turned us toward Dawson's window. We looked like a photograph of ourselves—Suki said it. And as we watched ourselves laugh, the sun slid behind some clouds and I suddenly saw past our reflection in the glass into the store, to a toolbox display and beside it, a man tall and dark—*my father, my father* whom I hadn't seen since last night—talking very close with someone, a woman, with short brown hair and enormous pink lips, *kissing* a woman, *kissing Rachel Cohen.*

"Shit." Suki said it.

I imagined myself reaching down and picking up a brick and hurling it at the window which would shatter and fall away and expose my father but before I realized that I would never do it and shrank a little inside, the sun shone brightly once more, obscuring everything on the other side of the window.

Kirby's was small as our family room and stuffy and the door creaked when you opened it so the old man who owned the place looked up when you came in. Whenever we entered, the man was bent over a newspaper on the counter, and though he always checked us out, he didn't say hi and neither did we. He spoke in a rumbly voice—"That all?"—when we piled our candy on the counter and he never smiled, but we didn't care.

Suki and I settled on four packs of Bazooka and two candy bead necklaces.

Then we went behind Kirby's, which was quiet and private. Near the back door was an old wooden box with green peely paint, for newspapers, I think, and we climbed up on top of it and Suki took out our cigars.

"Let's smoke," she said.

We sniffed our cigars, bit off the ends like we had seen them do in the movies, and lit them, making huge clouds of stinky smoke.

"Wanna put a spell on David Hanson?" Suki said.

"How we gonna do that?"

"I got one," she said.

"What d'you mean, you got one?"

"I found one in a book."

"Really?"

"I'll show you when we get back to my house," she said, and accidentally made a smoke ring.

"Cool," I said, and poked my finger in the center of the ring then pulled it out again.

"Are you okay?" Suki said.

"Why wouldn't I be?"

"You know—your dad," she said. "In Dawson's."

"I'm fine."

"You sure?"

"Yeah, I'm sure."

We sat smoking our cigars for a while, looking at them, rolling them between our fingers.

Suddenly, Suki said, "Maggie Barber got her period."

I didn't say anything and Suki said it again.

"How do you know?"

"She told me," Suki said, picking at a curl of old green paint on the box. "You haven't gotten yours, have you?"

When we were little, Suki and I had made promises to each other for our more grown-up selves to keep: we'd promised to have houses next door to each other; we'd promised to be maids of honor at each other's weddings; we'd promised to be roommates in college; we'd promised to double-date at the prom; and we'd each promised we would tell the other when we got our period. Though we would make all these promises sincerely, not one would be kept. Starting two months ago when I got my period.

I had stayed home from school that day with a stomachache. I had been watching TV in the family room and when I got up to go to the bathroom, I saw blood on the floor. When I checked the back of my legs to see if I had cut myself, I saw the red spot on my baby-doll bottoms. I began to cry because I knew what it was, and I knew my life would never be the same. I would get covered up by breasts and hips, and men would stare at them and I would have to act like I didn't notice or care. I would have to act like it was normal, like I had always had them. But no one would ever treat me the same. And I knew there would be something between me and Suki, something setting us apart. We wouldn't be just alike anymore. I stuffed some Kleenex in my baby-doll bottoms and when Cat got home, I told her and made her swear not to tell anyone. She said she was sorry, but it wasn't so bad, really, and she showed me how to use tampons. Cat was the only person I had told about my period; she had hers, so that made us even. But I didn't tell my mother and I didn't tell Suki and I didn't tell anyone else. And I never wore baby-doll pajamas again.

And now, here I was with my period again, my *third period,* feeling sort of sick and raw and sore, and Suki still didn't know. I'd hidden it from her when I got it last night and I wasn't about to tell her now. This was the decision I had made two months before: I wasn't going to say anything until Suki told me she'd gotten hers. I wasn't about to risk losing her over some stupid biology that had nothing to do with me.

"No—have you?" I puffed on my cigar.

"No. If you did get it, you'd tell me, right?"

"Yep." I kept my mouth busy with that cigar and puffed some more.

"Because I wouldn't want you to lie."

"Right."

"We promised, you know? We swore it on our blood sister-hood."

"I remember," I said, and I thought about the times we'd lit a candle and turned off the lights and pricked our fingers and min-gled our blood and promised things to one another.

"I'd really want to know." Suki brought the cigar to her lips and sucked her cheeks in, and the tip glowed like a hot nickel. *"Re-ally."*

"Really?"

Suki blew out a cloud of smoke and coughed a little. She swallowed. "We're best friends and I'd have to know."

"I'd tell you," I said.

Suki looked at me, then she looked down at the cigar in her hand and said, "You got your period, didn't you?"

I wanted to lie, I *meant* to lie, but I said, "Yeah."

Suki's mouth went flat and she snorted air out of her nose. "I figured. I mean, you almost have boobs. And you have some public hair."

"Sorry," I said. Then I said, "It's *pubic* hair."

"What?"

"It's not *public* hair. You said *public* but it's *pubic*—*pubic* hair."

Suki scowled. "It's *public*."

I laughed. "No, it's not. Where'd you learn the word?"

"I read it in a book."

"Thought so. You misread it. It's *pubic* hair."

"You just have to be right all the time, don't you? Okay, it's *pubic*. You happy now?" Suki puffed on her cigar and she didn't look at me. "You lied to me. You should have told me."

"I'm sorry."

"Who'd you tell?"

"Cat. Only Cat."

Suki puffed on her cigar and looked far away.

"I didn't even tell my mom. Really, I'm sorry."

"It's okay," Suki said, but after we smushed out our cigars and began walking toward Osgood Street, I could tell it was something between us.

The sky had grown completely gray and the air was thick and heavy as we climbed back up the hill on Meetinghouse Lane. No one stopped to offer us a ride. We didn't play escaped convicts and we didn't talk. When we got back to Suki's, she didn't even ask me in.

"See ya later," she said.

I picked up my bike and straddled it. I said I was sorry again and Suki just said, "See ya," and walked into her house.

I yelled after her: "What about the spell? Aren't you gonna show me?"

Suki turned and looked back at me. "Maybe tomorrow," was all she said, and she shut the door between us.

It was beginning to rain. I could hear the pelting of drops against the roof of the Domandis' station wagon, the hollow rattle of rain on their gutters. I pulled my jacket up over my head, tied the arms under my chin like ribbons on a bonnet and began riding back to my house.

My father had been kissing a woman not my mother. My father had been kissing my mother's best friend. My mother's Suki. He'd hit my mother, struck her, smacked her. He'd left bruises on her face, beneath her eye. He'd given her a fat lip. And he had spit on her, we could hear it. And now here he was downtown kissing Rachel Cohen in Dawson's Hardware, standing by a stack of toolboxes, kissing those huge pink lips.

ChapterFive

Underwear

Monday morning, my mother came downstairs late, after Mrs. Wyman had already picked Franny up for kindergarten, long after Dad had left for work. Cat would sleep till noon that day, our first weekday vacation day, which she would do any day she was forgotten about or allowed. Me, I was too restless to ever sleep like that. It seemed I listened while I slept since I would hear the first person rise in the morning and I heard everything that went on at night—it was as if I never really slept, my true self never slept but lay awake, coiled inside me, listening, ready. I couldn't sleep if someone else was awake. I couldn't really breathe deeply or let my arms and legs be long and loose until the house had been quiet, absolutely dark and empty of sounds and motion, for a long time. Even then, I had to sleep flat on my back, ready. I thought of myself as someone who only floated on the surface of sleep, waiting, my eyes closed like someone listening hard, listening for the smallest things. It seemed I always had a tightness in my body, in my limbs, in my throat, that went with the listening, a strained readiness. During the day, I was listening, too, though not as intently as at night, and this made me very spookable. Sometimes, Cat took a mean pleasure in waiting for me around corners, behind doors, in my closet, and watching me jump and scream when she showed her face. She didn't have to say anything. I could even be pretty sure she was there, hiding, waiting to leap out at me—that never made me any less spooked.

This morning, I would come downstairs when I heard Franny's small step in the back hall. I would feed her cereal and juice; I would comb her hair and dress her and walk her out to Mrs. Wyman's station wagon when Mrs. Wyman pulled in. Before Mrs. Wyman could ask, I would tell her that my mother was busy with something and that she said to say good morning and thank you. And Mrs. Wyman would smile and make me promise to pass along some friendly greeting to my mother, and I would promise, my evil, inside self would promise, all the while knowing I never would. And I would wave when Mrs. Wyman drove Franny back up the road and they disappeared around the curve. Then I would clean the kitchen, wash and dry the breakfast dishes. I would collect the linens from our bathroom and carry them to the laundry room. When I raised the lid on the washer, a pungent smell of sweaty socks filled my head and I wondered how long these wet clothes had been here. I poured in more soap and let the clothes wash again. Then I scooped the load from the dryer, cool and full of creases, and brought it to the kitchen table and began to fold. Cat's pale blue and green turtlenecks, Cat's jeans, Mom's pink top, Dad's chino pants, a tangle of knee socks and a mishmash of pastel-colored underwear. Mostly the underwear was Cat's and mine, cotton and simple, but there were also two silky pairs that were my mother's. It was funny—my mother's underwear seemed enormous, even though she wasn't, and I never could believe they really fit her. My dad's underwear would be with the whites.

Underwear was such a painfully private thing, about the only X-rated item you came in contact with in the normal course of things, if you were a kid my age—not your own underwear, of course (except under certain rare circumstances), but other people's underwear, most especially opposite sex underwear: boys' underwear, your dad's underwear, white cotton underwear with strange front pockets. Or if perceived, mentioned, *objectified* by someone else, then another girl's underwear or even your own underwear could become a disgraceful, tawdry item, a shameful piece of slander, something whose existence you would damn and whose ownership you would deny. For example, the year before, the morning after Cindy Davis's sleepover after we had all gathered our belongings, stuffed our T-shirts into our pillowcases, rolled our sleeping bags into spools, and were waiting up in the front hall for our mothers to come get us, Mrs. Davis suddenly appeared, displaying a small item pinched at either side between her thumbs and forefingers, draped between her two hands.

"Someone forgot something," she said in a musical voice.

It was a pair of underwear with pink and orange bows scattered all over it.

"Girls! Who belongs to these?"

I'd had to beg my mother for them, she usually insisted on plain pastel colors, but now they would have had to torture me to get me to call them *mine*.

Karen Bishop snickered but the rest of us sat quietly.

"No one?" Mrs. Davis held the panties high and turned them this way, then that, so everyone got a good look. I thought I'd faint.

Always helpful, Nancy Thing said, "Maybe there's a name on the label."

"Good thinking," Mrs. Davis said, but I could have told her not to bother looking. Though she always meant to, my mother never actually got around to doing that kind of thing—organizing, filing, labeling. Mrs. Davis searched the inside of the waistband.

"I can't believe these aren't anybody's." Mrs. Davis was relentless.

When I saw my mother pull up, I didn't wait for her to come to the door—I said thanks to Mrs. Davis and hollered "Bye" to the girls and ran out to the station wagon. I couldn't risk my mother's glimpsing the loathsome underwear, proof of the existence of my lying evil self, spread out flat and obvious where Mrs. Davis had left them on the side table in the front hall for everyone to see. My mother never mentioned their absence, but she never got me patterned underwear again. And of course, I never asked.

Underwear. Just the sound of the word could send kids into hysterics: in the lunchroom, Karen Bishop asked me, "What were you doing under there?"

When I said, "Under where?" she laughed riotously and got the other girls to laugh with her, at me, as if I'd just done or said something outrageous and embarrassing. I hated Karen Bishop.

Somehow it was as if you didn't want anyone to think you wore underwear. Cat told me about a movie star from a long time ago who bleached her hair white and didn't wear any underwear at all. I thought that was smart: not wearing any underwear at all guaranteed no one would ever see it. And someone's seeing your underwear—especially while you were wearing it—was like their taking something of value from you and it left you diminished. But this movie star who wore no underwear died before she even had kids, before she was even my mother's age, from having bleached her hair so white, Cat said, and then I thought of her as bleaching herself until she disappeared, bleaching herself out of existence. And I figured that had something to do with her wearing no underwear, and with everybody's knowing she wore no underwear. So it seemed clear to me that you didn't want anyone thinking you *didn't* wear underwear either. With one exception, which I discovered in second grade.

Because girls could not wear pants to school during this time, these underwear issues were a very big deal: we girls lived in constant peril of some boy's lifting our hems or climbing up behind us on the ladder to the slide or otherwise sneaking a peek at our panties, tarnishing our dignity and compromising our value as human beings. So at recess, we played jacks or Chinese jump rope or another quiet game where we weren't in danger of being exposed. But when I was seven, it suddenly occurred to me that I could guarantee no one outside my family ever saw my underwear unless I permitted it. Here's how it happened. One morning, early in the fall of that year (which was 1963), my mother was helping me dress for school when the telephone rang. I had already removed my green-checked baby-doll tops and Mom had pulled the dress down over my head when the phone sounded for the third time.

"Go ahead and put on your underwear, honey, and start on shoes and socks," Mom said and ran from my room. I pulled the white ankle socks onto my feet, then wrangled each foot into its proper shoe. I had just finished the buckles when my mother reappeared.

"Look at you! You're dressed. Good! Let's go brush that hair."

I almost said, *But can't you see I'm not wearing my underpants?* but as soon as the thought took shape, I stopped myself. No, she couldn't see; she couldn't tell that these were pajama bottoms under my dress! And who cared about anyone seeing their pajama bottoms? You could see them all you liked! You could drape them from the trees for all I cared! It was a real piece of luck and later, at recess, when I showed Suki and Karen Bishop and Nancy Thing, their eyes grew huge as if I'd done something illegal, which so far it wasn't, and they watched, stunned and envious, as I romped around the playground with the boys, climbing all over the jungle gym and the monkey bars and the slide. And when Curt Metzger began to chant, "I see London, I see France," I laughed and raised my own skirt and said, "They're *pajamas,* dumb-dumb!" and Curt Metzger's mouth hung slack and the other boys began to laugh and Curt Metzger ran off toward the teeter-totters. I ruled the playground that day! And the next day, Suki and Karen Bishop and Nancy Thing showed up in their baby-doll bottoms, too, and we all leaped and frolicked and tumbled all over each other and all over the playground. Soon, all but the most goody-goody of the girls in our class were wearing their baby-doll bottoms to school and it was as if we'd all been freed from some terrible handicap or curse. Before long, girls in the other second-grade class and even some in third grade were wearing their baby-doll bottoms and spirits were high! It seemed we were exploring territory that we'd always been banned from and every day during these baby-doll days felt like a holiday. And I think we'd have gone on this way until school got to be a regular paradise if Karen Bishop hadn't told Danny Dawes, who went on to tell Mr. Clark, who quickly told our principal, who made an announcement and sent a note to parents in the mail advising them of the situation and reminding them of our school dress code. After that, my mother checked my underwear before I left for school each day and the girls all got back to playing carefully and quietly on the playground and I *really* hated Karen Bishop.

After I finished folding the laundry, I stacked everything into a tower, tucking the underwears in the middle, and I returned it to the top of the dryer. Then I heard my mother's footfalls on the front stairs.

This morning, Mom looked like she'd been up all night, but I knew that wasn't so: they'd finally settled down around 2:00 A.M. Though Saturday night and Sunday had been quiet around my house, nobody really saying much, doing much aside from watching and waiting, Cat and I knew that anytime now, there'd be a fight, there *had* to be a fight—my father had stayed out all night Friday, which they probably would have fought over even if he'd done it before, which he hadn't—and it finally came last night.

I heard things crashing in their bedroom; I heard glass breaking. I heard things falling and coming apart. I heard my mother scream. I ran around in my room, looking for something, something that would help. My bureau, my closet, under the bed—*nothing!* I looked out a window and another window. I heard something shatter. I heard my mother scream. In my bureau, in my closet, under the bed—*nothing!* I felt like a bird panicking in a cage. Finally, I just crawled to the back of my closet, put my fingers in my ears, and rocked and rocked as if I were in a rocking chair and trying to go as fast as I could. After a while, I stopped and slowly drew the fingers from my ears and heard nothing. Back into my room, I still heard no noise at all. I sat on my bed for the longest time before getting back under the covers. Another long time had to pass before I could close my eyes.

Now, this morning, my mother wore a new bruise on her jaw, red and purple and flecked like a strawberry. She'd smeared a thick dry-looking peach-colored makeup over it, and over the bruise beneath her eye, but you could still see them like old stains in clothing.

The only other face bruises I'd seen before were on Billy Halliday. You'd have thought Billy Halliday was the world's clumsiest kid and not a former star of Little League because when you asked him where he got all his bruises and broken bones, Billy would always say he fell down. He would never mention his stepfather, Ivan the Terrible, mean as a snake, but every one knew Mr. Halliday was the cause. Still, Billy just said he tripped, he stumbled, he fell down. This was what my mother would say later that afternoon when Franny asked what happened to *her.*

When my mother came in the kitchen this morning, she went straight to the wet bar. She stooped down so I couldn't see her, but I saw the bottom of the bottle rise up above the level of the bar's counter, then heard the little suck when she pulled the bottle away from her lips.

The first time I saw my mother drink right out of a liquor bottle was about two months earlier. After school had let out that day, Cat had gone off somewhere with Stuart Haskins in his Rambler and I had ridden the bus home by myself. My mother's station wagon was in the driveway and when I entered the front hall, I waited a moment to feel for what kind of thing was going on, whether I could go in the kitchen for snacks or whether I should just head up to my room. I heard my mother's voice coming from the kitchen, rich and throaty. She was humming.

I moved through the dining room to the threshold of the kitchen and peeked. Standing at the wet bar with her back to me, wearing a full-skirted pink dress with a fitted top and sleeves small and puffed like babies' bonnets, my mother was swaying slightly from side to side, humming, busy with something in front of her. After a moment, she turned her head a little, raised a full bottle to her lips, her hips still swaying as she tipped her head back and drank right from the bottle, in long gulps, pausing twice to breathe. Then my mother made an airy "Aaah" sound, like someone emerging from cool water on a sultry day. She licked her lips and moved around to the side of the bar, to the faucet, and ran water straight into the bottle until it was full. And she was still humming. Then my mother twisted the cap back on the bottle's mouth and returned the bottle to its shelf inside the wet bar, gently easing the cabinet door shut. She did all this quietly, calmly, without hesitation, like one guided by a familiar pattern or following a well-trodden path.

With her eyes closed, her head leaning to one side as if it were resting on somebody's shoulder or as if someone were kissing her neck, my mother pressed one hand flat on her belly, held the other opened and raised it shoulder-height. Her lips were set in a peaceful smile and she began to hum again as she moved with tiny steps, turning slowly around the kitchen. Her skirt flared, her hair tumbled over her shoulder and swirled across her back as she pivoted and turned across the floor in front of the appliances, smiling and humming. I didn't know the name of the song, but I recognized the tune; it always made my mother pause—a ladle, a lipstick tube, a cigarette in her hand—and gaze off toward another place, another time when, I imagined, she was happy and in love. My mother spread her arms wide and began to twirl, then she opened her mouth and sang, "Daaaah, Dah-dah-daaaah," and I was astonished to see her now, like this, happy and smiling and easy, and for that moment I wanted to be her. Then my mother crashed right into the refrigerator, folded in on herself a little, like a closing flower. She was panting and laughing softly and she brushed the hair from her eyes and looked up and saw me in the doorway and giggled and blushed like a girl.

"You caught me," she said, still panting a little, smoothing her skirt and the back of her hair with her open hands, her face flushed and glowing.

The counter was covered with stuff, paper bags and other stuff, but no cookies. I opened the bread drawer and began to root.

"No snacks," Mom said, opening the fridge. "Sorry. I didn't have time to get to the market." Leaning into the fridge, she said, "Hey—here's an orange. You could have this." She reached back with the fruit in her hand, browning and puckered like it was losing air.

I shook my head. "No, thanks."

Mom frowned at the orange, shrugged, and tossed it back into the vegetable drawer. She leaned a little deeper into the fridge, then stood up and turned back to me with an armful of dimpled and deflated citrus fruit. "Wanna see something?" she said, bopping the refrigerator door closed with her bottom.

With one hand, she grasped two parched-looking lemons, brown and yellow as fall leaves; with the other hand, she palmed three shrivelly limes. Because they were lean and therefore small in their own way, and because she was in no other respect a large woman, it was easy to forget that my mother's hands were enormous, not wide and knuckly like my father's, but long and narrow, with pale, slender fingers that rested above her eyebrow when she cradled her chin in her palm.

My mother smiled and winked and then did the most remarkable thing: she tossed a lemon in the air above her, then a lime, then another lemon, slapping the first lemon back up as it fell, tossing up another lime and then she had all the fruit in the air, spinning, turning, the rim of an invisible wheel rotating around an imaginary hub, then a string of beads moving in a figure eight. My mother was juggling. *Juggling,* like a circus clown. Lemon, lime, lime, lemon, lemon, lime. She shook the hair from her eyes as she raised her face toward the ceiling and juggled higher. Keeping her back perfectly straight, she bent her knees and juggled lower. She tossed over her shoulder and under her leg. She caught behind her back and from beneath her bent knee. As the last fruit hung in the air, my mother spun around full circle, her hair and skirt flaring, and met it with an open palm and nodded. Then she took a little bow and when I hooted and clapped, she curtsied. My mother, juggling. My juggling mother. My mother the juggler. I'd thought I knew everything about her.

"I didn't know you could juggle," I said.

"Well, I guess you don't know everything." My mother kissed me, turned, and rolled the fruit onto the counter. For a moment, she just stood with her back to me. She didn't move at all. Then, from the drawer to her right, she retrieved a long knife and in one motion, she sliced a lemon cleanly in half. Without turning toward me, my mother said, "Go to your room now, Trisha."

And now, here she was, crouching on the other side of the wet bar, drinking from a bottle. I tried to say, *Hi, Mom,* but nothing came out. I moved my chair back from the table, scraping it against the floor.

The bottom of the bottle sunk behind the wet bar and I heard my mother clear her throat and close the door of the cabinet. Then she stood and nodded at me.

"Good morning, Trisha," she said, so plainly, so casually, as if she hadn't just drunk liquor straight from a bottle first thing after she woke, late, on a Monday morning, with a new bruise on her face. She moved toward the sink and ran some water.

I wanted to tell her to drink from the bottle if it made her feel better, but I didn't know how to say something like that.

My mother was wearing a red silk blouse and a black skirt and she'd tied a black ribbon in her hair. From behind, she looked so beautiful, her hair smooth and straight and pale next to the black ribbon, but when she turned around her face looked lumpy and uneven like a potato, due to the swellings and those bruises under the makeup like strange shadows on her face. Her eyelids were puffy and as she moved stiffly and slowly about the kitchen, I swear I wanted to take her and hide her—or run away with her where we could be happy and easy and she could dance and sing the words to the songs she only hummed.

"Cat up?" Mom said, wiping the sponge on the counter.

I said no but Stuart was supposed to pick her up around noon. "Oh?"

"They're going driving," I said.

"Is that what they call it now?" My mother smiled a wobbly punched-mouth smile, then said, "When Mrs. Wyman brings Franny home this afternoon, I want you two to come over to the shop, okay?" She removed the baked bean jar from the shelf above the cereal and poured coins into her open palm. She picked a few out with her other hand, slapped them onto the counter, then returned the extras to the jar. "Here's train money," she said, nodding to the small pile of change. "I've got to hurry, now."

Mom kissed me and looked into my eyes. She paused to smooth my hair back from my face. "You okay?"

I smiled. "Fine." I always felt fine, better than fine, when my mother came so close, touched my face, my hair, and looked into me and saw only the good things there. Those moments I knew she loved me and saw me as beautiful and for that time, I *was* beautiful and every good thing in me was shining and real and this was my true self. Looking so closely now at her wounded face, the purple-red bruises under that dry, pale makeup, the swelling under her eye, on her jaw, the tiny scabbed cuts here and there, everything felt different and crazy and dangerous.

After my mother left, I took my *Tom Sawyer* book and folded up in the comfy chair in the kitchen and read until Cat staggered downstairs at lunchtime, which came as a real relief because I was getting pretty sick of Tom Sawyer.

"Did Stuart call?" Cat was already dressed. She was wearing navy corduroys and a grey Harvard sweatshirt.

While Cat was gulping down a shrimp cocktail glass of juice, a horn sounded from outside. Cat glanced out the window and smiled and the horn honked again. I hurried over and looked out at Stuart's Rambler.

"That's Stuart's car," I said. "Stuart's here."

"No kidding," Cat said.

"Aren't you going out?"

"Eventually," she said, and then we heard the smack of the door knocker. "Wonder who that could be," Cat said, tossing her hair over her shoulder as she turned then ran for the front door.

I heard Stuart's voice but not what he said. Then I heard Cat's laugh and she called out, "Bye!" before slamming the door shut behind her.

From the dining room window, I watched Stuart and Cat heading for the Rambler. They were holding hands and every couple of steps, Cat raised her right foot high behind her and slapped its side against Stuart's bottom then continued walking, not missing a step. Stuart Haskins wasn't very handsome—he was thin and short, only an inch or two taller than Cat, with dull brown hair touching his shoulders, a round face, eyes that bulged so it seemed he was always on guard—really, he looked a lot like Peter Lorre to me—but he was a boy and he had a nice smile and pocket money from a weekend job and, most of all, he had that blue Rambler and when it worked properly, that meant escape and I guess that meant a lot to Cat. After a minute or two of fooling around, Stuart's grabbing Cat's foot and Cat's hopping toward the Rambler, openmouthed, shrieking and laughing—I could hear her from the dining room but as if my fingers were in my ears—they finally jumped into the front seat and kissed a lovers' lane kiss. Afterward, they took turns smoothing their hair in the rearview mirror. Then Stuart started the car, wheeled back out of the driveway, and took off up the street, leaving rubber. They were going driving, maybe to Hood's Pond or

Chebacco Lake, somewhere woody and private, and maybe they would make out there.

Just before two o'clock, Mrs. Wyman dropped Franny off from kindergarten. Franny could have gone to half-day kindergarten at the public elementary school but Mom said Mrs. Wyman gave little kids a better start in her private kindergarten. I thought it probably also had something to do with the fact that Mrs. Wyman would pick up her pupils and bring them home afterward. I had to give Franny her snack and help her into play clothes and pack her pink-checked bag with her Barbie, Barbie clothes, *The Lonely Doll,* her stuffed dog Mookie and a baggie of cookies, so I could take her on the train over to Ipswich, to Old Stuff, where Mom would be working until five.

We had to walk downtown to the depot, a long walk for a little girl so I let Franny ride me piggyback part of the way. We sang songs—"100 Bottles of Beer on the Wall," "I've Got Sixpence," and "When the Hearse Goes Rolling By"—and we played a geography game.

As we were climbing the stairs up to the platform at the depot, I heard, *smack-smack* and there across the street a storm door was bouncing in its weathered frame and Billy Halliday was heading off up the street toward the center of town. He had a long, determined stride.

"Why'd you stop?" Franny took my hand. "What're you looking at?" She glanced across the street where I'd been staring, toward the raggedy house, unpainted for so long you couldn't tell what color it had been.

It suddenly occurred to me that Billy Halliday was growing up just like my father had on that same sorry street and then something came in my mind that was so strange I didn't know what to make of it: I found myself thinking that my father could have *been* Billy Halliday.

Franny pulled on my arm. "Why're you looking at that house?"

"No reason."

"Come on, then, you alligator!" Franny scooted past me up the depot steps and ran ahead to the bench facing the tracks where we usually set our things while we waited for the train, but signs saying *Wet Paint* hung at the back of the bench now.

I called to Franny to watch out for the paint and though she wasn't yet within arm's length of the bench, Franny recoiled from it as if it had burst into flames.

"It's not gonna *hurt* you," I said, setting her bag at the base of a lamppost.

Franny pointed a tiny finger at the bench, then poked it.

"Don't touch," I said.

Franny brought her fingertip close to her face, then pointed it at me. "Look, blue paint. Just like Mommy."

I took *The Lonely Doll* from Franny's bag. "Want me to read to you?"

"Mommy keeps having paint on her."

"What?"

"She has blue paint on her—mostly just on her arms and her stomach and her legs."

"What are you talking about?"

Franny rolled her eyes as if she were losing patience with me. "I see it all the time when she lets me take a tub with her. It's blue and purple and black and it gets on her stomach and her arms and legs and it doesn't wash off. She has it on her face now."

"That's not paint," I said, then I stopped.

"It is *so* paint."

"Okay." I held the book up to her. "Want me to read this to you?"

"Why does she get it on her?" Franny said.

"I don't know, Franny. Okay? I don't know. Let's drop it. Do you want me to read this or not?"

"Not," Franny said, and she glared at me.

While we waited for the train, we played on the platform pretending we were war refugees escaping to Switzerland, except

Franny kept thinking we were soldiers running away from home which I told her didn't make any sense. And then we heard the rumble and screech and while I held onto her, making sure she didn't fall off the platform, Franny and I peered down the tracks staring hard, trying to conjure the train. When it finally rounded the corner, rocking a little from side to side, Franny began to wiggle and holler, "It's the train!" and I tickled her, making her shriek and wiggle some more.

On the train, Franny and I found an empty car and I flipped one of the seats back so we could face each other and have a private place. When the conductor came down the aisle I said we were going to London and Franny laughed and the conductor punched two tickets to Ipswich and asked for forty cents. The conductor wore glasses with lenses thick and grey as the bottoms of my parents' rocks glasses and we couldn't see his eyes and that made us stop laughing and get small and quiet—as if he could see us really well with those glasses, maybe even see inside us, like it always seemed my mother could. Then he left the car and I said, "What a crab."

Franny stared at me, glanced out the window, and stared at me again, this time with a flat mouth and narrowed eyes.

"What? He's your best friend?" I said.

Franny blinked and kept her mouth flat.

"What?"

"How come you get to ride backward all the time?"

"I don't."

"Yes, you do," Franny said, brushing the bangs from her eyes with her fingertips. "Every time. How come?"

" 'Cause I'm older."

"That's not fair. You'll always be older and then I'll never get to ride backward." She pouted and stared out the window, avoiding my eyes, and this was beginning to spoil my mood. The train always made me feel hopeful and adventuresome, made me believe in unlimited possibilities and faraway lands where no human has drawn a breath. Sometimes, on a very still winter's night when the cold emptied the air of clouds and voices and things in motion, I could hear the train whistle from my bed and it would strike a spark in my heart, send shivers up my neck, down my back, through my bones, and fill me with thoughts of a world that lay beyond Salem and the North Shore.

"Okay. *You* sit here," I said, and Franny and I switched places.

She scooted back into the seat until her legs were dangling, and she held her head high and peered out the window, blinking slowly, smiling triumphantly. But soon, Franny's face paled, her lips grew ashy, and her head began to bob with the train as it rocked on the tracks.

"I'm gonna puke," she moaned, and I quickly lifted her back onto my seat.

"Put your head between your knees," I told her and began to rub circles on her back. "Breathe slowly," I said. "Take deep breaths."

After a few minutes, Franny raised her head and looked around. Her eyes were bright again and the pink had returned to her face.

"I'm not gonna puke anymore," she said, adding thoughtfully, "How come Mrs. Cohen's always puking?"

"She isn't," I said. "And don't say *puke* say *vomit.*"

"Yes, she is," Franny said. "She puked two times yesterday when she came over."

"She didn't come over yesterday," I said. For Franny, all past days were yesterday.

"Well, the last day she came over she puked. And she puked another day, too."

"Vomited," I said.

"Vomited," Franny said.

Maybe Rachel Cohen was sick with a disease, a fatal disease. Maybe she would die and leave Lydia and Perry orphans and Mom would have them come and live with us. Lydia would steal all my things and Perry would break what his sister didn't want and our lives would be ruined. My mother would do that, too—adopt Lydia and Perry, I mean. She loved people who were worse off than she was. I think they made her feel like a cat person. I think she figured that they would never leave her. And I guessed that was why she married my father.

Just then, the compartment door hissed open, admitting the conductor again, who called out, "I-I-I-Ip-swich, I-I-I-Ip-swich," as if he were calling a dog with that name, and Franny jumped up and scurried to the door as if that dog were she.

To get to Old Stuff, we had to walk past the Iron Horse Bar, where grizzled men in dark clothes and boots heavy with mud were making a noisy scene on their way in and out. As we ducked around them, the men noticed us and one said something I didn't catch and the others looked at me and laughed and it made me feel sick and as if I had been touched somewhere private and clean with dirty hands. From the other side of the hazy window of the Iron Horse Bar, a sign promised *Free Beer Tomorrow* and Franny asked me to read the sign, like she did every time, and then asked why all the men didn't just go tomorrow so they wouldn't have to pay.

"Is it 'cause they want it *now*?" she said, slowing down, glancing back at the sign and the men.

"Of course they want it *now*," I said, squeezing her hand tighter, hurrying her along the sidewalk. "But that's not what the sign's about. It's a *joke*."

Franny said she didn't get it. When we reached the front of Woolworth's, we stopped and I tried to explain it for the thousandth time.

"Each time they go, it's free beer *tomorrow*, never *today*."

But Franny frowned and said, "That's not funny. It's unfair. There's no free beer at all, ever. It's a *lie*."

I told her she was too young to understand, but I knew what she meant and of course I knew that, in a way, she was right.

Old Stuff was located on the first floor of an old fisherman's house, a two-storied clapboard building weathered to a soft charcoal on a small, steep hill about five minutes from the center of Ipswich. A sign saying **Antiques** dangled over the stone wall at the base of the granite stairs leading up to Old Stuff.

As we opened the door, a bell above the threshold clanged into the quiet shop. The place smelled of old, dusty, dry things, acrid, rusty plumbing, stale tobacco, faded perfume. The floorboards, pale and narrow, creaked with our footsteps. Through a haze made dense by the afternoon sun, we could see Mom behind the counter, puffing on a cigarette.

Franny shrieked, "Mommy! Mommy!" and ran behind the counter to her, dropped her head in Mom's lap, hugged her about the waist, and wiggled her bottom in the air like a puppy.

The peach makeup Mom had smeared on her face had begun to fade, revealing the purple on the cheekbone beneath her eye, the red and purple on her jaw. Paint, Franny had called it, and now she said it again, laying a small finger on Mom's jaw. "Paint," she said, and Mom batted her hand away.

"It's a bruise," Mom said. "I fell down last night." When she saw me glaring at her, she added, "I tripped over something."

And then, without any knowledge I would do so, I said, "No, you didn't."

I couldn't believe I said it.

My mother's eyes grew huge; she couldn't believe it either.

Words like these only got spoken inside me by my evil self and I was the only one who ever heard me say them. They never made their way up my throat, to my mouth, past my lips. My inside self always swallowed them, pushed them down, kept them down.

My mother's lips were parted and her eyes were still huge and I thought she might leap up from her chair, reach across her desk, and smack me in the face, but instead, she coughed and glanced to her right, toward a grey-haired woman in a navy jacket who stood at the side of the room before a wide buffet inspecting a china set displayed there.

"I want you both to be quiet and go sit still outside the shop," she said softly and quickly. This was what we always ended up doing when we came here, unless it was raining or snowing in which case we had to stay in the back room with all the cardboard boxes and cobwebs and broken furniture and cracked china and a stinky brown-bowled toilet that ran all the time.

I suddenly felt I'd won something, not something trivial, like what I won when I won a fight with Cat, but something worth winning, though I couldn't have said what it was.

In a dented copper tub by the cash register was a stack of old, tattered magazines and comic books and Mom told us to take one and get out of the way. By then, it was three-thirty and Mom was drinking out of a Styrofoam cup and I knew it was liquor. I could smell it. She bit her way around the edge of the cup, like I do, but she left little red lipstick smiles like the decoration at the edge of a wedding cake. There was something wrong with me and Franny lying on a battered old sofa with rusty springs and fluff sticking out of it in the thin musty light of the back room, or our sitting there on the steps out in front of Old Stuff reading comic books, people in cars looking up and staring at us as they passed, people coming into Old Stuff looking down at us, checking us out, as if we might be for sale, too.

As I took a comic book from the copper tub called *Nancy's Naughty Nursery Rhymes,* I glimpsed something resting on an old cedar chest, in shadow, something familiar but out of place, and then I recognized it. "Isn't that Gramma Hattie's Bible?"

Ever since I could remember, the Bible had sat on a cedar chest at the foot of my grandmother's bed. It was enormous— bigger than a phone book or the unabridged dictionary—and it was dark and wholly present. Its cover was made of a thick carved leather. Inside, in handwritings generous and flowery, small and shy, straight and noble, were the names of my ancestors all the way back to the original owner of the Bible, Mary Sloane Warwick, who had entered her name and birthday—May 12, 1783—and the names and birthdays of her husband and her four children, along with their death days. Here and there pressed between pages throughout the book, you could find remnants of these people: faded roses, daisies, and columbine, flat and dainty and dry; long braids in blonde and brown, coiled or stretched out like book-marks; poems and letters, written in these dignified old hands; and a grey silken badge that read:

WE MOURN

THE

NATION'S LOSS

ABRAHAM

LINCOLN

April 15, 1865

"Yes, it was my mother's Bible," Mom said, staring into an open book of numbers in front of her. "Now, you girls get moving."

"You're selling it?"

Mom didn't look up. "That's right."

"Why are you selling it?"

"That old thing?" She took a gulp from her cup. "For one, it's hell to dust. And for two, it's been sitting for years in a box in the attic without anyone missing it. And it's not as if we don't all have our own Bibles. Now, enough—you two get going."

Mom returned to her book and Franny said, "Let's *go.*" I wanted to say something else—*But it's our family. How can you care about strangers' old stuff and not your own?*—but words wouldn't come.

Outside, Franny and I scooted to the edge of one of the cold granite steps in front of the shop and I began to read the book out loud until I realized it was dirty. The only poem I remember now is this one:

> Friends may come and friends may go
> And friends may peter out you know.
> But we'll be friends through thick or thin,
> Peter out or peter in.

I knew *peter* wasn't the name of a boy and I knew that, just as Mom made us wait in the car when she went into the package store, she should have kept this thing away from us.

Later that afternoon, some of Mom's new friends dropped by Old Stuff. They passed right by us on the stairs. Only one person seemed to notice us—a man who glanced at Franny, then remarked to me, "Cute little boy."

I smiled and nodded and slipped my arm around Franny's shoulders. I didn't want to give anything away.

Franny wriggled free and said, "I'm not a boy!" but the man had already passed.

From where we sat, we could hear Mom and her friends talking, telling jokes, laughing while they all drank liquor out of Styrofoam cups. These people were antique dealers and they really seemed to like Mom but ignored Franny and me. They didn't know our names and we didn't know theirs.

Though Old Stuff officially closed at 5:00 P.M., at 5:10 Mom was still talking and drinking with Tilly, who'd arrived just before closing after everyone else had left. When she saw Franny and me on the steps, Tilly seemed to wince, her lips quickly stretching wide and flat like a rubber band pulled at both ends and just as quickly they snapped back into a tight pinch of flesh radiating a handful of short, thin lines as if she had a mouthful of pins. I couldn't even see her eyes behind her horned-rimmed glasses. I didn't like Tilly.

"Glad to see you're staying out of your mother's way," she said, and proceeded into the shop. Before Tilly was through the front door, Franny had jumped up and turned toward her, sticking out her tongue.

For a few minutes we heard laughter, then nothing. I walked softly toward the front door and Franny tiptoed behind me. I opened the door carefully, just a crack, not enough for the bell to ring. I turned to Franny and brought my index finger to my lips. Franny nodded. We could hear Mom talking softly. I heard her say, "Rachel Cohen." Then she said, "Puke."

I closed the door and tugged on Franny's sleeve and though she looked cross, she followed me back to our place on the stairs.

"We just have to wait," I said and Franny began hopping up and down between two steps.

"See?" she said. "Mom said *puke.*"

"Mom can say anything she wants," I said. "She's the mom."

"And she was talking about Mrs. Cohen."

"I know."

After a while, Franny sat back down with me and we played hand-clapping games. Then we hopped and skipped up and down the steps. The sun was setting, the light growing thin and cold and gray and still no sign of Mom and Tilly. An old man and woman in dark clothing, arms linked, moved slowly along the sidewalk. They were looking down and the woman was talking.

"It's *imminent.* I-m-n-i-e-n-t. *Imminent.*"

"I-m-i-?" the man said, still looking at the ground.

"I-m-n-i-e-n-t," the woman spelled out again, slowly, loudly, not looking at the man. We could still hear her spelling after they had rounded the corner and disappeared.

Franny and I were both staring after them and suddenly Franny said she wanted to go for a walk.

"You can't," I said. "Mom'll be wanting to leave soon."

"Then I'll walk myself," Franny said, heading down the stairs toward road.

"No, you won't." I jumped up and grabbed her arm.

Franny sneered at me and tried to shake me off. "You're not the mother. You can't tell me what to do."

"Oh, yes I can," I said, pulling her back to the stairs by the arm.

Franny started screaming: "No! No! You're not the mother!"

Then I heard Mom's voice from behind me: "Do what your sister says," and I saw the defeat on Franny's face and I felt sorry for her. It was hardly a fair fight before Mom stepped in, but at least it was one-on-one.

So that Dad could pick up hay from the Afalfa Farm on the way home, Mom and Dad had switched cars that day and we were riding now in Dad's Impala. Franny stayed in the backseat to let us know she was sulking. The entire drive from Ipswich, through Hamilton and Wenham and most of Beverly, Mom was silent, staring at the road, exhaling audibly now and then. When we reached the south side of Beverly, the bridge to Salem was up and after a few moments of waiting, I turned on the radio.

A rich, bassy voice was saying, *". . . as soothing as the sea. The time now is five-fifty-seven."* After three clangs of a buoy bell, sounds of surf crashing and seagulls calling, the same voice said, *"This is wish radio, WSSH, one-oh-three on your FM dial, where all your dreams—"* Mom turned the knob of the radio and there was silence.

Suddenly Franny was leaning over the front seat, between Mom and me, showing us the coins in her open hand. "Look, you guys. I found this money on the floor. How much is it?"

"Fifty-two cents," I said.

Franny lowered her eyebrows.

"Twelve candy bars and two cents of penny candy," I explained.

"Wicked!"

"Toss it in my purse," Mom said.

Franny looked outraged. "It's *mine!*"

"And where'd you get it?" Mom asked.

"On the floor back here."

"And whose car is this?"

"Daddy's," Franny said.

"And who else's?"

Reluctantly, Franny said, "Yours."

"So whose floor is that?"

"Daddy's and yours," Franny said sadly, suddenly seeing the conclusion Mom was about to draw.

"So whose money is that?"

"Mine," she pleaded. "I found it, Mommy. Please let me keep it, *please?*"

Mom scrutinized Franny in the rearview mirror. "I'll make a deal with you," she said. "You can keep it if everything else you find is mine. Okay?"

"Okay." Franny smiled and sank behind the seat to resume hunting.

I stared at Mom who was tapping an index finger on the steering wheel. Then from behind us, Franny's voice: "I found a button!"

"Good," Mom called back to her.

"Hey, here's a pen." Franny leaned over the seat again and showed us. Everything was a prize now.

"Great," Mom said. "Toss 'em in my purse."

"Hey, look!" Franny hollered and tossed something made of silky fabric over the seat.

"What is it?" Mom said.

It was pink.

I didn't want to touch it.

I couldn't look at it.

I could see a ship with a tall mast in the harbor moving toward us. Cars stretched in long lines from both sides of the gap in the bridge.

"What *is* it?" Mom said.

Soon, you could see the mast move above the cars in front of us, slowly, smoothly, as if on wheels, but the ship was no longer visible.

"Clothes," Franny said.

Mom looked at the thing lying in a small pile between us on the seat.

Franny picked it up carefully, pinching it between the thumb and forefinger of her little hand. She wrinkled her nose. "Underpants," Franny said.

The mast glided past the cars.

I didn't say anything.

"Let me see." By the expression on my mother's face, it was clear they weren't hers. She grabbed them, held them by the waist band. The raised flaps of the bridge began to lower and the ship quickly grew small as it slid away from us, out of the harbor toward the ocean.

"Are they yours, Mommy?" Franny said.

Traffic ahead of us began to move; cars from the Salem side began passing by.

"Be quiet." Mom gathered the panties into her fist and stuffed them into her purse. Then she put the car in gear.

After this, my mother's face was set hard and mean and nobody spoke the rest of the drive. Not even Franny.

When we got home, the house was dark and still, no sign of Cat or Dad. In the kitchen, Franny turned on the little TV while Mom fixed herself a drink, then began to fuss in the fridge. She removed a plastic container, dumped its contents into a frying pan, turned on the burner.

"What're we having?" I said, moving toward the stove. I could see the stuff filling the frying pan—shiny, small brown things the size of peach pits.

"Chicken hearts," Mom said, pouring another drink.

I looked over at Franny who opened her mouth and stuck out her tongue. "How 'bout if Franny and I have peanut butter and jelly?" I said.

"Do what you like," Mom said.

"Peanut butter and jelly!" Franny called from the table.

After I made the sandwiches, sliced them into triangles, and put them on plates, Mom told us to take them upstairs and eat in the family room. The chicken hearts were sizzling loudly on the stove and an acrid, meaty smell had taken over the kitchen. Mom had chopped all the lemons and limes in the fridge and now they sat in tangy puddles, dozens of small wedges all over the counter.

"Where's Dad?" I said.

"Working late," Mom said, rooting through the junk drawer next to the stove.

"When's Cat coming home?"

"Couldn't tell you." Mom lit a cigarette, dropped the match in the sink. "I think she's having dinner at Stuart's." She stuck her tongue out a little, pinched something off the tip. "Now get going," she said, picking up the telephone receiver, starting to dial.

Up in the family room, Franny and I ate our sandwiches, watched *I Love Lucy* and *Patty Duke* and then Franny said she wanted dessert.

I told her I'd get it.

"Get cookies," Franny said. "No fruit."

From the dining room, I saw Mom sitting beside the phone, smoking, drinking from her blue cup, and on the little table next to her, a bottle of clear liquor, open and half empty. She refilled her cup with liquor, waved the bottle in the air as she said, "A son of a bitch is what he is. A goddamn lousy son of a bitch." She took a gulp from her cup and said, "And a goddamn sneaking cheating panty hider."

When I returned to the family room empty-handed, Franny pouted and looked like she might even cry. "Where's dessert?"

"We have to wait," I said.

"Why? Why can't we have it *now*?"

"We just can't, okay? We'll just wait a little bit. Hey, and besides—guess what? *The Twilight Zone* is on."

"Yay!" Franny said. "Then can we have dessert?"

"We'll see, okay?"

But when I tiptoed down again after the show, Mom was still on the phone. She seemed angrier now, she was talking louder, still swearing. The liquor bottle was almost empty.

Back up in the family room, Franny was distracted by another TV program and didn't seem to notice I'd come back again without dessert.

"I love that pig," she said, laughing, pointing at the TV.

During the commercial, I got up and went to the bathroom and when I came back, Franny was gone. As I headed toward Mom and Dad's bathroom, I heard screaming, steady and high-pitched, coming from the first floor.

I ran down the stairs. Franny was wailing.

It must be Mom.

Franny was shrieking. As I tore through the dining room I could see a foot, a leg, a body lying on the floor. Franny was standing beside it, her head tipped back, her face raised to the ceiling, screaming her heart out.

"She's dead! She's dead! Mommy's dead!"

I stared at my mother's face. It looked wholly blank, neither dead nor alive. I put my hand on her chest. I had to close my eyes to feel but I couldn't feel anything. Franny was screaming too much.

I hollered, *"Quiet!"* but Franny kept screaming. I got up and shook her and yelled, *"Stop it! Shut up! Shut up!"* and she did shut up and I kneeled down again and *there.* Mom's heart was beating. I opened my eyes, saw my hand rise and fall with her breathing. "Look—she's okay, see? Look at her breathing." I pulled Franny onto her knees beside me. "Look." Franny was staring at me, stunned, and I took her hand, brought it down to Mom's chest with mine and our hands rose and fell with our mother's breathing. Softly, now, I said, "See? She's breathing. Feel her heart? She's all right. She's fine."

Franny smiled weakly and nodded. Her face was wet and flushed. "Why's she on the floor?"

I looked at my mother's face. In this light, her bruises just looked like dirt smudges, like what you might have after playing outside all day. Her mouth was opened slightly, but neither smiling nor frowning. Like the rest of her face, it failed to express anything at all as if she were lost in a dreamless sleep, or made of wax.

"She's resting, I guess."

"Why not in her bed?"

"Franny, I don't know."

Franny leaned into me and said, "I wish Cat was here."

"Me, too."

After failing to wake her, Franny and I spread a blanket over Mom, tucked a pillow under her head. Then Franny turned on the little TV and I stepped over Mom and got two tonics from the fridge, a box of crackers from the cabinet. Franny and I sat at the kitchen table and waited for Mom to wake or for Cat or Dad to come home. We kept watching TV and looking over at Mom lying so still on the floor.

Around ten o'clock, just when a car pulled in the driveway, Mom moaned, then turned her head to the side and vomited onto her hair. I hurried over to her, held her head up while she coughed to make sure she didn't choke and I heard Cat holler, "Anybody home?"

"In here," I yelled, and Franny ran to meet her, saying, "In here, Cat! Mommy's resting on the floor and she just puked."

"Would someone please get some towels or something?" I said. "There's puke all over the place."

"Jesus," Cat said, hurrying into the kitchen. "What happened?"

"We were watching TV upstairs and Mom went to sleep here," Franny said.

"Franny found her about an hour ago," I said. "She was drinking all night."

Cat rolled her eyes.

"When we were driving home from Ipswich, Franny found a pair of women's panties in the car. Dad's car. They weren't Mom's."

Cat stared at me. After a moment, she said "Jesus" again. Then she grabbed a stack of towels from the linen drawer. "Wet these," she said, handing me a wad of towels. "Warm water."

Franny began whining. "What should I do?"

"Franny, your job is to go find something good on TV, okay?" Cat said.

"But what about Mommy?"

"She's fine. Now, you've got a job to do, okay? Will you do it?"

"Okay," Franny said gravely, and moved across the room to the little TV and began turning the knob, watching the screen. Soon she settled into a program, but from time to time I would look over and see her staring at us.

Cat began mopping up the vomit with wet dish towels, dumping them in a garbage can.

"Shouldn't we save these?" I said, nodding at the dish towels in the garbage can.

"For what?" Cat said. "If she wants them, she can rescue them."

"Why're you so mean?"

"*Mean?* Jesus, Trisha, it's not mean. It's *her* mess."

Cat wiped Mom's face, her lips, her chin. She smoothed the towel lightly over the bruises, wincing and biting her own lip, though Mom couldn't feel anything.

"Help me," she said, and I grabbed a soapy towel and began wiping the vomit from my mother's ears and hair, trying to see it without looking at it. Trying to see her without seeing the damage and the sickness. "You know, we should probably just let her lie here like this so she'll have to deal with it when she wakes up."

"Cat!"

"*What?*"

"You're *sick.*"

"Why?"

"She wouldn't do that to *us.*"

"What're you talking about?" Cat chucked another towel into the garbage can. "She *is* doing that to us." Cat shook her head at me, made that goose face of hers to show me what a jerk she thought I was.

"Let's get her up so we can clean the floor," Cat said, and together we pulled her arms and sat her up but she wouldn't stay like that on her own—she kept slumping forward and falling back, heavy and unbalanced. We were on either side of her, each with a hand on her back and a hand on her shoulder. She was wearing her red silk blouse and it was wet with dark patches now and I kept thinking it looked like she'd been stabbed, like she was bleeding under those dark places.

"You've got to hold her," Cat said, and I looked at my mother, her hair all stringy, her shirt all covered with those wet splotches and with vomit.

"What do you mean *hold her?*"

"Put your arms around her, keep her up."

"*You* hold her."

"Okay, then you can clean the puke off the floor."

"But look at her; she's disgusting."

"Let's get this shirt off," Cat said, like that, "*this* shirt," not

"*Mom's* shirt," as if speaking the whole truth of it had gotten to be too much for her, too. "Come on, help me."

Cat began unbuttoning Mom's shirt from the top so I started in on the bottom buttons, small luminescent bead-buttons like red pearls on her blouse, one of her favorites. She'd ordered the blouse from a catalogue one Christmas to wear with her black velvet skirt. Now that it was a little older, she wore it more casually, but she still treated it with special care, never hand washing it but taking it to Murray the Dry Cleaner instead.

It was hard to believe that this was our mother and we were undressing her. Our mother who'd undressed us and bathed us and fed us a thousand times. That, not this, was the natural thing. When we got to the middle buttons, I stopped.

"You do it," I said to Cat.

Cat unfastened the last buttons, exposing my mother's plain white bra and the stomach she took such pains to keep flat and sucked in whenever it was uncovered. Cat breathed in loudly and said, "Sweet Jesus" because here on her stomach were two enormous bruises, a large yellowing bruise on her right side just beneath her ribs and a deep purple and red bruise the size of a saucer almost in the center of her stomach. And here and there were shadows of old bruises, blue, brown and yellow half-dollar-, quarter-, nickel-sized ghost bruises.

"Let's do one arm at a time," Cat said, and reached around Mom's back, sliding a hand under the collar of the shirt onto Mom's shoulder. "Okay, I've got her," she said. "Pull the shirt off this arm." This was much easier to say than to do but eventually, after Mom had slipped out of our grip twice and had fallen again into the vomit on the floor, smearing it on her skin, on her hair, on her back, we wrangled each arm out of the shirt and Cat tossed it into the garbage along with the dish towels. There were old and new bruises on her arms and back.

"Hold her up," Cat said, and I put my arms around my mother but she was heavy and kept falling back onto the floor. "You have to hold her around the middle," Cat said.

So I did. I leaned into my mother, put my arms around her; I had to smash the side of my face against her and hold her tight with all my weight so she wouldn't slump back down onto the floor. I had to hold her so her head fell forward or her hair would cover her back and Cat couldn't clean it. Her skin was cool and rubbery and moist and though there was still a trace of perfume in her hair, she stunk like liquor and spoiled milk and I kept my eyes closed and said, "Hurry, Cat."

"Keep her *forward*," Cat said, and I had to move in closer to her, almost on her lap, and her hair covered my face and it was like I was hugging my mother, and it was like she was dead.

Finally, Cat said, "Okay, good enough," and I dropped her back onto the floor as if she were just some big dumb doll. It felt wrong to have her so much in our control. It made me feel crazy or evil.

"We should try to get her up to bed," I said.

"Guess so," Cat said.

"How?"

"We'll each get under an arm," she suggested.

We sat our mother back up again, each of us squatting on one side of her, under her arms. Cat counted three and then we both stood. Though she didn't seem awake, Mom must've been aware of what we were trying to do because it was as if she helped us get her up and just as we were ready to walk her, suddenly Franny was in front of us.

"She's not sleeping," Franny said.

"No, she's not sleeping," Cat said. "She's sick, Franny. We're putting her to bed. Would you wait for us here?"

Then we walked Mom through the dining room and up the back stairs and to her bedroom. We flopped her onto her bed, took off her shoes and her skirt and her pantyhose and then yanked and pulled and shoved her into place on the bed. I hated to touch her cool, moist skin, like sick skin. I hated to look at her in her underwear and bra like that, all pale but bruised and vulnerable, so much skin, so much white sick bruised skin, but her clothes were splashed with vomit so what else could we do? Then Cat pulled a blanket over her and we shut the door to her room.

Later, after we finished cleaning up downstairs, and after we put Franny to bed, tickled her, covered her in Monster Repellent (Cat's eau de toilette) and sang her the song about Silly Lilly and the Garbage Boys, Cat came into my room with me and said, "Don't tell Dad."

"Why not?"

"He just doesn't need to know, is all," Cat said. "Besides, she won't remember anything tomorrow anyway. What would be the point in telling *him*?"

I was sure we'd get in trouble for undressing our mother. I could hear her say, *"How dare you!"* and I could hear her call us stupid. But she never did.

We didn't get in any trouble for that night. Dad never found out and Cat was right, Mom didn't remember it—or if she did, she never mentioned it. In time Franny seemed to have forgotten it, too. Cat and I never talked about that night again. But I will never forget.

ChapterSix

What Do You Want to Show Me?

When I first woke Wednesday morning, looking out the window from my bed I could see colors returning after a long New England winter. I could see the pale morning blues of the sky, white-blues and grey-blues, the soft green leaves and tiny hard buds and pale pink-white blooms on the tree outside my window, the cherry tree I would climb down if I ever ran away. These colors were so weak, so fragile, it was as if without care they would fade and disappear altogether and with them, spring, and summer would never come and winter would return for good. I looked over to the shed and the chicken coop and beyond, to the start of the main meadow that lay beyond the blackberry patch. I looked past the little apple orchard by the woods to the south, across to the vegetable garden, over the smooth lawn all the way to the well house. Behind it, at the far edge of the meadow was the barn, a point on the circle of woods surrounding our land like a moat. Animal tracks dotted the meadow, black from here in shiny grey. Some mornings I woke and spotted deer out there; sometimes there were even babies that wobbled and teetered and fell to their knees like newborn colts. It didn't have to be morning to see squirrels and chipmunks and rabbits, of course, though you could see them then, too. And lots of mornings there were raccoon and sometimes even foxes, porcupines, and groundhogs.

The first time I saw a groundhog I thought it was a beaver, all round and arched and moving slowly through the garden, and I woke my parents. My father sprang from bed and hustled to the window in the hall between our rooms. He stared for a moment, blinking at the window, before he said, "Groundhog." Then he hurried back to their room and I thought maybe he'd be getting his binoculars for a closer look or his camera with the long lens so he could take a picture but he returned a few moments later with the shotgun he kept in a long green flannel sack at the back of his closet, something Cat and I were never *ever* supposed to touch. Before I could say anything, he had opened the window, crouched down and rested the barrel on the sill. He was very still and solid and somehow he created a thick silence that froze me so I couldn't move or speak. When he pulled the trigger, the shotgun jumped against his shoulder as if it were the thing that had been shot and the sound cracked in my ears like a thunderclap. My father looked at me and nodded his head, once. Then he rose, still sleepy warm in his pajamas, and walked back to their room with his shotgun, closing the door behind him. The shot was still in my ears, like the flash from a camera remains in your eyes long after your picture has been taken. I looked out the window, but I couldn't see the groundhog. I climbed into bed with Cat and lay there for a long time, listening to the shot. One shot.

That was a long time ago, B.F., and things were very different now.

Something had come into our family since then, something that seemed to change the space of a room or its tone, like new furniture or an unfamiliar smell or the presence of a stranger. It crept in quietly, almost imperceptibly, like a black cat into shadows and you could only know it was there indirectly, by my mother's bruised face or her quick slap on the table or her giving you till the count of three to disappear; by my father's narrowed eyes or his substantial absence or his odd arrival in your room late at night. Sometimes its effects were wild and furious, making my mother and father scream swears or throw things at each other or drive off into the night; sometimes it made everything dark and cold and slow, made my mother drop her head on her folded arms and weep at the kitchen table, made my father sit alone with a drink in the growing darkness of the living room, blank-faced, rigid and brooding.

Moments like those were huge and heavy and you would think they would never end, that this was life now and that this was how things would always be. But then, suddenly, the moment would be over and my mother and father would storm to separate rooms, or one would take off out the front door, not, I think, out of rising anger but because the thing was losing its power, the anger was running out, and they weren't sure how to face each other so abruptly in the calm and quiet afterward. Sometimes I thought this thing depended on their fury, couldn't exist without it, *fed* on it, so that if my parents could stop fighting, just for a while, maybe then this thing would die.

Those days, because of this black shadow in our lives, in our house, I found myself believing in the powers of things you couldn't see, not just this black thing and not just regular invisible things like

music or electricity; I found myself believing in magic and witches
and ghosts. Though Suki and I had agreed not to believe in ghosts
we said Hail Marys whenever we were worried about them, like
when we left Burying Point. I found myself thinking that that was
what my family had now, that that was what this blackness was: a
ghost. We were haunted. I couldn't get rid of the thought and along
with it, the idea that it was some old dead relative—Samuel Wilde
or his hung-as-a-witch daughter Sara—reaching forward from his
place in dead history, our history, into real space and time, making
the rest of us suffer as he had suffered. I didn't how else to make
sense of all the things that were happening then.

But the change in our family wasn't something we talked
about, like we never talked about Sara Wilde, hung as a witch, and
when we used to ask about her, Mom would say what's past is past
and let it be. Like we never mentioned the liquor bottles we would
find, stashed, half full, here and there—behind the sofa, lying in the
foot warmer, standing inside boots; like we never mentioned the
constant presence of Mom's blue tumbler, always full and jangling
with ice, and her night breath becoming day breath, too, or her
speeding off in the station wagon and not coming home or phon-
ing. And we never discussed the grocery bags stuffed with bills in the
back hall closet, or Dad's losing ten acres, almost half our land, to
Manny Thompkins in a poker game, and his not coming home Friday night. Nobody talked about the fact—and we'd heard Manny's
voice booming in the front hall, we all knew it was a fact—that Dad
had till April's end to hand Manny thousands of dollars or Manny
would sell the land, our land, to John Horton at Taylor & Sons
Real Estate Company for development. We knew about these
things, these were some of the weapons my parents used against each
other when they fought, but they must have been too potent for
regular, casual discussion in the calm, clear light of day because no
one ever mentioned them. Certainly, I was not interested in bringing them up; I had been raised among many things I knew nothing
about except that I was never to ask after them or to even to ac-

knowledge their existence. Unlike Cat, I was not tempted to break this unspoken rule.

So now there were nights my father came home so late it was morning and days my mother would not get out of bed at all and yet no changes in our behavior were required—in fact, what was required was that our behavior *not* change. After my mother found someone else's underwear, *another woman's panties,* in my father's car, the night and day were just like this: hours after Cat and I put our mother, then Franny then ourselves to bed, Dad came home, poured a drink, and staggered up to the guest room only to rise two hours later to leave for work. Tuesday Mom remained in her room, in her bed all day, getting up just five times, three times to use the bathroom, twice to make drinks following the remedy—a kind of spell, really—that my father subscribed to: *a hair of the dog that bit you cures the wound.*

And all day Tuesday, it rained. Cat and I stayed in the family room reading books, playing with the Ouija board, trying to hypnotize each other with Cat's gold locket and listening for Mom. As if we were simply finding something for our bored eyes to fix upon, as if it didn't matter one way or another what we saw, and without mentioning the fact that we were doing this, Cat and I kept looking out the family room window down onto the driveway where the station wagon was parked, making sure no one had come or gone, I suppose.

When Dad got home at the usual hour, he poured himself a drink and went straight up to the guest room. Cat and I were ready, we'd braced ourselves, and that night we talked in whispery voices, made our own dinners and dinner for Franny, walked lightly on the stairs and hardly spoke outside the family room. Without our asking, Franny did the same and the three of us in our long pale nighties were like ghosts in the house, silent, watchful, and unnoticed. Suki hadn't returned my phone calls and I kept hoping she wouldn't now—the phone's ringing would have been too much and I wouldn't have known how to be with her right now. When I went to bed that night, the muscles in my back and neck and shoulders ached and I suddenly felt I'd been holding my breath all day.

So, this morning when I woke and looked out and saw the sun rising into a pale sky casting a gentle light across the meadow, I was ready for anything. For a long time, I petted my cat, Pip, while listening, waiting, until finally, I heard Franny's voice, then my father's, then their footfalls on the back stairs. When I entered the kitchen, Franny was already dressed, eating cereal at the kitchen table and my father sat beside her with a cup of coffee but he wore casual slacks and a turtleneck, not his work clothes.

When my father said, "I'm taking the day off," the thing already coiled inside me twisted tighter.

I knew Cat would be out all day with Stuart. She'd told Mom they'd be going to Boston, to the Fine Arts Museum.

After Mrs. Wyman collected Franny, my father told me to rake the side yard and then he left; he was going to do errands, he said. My mother was still upstairs in her room, not sleeping. I could hear her. She wasn't pacing, but she was up, looking at something I thought. Reading, maybe, though she crossed the room from time to time so she wasn't lost in a book. I imagined her taking her grey metal box with the combination lock from under her bed; I imagined her dialing up the secret code on the lock and raising the box's lid. She would take out the documents and certificates, one by one, and read them and I imagined them bringing her some understanding, some wisdom or hope that she needed right now.

While I was outside raking, I heard Stuart Haskins's horn, then peered around the side of the house and saw his blue Rambler back out of the driveway and wheel off down Wilde Road with Cat's pale head on the passenger's side. I raked for a while but there wasn't much debris left over from fall. Back inside the house, everything was quiet now. Only my mother and I were home; she was silent in her room. Up in the family room, I lay on the floor with Maggie. I rubbed her stomach then her chest above where I imagined her wormy little dog heart beating. I turned on the TV, low, and listened for my mother.

A movie called *The Leech Woman* was on. A beautiful dark-haired woman had to drink the fluid from the spines of men in order to preserve her youth. Otherwise, she would shrivel up and become a hundred years old. The woman wore a ring with a hook on it and while she was kissing a man she had to jab the hook into the back of his neck. The man would die, the woman would drink from the ring and stay young.

After the movie, I went out front on the breezeway. There was a bench out there and two white pillars. I put my arms around a pillar and kissed it. I leaned around the side of the pillar and kissed it some more.

"Looks like he's getting pretty fresh." I stood up and saw my father. He was carrying a small brown paper bag with DAWSON'S HARDWARE printed in red on the side. He was laughing.

When Suki finally called that afternoon, I was upstairs reading. She asked if I wanted to ride bikes. She said she wanted us to go to Candlewood Forest; she wanted to show me something but she wouldn't say what.

We decided to meet at 2:30 at the sandpit, a hole in the ground left from some sort of construction years ago.

I headed for the kitchen and as I entered I saw my dad leaning against the far wall looking into the coffee cup in his hand. When he glanced up at me, I saw the storm in his face. My mother was by the sink, beating something in a bowl. Her whole body shook.

"Mom?"

She looked at me with sad, red eyes. The bruise on the her cheekbone under her eye was starting to yellow; the one on her jaw was almost black in the middle, light purple on the edges.

I started to say I was going to ride bikes with Suki but my father said, "Get out." When I went to speak again, he said, *"Now."*

As I crossed the dining room toward the front hall, I heard my mother holler, *"Ten thousand dollars, David!"* and as I pulled the front door closed behind me, I heard her scream, *"Stop!"* and something shattered on the kitchen floor. I felt kind of crazy in my insides and that angry thing inside me tightened.

$\mathbf{S}$uki had a boy's stingray bike with a banana seat and she called it *Stinger.* Mine was *Star,* a regular girl's bike, but a sparkly blue. When we were younger, Suki and I could only be alone to explore our backyards and we had to be accompanied by an older kid, Cat or Suki's brother Kenny, in order to ride anywhere—never all the way downtown or to Devil's Rocks or to Burying Point—but now we were twelve and the world had grown because we were allowed to ride on our own and we could go anywhere. We would ride side by side, calling to each other, laughing, and sometimes it felt as if the rest of Salem were rushing by us and we alone were still. Sometimes we pretended our bikes were motorcycles and we turned the handlebar grips and made revving noises but mostly we pretended they were horses and we were cowgirls or Indian scouts. All over Salem were meadows and woods with bridle paths and ancient Indian foot trails and we knew all of them by heart. Because we rode everywhere.

Now, as I rolled down the hill to the sandpit, I could hear my mother again: *Ten thousand dollars, David!* Her face was lumpy like an old foam pillow and splattered with strange colors you didn't see on normal skin—yellow, purple, black—while she yelled at my father about ten thousand dollars. She must have been talking about the money he'd need to get our land back. *Ten thousand dollars!* Without it, they'd start building houses in our meadows and up in our woods, modern new houses on this old land.

I arrived before Suki and headed down into the sandpit. I remembered hearing a story from some kid about a car that crashed in here. The kid said there'd been a family in the car and everyone was killed and their bodies were still here under all the rocks and dirt and gravel. Though I didn't really believe it, I felt funny being here alone.

"Hi!"

I jumped and my whole body shook. "Don't scare me like that! God, you really scared me."

"Sorry," Suki said, laying her bike on its side.

We were dressed just alike: boys' sneakers, blue jeans, sweatshirts.

"Come here," I said, walking toward a big rock. Suki followed me. "Did you ever hear about the car crash?"

"Yeah," Suki said. "John van Aiken told me. He said they're still here, under this rock." Suki kicked at the rock with the toe of her sneaker. "John van Aiken said there was a baby—two parents and a baby. He said they were going really fast and went off the road and crashed in here and the car exploded into flames. Afterward, the neighbors came and put dirt over the bodies."

"Really?"

"Yeah, but John van Aiken is a wicked liar," Suki said. "He said he felt up Patsy Ballard's older sister and he never did. Patsy said she was watching the whole time and they never even kissed."

"Maybe he did feel her up," I said. "It would be just like Patsy to lie."

"No way. Patsy's sister wouldn't let anybody feel her up." Suki leaned close to me and whispered, *"She stuffs."*

Then Suki said she had to pee and she took off out of the sandpit toward the woods. I walked backward, keeping my eye on that big rock, picking up stones and chucking them at it, heading out of the sandpit, moving carefully until I heard Suki yell, "Jesus!" Then, "Come here!"

I turned and hurried toward the woods. "Where are you?"

"Here." Her voice was coming from a clump of bushes. Behind them, Suki was squatting on the ground turning the knob on a black box tall as a stereo console and wide as a TV set.

"It's a safe!" Suki said.

It was a safe all right, *a real safe.* It had a knob with numbers around it and a black handle and gold trim framing the door. And it was locked. We tried turning the knob, we hammered at the hinges with rocks and pried at the door with sticks, but it wouldn't open.

"Should we get my dad?" I said. "He's home today."

"Nah," Suki said. "Let's get Perry Cohen."

The Cohens' house was less than a quarter of a mile down the road from the sandpit and Perry Cohen was the biggest kid we knew though, as I've said, everyone thought he was mental and everyone was scared of him. Everyone except Suki.

We rode to the Cohens' house as fast as we could; we rode standing on our pedals; we rode hollering into the fast air. *A safe!*

Suki yelled, "Money!"

I yelled, "Gold!"

"Diamonds!"

"Emeralds!"

When Suki hollered, "Top-secret secrets!" we both cracked up.

But Mrs. Cohen told us Perry was at his Pilgrim Fellowship meeting and wouldn't be home till four o'clock. Mrs. Cohen looked at us funny and I wondered if she'd seen us when she was kissing my father in the hardware store. Suki said we'd be back later and we headed off down a path alongside the Cohens' house. I called to Suki to wait up and when I reached her, I said, "You sure you don't want to get my dad?"

"We can wait," she said, and looked at her wristwatch. "It's just an hour. Besides, there's something I want to show you." Suki grinned and took off on her bike toward the woods you had to cross to get to Candlewood Forest. It was a pain to bring bikes into the woods—there was a steep hill and even a swamp—but there were trails in Candlewood Forest, packed dirt trails, and the trees in the forest were straight and skinny with most of the branches so high up they didn't hit you as you rode. The floor of the forest was soft with pine needles. It smelled good and made a nice crispy sound when you walked. Candlewood Forest was very private.

"What do you want to show me, anyway?"

"I can't tell," Suki said.

"Is it a fort?"

"No."

"A new place to play?"

"Kind of," Suki said. "You won't be able to guess, so don't bother."

After a minute, Suki said, "Don't you hate Rachel Cohen?" in a way that made it clear that she did but I didn't say anything.

When we reached Candlewood Forest, we got on a trail, packed and smooth and we could ride one-hand. We pretended we were riding horses, posting on our bikes, hitting make-believe haunches with sticks we picked up off the ground.

"This way," Suki hollered, and I followed her off the trail, down a hill. I had to swerve to miss some trees and it felt like I was going too fast. Suki took a sharp turn and skidded on the pine needles. I slowed down for the turn, then tried to catch up. We came to a place where the trees thinned out and Suki stopped and got off her bike.

I couldn't see what was special about this place.

"Look at these," Suki said, touching a thin root that stuck up and arched out over the ground.

"So?"

"Watch." She took off her sneakers, then her pants, and lay down on her stomach in the pine needles. "Look down here," she said, and I looked and saw the root rubbing between her legs, against her underwear, as she moved. She made her hand a fist and settled it on the ground under her face. She dropped her lips on to the side of her fist and began kissing it.

"What're you doing?"

"Pretending it's Bruce Hartman," she said. "Try it."

I took off my sneakers and my pants. Then I got on top of a root, closed my hand into a fist.

"Who do I pretend it is?"

"David Hanson," Suki said. "You like him."

I moved so the root rubbed against me and though I'd meant to, I didn't pretend it was David Hanson I was kissing. Instead, when I closed my eyes, there beneath me was Billy Halliday with his sleepy brown eyes and his soft, soothing voice and I was kissing him and he was kissing me back and suddenly, a jolt went through my whole body and I stopped. I just lay there on the pine needles.

After a minute, I started to put my jeans and my sneakers back on. "How'd you find out about this?"

"I came back here by myself a few days ago and I decided to ride off the trail. Then I stopped here," Suki said as she finished tying her sneakers. "And I just did it. That's all." She looked at her watch again and said, "Hey, maybe Perry Cohen's home now."

I'd forgotten about the safe.

"Arriba! Arriba!" Suki hollered, like the Mexican cartoon mouse, and we scrambled to our bikes.

At the Cohens', we found Perry in the yard chopping wood. We rode right up to him but we didn't actually get off our bikes; we just stood astride them while we talked.

"We found a safe," Suki said.

"A safe?" Perry held the axe with both hands. I could see the muscles slipping beneath his skin as he raised and lowered the axe though he wasn't cutting wood anymore.

"You know, a safe," Suki said.

"A safe," Perry said again. "What's in it?"

"That's what we want to find out," Suki said. "Will you help?"

Perry said he'd get some tools and meet us at the sandpit.

Suki and I rode ahead and when we got there, we left our bikes, and climbed the hill behind the sandpit.

"Want a cigarette?" I said, digging the thin rumpled pack from my jeans pocket.

Suki smiled and I pinched two from the pack and we lit them.

We tried to blow smoke rings. We tried to French-inhale like Suki's sister Laura always did, a thick ribbon of smoke from mouth to nose. We tapped our ashes onto our jeans and rubbed them in. And all this time we weren't saying anything, just smoking and digging into the dirt with our heels and sitting close together. Then

Suki pried a stone out of the ground and chucked it into the sand-pit. I got a stone and threw it in, too. Then we were both throwing stones, and though neither of us said so, we were aiming for that large rock. I could almost see the family in the car under the rock, the skeletons black and gristly like barbecued ribs, the dad's hands still on the wheel, his jaw clenched in a gruesome smile, the mom's arms above her head, her jaw wide open. But in the back, the baby was just a little black bundle, a quiet pile of coal.

The sun was sinking behind the trees and it was beginning to get cold and Suki said, "Where *is* he?" when at last we saw Perry Cohen moving slowly down the path carrying a sledgehammer and a metal rod, lumbering like a bear. We tossed our cigarettes into the sandpit and tore down the side of the hill.

"What took you so long?" Suki said.

Perry put a big hand in his hair and shrugged his shoulders. "Where's this safe?"

"Follow me," Suki said, and she took off toward the woods.

Rubbing his hand across the top and down the side of the safe, Perry said, "I've never seen one of these before." He squinted and added, "In real life, I mean." Then he shoved the safe onto its back. He stuck the metal rod in the crack of the door and came down hard on it with the sledgehammer. Nothing happened. Perry belted the rod again. Then he rolled the safe onto its side, lifted the sledgehammer high over his head and came down so hard on the hinge the whole safe jumped. The hinge was busted.

Suki clapped her hands. "Now do the other one."

The second hinge took longer, but Perry finally broke it, too.

"Stand back," he said, and knocked the door off the safe. He bent down. "Nothing in here."

Suki rushed forward. "Let's see."

She squatted in front of the safe right next to Perry who was still holding the sledgehammer.

"Oh yeah?" Suki reached in and took an envelope from the safe. She waved it in the air, laughing, then tore it open and removed money from it.

My heart beat hard. "How much?"

Suki stared at the bills. Her eyebrows were low. "Three dollars."

"Is that all?" I said, examining the empty envelope then peering into the empty safe.

"Wait a minute," Suki said. "These aren't normal dollar bills—see how that seal and the numbers are blue? And look: across the top it says *Silver Certificate.* I bet they're worth a lot of money."

I stood behind her. The light was failing.

Suki gave me a bill. "I guess we should each get one," she said, and turned to Perry. "Here. This is yours."

Perry took the bill. His eyes were wide, like no one had ever given him anything before. He studied the bill, turned it over and sniffed it. Then he tore it in half.

"What'd you do that for?" Suki yelled.

"Now I have more money." Perry was smiling.

Suki told him to go home and put his money somewhere safe. Perry moved toward her and I thought maybe he was going to hit her but he leaned down and kissed Suki on the cheek. I waited for Suki to wipe her face with the back of her hand and say, "Gross!" but she didn't, she said, "Thanks, Perry. Go home now," and at that moment, I knew there was no one in the world I loved like I loved Suki.

Perry smiled, then grabbed his tools and trudged off. Suki and I got our bikes.

"Don't tell anyone," Suki said.

"About what?"

"Candlewood Forest."

"Okay."

"See you tomorrow," Suki said, and started pedalling away.

"See you."

I rode standing the whole way home. I thought about Candlewood Forest and I wondered if I was still a virgin but

I wasn't exactly sure what a virgin was and somehow it didn't seem to matter. Any guilt I might feel could easily be swallowed up by the dark thing inside me.

Then for the first time since we found it, I wondered about that safe and how it got there by the sandpit. I thought of all the times I'd dug for arrowheads and fossils and gold; I thought of my father roaming around the beach and through our meadows and woods with that metal detector looking for riches. And I wondered how long that safe had been there, in the sandpit, whether it had always been there, all those years we'd been messing around there, all those times we'd hunted for treasure there, and we just never found it before. And it occurred to me that maybe that was what the world was like, full of amazing treasures hidden in safe places, things you wouldn't find until you weren't looking for them.

Coasting down the hill to my house, the last rays of the day poked through the trees and the rush of cool air filled my eyes with water and suddenly everything looked soft and washed in gold and it felt like early morning, a summer morning, fresh and cool and long ago now. Cat and I are squatting in the garden, picking peas into the laps of our nighties. We toss peas to Maggie who is a puppy with a young, clear heart and she bites at the air and tumbles in the dark earth. My head is filled with the smell of that good earth, rich as coffee. I love the feel of it, soft and cool and moist under my feet, in between my toes. I love tasting those little peas, biting them out of their pods, throwing them to Maggie, who is playful and strong. I love watching my parents survey the property, drinking coffee from blue mugs, talking about things we don't understand. They move slowly. They hold hands. When they kiss in front of us, my heart beats high in my chest. Cat and I chase Maggie through the garden. Our nighties flutter about us, ruffled hems, light cotton, light colors.

My mother and father come close and I hear my mother say, "like two little butterflies" and I picture that, *two little butterflies,* and I laugh. My parents squat beside Cat and me in the garden and they eat peas, too, and my father points to the meadow, which seems to be dusted in silver. My mother points out the dark paths meandering through it toward the forest and says these are animal tracks and my father says she may be right—unless, of course, this is a magic meadow and these are really fairy trails. In that case, the fairies come at night and dance in the meadow and sing magical things to protect us all and keep us safe. When my father says this, he sprinkles a little dirt over my head, then Cat's head, and we laugh and my mother laughs and I feel we are fairies.

Thinking of all this now, I ached in my bones and had to stop by the side of the road. I had to let my bike drop and I hurried to the stone wall by the road because I needed something solid to grab onto so I wouldn't suffocate in the feeling rising up over me, so I wouldn't die and fade into the past with that time that I'd suddenly seen was gone forever. I concentrated on my breathing and tried to keep my stomach low in my body and then it occurred to me that maybe, if we wanted, we could *make* it be that time again. Maybe my mother and father had forgotten how happy we were then. When I reminded them, of the peas and the magic, of their coffee cups and how they would kiss, they would want to make then now, too.

When I got home, I dumped my bike between the cars in the driveway and ran into the house.

None of the lights were on downstairs. I hurried up the back stairs to my parents' room. Their door was closed. I could hear voices from inside.

I sat at the top of the stairs, to see what kind of thing was going on. At first, I just heard regular voices. Then there was a loud crash and the door to the room opened. My mother bolted past me down the stairs and then I heard the front door slam. My father stood beside me. I was holding my dollar bill.

"Dad?"

He looked down at me as if he didn't know me. There was a darkness in his face. Then he ran down the stairs, too. I heard the front door slam again.

The door to my parents' room was open and inside I saw clothes strewn all over the bed and on the floor. My mother's clothes. Some were ripped, torn into pieces so you didn't know what they had been. Bureau drawers had been turned upside down and stockings and underwear and my mother's jewelry were scattered everywhere. And on the bed, on the bureau, on the windowsills and the walls, were globs of shaving cream. I watched as a puff slid off the edge of the bureau and down its side, landing in a quiet pile on the floor.

I found Maggie in the guest room sprawled out on the carpet. I put my hand on her chest to make sure she was breathing. I imagined the worms escaping from her heart, weaving their way outside, winding around it, tight, tighter, squeezing the soul out of her.

I looked out the window, down onto the driveway. Floodlights were shining on the asphalt. Both cars were gone and my bike was lying where I had just left it, the front wheel spinning, slowly, the spokes shining clean and silver in the light. From the guest room window, my bike looked small and fragile, like something made from a paper clip, like something that could be smashed between a thumb and forefinger.

Chapter Seven

I Saw Everything

The spring of the year I turned twelve was the first spring in the life of my cat, Pip, who was born on a still, blue morning in late October, the last of our cat Eartha's second litter. It was 6:00 A.M. and cold and the grass on the lawn crunched under our feet, stiff with frost, as Cat and I brought steamy buckets of water and milk down to the barn for Misty and the chickens and the cats. The lock on the barn door was frozen shut on the latch, so Cat slipped off a mitten, and tried to pry the latch loose with her bare, damp hand. Her fingers froze to the lock. I don't know what she was thinking when she leaned up to the lock and stuck her tongue on it, next to her fingers, but her tongue became fixed to the lock as well, and I couldn't help but laugh at the sight of Cat balanced on tiptoes, stuck to the front door of the barn like that. She couldn't even yell at me, though she made these gurgly throaty noises, the kind you make when the doctor tells you to open up and presses the back of your tongue with a Popsicle stick. I finally got my parents and they got Cat free somehow. Cat was angry at me for having laughed but she got to go back up to the house and be babied while I finished the chores alone.

While I was tapping the ice out of the cats' milk bowl, I heard a soft cry, like a baby, then another. The sounds were coming from a darkened corner of the barn, where I found Eartha lying on her side in the hay, small animals scattered around her. At first I thought they were field mice she had caught and killed, but as I approached, I saw that they were moving. Then Eartha made a sharp noise like someone had pulled her tail. She was breathing quickly and all the muscles in her body squeezed in and made her smaller and there, from beneath her tail, something that looked like a large wet plum began to emerge. When Eartha curled down and began to tear at it with her teeth, I saw a tiny head, angular like a puppy's, and Eartha gnashing at it, devouring all the wet skin around it and I thought she would eat it and I went to hit her when she began to stroke it, firmly, with her tongue. It was the fifth kitten. After she had finished cleaning it, she lay back down and made a sharp cry again and went tight and a sixth sac slipped from her. It held a tiny black-and-white kitten, much smaller than the others. I called her *Pip.*

Pip was puny, the smallest in the litter, and when the other kittens attached themselves to Eartha's side, Pip was left trembling in the hay.

"Isn't she the sweetest?" I said to my mother.

My mother told me that Pip was the runt, she was the weakest, she wouldn't be able to compete with the other kittens for milk and she would die. After that, I would get up early and trek down to the barn in darkness, spend frigid mornings before school in the hay, holding Pip to a nipple, pushing the other kittens aside. During school I would stare at the clock, trying to make the hands sweep around faster, hoping Pip would hang on until I got home. Then I would be back in the barn until dinnertime, when Cat would come down and say: "Mom's really mad at you. You forgot to set the table." More than once Mom sent me to bed right after dinner for forgetting my chores and I kept accumulating points on the Demerit List, so it seemed I was always being spanked. But soon the worst of winter was over, and Pip had made it.

We gave away all the kittens but Pip, who purred almost constantly and was as devoted as a dog. Each afternoon, I would find her waiting for me at the bus stop, playing on one of the large rocks or climbing in the cedar tree. Mornings I would wake with Pip at my side, tucked under my arm like a doll. And on dark bleak nights, nights when my parents would rage around the house and Cat and Franny and I would cower in our beds, I would hold Pip tightly in my arms and, remembering the snowy mornings I had held her to Eartha's side, I would feel safe.

This night, the night of Friday, April 12, 1968, was the night of my parents' barbeque and Cat and I had to help get ready. We worked at one side of the kitchen table shaping hamburger into patties, spreading sweet tomato sauces on chicken breasts and ribs, stirring dips, arranging deviled eggs and stuffed celery on trays. At the other side of the table, Franny had been shaping green clay into people, sneaking blobs of clay into her mouth when she fake-coughed, though I told her not to eat clay and Cat said it would give her diarrhea. Franny had kept saying, "I'm *not*." Now she was messing with paper clips, bending them and fastening them to her teeth, pretending she had braces, and I could see tiny green flecks rimming her gums and stuck between her teeth as if she had just eaten pale spinach.

Mom was drinking from her blue cup, making ice cubes, chopping vegetables, not saying much.

"Who all's gonna be here?" Cat said, sprinkling paprika on the eggs.

"You'll see," Mom said. It was late afternoon and my mother had already dressed and she looked beautiful: she had curled the ends of her hair and she wore Ribbon Red lipstick; her eyes were bright and the bruises on her face had almost disappeared.

"Are the Cutlers coming?" Cat said.

"They have other plans."

"Can I have Lisa over?"

"No," Mom said.

"Can I have Suki over?" I said.

"No. No one can have anyone over."

Once people started arriving, Cat and I got to pass around platters of hors d'oeuvres and ask people if they wanted a drink. My mother said, "Don't you dare ask if they want *another* drink, do you hear me? One should never be made to feel as if anyone's counting. Just ask if they would like *a* drink."

I had never seen many of the people who came that night. A very old couple with white hair sat in the living room, talking quietly, sipping cocktails. The woman said, "No thank you, dear," when I asked if I could get them anything. Most of the people were younger, though, my parents' age I suppose, and they stood around outside laughing and drinking. When Rachel Cohen arrived, she was already drunk, Cat said, and she was smelling like honeysuckle and wearing big sparkly earrings. She giggled and said, "Swell outfit, Molly. I'll have to borrow it sometime."

Mom was wearing tight red slacks and a white linen blouse and she was the spitting image of Lauren Bacall, Rachel said. Mom glared at her but didn't say anything at all.

Mrs. Cohen hurried over to Cat, took Cat's face in her hands, and kissed at each cheek, not touching them with her big pink lips. "I hear you've got a big horse show coming up!" she said.

"Not till May," Cat said.

"That's just marvelous!" Rachel said. She smiled, kissed at Cat's cheeks again, and hurried off.

My father spent a long time talking with Rachel Cohen and a woman with orange hair and pure white skin. Rachel Cohen didn't even look at the woman; she just kept her arm looped through my father's and stared up at the side of his face. The orange-haired woman wasn't sick, I could tell, but she had almost no color in her skin, just a pale pink stain spreading from above her lips onto her cheek, like an old juice stain. When I asked this woman whether she would like something to drink, she scowled at me and told me to go help my mother in the kitchen.

There was a very loud woman in the kitchen with my mother. She had short black hair teased up high and a pointy nose and she was wearing a black see-through blouse and a black-and-white polka-dot bra. I had met the woman before, but I couldn't remember when and I couldn't remember her name. Suddenly the woman was staring at me, checking me out, looking me up and down.

"Trisha, dear, I believe you're getting boobs." Before I could say anything, before I could even have guessed how I felt, the woman must have noticed I was staring at her shirt, at the polka-dot bra underneath. "Like my peek-a-boo blouse?" she said.

My face was burning and my mother said, "Trisha, why don't you go circulate?" She shoved a tray of tiny hot dogs into my hands. They were like little penises in tiny white cradles. I tried not to look at them.

Outside, Cat was standing with Manny Thompkins, who was showing her tricks he could do with his face and head: touching the tip of his nose with his tongue, crossing one eye while rotating the other, and wiggling his ears. Since he wasn't here in his official capacity as chief of police, Manny Thompkins was wearing a red shirt under a dark blazer. He had been at our house plenty of times before, for poker games and for cocktail parties, though I don't think anybody wanted him here now. Manny Thompkins was about to sell ten acres of our land to Taylor & Sons Real Estate, who would

cut it into tiny parcels and chop down trees and chew up the earth
and ruin the space forever, just as they were ruining it near Suki's. I
imagined one day waking in my bedroom, sitting up, and looking
out my window at houses up in the blackberry patch, in the woods,
and in the main meadow. But my father said he'd been on such a
losing streak lately he was sure he'd be winning soon and he'd be
able to buy back the land before Manny's deal was finalized. He had
two weeks.

Manny Thompkins's lips were what my mother called *liver
lips*—thick and purple and fleshy—and now they were parted showing his short, square teeth as he smiled and poked Cat with his big
fingers. Cat was not laughing. Manny said, "But you *must* be able to
cross your eyes."

I looked at Cat. "Dad wants you." I said it smoothly and
easily, like a natural born liar, and Cat smiled and hurried off. For a
moment I wondered at myself, lying like that—not hesitating, not
even feeling guilty, I realized, not in the least.

Everyone was going on about how cute Franny was, and it was
true. That night, she wore a tomato-red dress with bright fruit
shapes appliquéd on the front. Early on, she scooted around, offering people cocktail napkins and potato chips, calling them *sir* and
madam. Later, she introduced everyone to her stuffed dog Mookie.

Some of the people who came were antique dealers. Some
were Mom's new friends like Janie and Tilly. Some people said they
owned junk shops and chuckled. They stood together in circles, gos-
siping and arguing about prices and reproductions and something
called *end-of-the-day glass*.

People in one group were talking in muted voices when I approached.

"Something something Jewish," a thin man was saying.

A woman with a dark mole on her chin said, "She claims
they're *German*."

Someone squeezed my shoulder and I flinched.

"You must be one of Molly's girls." The bald man behind
me was wearing a bright plaid jacket and lime green pants, clutch-

ing a drink, standing at the edge of a circle of other men with
drinks.

When I said I was, he asked my name and called me *kitten,* as
if I were a little kid.

"Trisha, right?" someone else said. This man had thick black
hair slicked straight back and a flushed face. He was wearing a ripped
brown sweater and dirty jeans.

"And you're twelve—am I right?"

I didn't say anything.

"I know all about you girls." Smiling, the man rocked forward
on his toes, then back on his heels.

"Are you an antique dealer?"

The man snickered and looked at the other men in the group.
Some of them laughed.

"Hardly. I'm a food broker. Jack Masterson." He put his hand
out to me and I shook it. The only other time I could remember
shaking hands was with Reverend Pinkham at Gramma Hattie's funeral. I didn't know what a food broker was and I wasn't going to ask
but Mr. Masterson said, "I call myself a *food broker,* Trisha, but really,
I deal in damaged and surplus food products: dented canned goods,
fatty meats, irregular bottled liquids, overstock. I deal out of my
truck, sell to the public at a discount. That's how I know your mom."

"Does anyone want anything?" I said, offering the tray of little hot dogs, and Mr. Masterson patted his belly and said something
about a diet but took one anyway, slid it lengthwise into his mouth.
I looked down at the tray at all the little hot dogs and suddenly I
thought of Mr. Nealy, Burying Point, the red-faced man, and I
thought, *All the men here have penises,* and my knees felt soft and rubbery.

"Thank you, sweetie," the bald man said and patted my head.

The sun had set when my father finally got
around to laying the meat on the grill. People cast long shadows as
flood lights illuminated the lawn. My father wore an apron that said

Kiss the Chef, and he kept asking me to go get things: a spatula, an extra plate, the salt and pepper. From just outside the kitchen door, I heard my mother talking.

"No, she's not pretty, but Trisha's very cheerful," she said, and something inside me collapsed and I felt I'd been punched in the stomach and I thought I would throw up. I ran to the side of the house, into the shadows, and though my head was filled with breathing, I kept hearing her. *No, she's not pretty* . . . I fell against the side of the house. It was true, of course, I wasn't pretty, and I knew it, I'd always known it—any ugly girl, especially one with a pretty sister, knows she's ugly—but it made me sick to hear it now especially with the other thing she said: *Trisha's very cheerful.* I felt broken and defective; I felt like a stranger.

After a time, I hardened myself and walked back into the light and into the house.

My mother and the woman in black were taking plastic wrap off bowls, stocking trays with paper napkins and plates, chattering and laughing.

When my mother saw me, she said, "Here," and held out a tall glass filled with ice, clear liquor, and a wedge of lime. "Take this to your father." As I reached for the glass, I watched it drop from her hand and shatter on the linoleum.

The woman in black said, "Jesus Christ."

When I stopped to pick up pieces of the glass, my mother quickly drew in a breath. "Just get out."

My throat felt thick as I ran from the room, ran outside to look for Cat. Somehow, she'd wound up standing with Manny Thompkins again. Behind them, my father was flipping hamburgers at the grill and while four or five people looked on, a man in a bright yellow sweater flounced over and kissed my father and everyone laughed. The bald man in lime green pants grabbed a bottle of brown liquor from a tray and emptied it into his mouth; a tall blonde lady slapped him on the bottom and they cracked up. Three women stood close together, talking seriously in busy concerned voices. Mr. Masterson, the used-grocery man, jumped up on a woman's back and they shrieked as the woman staggered around the lawn. I watched a man turn his head and spit into my mother's flower bed beneath the picture window. I watched a woman grind a cigarette into our lawn with the toe of her shoe. I sat down on the grass and pulled my knees to my chest. I could smell the dirt.

"Burgers!" my father yelled.

Cat rolled her eyes as she walked by me toward the house, Franny in tow.

Franny had her Mookie dog tucked under her arm and she was whining, "But I don't want to go to bed," and Cat was saying, "I know. I know." I watched Manny Thompkins watch my mother walk from the kitchen door over to my father. She was smiling, moving in long strides, her head held high, her hair gleaming in the floodlights from the house.

Manny Thompkins took a few steps toward me and said, "Your mom's a fine woman." We both looked over at her, standing with some men and women near the grill, listening to one of the women. When the woman stopped talking, everyone laughed, my mother laughed, tossing her glossy hair, showing her white, even teeth. Manny Thompkins put his arm around my shoulders and breathed in loudly through the nose. "A truly *fine* woman."

I nodded. "She's very pretty."

Manny Thompkins shook his head and brought his face close to mine. "Your mother's not *pretty.*" His eyes were glassy, his face flushed. "Your mother's not like other women." I could see Manny Thompkins was trembling when he added, in a whisper, "Your mother is *heavenly.*"

Heavenly. My mother, *heavenly!* Suddenly, I saw a gleaming halo and feathery white wings that raised the words up above the liquor mouth from where they'd come and they seemed to float before us, above us, and to be real and solid and therefore true. *My mother was heavenly!* No matter that it was Manny Thompkins who said it; these words elevated me, also, lifted me up, took me in their soft embrace and soothed me.

Just then, Manny Thompkins lurched and staggered forward

with Jack Masterson's slap on his back. Mr. Masterson chuckled as he walked past, calling back to Manny, telling him to wake up.

Manny Thompkins nodded and cleared his throat and then he began walking me toward the grill. "So how d'ya like your burgers, little lady?"

"Rare."

"What? Dontcha like 'em cooked?"

"I like them rare."

"And what d'ya like to have on 'em?"

"I don't like anything on them."

Manny turned to my father. "What? Your girls like raw meat? You teach 'em that?"

My father ignored Manny Thompkins and handed me a paper plate with a hamburger on it.

I returned to my place in the grass and watched my father as he peppered and flipped and served the meat. This didn't feel like our yard, the place where we built snowmen, ran through the sprinkler, played with Maggie. It seemed like a place I knew from books or somewhere I had visited long ago or in a dream. I watched the people on the lawn, all in motion, drinking drinks, shifting their weight, gesturing with their hands, shaking their heads, stamping their feet, getting loud, laughing loudly, talking loudly, almost yelling at each other.

I saw my mother coming out the back door carrying a platter of chicken, the chicken Cat and I had washed and covered with sauce. She set the platter on the card table next to the grill and gave my father a serious look. Rachel Cohen said something to my mother but Mom just glared at Dad. Then I heard her, say, "Damn you," and she turned and walked back toward the house and inside I grew tight.

A bright light flashed and everyone turned to look. Cat was taking a picture of three women, now all smiling for the camera, arms circling one another's shoulders.

"Hold this," Cat said to me, dropping the camera into my lap as she went for the grill.

I finished my hamburger and folded my plate in half, then again.

Cat returned with a hamburger and some cole slaw.

"I wish they'd leave," I said.

"Me, too," Cat said. "Mom and Dad are drunk." Cat took a big bite of her burger.

After a moment, I said, "Are the Cohens Jewish?"

"There aren't any Jews in Salem. I think they're German. Why'd you ask?"

"I thought I heard somebody say it."

Cat bit into her hamburger again, chewed the food to the side of her mouth, and said, "Well, if they are they're going to hell."

"What d'you mean?"

"All the Jews are going to hell."

"Why?"

"Because they killed Jesus, stupid."

"No, they didn't. It was the Romans," I said.

"The *Jews*. Read Matthew and John."

"They're *all* going to hell?"

"Yeah."

"How come they're all going to hell? None of the Jews now were even around then."

"It's a sin they all carry." Cat took a forkful of coleslaw. "They're like a family and the sin gets passed down like a trait. Like curly hair." Cat raised her eyebrows and winked at me. She looked around at the people. "There could be Jews here—who knows?"

Rachel Cohen was still over by the grill with Dad. She didn't look like she could kill anyone; she sure didn't look like someone who would kill Jesus.

While Cat ate the rest of her dinner, we watched Dad, who sat with Rachel Cohen and the woman with orange hair, and Mom, who was hurrying around, offering people drinks and salads. From the darkness, Pip suddenly appeared between my father and the woman with orange hair. The woman grabbed Pip around the mid-

dle and held her out in front of her, saying, "You rotten little thief—
trying to get my dinner, were you?" She must have been squeezing
tightly because Pip began to squirm. As the woman continued her
scolding, Pip reached a paw out and took a swipe at the woman's
face.

"Goddamn it!" the woman screamed and hurled Pip to the
ground in front of her. Rachel gasped and my father dropped his
plate and looked at the woman's face. I ran over.

"That damn cat attacked me," the woman said and raised her
hand to her cheek. "That cat could have blinded me."

"Get her out of here," my father said.

I took Pip in my arms and hurried back to where Cat was still
sitting.

Cat brought the camera to her face. "Say cheese."

Pip leapt from my arms and the flash dazzled my eyes, like
lightning, leaving a bright dot that floated in front of the people eating, drinking, laughing on our lawn. Cat took a picture of some
people gnawing on ribs. She said "Cheese" to my mother and
Manny Thompkins and the woman in black. She said "Smile" to
Mom's friends Rae and Tilly, who were eating from paper plates on
their laps. A couple smooched for her, their faces touching.

"Both look at me," Cat said. "And smile."

The couple obliged and blinked and shook their heads after
the flash went off. Cat asked people to assume strange positions: a
woman stepped on the chest of a man, hands linked above her head
in victory; two women held a man on their shoulders; a blonde
woman, leaning forward, hand on hip, blew a kiss to the camera.
"Do something," Cat said to Jack Masterson, and he swung around
and pulled down his pants. Someone lobbed a roll at his bottom and
Cat turned away.

Mom and Manny Thompkins were both heading toward the
grill for seconds and Cat stopped them and asked them to pose.

"What should we do?" my mother said.

"Whatever you like," Cat said.

Manny Thompkins slipped his arm around my mother's waist and Cat snapped a picture. My mother giggled and put her head on Manny's shoulder.

"Great!" Cat said, and the flash cube sparked and rotated again.

Stepping to one side, Manny Thompkins took my mother in his arms and leaned her way back. My mother was laughing. Cat took another picture. Everybody was watching. Manny Thompkins looked down at my mother suddenly, as if surprised to find her in his arms, looked back at the camera, and then kissed her. Some people started hooting. Someone whistled. People clapped. The flash went off again, then again, and Manny Thompkins was still kissing my mother. My mother began shaking her head and pushing against Manny Thompkins's chest. Nobody did anything. Whistles. Clapping. My mother struggling. Finally, I ran up and started hitting Manny Thompkins on the arm. I hit him with one fist, hit him on his big, thick arm covered with a dark web of hair. I looked at that arm, at the hair, and hit as hard as I could. Manny Thompkins set my mother back on her feet and stared at me, like I had said something, done something, shocking. Then he started laughing. Everyone else started laughing, too.

I ran away, down to the barn, where I found Pip in the hay. I curled myself around her and lay there for a long time, wishing my mother would come to me, listening to the hooting and laughing and chattering up at the house. After a while, it sounded like people were chanting: "Bag of watermelon seeds, bag of watermelon seeds." Slippery, black, shaped like tears.

I was lying now in the very place where John Hathorne had attacked my eight-greats-aunt so many years before and though I'd heard the story from my Gramma Hattie, I couldn't really believe it, that this was the very same place, I mean—at least, I couldn't believe it in the same way that I believed that I was lying here in the hay and that Pip was lying with me. Somehow John Hathorne, Sara Wilde, Samuel Wilde, the witchcraft examinations, the crazy fits of the accusers in the First Church, our church, where the examinations were held, the hangings on Gallows Hill—all of these people and all of these happenings were as real as the sound of Misty shifting her weight in her stall, the smell of chickens and oats and horse and hay, this very barn whose rough walls I could touch, whose heavy door I could bolt. How was I supposed to believe that?

And still my gramma told me this about Sara Wilde and John Hathorne and 1692 as if she had been a witness, as if she had seen it all with her own eyes. She said that after Sara Wilde smacked him with the shovel, John Hathorne said things to his housemaid, Ann Burroughs. He said Sara Wilde was creeping around outside their house at daybreak. John Hathorne told Ann Burroughs that he heard Sara Wilde call her name. And the housemaid began to think Sara Wilde was like the others. Ann Burroughs became convinced that Sara Wilde was appearing in her room late at night in the form of a cat, and she told this to her master, John Hathorne, who had suggested that witches often appear to their victims late at night, in their bedrooms, in the form of a cat. And like seventeen of the other people executed for being witches in the spring and summer and fall of 1692, my eight-greats-aunt was hung on Gallows Hill, the Witches' Hill, not even a mile from her house, from *our* house, from *here,* in Salem Town.

When I opened my eyes, hay scratched my eyeball. There was hay in my mouth. Pip was curled up at my side. It was very quiet. Crickets. The rustling of feathers. The buzz of the night in my ears. The party noises had stopped: no babbling, no clinking of glasses, no shrieking-whooping-hooting sounds, no howls of laughter.

From the well house, I saw my father dragging a trash bag across the lawn, my mother sitting where Rachel Cohen had been by the grill, talking.

As I trudged up the hill, I heard her holler, "—because you can't keep it in your pants!" She paused, then yelled, "And the decision is *not* yours to make."

When my mother noticed me making my way toward the

house, she said, "Or maybe we should ask your children what they think."

My father picked up a napkin from the grass, crumpled it in his fist, and dropped it in the garbage bag.

My mother snorted, stood up, brushed off the back of her pants, and went into the house without saying anything.

"Dad?"

"Shut up."

Cat came out the back door carrying a cocktail. "Here you are, Dad."

My father took the drink from her and polished it off in one gulp. Cat stood looking at him.

"Damn your mother," my father said, just as my mother appeared behind him.

"What's that?" Mom was holding her blue tumbler, tracing circles with it in the air. The ice cubes made a rushing sound against the sides of the tumbler.

"I said *damn you!*" My father hurled his glass toward the back door but it made no sound as it disappeared in Mom's flower bed. Then he stalked off around the side of the house and into the shadows.

My mother started laughing.

"I'm going to bed," I said.

"No," my mother said. "Sit down. You, too, Cat. I think your father is about to perform for us. He's really very talented, your father—bet you didn't know that. Oh, there's lots you don't know about your dad. Let's just see what he's gonna show you now." I didn't know what she was talking about. Maybe this was something that they always did when they fought and we hid.

"But I'm tired," Cat said.

"Sit!" Mom said.

I sat down where I stood and Pip jumped in my lap. Cat squatted down next to me, close, and started to rub Pip's ears.

Then we heard my father moving toward us through the darkness. We heard him because he was groaning and making a loud puffing sound. I could see his shape, black and dense in the darkness, and he was staggering, carrying something, making a snorting noise. Then he grunted and lurched forward into the light. His arms were straight and I could see the muscles straining against his skin, like they might burst out of it, as he moved slowly with the huge rock. It was one of the rocks from the bus stop.

"Oh, big man!" my mother yelled. She set her cup next to her on the ground and bit her pinkies and made a loud, sharp whistle. "What are you going to do, big man?"

My father came at us, at Cat and me. I held my breath and Cat wrapped her arms around me, tightly. Dad kept coming and Mom didn't say anything.

Pip jumped from my arms.

Lifting the rock over his head, snorting and panting, my father went after Pip.

Pip was sitting there in the grass, now, licking a paw.

I could feel my heart wild in my chest but I couldn't move. I couldn't make a sound. I wasn't even there.

"Big, tough man!" my mother yelled. "Is the big mean man gonna squish the little kitty?"

I saw my father bring the rock down onto Pip with both hands. They were still in the light. I could see everything. Blood on the rock, blood on my father.

Cat stood up. She didn't say anything. There was no sound at all.

Dad was motionless. His eyes were wide open and fixed on the barn, or on some point far away. His shoulders were hunched forward, his arms curved at his sides, his feet wide apart and he seemed to be waiting for something, or expecting something, some signal, to direct his actions.

I got up and ran.

I ran past the well house, the barn, past the compost heap, along the fence at the back of the meadow to the woods.

I scrambled up a trail, branches scratching at my face and arms, clawing at my shirt.

Soon, my throat was burning, my heart was in a rage in my head and chest. I kept slipping on the pine needles, but I grabbed a root, a trunk, a limb and pulled myself up and ran until I reached the cool mossy clearing and dropped to my knees.

My ears were ringing and my head was filled with breathing and pounding. I fell onto my side, pulled my knees to my chest, hard.

When I closed my eyes I saw my mother's teeth biting into her pinkies. I saw my father with the rock raised above his head, coming toward Cat and me. My father, wild and fierce, teeth straight and close like a zipper. Then I saw Pip's body, trembling, black and shiny.

I rolled onto my back. I listened for sounds, then opened my eyes. Faint stars rose and fell at the edge of my vision, and then I saw stars everywhere—real stars, bright and clear, tiny, sparkling white.

I would have to be very careful. I would be obedient and polite. I would watch my step.

ChapterEight

Green Pastures

I was hiding at a place tucked back up in our woods that Cat and I called *Green Pastures* where, in a clearing surrounded by trees, moss spread out like a rich green lawn, like a plush new carpet, deliberate, thick and even. No path led to this spot in the woods; to get here, you had to know just where to turn off the regular trail and then you had to be small and not mind being scratched at by the underbrush and pay careful attention to the slope of the land or you would pass right by Green Pastures and head off toward Route 62 or Gallows Hill. Cat and I discovered this place when we were small and we always kept it a secret. Cat named it *Green Pastures* after that place in the Bible where the Lord maketh you to lie down and restoreth your soul, and the name seemed just right: the moss was thick and soft and green with life and the branches on the trees surrounding the place reached up high and protective, keeping you dry when it rained or snowed and cool when the sun beat down in a cloudless summer sky. Though lots of places seemed magical to some degree back then, full of secret histories and hidden purposes, Green Pastures was unique in being completely private and cut off from my parents and other kids and everyone else who wasn't an animal, a ghost, or Cat and me.

More than once I had wondered if this spot was here, if the moss had grown thick and abundant like this, when Sara Wilde was alive and whether she'd ever found it and lingered here in this slow, rich place like Cat and I did. I wondered if, on sultry afternoons, she might wander up here and stretch her bare legs on the cool moss and look up at the treetops and at the bits of blue sky behind them, and wonder about the universe and her place in it. Maybe, like me, Sara Wilde would close her eyes and let her head fill with all the rich, nameless, woody scents and maybe she, too, dreamed of other worlds, places where the sun was always shining and soft breezes always blew, where the parents were calm and happy, and where your inside self could be your outside self because it wouldn't be hard and nasty and vicious—it wouldn't have to be: there would be nothing to make you split in two like that, to make you coil around yourself so you could keep safe.

Now the damp of the moss and the chill of the night made my body shake and my teeth chatter and I could feel my bones. The stars were hidden by clouds. Through the branches of the trees, I could see the moon behind the clouds, glowing, like a luminous pearl behind a sheet of cotton; I could see the lights of the house shining low and dim. Someone was still up. I sat on the moss, aching with the cold, hugging my knees, making myself solid and hard and compact, until I was numb. Anything could be going on up there.

From the far side of the meadow I could see the flood lights casting a freakish glow on the lawn, but no one was around. As I came up the side of the lawn, I saw the garbage bag my father had been dragging behind him lying by the barbeque now, black and lumpy, stuff strewn around it. Chicken bones and blobs of cole slaw and half-eaten hamburger rolls were spilling out of it and everything was covered with ashes and dirt. Greasy napkins and cigarette butts, beer cans and empty pickle jars were scattered here and there, on our lawn.

And a few yards away, just beyond the reach of the shaft slanting down from one of the floodlights was the rock from the bus stop, heavy and solemn, here in the middle of our lawn. It was the rock that had a small impression on its narrower end, where water would collect when it rained. When I was little, Cat would leave things in the hole for me to find—a piece of Bazooka or a ribbon marble, once even a turquoise ring.

I could see dark splashed up from the bottom of the rock and I sank to my knees on the lawn.

"Pip." I said it out loud, and then I called her, as if it were really possible that nothing had happen, as if she really might come running now and make the rest of the night, what I knew and what I had witnessed with my own eyes, false.

Just a short time ago, I had been here in this very place with Pip on my lap. Cat had taken a picture.

I stared at the rock. I imagined that under it was a flattened, broken body and I saw that a line had been crossed.

The back door was open.

I walked in and called, "Hello?" but no one answered. On the floor of the kitchen, my mother's old pine shelf broken, splintered, more broken china, broken things.

From the back hall, I could see my mother on the floor of the living room, sitting cross-legged, slouched over. She was clutching her blue cup. A cigarette was burning in an ashtray by her knee and she was facing the spot where the Christmas tree went each year.

Last Christmas eve, I came downstairs and found her in just this place, alone in this room that was dark as coal except for the colored lights of the tree and the red glow on the tip of her cigarette. Her smoke swirled up toward the angel at the top, then disappeared. She was just sitting there on the floor, all by herself, weeping softly, rocking back and forth, at the foot of Samuel Wilde's chair. And it was as if she wanted to be alone since she yelled, "Out!" when I said, "Can I come in?" But it was also as if she wanted us to know she was so sad and so alone because she left the doors to the living room wide open, and she didn't come up and kiss us good night.

There was no Christmas tree now and with only the thin light from the lamp behind her, I couldn't make out whether she was crying and I said it again, "Can I come in?"

Mom took a sip from her cup. She held something in her left hand.

I waited until I heard her swallow before I said, "Mom?"

"No," she said, not turning her head, not looking at me. She set her cup on the floor, then took the object into her right hand. I could see it was the pair of iron scissors from the wall but she wasn't admiring its homeliness now; she held it with the blades closed across her palm; she held it like a dagger.

I couldn't move.

"Out!" she yelled.

I watched her raise her hand to her face. I heard her sob. I wanted to hold her and stroke her hair and tell her everything was okay but I would never have enough power to comfort my mother.

I took off up the back stairs.

The door to my parents' room was opened and the lights were on but no one was around.

I found Cat in the family room, sitting in the dark, holding her knees to her chest, small at one edge of the couch.

"Trisha," she said.

We held each other and I kept saying, "It's okay. It's okay," and I tried to think *Nothing happened* because somehow that was how we would act tomorrow, like nothing had really happened.

Cat didn't say anything.

"Where's Dad?" I said.

"He took off." Cat squeezed my hand. "I'm really sorry about Pip. Really, I'm so sorry." She said this softly, and she looked sorry, too—her eyebrows were raised and her forehead was wrinkled and I thought she might cry.

There was no noise in the house.

No noise at all.

I got up and turned on the TV. We heard a zapping sound, then a woman's head wrapped in bandages, hooked up to a machine, slowly resolved itself on the screen. Organ music was rising in the background and sparks were flying all over the place. Cat and I sat close and held hands.

"Where'd you go?" Cat said.

"The woods. Green Pastures."

"I looked for you in the barn." The room was filled with a silver light.

"Cat?" I said, but when she said, "Yeah?" I didn't know what else to say.

She leaned over and hugged me.

Zapping sounds filled the room.

We both jumped when we heard the front door slam. We hurried to the window and watched Mom back out of the driveway in the station wagon.

I looked at Cat. She looked so young and pale.

Someone was screaming on TV.

Cat pushed the ON/OFF button and walked me to her room. She cleared some space from her bed and pulled back the covers. We got in, but it was as if we were not alone, as if something else were there with us, breathing up most of the air, making her room seem full, almost too full for the two of us to sit there like that, on her bed, waiting—for what, I didn't know.

Deep in the night, I woke to a peculiar smell, like what smolders beyond the chemicals and perfumes at the beauty parlor, and a strange sound, a voice I didn't know, and then I realized I was in the air, I was being carried, but I was so full of sleep my eyes wouldn't open until I was surrounded by cold and the sound of someone crying. It was dark and I was out in front of our house, being carried across the front lawn toward Franny, who was sitting near the bus stop with Cat. Franny was crying and Cat was holding her on her lap, rocking her, stroking her hair, saying, *"Shshsh, shshsh."* Maggie lay on the ground beside them, not moving, as if she'd been sleeping there for a long time, or as if she were dead. It was nighttime and Cat and Franny were in their nighties and so was I and I almost called out to them until I realized it was Mr. Nealy who was carrying me and my throat closed. I couldn't answer him when he set me on the ground beside my sisters and asked, "You okay?"

He said something to Cat, then hustled back to the house. I watched Cat as she rocked Franny who had stopped crying and was sucking her thumb now, rubbing the head of her stuffed dog Mookie against the side of her face. While Cat rocked slowly, whispering, *"Shshsh, shshsh,"* I thought how much she looked like Mom with her long pale hair and her bow lips and I moved closer to her so I could feel the rhythm of her rocking.

"Trisha, there's a fire," Cat said, calmly, as if she'd said something else, something ordinary and expected.

I was cold and leaning into Cat, feeling soothed by her warmth, by her rocking.

I remembered my mother's saying if anyone dropped a match in the house, it would go up like a haystack and suddenly I imagined the whole house ablaze, burning down to the frame, then collapsing in on itself in flames, like in that scene of Atlanta burning in the movie of *Gone with the Wind*.

Soon, three fire trucks would arrive at our house and we

would remain here on our lawn, three little ghosts, invisible and without a claim to the house or the barn or the land or anything else. Two of the fire trucks would park behind us on the road; one would pull down into the driveway. Men in black rubber clothes with hard black hats would rush by us and into our house carrying long-handled axes—I imagined them chopping up all our things— but the fire would already be out. Mr. Nealy would have put the fire out himself before they showed up. The men would all stand together for a time. Mr. Nealy would lean into the door frame, both feet inside our house, in the front hall, as if this were his place, and the firemen would shuffle their feet and fuss with their hats and shift their weight on the breezeway. They would all talk together on the breezeway and we would listen. *Where are the parents,* they'd want to know, and *How old's the oldest.*

Cat would lie and say she was sixteen when Mr. Nealy asked because she knew that was the age they'd need her to be in order for them to leave and leave us alone. When Mr. Nealy asked for the third time where our parents were, Cat would say, again, that she didn't know and I wouldn't say anything at all.

But Dad would return home before Mr. Nealy and the firemen had left. He'd pull over at the bus stop, nose to nose with the first fire truck, and he'd hop out of the Impala and hurry over and ask Mr. Nealy and the firemen what had happened. One of the men would tell him that there'd been a small fire in the living room, probably started by cigarette ashes dropped in a wooden wastebasket. The basket burned and ignited the fringe on the Oriental rug but, aside from some charring of the floorboards, nothing else was harmed. We would be very lucky Mr. Nealy happened to be cruising by just then, the man would say. We would be very lucky he had such a keen eye and happened to notice the glow in the window downstairs. My father would nod and smile at Mr. Nealy who would nod along with him, though Mr. Nealy would be lying now: he had already told Cat and me that it was the front door standing wide open that caught his eye; he didn't even notice the flames until he leaned into the front hall to pull the door shut. Then suddenly, Dad would turn to us, a loving father now, his eyebrows raised, his mouth opened, all concerned. He would squat down and put his arms around the three of us.

"Aw, Booboos!" he would say, as if he really meant it.

Then he would lie to Mr. Nealy and the firemen. He would say that he'd woken and found he was out of cigarettes so he'd gone to the Esso station to buy a package from the machine. My father didn't smoke. Then he'd add that my mother must have woken after him and done the same; he'd say she must be on her way home right now; he'd say she'd certainly be here any minute. He'd thank the firemen and shake Mr. Nealy's hand. Then my father would take Franny in his arms and say, "Come on, Booboos," and we'd all walk back to the house. On the breezeway, he'd pause and turn and wave and tell us to wave, too, and I'd imagine what the men saw when they looked down here at us—a loving dad, happy, safe kids—and I'd hate it, I'd hate him, inside and out.

When I woke Saturday morning, my room was filled with a cold gray light and I was alone in my bed with Cat. Normally, Pip would be tucked under my arm, pulled close to my side. Normally, she would wake when I woke. She would purr and rub her face into mine and knead the blanket till we got out of bed. As we rushed down the stairs, I would step carefully, in case Pip should be under one of my feet as she wove her way between them, but she never was; we never got in each other's way at all.

Last night, after putting Franny to bed, Dad asked Cat and me if we knew how the fire started.

"You girls weren't smoking cigarettes, were you?" he said, earnestly, and he had a stern look on his face, as if either of us smoking cigarettes would be something that *mattered,* and it made me want to laugh. It made me want to hurt my father. That thing inside me wanted him dead and sorry and in pain.

Cat said no; she said we had no idea how the fire started. I didn't say anything. Dad let it go, said good night, and headed into the kitchen. We went upstairs to Cat's room and climbed into her bed. Cat left her door open and we watched Dad as he hurried down the hall toward the family room with a bottle and a glass full of ice. We heard him turn on the TV. We heard him flip the channels until he found a station that was broadcasting. It was some kind of church service but he kept it on anyway.

"Let's sleep in your room," Cat said.

My mother had not returned last night and all was quiet now. Daylight seemed to dispel the chaos, leaving a kind of calm in its place, but a temporary calm, like what's found in the eye of a storm, thin and unpromising like this morning light, nothing to make my inside self relax and uncoil and be easy in any way. My father only slept a short while; I'd heard him rise at five o'clock. I had heard him trudge down the stairs. I had heard him in the backyard, grunting softly as he lifted and carried heavy things.

I sat up now and looked out my window and saw the clouds were moving on and it was becoming a clear, sunny morning. The lawn was the same old lawn. The barbeque and the card table were gone. No garbage. No rock. Just a dark stain like a mud puddle in the grass.

But nothing was the same. A line had been crossed and now time wasn't real time anymore. What happened now had no relation to what happened earlier. Suki and Billy Halliday, riding bikes and finding a safe—these things happened to another girl at another time. Anything could happen now.

And now, as I lay in bed, listening to my father and Franny making their way down the back stairs, Franny's footfalls small and abrupt, Dad's heavy and hard, I heard the train whistle sound, long and low and so close, and I imagined myself running to catch that train and hopping on and riding it far away, deep into the country, late into the day, deep into the night. And then I saw images of the night before, disjointed and vague like memories of a dream: leaning way back, a man drinks from a bottle while people count out loud and someone claps; there is a piercing screech like a crow but it's a woman bent over at the middle, laughing, her mouth so huge you can see the metal in her teeth; a roll bounces off Jack Masterson's bare bottom. Manny Thompkins; my mother; my father. The rock from the bus stop.

And now Pip was dead. My father brought the rock down onto her. My father murdered her. It couldn't be true, but knowing it made me crazy in my mind.

Now I heard Cat sigh a waking sigh and I opened my eyes again and looked over at her.

"You okay?" she said.

I nodded.

She squeezed my arm. "You sure?"

"Yeah."

We slipped on our robes and went downstairs together.

Franny was sitting at the kitchen table with a glass of milk, eating crisped rice from the box, looking at the funnies when we walked in.

Inside the fridge, there was no orange juice. No doughnuts or sugar cereals or fruit cocktail in the cabinets.

Dad was sitting on the step stool reading the newspaper, sipping from his coffee cup, tapping his foot, as if he were a normal, innocent father on a regular Sunday morning.

"Dad, we don't have any food," Cat said.

"We don't?"

Cat began shifting things around in the freezer, crinkling plastic. "Mom hasn't bought anything for *days*," she said.

"Well, we'll have to do something about that, won't we?" Dad said and he smiled at her and sipped from his coffee cup as if he weren't a murderer at all.

"Where's Mommy?" Franny asked.

Cat and I pretended she hadn't said anything, but when she continued whining, Dad said, "She'll be back soon," and I wondered if he believed it.

Dad folded his paper, then folded it again and slapped it on his thigh. "Cat, Trisha, come over here."

We moved toward Dad who remained seated.

"I'm not gonna bite," he said, but neither of us moved closer.

"Okay, look—I just want to say I'm sorry about last night. I really am. Things got out of control. Things got way out of hand. I'm sorry."

Neither of us said anything.

"Trisha." Dad reached toward me and I stepped back. "Look, I just wanted to say I'm sorry about what happened to your cat." He sounded almost angry now. "I really am."

I didn't say anything.

"Hey, if it would make you feel better, why don't you go ahead and hit me?" My father extended his arm out toward me. "Go ahead, hit me."

"She doesn't want to hit you, Dad," Cat said, but Cat was wrong. I did want to hit him; I wanted to hit him with that rock.

My father folded his arms across his chest. "Well, we have to let it go now. What's done is done. It's really unfortunate but it'll never happen again."

The way my father spoke, you'd have thought he was talking about damage caused by a hurricane or a tornado or some other natural disaster.

Suddenly, my father stood and clapped his hands. "So, what does everybody think about getting groceries now and going out for pizza tonight?"

Franny bounced in her chair and began clapping her hands. "Yay, pizza!"

At Buster's Market, Cat and I got stuff from the shelves while Franny rode in the cart, kicking her feet against the side and making an awful racket till Dad promised her a candy bar if she stopped. Franny was really too big to ride in the cart like that, but when Dad said something about it, she told him, "Mommy always lets me," and he let it go. I kept a distance from Dad—I had all day; I felt as if I might hurt him somehow if he got too close. But I watched him, especially with his being so near to Franny.

We got Twinkies and colorful cereals with marshmallows, caramel popcorn, cheese popcorn, barbequed potato chips, peanut butter and marshmallow fluff, tonic and boxes of ice cream on sticks and TV dinners with a toy surprise in each package and Dad kept lowering his eyebrows and half smiling, saying, "Are you sure your mother lets you have these?" and Cat kept saying, "All the time."

That afternoon, Dad was busy upstairs—he was always working on projects around the house but usually they involved hammering or sawing or staining or sanding and usually he did most of the work in the garage or the basement. Today, Dad was moving things around in his and Mom's bedroom, opening drawers and closets, carrying things downstairs and out the front door. At first, Cat asked him questions—What was he doing? Did he want a beer?—but he answered gruffly, not looking at her, so Cat decided we should all stay in the kitchen and out of his way. When we had to go upstairs for something—to get a book or a sweater—we moved quietly and we were careful not to let him see us. We put things back when we used them; we cleaned up after ourselves. It was like we weren't even there. Even Franny was careful and contained that afternoon: she spoke quietly, ordered her toys on the floor by the easy chair when she was done with them, cleared her own snack dishes from the table, set her shoes side by side when she took them off.

While Cat and I baked oatmeal cookies, Franny sat on the easy chair flipping through *Are You My Mother?* for the thousandth time, watching reruns of *Route 66* and *The Rifleman* and part of a movie called *City Beneath the Sea.* And all the while, she sucked her thumb, rocked back and forth, and hugged her stuffed dog Mookie. Grey fluff from the chair was sticking out of her nose.

"Where is my mother?" Franny said, not looking up from her book.

"Are you reading or are you asking?" Cat said.

Franny thought about it. "Both," she said.

"She'll be back," Cat said.

"Why did she leave?"

"Just read your book," Cat said.

After we had pulled the last batch of cookies from the oven and set them on the rack to cool, Cat leaned across the kitchen counter and looked out the window facing the front yard. "Jesus God!"

"What."

Cat nodded toward the window and whispered, *"Look,"* and I got on my tiptoes and looked out the window and there, at the bus stop, by the road, was an enormous pile of stuff, things, personal things, like what you saw in front of people's houses when the Salvation Army was making a pickup: cardboard boxes with clothes and shoes falling out of them, lamps and stacks of books, armfuls of dresses and blouses still on hangers, a row of suitcases, hat boxes, an old sea trunk, a pair of figure skates, a tennis racket, a green velvet pillow with *Mary Elizabeth* embroidered on it.

"That's Mom's pillow," I said. Gramma Hattie had made it for her when she was sixteen and Mom had always taken special care of it.

"It's Mom's *stuff*," Cat whispered.

Neither of us moved for a moment, we just kept staring at our mother's belongings, heaped up out there like that, all exposed, for anyone to see or take or harm. We kept looking at the pile, as if we might see something about it that explained it, that made sense of its being there. The pile covered the entire area where we would wait for the bus, from the edge of the road all the way to the rocks at the edge of the front lawn. Then I noticed the rock from the night before, returned to its usual spot looking as it always did, as clean or dirty as it always was, as if it had been there all along.

Suddenly, Dad was behind us. "Catherine, Patricia," he said. His voice was flat and measured. "I'm only going to say this once. That garbage out there is off limits. Do you understand?"

"What's Mom's stuff doing out there?" Cat asked, as if she hadn't heard him.

"Off limits."

"Dad, it's all Mom's stuff." It was as if Cat couldn't hear him. "Her things, her pillow, her—"

Dad spoke with his lips tight across his teeth. "This is not open for discussion." With the light behind him from the picture window, Dad looked dark and enormous. He turned to the wet bar, exhaled loudly, squatted down, and began rooting in the cabinet.

The phone rang and Dad answered it.

"Rachel," Dad said, as if she were an old friend he hadn't spoken with in a long time. He turned his back to us and talked softly into the phone while he poured himself a drink.

Cat and I sat at the kitchen table with Franny. She was glancing from her book to the TV.

Franny began to read out loud: " 'The egg jumped. It jumped, and jumped, and jumped! Out came the baby bird! "Where is my mother?" he said. He looked for her.' "

Cat said, "I bet she'll never even say she's sorry."

"Who?" I said.

"*Mom.* Who else?"

"Sorry for what?"

"Listen, sisters!" Franny said. " 'He looked up. He did not see her. He looked down. He did not see her.' "

"*For what?* Are you mental? For leaving us."

"Be quiet!" Franny hollered.

"It's starting," Cat said, and *The Munsters* came on the TV.

After a few minutes, we heard Dad say, "Half hour. Okay. Good. Bye now." Then he hung up the phone and sat down with us.

An advertisement for *What's My Line?* came on the TV screen.

"What's a line?" Franny said.

" 'I love you with all my heart,' " Cat said. " 'I will never let you go.' Stuff like that."

"No, it's not," I said. "It's what you *do.*"

"What's *my* line?" Franny said.

"Pest," Cat said.

"Daddy, does the Easter bunny come tomorrow?" Franny said. She'd been asking about it for days.

When Cat said, "Nope," Franny wriggled in her seat and said, "Yes, sir! I know he does! Mommy said he comes on Sunday!"

"He comes *tonight*," Cat said, and smiled.

"That's what I meant," Franny said. "Or tomorrow early *early.*" Franny stuck her finger in her nose. "Why did Mommy leave? Doesn't she like us?"

"Stop it, Franny," Cat said. "That's disgusting."

"You're not my mother," Franny said.

"Stop it, Franny," Dad said absently, and finished off his drink. "So, who wants pizza?"

"*Pizza!* Yeah!" Franny hollered.

"I invited the Cohens to come with us," Dad said.

"Can't we do anything just us?" Cat said.

Dad ignored her. "The kids can't come but we're getting Rachel in fifteen minutes so we'd better get moving."

When Dad backed the Impala out of the driveway, Franny leaned her face close to the window and said, "Hey! What's all that junk?"

"Junk is exactly what it is," Dad said into the rearview mirror. "Junk. Garbage." He stopped the car and turned around and looked at Franny in the backseat. "And you're not to touch it, do you hear me? You leave that garbage alone or I'll blister your bottom, I swear."

Franny looked wounded and when Cat said, *"Dad!"* she began to cry and Dad softened a little. "Just leave it alone, okay?"

The Riverview was a pizza place in Ipswich, the only one around. Half of it was dark with dim colored lights, illuminated beer signs, and a tall bar with high stools—not the metal kind bolted to the floor like in Reynold's but wooden stools with backs and arms. Near one of the walls was a pool table but Dad said we were too young to play. The other part of the Riverview had booths with red vinyl upholstery and a dance floor and a bowling machine.

Dad and Rachel Cohen slid in on one side of a booth and Franny, Cat, and I got in on the other.

The Riverview had a good jukebox and Dad gave Cat and me change to put in. You could get three songs for a quarter. Cat put on "Satisfaction" by the Rolling Stones and I danced to it. The waitress taking our order nodded her head toward me and said to Dad, "That's nothing. I do that in bed with my husband every night," and Rachel Cohen laughed. I sat down feeling miserable, embarrassed, and dirty. Dad ordered a large cheese pizza, two vodka martinis, and three Shirley Temples. When Cat said she wanted a 7UP, I said I did, too, and so then, of course, did Franny.

Franny skipped over to the bowling machine and picked up the canister of powdered wax. She sprinkled some wax on the floor and came running back to the booth with the canister. "It's cheese!" she said, putting the canister on the table.

"No, stupid—it's wax," Cat said, and Franny frowned.

When the waitress brought our 7UPs and Dad's and Rachel's cocktails, she said, "Anything else I can get you folks?" and Dad raised his hand and put up one finger and said, "Don't go any-where." Then he polished off his drink and handed the empty glass back to the waitress. "Another one of these," he said.

The waitress smiled and winked at Dad. "Now you're my kind of man," she said, and Rachel Cohen slipped an arm through my father's and said, "Mine, too."

Franny asked the waitress, "Are you my mother?" and giggled.

"No, honey," the lady said. Then she nodded at Rachel Cohen. "That's your mother," she said, and bustled off with my father's empty glass.

Franny scowled and hollered after the woman, "No, it's not!" and Rachel Cohen cleared her throat.

And then I thought about my mother, about her things out by

the side of the road, just all heaped up out there for anyone to take or mangle or destroy, and I wondered where my mother could be. Maybe she was home right now putting her things away, but I couldn't imagine that. I couldn't imagine her doing anything other than thinking about us. And drinking.

A teenage boy walked by our table and Franny reached out from the booth and swatted his arm.

"Are you my mother?" she said, and cracked up.

"Cut it out, Franny," Cat said.

"No," Franny said. "You're not the boss."

"Franny, settle down," Dad said.

When our pizza arrived, Dad served the pieces to us and started talking about what we were going to do the next day.

"As you all know," Dad said, "tomorrow is Easter."

"Will Mommy be home?" Franny said.

Rachel Cohen cleared her throat again, looked at Dad, then excused herself for the Ladies'.

Dad shook his head. "I thought we could do something together for Easter—just the four of us."

"But didn't Mom invite people over for Easter dinner?" Cat said, speaking with her mouth full. "I'm pretty sure she did. I'm pretty sure she invited the Cutlers and some other people." A thread of cheese was stuck to Cat's chin and it waggled as she spoke. I smiled, but I didn't say anything.

"*What,*" Cat said, looking at me.

"There's a booger on your chin," Franny said, and laughed.

Cat wiped her chin and looked at her napkin. "It's *cheese.*" She rolled her eyes. "Anyway, people will be expecting to have dinner with us."

"Well, it looks like that's out now," Dad said. He took a sip of his drink. "So I was thinking maybe we could get away somewhere, do something a little different."

I groaned and Cat said, "Why don't we go to Animal World?"

"I was thinking we'd go to Castle Bay," Dad said.

"Where's Mommy?" Franny said.

"Why not Animal World?" Cat said.

Animal World was a kind of park in New Jersey. Mom and Dad had taken Cat and I there years ago, when we were little. You got to drive around on dirt roads that circled through fields and woods, but you had to go slowly so you wouldn't hit any of the animals. I remember some lions sleeping at the edge of a meadow and a buffalo behind a wire fence, but that was about it. Now it was April and Animal World was opening for the season.

"We haven't been to Castle Bay for such a long time," Dad said. "I thought it might be fun."

"When's Mommy coming back?"

"Hush," Dad said, leaning across the table, patting Franny's arm.

"Not Castle Bay," Cat said. "I hate Castle Bay."

I liked Castle Bay but I didn't want to go there, either. It felt wrong. Easter we should be hunting eggs in the churchyard then having a nice dinner. Easter we should be with Mom. I wanted to say these things but my voice wouldn't come.

"Can't we go to Animal World, Dad?" Cat said. "They have a wildebeest this year and they have a new petting zoo."

"I've already made the reservations for Castle Bay."

Cat clicked her tongue and looked down at the table.

"Hey, we'll have fun," Dad said. "We'll have a suite and a color TV and you can order room service."

"Is Mrs. Cohen coming?" Cat said, snidely, glancing toward the Ladies' room.

"Nope, it'll just be the four of us."

When Dad pulled up to the Cohens' house, Rachel said, "Night, girls," all cheery and sweet, and Dad told us to sit tight, he'd be right back. Then he walked Rachel Cohen to her door. Franny was asleep with her head in Cat's lap. Cat and I watched Dad and Rachel Cohen talking under the dim yellow bulb at the top of her steps. Then Dad opened the screen door and Rachel went inside the house.

When Dad stepped in after her, Cat said, "Christ."

The door closed behind them.

"And she's Mom's best friend," Cat said.

I didn't say anything.

About twenty minutes later, the door opened again and Dad hustled out, calling, "Good night!" and waving behind him.

As we cruised down the hill at the end of Wilde Road, I could see Mom's stuff still piled up at the bus stop, a dark vague mountain of personal things, things that mattered to her. Things she had cherished and saved specially. Things she would be sad to lose. Franny was awake now and she began to whimper but before any of us could even say anything, Dad said, hey! we could watch *Voyage to the Bottom of the Sea* on TV but he called it *Voyage to the Bottom of the Bathtub* and Franny cracked up. Cat said it wasn't on and stomped into the kitchen.

We sat around the kitchen table watching *Pat Boone in Hollywood,* and Franny kept asking who all the stars were. We drank orange soda, ate our new snacks, read the bags and boxes they came in. Franny was munching on frosted cereal with marshmallows, something Mom would never let us get, straight out of the box, something Mom would never let us do.

During a commercial, Cat said, "Daddy, can't we please, please, go to Animal World?"

Without looking at her, with both hands on his drink, Dad made his mouth tight and said, "Drop it, Kitty."

That night, I slept in Cat's room. I didn't ask and she didn't say anything about it when I crawled in, as if she'd been expecting me.

I thought of my mother's things piled up by the road at the bus stop like that. It felt like it was keeping us in, and Mom out. All Mom's things were so exposed there—her scrapbooks and her clothes and her velvet *Mary Elizabeth* pillow—and it felt like she was in danger, too.

"Are you okay?" Cat whispered it though Dad was in his room with the door closed on the other side of the house.

"I'm scared." I whispered, too. "What's going to happen?"

"I don't know. 'The secret things belong unto the Lord.' "

"Do you believe that?"

"Kind of. I believe in God. I believe God will help us."

"You do?"

"Of course. Remember that psalm: 'God is our refuge and our strength, a timely help in trouble'?"

"Yeah. Will you say the rest of it?"

" 'God is our refuge and our strength, a timely help in trouble; so we are not afraid though the earth shakes and the mountains move in the depths of the sea.' Then there's a little more about water and mountains and then, 'There is a river whose streams bring joy to the city of God, the holy dwelling of the Most High; God is in her midst; and she will not be overthrown, and at the break of day He will help her.' "

I said, " 'At the break of day, He will help her.' "

"Yeah."

"That's all?"

"That's all."

After a moment, I whispered, "Will you say it again?" And Cat would repeat the psalm as best she could and I would try to remember it, to repeat it to myself as I waited for sleep, but part of a different psalm would come into my head and fill it: *Oh, that I had the wings of a dove to fly away and find rest!*

ChapterNine

Easter Morning

Easter morning, Franny was the first to get up. It was still dark out. Clutching the hem of her nightie in one hand, her stuffed dog Mookie in the other, she tiptoed down the back stairs through the dining room and into the kitchen. The refrigerator door made a little suck-pop sound when Franny opened it to get the chocolate pudding. Dad had made the pudding the night before, as a bribe, Cat said, so we wouldn't argue about going to Castle Bay.

Franny ate the remaining chocolate pudding, which was

enough for two, followed by three slices of American cheese. Then she went into the dining room and checked out the Easter baskets at our places on the table. Cat's was pink, mine was blue, and Franny's was yellow. Somehow Dad had remembered this. Each basket contained a sugar egg decorated with ribbons of hard white frosting and a little bunny scene inside. We each had two solid chocolate rabbits, a white chocolate caramel pop, six hot-pink marshmallow chickies and handfuls of bright jelly beans tangled in the shiny green tinsel in the bottom of the basket. Franny spent a while in the dining room, comparing the baskets, making sure she wasn't shortchanged, making sure Dad didn't play favorites—or that if he did, that that favorite was she.

I woke with a start that morning—*something's missing*—and then I remembered Pip. I lay awake in Cat's bed for a long time, listening, waiting, thinking of my father, thinking of Pip. When I heard Franny's small steps on the back stairs, I got up and tiptoed down the front stairs and began spying on her, but Franny was a little girl, only five, and I knew she wanted to wake us up, so I went to my room, got into my bed, and pretended to be asleep when Franny threw the door open and said, "Trisha! Wake up! It's Easter!"

I made her coax me out of bed, then I followed her into Cat's room. Franny pulled on Cat's arm until Cat was half on the floor. Cat smiled and let the rest of her body slip off the bed but she was still faking being asleep. Franny began tickling her, then leaned her face into Cat's until they were nose to nose and hollered, "Wake up!" Cat laughed and began poking at Franny's sides and Franny giggled and screamed, "Stop! Stop!" as she fell onto the floor with Cat. Cat kissed Franny's head and gave her a noogie, then stood and picked her up and carried her down to the dining room.

Cat took her place and sat with her hands folded in front of her, in front of her basket, on the table.

"Sit down," Cat said solemnly. "Today is the day of the resurrection of our Lord Jesus Christ and we should pray."

Franny and I took our places and folded our hands.

"Let us bow our heads," Cat said.

Franny and I lowered our heads and closed our eyes.

Cat said, "Dear Lord," and cleared her throat. Then she blurted, "It's really dandy You gave us this candy! Yay, God!" and Franny and I laughed. Cat was always coming up with cool stuff like that.

"Come on," Cat said, grabbing her basket and heading for the front stairs. We followed her up to our bathroom, where we found her sitting in the tub. Franny and I got in with her. We sat in a line, eating candy from our baskets. We sat in silence, my legs circling Franny, Cat's circling me, sucking at the bunnies, counting jelly beans, licking the sugar eggs.

After a while, the door opened and the light turned on. It was Dad.

"Booboos!" he said, and rushed off. He came back in a few minutes with the camera. "Smile," he said and the flash bulb went off, leaving a hot bright dot in its place. "Let's make breakfast," he said. "We've got a trip to take today!" We all climbed out of the tub and scrambled downstairs with our baskets.

Dad had put bacon on the griddle and now while he sifted flour into a bowl, he was singing a song about fried ham: "And after the macaroni, we'll have popcorn, peanuts, and pretzels . . ." He seemed so happy and so light, like someone who didn't have anything weighing him down.

When he said, "Salt, Trisha," I reached across the counter for the shaker on the windowsill and I saw the heap of my mother's things still out front. Though the wind seemed to have tipped some boxes, blown over a lamp, and scattered some papers, a hat, and a basket along the road, it didn't look like anything had been touched. Still, the pile sat there, frightening, exposed, spreading as if it were bleeding, as if it were an open wound.

"Three eggs," he said to Cat, who was leaning against the fridge. "And the butter," he said.

Dad scooped batter on a greasy skillet and made toast while Cat and Franny and I set the table.

"Man your stations, ladies," Dad said.

Franny ran back to her place, climbed up on the chair and kneeled in it. Dad handed a platter of bacon to Cat, who handed it to me, and I put it on the table. Franny grabbed a strip and started chewing on it, holding it with both hands. A plate with four slices of toast passed from the counter, to Cat, to me. Then came the pancakes.

Just as I set the plate of pancakes on the table, the phone rang.

"Hello?" Dad said in a cheery voice. And then he stopped smiling and suddenly his voice and mouth were flat. "Hello, Molly."

"It's *Mom!*" Franny said, clapping her hands and wiggling on her chair. Cat told her to hush up.

Dad pulled the phone away from his face and said, "Go ahead, girls. Don't wait for me." Then he sat on the stool near the stove and talked softly. His forehead wrinkled and his mouth grew tight. Then he lowered his head, pinched his nose between the eyes and rocked back and forth. He mumbled something but I only heard the word *house.*

"These are terrible!" Franny spit the food back onto her plate.

"Quiet," Cat said, turning her head sharply toward Dad.

"But they're all runny in the middle," Franny said, and she was right. I looked at the one I had just cut, deeply tanned on the outside, but oozing batter onto my plate into the syrup.

"Give me your plates," Cat said softly. Franny and I passed Cat our plates and she scraped them onto hers and handed them back to us. Dad's head was still lowered, as if he were looking at the kitchen floor, when Cat sneaked off to the bathroom carrying her plate.

Suddenly, Dad said, "Jesus Christ! You'll *get* it back." He paused and said something about her stuff.

Cat returned to the table and buttered some toast. She looked at Franny. "Don't say anything."

Franny shrugged her shoulders as Dad said, again, "You'll *get* it back," then hung up the phone. Dad just stood there for a minute with a clenched jaw, breathing deeply. Then he looked up quickly as if he had suddenly remembered something. He smiled at us. "How's breakfast?"

"Fine," Cat said.

Franny made a face but she didn't say anything. Dad poured himself a cup of coffee and sat down at the table. "Something wrong, Franny?"

"I don't feel good. I have a tummy ache."

"Better lie down," Dad said. "We have a little trip to take today and I don't want you feeling bad for it."

"Yeah," Franny said. "We're going to Castle Bay."

"To Castle Bay," Dad said. "We need to make a little money here." He laughed awkwardly. "Actually, I think we'll have a good time."

"I hate Castle Bay," Cat said. "Please let's go to Animal World, Dad."

"We've already talked about this." Dad said it in a low voice and he didn't look at Cat.

"But Franny's never even *been* to Animal World," Cat said, and then Franny started whining about going to Animal World and Dad stood up.

"We'll go another time." Dad refilled his cup with coffee and sat back down.

Cat stared at her plate.

Franny said, "Do they have bears at Animal World?"

"I think they have a cocktail lounge at Animal World now," Cat said, and I knew she didn't believe this.

Dad didn't say anything but he looked at Cat with narrow eyes and he held his jaw tight.

"How come we never get to do what *we* want to do?" Cat said.

"Yeah. Let's go to Animal World," Franny said.

"I said we're going to Castle Bay," Dad said. "I said that's final."

"Is Mommy coming with us to Castle Bay?" Franny asked, and

Cat slapped her. Franny gasped and looked shocked and *I* was shocked and I hollered, *"Cat!"* and Franny began to cry.

"She hit me, Daddy." Franny was wailing.

Dad didn't say anything but slowly he stood. He held the coffee cup in his fist. He was glaring at Cat.

Franny clambered down from her chair. "Daddy, she hit me!" Franny said, sobbing, her face flushed and wet with tears.

My father looked enormous and as he turned away, I imagined him drawing back and hurling his coffee cup at Cat but just then, Franny made a little whimper noise and threw up on the floor.

Dad cleaned up while Cat and I washed Franny and put her to bed. Franny didn't have to go to church, Dad said. He would call up her sitter, Cindy Carter, and see if she could come over for an hour.

While Dad phoned Cindy, Cat and I put on the new Easter clothes Mom had bought us: navy blue dresses with crisp white collars and cap sleeves, shiny patent leathers, white cotton gloves, and navy blue hats circled with white ribbons. When I went downstairs to show Dad my outfit, I heard him on the phone in the kitchen.

As I crossed the threshold, I heard him say, "I *do* love you," and I stopped and stood where I was by the wet bar. A can of tomato juice and a bottle of vodka sat by a glass which I supposed was filled with both.

"Next time I see her," Dad said. "I'll phone you tonight then. B'bye." And then he added, "Rachel?" And then I heard him hang up the phone.

I picked up the glass and raised it to my mouth. It wasn't so bad—just tomato juice with a sting. I swallowed and filled my mouth again.

"How long have you been standing there?" Dad said, replacing the receiver on the base.

I shrugged my shoulders and swallowed.

"Give me that," he said, annoyed, and grabbed the glass from my hand.

I left the room.

Upstairs, I sat on Cat's bed, watching her brush her hair, put on lip gloss, and brush her hair some more.

"You okay?" she said.

I shrugged. "I *do* love you," he had said. "Rachel?" he had said.

"Why don't you go finish getting ready?"

I nodded but I didn't move.

Cindy showed up at around nine-thirty. "Is Goodwill making a pickup?" she said.

"You mean the garbage out front? If you see anything you want, just take it," Dad said. "Help yourself."

Cindy said, *"Thanks!"* and smiled and not even Cat could say anything.

We all kissed Franny and drove off in the Impala.

As usual, Reverend Pinkham was standing inside the doors of the First Church greeting the congregation before the service. When Reverend Pinkham shook my father's hand and looked concerned and asked where Mom was this fine Easter morning, my father lied and said she was sick, which I thought must have been something like lying to God, which I knew had to be some kind of sin even though we were Protestant and, unlike the Catholics, Protestants didn't seem to care much for sin. During the service, Cat and I whispered about Joe and Steve Watson who were sitting with their parents in the pew in front of ours, until Dad said, "Shush!" I kept thinking we weren't in our regular place; everything looked different from where we were now.

And then, not for the first time, I thought about the fact that this was the same place, the same church, where John Hathorne examined my eight-greats-aunt, Sara Wilde, 276 years before. It was a different building then, a fire had destroyed the original structure, but it was the same church, the same space where my aunt was tried and found guilty and sentenced to hang by the neck till dead on Gallows Hill.

I thought about Sara Wilde up at the front of the church

where Reverend Pinkham stood but now, everyone was quiet and respectful, listening, thinking they were hearing the truth, while back then, no one would have believed Sara Wilde, if they'd heard her, and no one could have heard her, if she'd spoken at all. The church was a madhouse then, with those girls, those famous girls, screaming and contorting and carrying on, the congregation jeering and heckling, and John Hathorne hollering, pounding his fist, demanding a confession.

Sitting here now, I wondered how Sara Wilde felt then. She saw what was happening around her but it couldn't have made sense: people were turning on each other, friends against friends, family against family. Dark, violent forces were loose in the world, forces Sara Wilde couldn't see or understand or make herself safe from. Sitting in this church in the middle of that chaos, she must've felt crazy and numb and far away. Maybe she imagined herself up in the rafters of the church looking down on all those insane people—those girls and those spectators and John Hathorne—and I imagined that now, her looking down on them, wanting to drop things onto them, to hurt them back, yes, but mostly just to stop them. I imagined her wanting to hurt John Hathorne and I imagined her wanting to hurt her father, for letting this happen, and her mother, for abandoning her to her father's care. When I closed my eyes to make the picture come clear in my head, I saw this regular congregation here now and it was me I saw up in those rafters. And then I supposed that maybe it was possible that all those years and centuries ago, Sara Wilde had felt just like I felt right now.

A lock of Joe Watson's hair was sticking almost straight up in the back, like Suki's, but Steve Watson's hair was smooth and flat. A shiny round bald spot crowned their dad's head like a little cap and their mom wore a satiny white bow in her dark hair. After church, Mr. Watson might stop at Kirby's for the *Boston Herald*; maybe he would give Joe and Steve a quarter each for candy. Later, Mrs. Watson would make a nice Sunday dinner. She would be happy to have such a family and she would say so in the grace.

For the rest of church, I thought about our trip to Castle Bay.

That afternoon, the four of us would be driving there for some fun, Dad said. We would be guests of some casino. Dad would be given a suite and Cat would turn on the TV and we would watch some old romance or a Western and we would bounce on the bed. Meanwhile, Dad would be at a blackjack table, gambling. Every time we came to Castle Bay, he would bring three white envelopes with him: the first was marked *Okay,* the second had *Careful* written across it, and the third said *Are You Sure?* with the *Sure* underlined twice. I don't know why he bothered writing these things on the envelopes, because from the way he would charge into the room and grab one from its hiding place, ripping it right open, it didn't seem he ever read them. On a good night, Dad would come upstairs to visit with us. He would tell us we could order room service and he would be smiling. On bad nights, he would storm upstairs three times—the first two to get envelopes, the last to go to sleep.

On the drive back from church, Cat asked again if we could go to Animal World and Dad didn't answer her. We drove straight home and I kept thinking it was possible Mom would be there when we pulled in. It was possible that she would be making us a dinner, baking something sweet, and that when we walked into the dining room, we would hear her humming. But when we got home there was no sign of Mom's station wagon and her stuff hadn't moved from the bus stop.

Franny was feeling a little better now. She hadn't thrown up again, Cindy said.

Dad ruffled the hair on the top of Franny's head and asked her if she wanted to go to Castle Bay. "Do you think you feel well enough?" he said.

Franny said, "Yeah! If I can wear my dress, too."

"You bet!" Dad said. He pulled his wallet from the inside of his jacket. "You girls go pack your bags and help Franny get ready."

As we were leaving the room, Cindy said she'd had a chance to look at the stuff out front while Franny was resting and she'd decided to take three of the handbags, the tennis racket, and the hair dryer, if that was all right. That was just how she said it, too—"*the* handbags," "*the* tennis racquet," "*the* hair dryer"—as if they didn't belong to anybody.

Cat cleared her throat loudly and Dad said, "Get a move on, girls." And then he handed Cindy some bills and told her to go right ahead and help herself.

That thing inside me twisted tighter and I felt it could've leapt out of me and wrapped itself around my father's neck and choked the breath out of him right there on the spot but Cat squeezed my arm and said, "Come on," and I followed her upstairs.

While we packed things for ourselves and Franny, Cat had a tight mouth and her movements were abrupt and almost violent and she kept exhaling loudly. When I asked if she was okay, she said, "Am I *okay*? Of course I'm not okay. How could anybody be okay when we haven't seen our mother for two days, our father killed your cat, and now he's getting rid of all her things and we're going to Castle Bay for Easter so he can gamble. Doesn't something seem not okay about that to you?" Cat's face was red and she was shaking. Then she said, "Trisha, if it weren't for you and Franny, I swear I'd run away."

I could hardly speak and when I did my voice was small as if someone were stepping on my neck. "Promise you won't."

Cat looked down at the suitcase and said, "I won't."

Dad made all the last-minute preparations for the house, like feeding the chickens and Maggie and the cats, and giving Misty extra hay and water, and turning on lights in the living room. When we left the house, he took a key from his pocket and locked the door behind us.

I had never seen the front door to our house locked from the outside before. I'd never even known there was a key.

Chapter Ten

Are You <u>Sure</u>?

The drive down the Garden State Parkway took two hours and twenty minutes. Cat got to read the map. To get to Animal World, we would have had to take the turnpike and at around Union, Cat started saying, "It's not too late to get on the turnpike, Dad. It looks like we can get it at Fords."

Dad just said, "Caaat," stretching it out a little and making it sound like a question. Cat didn't mention Animal World again.

Cat and I had packed coloring books and crayons, *Are You My*

Mother?, The Runaway Bunny, and *The Lonely Doll* for Franny but she just lay quietly next to me on the backseat, dozing. Cat and I sang songs, played the alphabet game with license plates, and for long periods just stared out the window in silence. We stopped twice, once for lunch at a pie shop, and then again when Franny had to go to the bathroom.

The pie shop looked like a Howard Johnson's: it had aqua walls and orange booths and colorful place mats with jokes and puzzles. In the front by the cash register, a glass column-shaped display case held rotating shelves of large fluffy pies. Dad said I hardly touched my tuna melt but I could still have dessert since it was a special occasion, since it was Easter. Franny was sipping Coke and didn't want any pie. Dad had apple and Cat and I ordered strawberry. It turned out that the pies looked much better than they tasted: the strawberries were bitter and covered with a thick, sticky, sweet jam; the white fluff wasn't even whipped cream but something chalky and musty tasting. After lunch, Cat had to go to the bathroom and so did I but Franny said she needed to lie down and Dad hurried her back to the car.

When we had been driving about twenty minutes, Franny said, "Can we stop?"

Dad groaned—"You should've gone at lunch"—but he took the next exit and we pulled into a BP station. We parked next to a pump and Dad said, "Fill 'er up" to the boy who came to the car window. The boy was wearing a blue uniform with *Ron* written in green on the breast. On the other side of the pump was an old Negro man stretching next to his sedan. Inside the sedan was a big kid who was not a Negro. The kid had huge, pale eyes and he was talking to no one and looking out the window at us. The kid was maybe sixteen years old. He made me think of Perry Cohen. I opened the car door for Franny.

"Want me to take you?" Cat said.

"No, I can take my own self," Franny said, climbing down from the car.

"You have to ask the man for the key," I called to her as she ran toward the glassed-in office clutching Mookie, never even seeing the kid in the car on the other side of the pump as she hurried by. But Cat and I stared at him.

The kid's head seemed to be touching the ceiling of the car and he looked fat, his face a huge bowl of bread dough with those big pale fish eyes that followed Franny as she ran by. You could see the whole of the colored part of his eyes, they were that huge, like something behind the boy's eyeballs was pushing them out of his head.

Cat hit me hard with her elbow and said, "Don't stare," but we both did.

When the Negro man wandered into the body shop for a look at something, Fish Eyes got out of the car and walked toward the office. He was wearing a blue T-shirt and his shoulders were rounded as if he were carrying a great weight on his back.

Franny was in the bathroom. Dad was trying to tune in the radio while the gas pumper named Ron washed the windows and checked the oil. Then he came up to Dad's window with a small clipboard and a pen. Dad signed the little form on the clipboard, took a sheet and his card from Ron in exchange for the pen, and went back to the radio.

In the office, a man was bent over, leaning into his hip, writing on a counter. I hit Cat's arm and she told me again not to stare. As Franny came running around the side of the building toward the office, the fish-eyed kid began moving up on the man, who was still writing. Franny was skipping past the tire display when the kid grabbed the man from behind and began squeezing the man's neck in the crotch of his right arm, lifting the man off the ground and wheeling him around. The man started making a loud ratchety sound and grabbed at his throat, at the kid's arm across his throat, with both hands. The man's eyes were huge, too, and his face looked sunburned. The kid was shaking and his fish eyes grew even larger and his face was shiny. He began to edge the man through the door when Cat yelled, "Run, Franny!" and Franny crashed right into the man. The kid took a step back, still gripping the man, and he stared at Franny, and Franny stood staring at him. It seemed everything stopped here for a moment.

Then the Negro man was screaming, "Phil! Phil! No!" and Ron, who had pumped our gas, was already in the office, trying to get Phil off the man. The Negro man got his arm around Phil's neck and Ron helped him wrestle Phil to the floor of the office. Dad was out of the car, running toward Franny. He picked her up and ran back to the car.

"Let's go," he said, putting Franny next to Cat on the front seat.

"But Mookie," Franny said. "I forgot Mookie."

Dad didn't say anything as he turned the wheel and we sped out of the gas station.

Franny started to cry. "*Mookie!* We have to get Mookie, Daddy! We have to go back!"

My father didn't look at her.

Cat put her arms around Franny and whispered softly to her. Franny was crying and Cat rocked her and stroked her hair and whispered, "Hush, hush," like the old lady in *Goodnight Moon.*

"But *Mookie*! I want my Mookie back!"

Cat whispered, "I know, I know. Now, shush."

When Franny hollered, "Daddy, I need my Mookie dog!" my father yelled, "Enough, Franny!" Then with his jaw clenched, he added, "Not another word out of you."

The rest of the trip to Castle Bay, we were all very quiet. Eventually, Franny crawled into the backseat with me and lay down. From time to time, she would start sniffling and moan, "Mookie." But mostly, she slept. Dad turned on a classical station and kept looking in the rearview mirror.

"I smell the ocean," Cat said suddenly, and rolled down her window to let in the salty air. "We must be there."

"We're here," Dad said.

We passed large concrete buildings with flat scrubby lawns

and bright billboards on their roofs before we pulled up to the Marina Casino.

I shook Franny gently. "We're here."

The entranceway made it feel like we were going to the theater: there were lots of light bulbs and mirrors and glass doors with shiny handles.

I helped Franny out of the car and she rubbed her eyes and began sobbing. "Mookie! I want Mookie!"

I whispered to her, "You can't talk about Mookie now. We'll figure something out later. Okay?"

Franny nodded but her mouth stayed small and pinched.

Cat came around from the other side of the car and stretched her arms and said, "Can we eat?"

Dad said, "Soon, Kitty," and nodded to a man in a maroon outfit who then slid our luggage onto a silver cart and rolled it into the hotel. Our suitcases looked so strange there—Dad's was blue-and-green plaid like a kilt with dark leather trim, and the one Cat and Franny and I were using was purple with hot-pink flowers and neither of them looked like they belonged there, on that shiny, modern cart in this casino-hotel.

A man older than my father wearing the same maroon costume took the keys from Dad and drove away in the Impala and it felt like we would never see it again and we would be stuck here forever in Castle Bay. Loud music was pumped into the entranceway and it grew louder as we approached the lobby, passing people wearing glamorous clothes—suits and ties, high heels and silky dresses, black and white and shiny gold; some people were laughing, some were just talking.

Cat and I held Franny's hands and followed Dad through the lobby up to a tall counter with maroon carpet up the front. Being inside the hotel was like being inside of a big jewelry box—the bright lights and silver rails, shiny mirrors and glass doors made the whole place sparkle. To our left, little bells and sirens were going off and bright lights were flashing. That was the casino. You could see the slot machines from the lobby; you could hear laughter, cheers, and the sound of flowing coins. People were carrying white buckets filled with quarters or nickels. They were dressed up. They were drinking drinks. We weren't allowed in there.

The first few times we came here, I begged Dad to bring us into the casino with him, but he would always say *no* and I would always end up crying. Then one time he hit me and I never asked again after that.

We had to wait around while Dad signed some papers and got the key. Cat tried to keep Franny from thinking about Mookie—she taught Franny a hand clapping game and then told the story about the ghost with the bloody finger—but still, every few minutes, Franny's face would wrinkle up and turn red and tears would start slipping down her cheeks.

Finally Dad said, "Come on, girls," and we all followed a guy in a maroon costume to a glass elevator that took us to the top of an atrium. You could see all the way down to a fountain, shooting water up at the base of the atrium. Shiny chrome railings circled the atrium on each floor. Franny looked down from the elevator and started to whimper.

"Just don't look," Cat said, and Franny closed her eyes.

To get to our suite, we had to walk around the perimeter of the atrium. Franny stayed near the wall, holding Cat's hand, and she kept straining to look toward the atrium, even though it scared her so much. Dad walked ahead with the guy in the maroon costume who brought us to number 1211.

Our suite had two rooms: a living room with a pull-out sofa bed, where Cat and I would sleep, and a bedroom with a king-size bed for Dad and Franny. The living room had a sitting area with a round table under a chandelier and some stuffed chairs. There was a desk, a straight-backed chair, a color TV, a radio, a telephone, and a little refrigerator packed with tiny bottles of liquor, cans of soda and beer, chocolates and crackers and nuts. The bathroom was all mirrors except for the ceiling and it had a telephone, too. In the bedroom was another TV and another telephone. Behind the bed was a wall of mirrors; facing the bed were built-in closets, panelled with mirrors. And the whole place had plush maroon carpeting that made you feel you were dragging your feet.

The guy in the costume told us our luggage would be up in fifteen minutes and he asked if there was anything else he could do for us. Dad said, "No, thanks," and handed the guy a bill. Cat went for the fridge.

"Can I have some of this?" she asked, holding up a cylinder of chocolate.

"Why don't we go down to the restaurant and have a snack?" Dad said. "Then everybody can have what they want."

The hotel had a bar and three restaurants—one was darkly lit and fancy-looking, one was a steak house, and one was a deli. We went into the bar, since Dad could have a drink there, if he wanted, and we could have Shirley Temples and peanuts and Goldfish. We were all still dressed in our Easter clothes and people watched us walk in and sit down at a booth. Stained glass lamp shades hung down over each booth and old colored signs hung on the walls. A woman in a short green velvet skirt with many petticoats and a ruffly white top asked us what we would like. Dad ordered a special kind of vodka, on the rocks, with lime. Cat said she would take a 7UP, so Franny and I did, too.

"I wonder what movies are on," Cat said, poking at the peanuts.

"I wish I had my Mookie still." Franny began crying.

Cat said, "Hey, I know—we'll stop and get him on the way home, okay?"

"He won't still be there," Franny said.

"Sure, he will," Cat said. "Of course, he will. That's it. We'll just stop and get him on the way home."

Franny looked at Dad. "Can we?"

"Sure," he said, all easygoing and cheerful. "You bet!"

Finally, Franny smiled. "Oh, my Mookie!" and I couldn't understand why we hadn't thought of it sooner.

The waitress brought our drinks on a big round tray and she set them at our places at the table. Cat's and Franny's and mine each had two maraschino cherries skewered with small plastic swords. Dad gave her a twenty dollar bill and told her to keep the change and winked.

"What about food?" Cat said.

"Here're all these yummy peanuts and crackers." Dad slid the bowl of crackers toward Cat. "And if you're still hungry later, you can order room service."

"I have to go to the bathroom," Franny said.

"I'll take her." Cat got up and held Franny's hand and they left the bar.

Dad didn't say anything. He looked down at his drink, then off across the room as he lifted the glass to his mouth. I stared at a Hires root beer sign on the wall by our booth. It was shaped like a bottle, with a thermometer running down the middle of it. I wished I owned that sign. I imagined the lady in green velvet watching me stare at the sign, then coming up to me and saying, "Honey, you really like that sign, don't you? Why don't you take it? It's yours." People were sitting on stools at the bar—a woman in a shiny silver pants suit was talking with a bald man wearing a red tie; a dark man wearing a gold chain around his neck sat alone; and three women Mom's age were leaning together, smoking, talking loudly. I wondered where my mother was and what she was doing. I tried to imagine her thinking of us, missing us, but I couldn't. I couldn't imagine my mother at all. When I tried to picture her face, all I could see was my mother's stuff by the bus stop at the top of the driveway. When I tried to hear her voice, I could only hear my father's: "You'll *get* it back." That's what he'd said to her on the phone this morning. He'd said it twice.

"How much did you bring, Dad?" I said.

"How much?"

"How much money."

"None of your business."

"Sorry."

He said, "No, honey, I'm sorry," and he reached across the

booth for my hand. "I'm just a little tired is all. But, hey! Look, we're here to have fun. That's what this place is about, that's the whole idea in coming here—to have a good time, okay?"

The waitress returned and asked if she could get anything else and Dad smiled and said he'd like a refill and winked at her again.

Just then, Franny came running up to Dad's side of the booth, Cat following behind.

"Daddy, they have a gift shop," Franny said. "They have these stuffed animals—a really cute giraffe, a black bear, and there was this little lion in a pink dress with a hat on. Can I get one, Daddy?"

"Sure," Dad said. "Why not? It's Easter. Everyone can get a present."

Dad took a fifty-dollar bill from his wallet and gave it to Cat. "You make sure everyone gets what they want," he said, and handed her the bill. "You too, Trisha. Go ahead now. You all go get yourselves a present. From me."

Franny was the only one who wanted anything. She took a while comparing and squeezing different animals.

"Move it, Franny," Cat said, and Franny picked a fluffy, light brown kangaroo with a removable baby in the pocket.

"I'm going to call him *Chester*," Franny said. "He'll be my friend till Mookie gets back."

"It's a *girl*," I said.

"I don't care," Franny said.

After we finished our drinks, Dad brought us back up to our suite. Cat turned on the TV and flopped onto the sofa. Franny sat at her feet, holding the kangaroo and sucking her thumb, tracing circles around the tip of her nose with the knuckle of her index finger. Dad removed the envelopes from his jacket pocket. He put the one marked *Careful* in the outer flap of his overnight bag.

"Kitty, I want you to take this envelope and hide it for me." He was holding the envelope out to Cat. It was the one that said *Are You Sure?*

Cat said, "You want me to hide it?"

"Look, I've changed my mind. I don't want to touch this money. I don't even want to know where it is. So please, honey, hide it somewhere and promise you won't tell me where it is."

"Even if you ask me?" Cat was staring at the envelope in his outstretched hand.

"Absolutely," Dad said. "You've got to hide it and promise me that, no matter what, you won't give it to me."

Cat said, "Okay, I promise," and took the envelope.

"Now, girls. It's three-thirty. I'm going down to do a little gambling. If you need me, I'll be at the blackjack tables. You can have me paged there. I'll be back around dinnertime, but if I'm not here by six, go ahead and order room service. Be good and have fun." Then he kissed each of us and left.

"Where're you going to hide it?" I said to Cat.

"I don't know." Cat began looking around.

Franny clapped her hands. "Hide it under the bed."

"Don't be stupid," Cat said.

"Hide it in your purse," I said.

"That'd be the first place he'd look."

"How much is it?" I asked.

"I'm not going to open it." Cat raised the envelope to the light. "You can't see through the paper."

"Hide it in your suitcase," Franny said.

Cat ducked into the bathroom and came out with a Kleenex box.

"I could put it in here." She removed a wad of tissues from the box.

"Yeah!" Franny tossed her kangaroo in the air.

"Or, wait a minute. Give me that thing," she said, grabbing the kangaroo from where it landed on the carpet.

"No!" Franny stomped her feet. "He's mine."

"I could put it in here." Cat pulled the baby from the kangaroo's pouch and slid the envelope in in its place.

Franny grabbed the baby from the floor and began trying to shove it in the pocket, too. "What about the baby?"

"Who cares?" Cat said. "It's perfect. Do you mind, Franny?"

"Yes!" Franny hollered, and stamped her feet again.

"Aw, please, Franny. You can keep the baby safe in your own pocket. Please?" Cat had her arm around Franny's shoulders.

"I guess so," Franny said, and began rubbing the baby against her cheek.

"Nobody tell," Cat said.

"Of course not," I said.

"Franny, this is a secret," Cat whispered.

"I'm not gonna *tell*," Franny whispered back, still rubbing the baby kangaroo against her cheek.

Then we all settled on the sofa and watched a Western about a gunslinger who rides into town one day, shoots three men, kisses a woman, then gets hired by the town to protect them from some outlaws.

"He's cute," Cat said.

Franny made a gagging sound. "He's *gross.*"

"Let's watch in the bedroom," I said.

Cat flipped on the TV and we all climbed onto the bed. Cat lay down on her stomach. "Let's play Walk on People," she said.

Franny and I got in line at her feet. Franny went first, stepping carefully on Cat's calves, shifting her weight from foot to foot as she moved up Cat's thighs, to her bum, onto her back. Cat was grunting and laughing a little, watching Franny walk up her in the mirrors on the closets. Cat laughed and grunted even louder as I walked along her body. I got to be next. It felt good to have Franny stepping on my legs and back; it almost tickled. Cat was much heavier and I felt the breath leave me when she stepped onto my back. I had my eye on her in the closet mirrors and I screamed when I saw her jump up above my back, only to come down with her feet straddling my body, laughing. We never put our full weight on Franny— she was too little—but we pushed down a bit with one foot up the length of her body. She liked it, too.

Just as we were settling down to watch the end of the Western, there was a knock at the door and Cat answered it. It was Dad.

"Well, it's not exactly a big winning day for Dad." Dad took the second envelope from his overnight bag. "Yet," he said, and smiled and winked. He ripped open the envelope and put the cash inside his wallet. Then he folded the wallet shut and returned it to his inside jacket pocket.

"Dad, maybe we should go home," Cat said. "Maybe it's not a good day for gambling."

"My luck's about to change." Dad winked again. "I can feel it," he added, and he hurried out of the room. I looked at Cat, who shrugged her shoulders.

I began to flip the channels, looking for something else to watch. The TV in Castle Bay had weird channels we didn't get at home, like channel 3 and channel 6. On channel 47 a movie called *Gidget Goes Hawaiian* was just starting. Franny and I lay on our stomachs watching it.

"Want some of this?" Cat said, holding up a chocolate bar from the fridge. "Or want some Easter candy?" Cat had emptied our baskets into a paper bag and brought it with us.

"Yeah!" Franny said. Cat peeled the wrapper off the bar and handed it to Franny. Then we all lay back down on the bed.

"Who's that?" Franny said.

"Moondoggie," Cat said.

Franny wrinkled her nose. "Who's Moondoggie?"

"Just watch," Cat said.

Before the movie was through, just when Cat had said we should order some dinner, Dad knocked on the door again. Cat let him in.

"I've just got to make some quick calls," he said, and went for the phone.

"I wanna take a bath," Franny said, and Cat said, "Okay." Cat went into the bathroom, turned on the water, came back out, and stared at Dad.

"Yes, I'll hold," he said into the phone. He looked around the room, then said, "Hello. I was wondering about getting some cash here." Then Dad read some long number from a green credit card.

Franny jumped onto his lap and Dad looked annoyed, but let her stay.

"Fine, fine," he said. "Castle Bay." He dug a pen and an empty envelope from his inside jacket pocket. "Great," he said, scribbling something on the envelope. "Thank you," he said, then, "Pardon me? Oh. Yes. Happy Easter to you."

Dad hung up the phone, shoved the envelope back into his pocket. "I have to go downtown for a little while. Then I'll be at the blackjack tables if you need me. I love you all."

He looked at us and I felt like he was a stranger. Then he kissed Franny, set her on the floor, then kissed Cat, then me, but somehow it was like he didn't really see us and he didn't really kiss us. Some of his liquor smell remained after he left the room.

I felt nervous and I could tell Cat did, too. She went into the bathroom, turned off the water, and said, "Okay, Franny. Come on."

I helped Franny out of her dress and tights. Cat said, "Franny! Come on!" and Franny ran to the bathroom in her undershirt and panties. Meanwhile, Gidget was trying to surf with some blonde guy who wasn't Moondoggie.

After her bath, Cat put Franny in some play clothes and Franny lay back down on the bed. Cat switched the channels, stopping at a black-and-white film with a woman singing in front of an open window. It was pouring outside the window and the woman stood there singing, not even looking out.

Franny said, "Can't we watch *Davey and Goliath?*"

"Aren't you guys hungry?" Cat said. "Let's order room service."

Cat got the gold-and-crimson folder from on top of the TV in the living room and spread it open on the bed.

Franny said, "Do they have jumbo shrimp cocktail?" and Cat put a little pencil check next to it on the menu.

"What about this?" I said, pointing to a shaded part of the menu called *Side Orders.*

"Excellent," Cat said, and she put checks next to the french fries and the onion rings. Then she said, "How 'bout three cheeseburgers?" and marked three Xs next to *Deluxe Cheeseburger Platter* on the menu. "What about dessert?"

"Sherbert!" Franny said.

"It's *sherbet*," I said.

"They have raspberry, orange, and lime," Cat said. "Which do you want?"

Franny said, "Uuuum" and I put my finger right on the menu: "Chocolate mousse!"

"Yes!" Cat said.

"Raspberry!" Franny began bouncing up and down.

Cat circled the chocolate mousse and the raspberry sherbet. She put Xs next to the Dutch apple pie and the chocolate cake. Then Cat dialed the phone and placed our order.

"Hello," she said. "Yes, this is suite twelve-eleven and we'd very much like some room service." Cat listed the food, adding grown-up phrases like "If you please" and "Perhaps we'll try" and "Could you recommend."

Franny fell asleep between Cat and me and we watched the movie until there was a knock at the door.

"Room service," the guy said to Cat, when she opened the door.

"Please enter," she said, and stepped back so the guy could roll the cart into the living room.

The guy was a teenager and, like all the other men working here, he wore a maroon costume. He smiled awkwardly at Cat and then lifted little silver bowls off the plates and showed us our food.

"Is that it, then?" he said.

"Is what it?" Cat said.

"Do you want anything else?"

"No, thank you," Cat said, and she signed the check.

The guy blushed and bowed a little, from the waist, as he left.

Cat and I began munching on the fries in the living room.

"What about Franny?" I said.

"Let her sleep," Cat said, getting up to turn on the TV.

We watched the end of the Gidget movie, eating most of the french fries, some onion rings, the chocolate mousse, and the Dutch apple pie.

"I wonder what makes this *Dutch*," Cat said, taking the last forkful of pie.

Just then, someone knocked at the door and Cat answered it. It was Dad. His hair was standing up, this way and that, as if he had just messed it with both hands. The top button of his shirt was undone and the knot of his tie hung low. His suit was wrinkled and there was a shine on his face. He reeked of liquor.

"Cat," he said. "Give me the money."

"Hi, Dad," Cat said. "Want something to eat? We just got room service."

"Listen, I need that money now. That third envelope."

"No way."

"Look, this isn't a joke. I've changed my mind. I want the envelope. I'm serious." Dad had moved close to her and he was looking at her with huge eyes but it was like he wasn't seeing her.

"No, Dad. *I'm* serious. You made me promise."

"Listen to me." Dad spoke louder now, moving closer. "I need that money." He smiled awkwardly.

Cat began backing up toward the bedroom. "Sorry."

"Where's the envelope, Cat?"

"I'm not telling."

"This isn't a game. I'm not fooling around." Dad lunged forward and grabbed Cat by the shoulders. "Where is it?"

"No, Dad," Cat said. "You made me *promise*. I can't tell you where it is."

"Give me the money!" Dad yelled it.

"But what about the promise? You made me promise and I promised." Cat was yelling now, too.

"Where's the envelope?"

Dad was gritting his teeth. He looked like he might bite her. I wanted to yell at him to stop. And I did—I yelled, "Dad! She *promised*."

Dad shook Cat and said again, "Where's the goddamn envelope?"

Cat didn't say anything and Dad let her go. He ran into the bedroom and went for her suitcase. He unzipped it and turned it upside down, spilling everything onto the floor. Dad fell to his knees and sifted through the clothes and teen magazines; then he searched the inner and outer pockets. Cat and I were watching from the doorway. We were watching to make sure Franny was safe.

"Goddamn it, Kitty, where *is* it?" He picked up the paper bag with all the Easter candy in it and emptied it on the bed. Some of it fell on top of Franny, who was still sleeping and didn't move.

Dad rushed past us into the living room, grabbed Cat's purse from the desk, and began rooting through it. Cat hurried over to the sofa and picked up Franny's kangaroo.

She tried to do it casually, but Dad looked up and said, "What've you got there?"

"Dad," Cat said, holding the toy to one side.

Dad tossed her purse onto the floor and began moving toward her, his arm outstretched, his hand open. "Give it to me, Cat."

"No, Dad." Cat drew her arm behind her back. "You made me promise. I promised."

A look came over Dad's face, like all the muscles in his face and neck had suddenly gone soft and then, calmly, he said, "You know, you're right, Kitty. I *did* make you promise," and he smiled a thin little smile. Cat didn't smile back but she didn't move as he came closer, smiling that odd smile, and she didn't move when he lunged forward and wrapped his arms around her and tried to grab for the kangaroo.

I began to hit Dad's arm. I hollered: *"No, Dad! No!"*

"Now, Cat," Dad said, batting at me, still going for the kangaroo. Cat wriggled out of his arms and ran for the door. Dad stumbled and Cat looked back at him. She had her hand on the knob when he regained himself.

Cat opened the door. She kept her eyes on him.

"Dad, *no*," Cat said. "You made me promise," she said. Then she ran out of the room. Dad followed her and I ran after them.

Cat was on the other side of the atrium, clutching the kangaroo, clinging to the railing, and Dad was edging toward her, one hand opened to her, saying, "Come on, Cat. Hand it over," in a singsong voice as if he were trying to be calm, but his voice was strained and trembling. I could see he was trembling all over, down to the fingers of his outstretched hand.

Cat was squeezing the kangaroo around the neck, backing up, saying, "No, Dad. I *promised.*" She was starting to cry. She was still in her Easter clothes, her navy dress and white knee socks, and suddenly she looked so young with her long blond hair and wide, open face wet with tears as she shook her head back and forth saying, "I promised you, Daddy."

I screamed, *"Leave her alone!"* and then Dad made a run for her.

Cat shimmied backward, but the floor was polished and slick and she fell on her stomach onto the tiles. Her legs were hanging over the edge into the atrium.

Cat screamed, *"Daddy!"* and I yelled, *"No!"* She was still holding the kangaroo. Her legs were kicking in the air behind her. She tried to scramble back onto the floor as Dad reached out. Then she was gone.

Dad was squatting by the edge of the atrium. His eyes were opened wide. His mouth was open and his face was shiny and grey. A clear bead sat at his temple. I watched it slide down the side of his face. He didn't move.

I ran to the railing and held on. The metal was cold and slippery in my hands. I felt something would grab my ankles and pull me down into the atrium. I squeezed the railing. There was a loud buzzing sound. I looked down and saw Cat, in the fountain at the bottom of the atrium, still holding the toy. People were running toward the fountain. The water splashing in the fountain didn't make any noise. Apart from that buzzing sound, there wasn't any sound at all. Cat wasn't moving. I might pull myself over the top of the railing and dive in after her. A man stepped into the fountain, took her in his arms and lifted her. I wanted to yell at him to leave Cat alone. But my voice was gone.

Then there was a crowd of people. There were men in blue uniforms with gold badges. Dad was talking to them. We were in the hotel suite. Franny and I were sitting on the couch with a lady with grey hair. Franny was crying and the lady was saying nice things to her in a soft voice, calling her *honey.*

"Something something accident," the men said.

Dad said something, too.

"Are you sure?" they asked.

Dad said yes. He said some numbers.

"Simply a question of liability," one of the men said.

Then Dad came over and had his arms around me.

I made myself small and hard and thin. I made myself a cold, sharp wire. I pulled my whole self in, inside my hard, cold, inside self. No matter what happened to me again in my life, my father would never be able to reach me. Flesh and muscle and bone would come between us, making him soft and far away, making me hardly here at all.

ChapterEleven

Down to the Dust

"What happened?" they asked.

Franny said she didn't know. She had been sleeping. She hadn't been there.

They asked me, What happened? What did I see? but I couldn't say. They understood, they said. They'd talk with me later.

My mother came down to Castle Bay late that night or early the next morning. She wept and got us food. Her eyes were bloodshot and her eyelids were pink and swollen. I was shocked to see the bruises on my mother's face, under her eye, on her jaw.

My mother tucked Franny in bed but I wouldn't go and she didn't try to make me. She rolled a comfy chair in front of the TV set and said, "Why don't you sit here, honey."

I climbed into the chair. Mom got a blanket from the closet and she wrapped it around me, hugging me with it. The blanket was pilly and itchy and it didn't smell like our things.

My mother drew back and looked into my face. "Everything's going to be okay," she whispered.

I looked at the marks on her cheek and her jaw and then I reached out to touch one. My mother took me in her arms again and squeezed me hard and kissed my hair and the side of my face. "Everything's okay," she whispered, but I could feel her crying, tremors through her body shaking mine, her tears on my face. Then she turned and pulled the button on the television set. Something took shape on the screen.

"You want to watch this?" she said.

"Sure, fine."

Mom nodded and smiled thinly then stood and moved toward my father on the other side of the room. He was on the phone talking softly. When he saw her approach he blinked rapidly and hung up. My mother looked at me and nodded again. "Watch your show now," she said, and turned to my father.

My parents spoke in hushed voices. They both wept, but not at the same time. It was as if they took turns, as if they each needed someone to comfort them so they could eventually stop crying. Otherwise, it seemed, if they cried together, they might cry forever.

Later the men came back and asked me again, "What happened?"

I knew if I told them, they would put my father in jail and never let him out. He was a dog person and everyone would be happy to see him caged.

We had been watching a movie. Cat had ordered room service for us. We had been eating french fries, onion rings, and chocolate mousse. We had poked our tongues through the holes in the onion rings, made them hang in front of our mouths, dangled the large ones from our wrists like bracelets.

Franny was asleep.

There was a knock on the door and Cat opened it. Dad was standing there looking like he just woke up. There were bags under his eyes. His face was shiny. The knot of his tie hung low. He made the whole room smell like liquor.

Cat grabbed the kangaroo and ran into the hall and Dad ran after her.

Cat wouldn't give him the kangaroo.

She had promised.

He had made her promise.

We had been hit before for telling lies or breaking promises.

Cat fell onto her stomach. Her legs were hanging into the atrium.

Dad ran toward her.

Cat's arms were stretched out on the tiles. The palm of her left hand was pressed on the floor and she was flexing her fingers, like she was trying to get some traction. In her right hand, she held the kangaroo by the neck. As she began to slip, Dad reached out for her. He reached for her hand with the toy.

He reached out, but not for her hand.

He reached out to grab the toy.

And then she was gone.

This was what happened.

And when the men asked me again, this was what I told them.

"It was instinct," Dad would tell me later, when we were alone. "Pure instinct," he'd add, but his face would be saying something else.

This was all he'd ever tell me. This was all he'd ever say to me about Cat's death.

The men looked at me but they did not write down what I said.

When they left, they did not take my father with them.

My father never went to jail, not for a day.

Nobody ever asked me questions about Cat's death again.

Everybody cried. Everybody sent flowers and wreaths with black ribbons. Everybody said how sorry they were about the accident. It was just like when Gramma Hattie died two years before, except she was old and this was Cat.

It was late April 1966, a Sunday, and Gramma Hattie was spending the afternoon. After dinner, Mom had gone out to pick up Cat from Lisa Cutler's house, and Franny and I were watching a movie in the family room. Gramma Hattie had stomach cancer. She was very weak and she wanted to take a nap. Right after my mother left, Gramma and Dad had had a big fight and I had tried to eavesdrop. My gramma didn't yell or even raise her voice but I could tell she was speaking very seriously. I heard her call my father a parasite. I heard her say he only knew how to *take*. My gramma said that maybe my mother didn't care how he treated her—there was nothing Gramma could do about that either way. Mom was a grown-up. But we were another matter. There were laws. The Child Welfare Department was not about to let him get away with beating his children. *Beating his children?* Had Dad beaten us? I tried to remember, but I could think of nothing like that, nothing at all extraordinary. Just spanking. No fists or whips or clubs. Just hairbrushes and belts and stuff. No real weapons. Kimmy and Dan Taylor's parents had a paddle that was just for spanking and it hung on the wall of the Taylor's family room, like a threat. I always felt sorry for Kimmy and Dan and glad that it wasn't us. But still, what they got was spanking. Beating, I imagined, made you like Billy Halliday with those black eyes and broken bones. We'd had bloody noses and bruises and cuts and Dad had even knocked out one of Cat's baby teeth but we had *never* had black eyes or broken bones.

My father was furious. He yelled swears at my gramma but she said she wasn't scared of him.

The back stairs were old and steep. Gramma Hattie pulled herself up them, grasping the railing hand over hand, like a mountain climber with a rope. She wore black shoes with laces and low heels, but still, one of the heels didn't make it onto a step. That's what Dad would say.

Franny and I heard the thud-thud-thudding down the stairs and we heard my father holler.

We ran to the back hall.

My father was at the top of the stairs. He was the only one who saw her fall. He was the first to holler, the first to call her *the body.*

"We mustn't touch the body before the police arrive."

Gramma Hattie's head was lying on her shoulder. Her eyes were open, bright blue and clear like a baby's. One of her arms was twisted behind her back. The other was at her side, bent at the elbow, like it might have been if she had been asleep. Her mouth was opened, like she was going to say something. But her head was touching her shoulder.

We all wore black then. And Reverend Pinkham told us Gramma Hattie was lucky. He said she was a good Christian woman and she was now in the hands of her maker. "Ashes to ashes, dust to dust," he said. My mother and father placed wreaths with black bows on Gramma Hattie's grave.

And now, we were back in Burying Point, wearing black again. Reverend Pinkham said some of the same things now that he had said at Gramma Hattie's funeral—about luck and being in heaven and "ashes to ashes, dust to dust."

My mother and father set wreaths with black bows on Cat's grave.

My mother collapsed in my father's arms, sobbing into his

shoulder. My father raised his face to the sky. His eyes were shiny, his mouth was open like he would scream but he was silent.

Everybody said how sorry they were about the accident.

Lots of kids from school were there, so many familiar name-less faces, so many children in dark colors.

Stuart Haskins came over to my parents carrying a bouquet of pink roses. He looked young and nervous and pitiful and out of place. His hair was combed smooth and he wore polished shoes and a dark suit made for a shorter, wider body. Stuart's face was shiny and pink and his eyes were bloodshot. When my father extended his hand to Stuart, Stuart didn't seem to know what to do with the flowers and he looked panicked. My mother reached for the bouquet and smiled and Stuart gasped for air and my father embraced him, patted his back, and gestured to Stuart's mother, who hurried over and walked Stuart back to his blue Rambler.

Our principal, Mr. Pearson, stood with our head custodian, Red Stultz, and our bus driver, Mrs. Lindall, and all the tenth-grade teachers. Some of the teachers had puffed eyes and swollen faces; some were weeping. You couldn't see Mrs. Lindall's face behind a short black veil but from time to time her shoulders shook and she plucked a hankie from her sleeve and slipped it up under the veil and made honking sounds. Mr. Pearson's hands were folded before his crotch making him look like an obedient child. His face was red and he looked dismal.

Of course, the Cohens were there and Perry embraced both my parents. He said how sad he was that Cat wouldn't be coming back. He said she was the prettiest girl he'd ever seen. Rachel Cohen kissed my father on the cheek, turned from my mother, and walked toward Lydia, who was standing at a remove, by herself under a birch tree. Mom's friend Janie came over and hugged my mother, then stood with her arm around my mother as if she were holding my mother up.

Mr. Nealy was there, of course, and so was the red-faced man. They wore dark suits and ties knotted at their throats. Mr. Nealy had to go home and change before he could cover Cat's coffin with dirt, so before everybody left, he was in his regular work clothes. While they were lowering the coffin into the earth, Mr. Nealy brought a handkerchief to his face, to his eyes, and he pinched the bridge of his nose with it. Then he shovelled dirt into Cat's grave. Later, Mr. Nealy and the red-faced man would speak with my parents, shake my parents' hands, and move off toward a sprawling old tree where Bob, the man from Reynold's Apothecary, was standing with Bettina Nealy, who wasn't half as huge now, here in Burying Point, as she had been all these years in my imagination. She wore plain black and her hair hung straight down, rich and thick and gleaming just as I'd remembered it. Her pale eyes were hidden behind dark glasses. Mr. Nealy leaned back against the tree and the red-faced man picked and scratched at the bark. Bob peeled the plastic wrap from a pack of cigarettes and they all smoked, Bettina Nealy, too. They shook their heads and kicked at the roots at the base of the tree and they all looked so sad.

Suki was there, too, of course, and she elbowed me in the side when Mr. Nealy's green truck first drove up the paved path toward the burial site, but we didn't say anything when he stumbled out of the truck or when the red-faced man appeared from around the other side. All the Domandis were there—Laura was wearing a plaid skirt and stockings. Mr. Domandi shook my parents' hands, said how sorry he was for their terrible loss, and Mrs. Domandi embraced my mother and wept.

There were so many people I didn't know at Burying Point that morning. They must have been parents of kids at school, Cat's friends' parents, the grown-ups we saw at the library or downtown at Buster's Market. Some of Mom's new friends were there—Tilly and Jack Masterson and some of the other people from the barbeque.

When everyone began to leave, Mom started sobbing, just weeping without even covering her face, just falling to her knees and weeping—her eyes squeezed shut, her mouth an open gash in her beautiful face, her whole body shaking. I wondered if for her, the funeral had been like a last bit of contact with Cat and now that it was over, so also was that contact and she felt she couldn't bear it. Dad squatted down next to her, put his arm around her and spoke to her softly. He dug a handkerchief from his pocket and offered it to her. My mother nodded and wiped at her face and dabbed at her eyes with it and then my father helped her to her feet. That day, all day, and for days to come, Mom and Dad would be gentle with each other like that—they would look after one another, speak softly and kindly to each other and be careful with each other's feelings. But they would be so unused to being this way together, so many years would have passed since it was natural and normal to them, that they would be uncomfortable together and therefore anxious to be apart.

While I was walking to the car, I turned and looked back toward Cat's grave and I noticed someone, Billy Halliday, sitting all alone at the foot of a tree, smoking a cigarette. He took a long pull off the cigarette, then flicked it into the air. I didn't see it come down. Then he stood and brushed the back of his jeans and reached down and picked up something off the ground and began walking with it toward Cat's grave. Flowers. A fistful of daffodils. Billy Halliday kneeled at Cat's grave, set the daffodils on top of all the other bouquets, and bowed his head. After a few moments, I heard him sigh. He raised his head and looked at the heap of flowers. Then Billy Halliday stood and walked away through the cemetery toward his house.

But Billy Halliday wouldn't go home that day, or any other day. None of his family would have seen him since they left for church that morning. Billy had stayed home alone and when the family returned from church, they would discover the house ransacked, Billy gone, things missing. It would turn out that I was the last person to see Billy Halliday and I would wonder if I'd been dreaming. At first, like everyone else, I'd think something bad must have happened to Billy. In the *Salem Evening News,* Manny Thompkins would be quoted as saying, "The child is missing, the place was robbed—of course, foul play is suspected." But Billy Halliday was no child and then I'd remember something: I'd remember Billy's saying, *One day, I'm getting on that train and I'm gonna take it far away from here. I'll get a donkey and mine for silver and have myself an adventure.* From then on, that's how I thought of Billy Halliday, smoking cigarettes, drinking liquor, riding around on that donkey, his pockets bulging with lumps of silver. And I'd think of him often, too, whenever I'd hear the train sound its whistle as it blasted through Salem into the night, into the rest of the world. I'd never worry about Billy Halliday and I'd hope to see him again in my life, but I never would.

        As Billy Halliday disappeared into Burying Point, I heard Franny wailing and I turned and saw Mom carrying her to the car, hurrying with her, kissing her hair. Reverend Pinkham was jogging along beside them, speaking to my mother. My father had run ahead to open the car door. For a brief moment, I saw myself following Billy Halliday up into the woods on the other side of Burying Point; we'd drink down all his stepfather's liquor and smoke all the cigarettes we could find and disappear into it all, putting clouds of smoke and liquor drinks between myself and all this sadness. Between myself and Cat's permanent absence.

    Mom hollered at me to get into the car. She was crying and nodding and thanking Reverend Pinkham. Dad was crying, too. He didn't make any noise like Mom and Franny, tears just slid down his cheeks.

    For an entire week it seemed my father cried—no noise, just tear after tear.

        After the funeral, I didn't want any time to pass— not like the poet says, not to honor her, though I wish that'd been what I felt. I didn't want time to pass because I didn't want Cat to slide further away from me. I didn't want time to come between her and me, making her more a memory than a person, making her less and less real. I would sit quietly by myself—no books, no television, no music, no people—which was the only way I could think of to hold onto her, to slow time down. I would sit alone in the living room in Samuel Wilde's rocker, finally understanding why he had done that, rocked alone in this room day after day, rocked himself to death here. Otherwise, if I were busy with things, time would rise up and cover Cat, pushing her deeper into the past and burying her there.

It seemed we never talked about Cat. Dad never mentioned what happened in Castle Bay except to tell me, that one time, in the kitchen, when no one else was there, "It was instinct, Trisha. Pure instinct." But while he spoke, he wasn't looking at me; he was glancing around the room, at this and that. And he would never say anything else to me about Cat's falling into the atrium.

About his letting Cat fall into the atrium.

My mother never said anything at all. When Franny mentioned Cat, she was either told to hush up or she was embraced and rocked which also silenced her.

The first few days after the funeral weren't like real days. Dad didn't go to his office. Mom didn't go to Old Stuff. Franny didn't go to Mrs. Wyman's kindergarten and I didn't go to school. We weren't used to all being home together at the same time and we weren't used to each other, or the world, without Cat. We were all careful with one another—none of us knew the rules now. Everything was fragile. Everything was outside of our control. We all wandered around the house silently. People we didn't know brought food for us in casserole dishes and lidded kettles but I didn't understand why since Mom was a fine cook. Why did her daughter's dying mean she couldn't cook? She wasn't going to work—what else was she supposed to do with her time now? These were the things Mom said to my father as she kept busy in the kitchen and fed the neighbors' dinners to Misty, Maggie, and the chickens.

I listened for Cat, those early days. I sat and rocked in Samuel Wilde's chair and held onto time and listened for her—for her stereo, for her laugh, for her step on the back stairs or in the hall. Once, I thought I smelled her eau de toilette; once, I smelled her incense.

Everything in our house, in my life, felt foreign and unfamiliar, far away and not real. I kept thinking it felt like I was watching a movie and the movie would end and I would wake in Cat's bed with Cat next to me, breathing in my face and laughing. But every day, I woke in my bed alone and when I'd tiptoe into Cat's room, though I could feel her all around me, it would be empty.

One morning, three and a half weeks, twenty-four days, after Cat died, I rode my bike alone down to Burying Point. Mom and Dad were at work. Franny was at Mrs. Wyman's. As I had done all these days since Cat died, I refused to go to school and my parents didn't make me. The monument company had finished the headstone for Cat's grave—the owners had been friends of Gramma Hattie's and Grandpa Percy's and they'd made it in a special hurry—and Mom and Dad had come down to see it placed the day before. I'd had to stay home with Franny. They said it would be overwhelming, they said it would be too much for us. But when I looked at the stone now, planted in the earth in Burying Point, I saw that, really, it was too little.

Catherine Anne Dalton
Our Beloved Daughter
January 24, 1953–April 14, 1968

At the base of the stone, vases of flowers tied with dark ribbons leaned together in the early spring wind. Wilting bouquets lay next to dry wreaths propped on stands. Black bows rustled; petals drifted off into the breeze. Six pale, dry daffodils lay by themselves off to the side of the stone. I searched around and found a rock the size of a crab apple. I kneeled in front of the stone and I began to scrape the rock across it. I wanted to dig something in it, something that said how much I loved her. Nothing here said that. Nothing here said that Dad traded this girl for the money she'd hidden, that he'd traded her for the possibility that he would win enough money to buy back land that had never been his to begin with. Just ten acres of land.

What was funny was that, really, we were the ones who owned that land, Cat and I—we walked and ran and rode bikes and horses all over it. We climbed the trees and made forts and found secret safe places. We knew which hills, which trees, gave the best view of the firehouse, Devil's Rocks, downtown. In this town, we knew the shortest distance between two points. We knew all the frog ponds and marshes and wading pools hidden deep in the woods. We knew the contours of the land. And we knew what everyone else did on it: we knew exactly where Mr. Perkins hid his liquor bottles so his wife wouldn't find them; we knew where the teenagers drank beer and smoked cigarettes, where the boys fondled *Playboy*s, where couples made out. We spent our life on that land. We knew it from the inside. We loved the land and we valued it more than anything, more than toys or books or even the ocean. But without us, the land was just empty space for grown-ups to claim and cut up and sell.

I stretched my arms around the sides of the stone but it was wide and hard and cold. I kissed the stone, kissed her name.

It was May, now, and Cat was to be in a horse show at the end of the month. She had a new hard hat and a new shirt still wrapped in plastic. Her room was exactly as she had left it. Her curtains were still closed. Her white gym socks were still balled up and stuffed inside her sneakers. A pair of her chino pants were still draped over the back of her chair. Her riding boots still stood by the door to her closet, matte with dust now. Cat's Lippizaner horse calendar was still opened to APRIL.

Every day, these days, I crept into Cat's room and looked around to see if anything had changed from the day before—if the month on her calendar said MAY, if there was an impression in the pillow on her bed, if the dictionary she'd left open on her desk had been flipped to a new place in the alphabet. But nothing was ever different. Everything was frozen now. Everything was the same now, for Cat.

It was May already, time was slipping by, and Cat was disappearing. I couldn't remember her voice or her laugh or how she smelled. Things were going on without her. Flowers were blooming; grass needed to be mowed again; summer was coming; but her calendar still said APRIL. Her clothes—the pants over the back of her chair, her sneakers and socks, her riding boots—still needed to be put away. The silver bracelets she'd set on her bureau were now dark with tarnish. The air in her room was musty and a layer of dust had settled over everything.

"Come back," I whispered, and my eyes were hot and the writing on the stone melted into a blur.

When I coasted down the driveway, the station wagon and the sedan were still gone. It was only eleven-thirty.

I bolted up to Cat's room; inside, nothing had been touched. I unzipped my jacket and carefully removed the daffodils from inside. The stems were all bent and mangled, so I snipped off the flowers and set them on Cat's bureau. I grabbed the pants draped over the back of her chair and I folded them carefully, then put them on the shelf in her closet where they belonged. I pulled the socks from her sneakers, tossed them into the hall and set the sneakers on the floor of her closet. I picked up her riding boots, brushed them off, and moved them to the back of her closet where she would have set them by now. I looked at the Webster's dictionary lying on her desk, opened to the Ts. I shut it, and stood it at the end of the row of books on her desk where she kept it. I grabbed the book on her night table splayed open, spine up; it was an old leather book, a volume of poetry, green with gold letters. Cat had set it there in haste. She never would have left it like that this long. I shut the book and wiped the dust from it and slipped it into my jacket pocket. Then I dusted her entire room—her window sills and her desk and her bureau and all her little things. I opened her curtains. I flipped her calendar to MAY. As I left Cat's room, I didn't pull the door closed behind me.

In my room, I took the silk flowers from the vase on my bureau and reached inside for the pack of cigarettes I had swiped from Mom. I glanced up at my wall and saw the horseshoe above my bed. Upside down. The wrong way. Cat had told me to fix it—it had to hang like a U—but I'd forgotten. And now all the luck had run out.

Downstairs, in the living room, I dragged the rocking chair across the floor to the window and pointed it northward, toward Gallows Hill. I lit a cigarette and inhaled the smoke. I didn't cough. I smoked the cigarette and began to rock, staring out the window at the trees. I tried not to think about anything and for three cigarettes, I didn't, I just stared and smoked and let my head be filled with smoke and trees. Then suddenly, I saw an image of my father with that rock from the bus stop, I saw him carrying it, wild-eyed and grunting, with his arms straight and strained, and it wasn't like a memory at all, it was like he was before me now, like it was real and really happening *now*. I crushed out the cigarette and ran out the back door.

I looked around but no one was there. It was cooler now and the sun was beginning to sink behind the woods. I took off down the hill and ran straight through the meadow and up into the woods, up the path toward Green Pastures. But when I reached it, I didn't stop there, I ran right past and kept going up deeper into the woods. I felt sure that as long as I was moving I would be safe. I ran beyond where Cat and I had ever gone, beyond where the path ran out. I ran through woods for a long while until I came to an eskar. From its top, I saw Prospect Street. I scrambled down into a little glen of trees and leaves and fallen limbs and then up the other side all the way to the hill.

Grabbing tree limbs and roots, I climbed and pulled myself up, scrambling and slipping a little on the leaves, until I reached the summit. Long ago, the hill and this land surrounding it had been cleared so it might serve its rightful purpose, so people and horses might scale it, so wagons carrying men and women and shovels and ropes might be pulled up to the top.

For a moment, I stood stock-still and looked around me at this old place, this old space. Maybe because it was only late afternoon and already the sun was setting, or maybe because this was such a desolate place—the grass the town had once tried to grow here had long ago been choked by thatch; the old trees were now crabbed and leafless, having been killed off by new, reckless underbrush and weeds—or maybe because this hill had somehow kept the horror of its history through the years, I felt myself filling up with a lonely, dark sadness.

Right here, on this very spot, early on the morning of August 19, 1692, my eight-greats-aunt Sara Wilde was hung by the neck till dead. For witchcraft, they said, though I felt sure it was for revenge.

From the gallows, Sara Wilde cleared her throat and spoke.

"Listen now, gentlefolk!" she said. Sara's hands were tied before her and she folded them in prayer then lifted them to her chest and said, again, "Listen now!"

The morning was clear and cool and Sara Wilde didn't tremble or cry but bowed her head and began reciting the Lord's Prayer. Grandma Hattie told me that had she stammered or stuttered or even coughed, the crowd would have known she was guilty—everybody knew that witches could not recite the Lord's Prayer without mistakes because they only said it at Witches' Sabbaths and then only backward.

The crowd was silent while Sara Wilde spoke and when she finished, people started yelling, "Cut her down!" and "Her innocence is clear!" until John Hathorne addressed them. He said that they should remember that God had revealed her guilt to his own housemaid and to a jury of townspeople and that they, good Christians, should not forget that the devil is often changed into an angel of light when his power is most threatened. And so the execution proceeded, and the eight people were hung. My many-greats-aunt Sara Wilde was hung. Right here on Gallows Hill. Gramma Hattie said it was the largest single execution of witches in the whole United States ever. My gramma said that afterward, Sara Wilde's clothes were stolen by the spectators—her friends, her neighbors—

and her naked body was dumped in a hole with the other people hung with her that morning. Her hand and a foot and someone's chin were left sticking out of the dirt when the diggers were through and everyone went home to eat. Right here where I was standing now. Her bones must be here beneath me now, I thought. Returning to the dust from which they came.

From up here now, I imagined smoke, many shades of gray, thick above the charred ruin of my house in the distance, fire trucks scattered around it, like toys forgotten on the lawn, trying to conjure a house, a family, from the ashes. In the other direction, on a hill not far from here, I could imagine the enormous red brick building, solid and austere, windows like eyes all fixed on me. The state hospital for troubled youth. Bad kids. Kids who smoked cigarettes and messed around in the graveyard. Kids who put spells on people and wished people dead. Kids who wanted to burn the house down.

I began to root in my pockets for cigarettes but I found the volume of poetry instead. The light was fading but when I opened the book, I could still read:

> The wrong of unshapely things is a wrong too great to be told;
> I hunger to build them anew and sit on a green knoll apart,
> With the earth and the sky and the water, re-made, like a casket of gold
> For my dreams of your image that blossoms a rose in the deeps of my heart.

And suddenly I saw it was true! I saw that somehow I had let all the blackness out of that thing inside me, that dark, evil murdering thing. Somehow it had loosened itself and uncoiled and bled itself out of me and now there was nothing there at all; nothing poisonous or deadly inside me to be me. When had it happened? I couldn't say but I could see that all that remained were thoughts and memories of Cat and they *were* blossoming a rose! A rose like I'd seen budding in my mother's lips. A rose sprung from an image of my sister who was the best of me and whom I could carry with me now, here, safe in the deeps of my heart.

That night, my father would sit with Franny and me and explain that he wasn't going to be married to Mom anymore and he would call her *your mother.* He was going to marry Rachel Cohen. Rachel Cohen was going to have his baby, who would be a sister or brother of ours. (The baby would turn out to be a girl and they would call her *Katherine* and everyone would call her *Katie.*) Dad would say that I would remain with Mom. Franny would go with him to the Cohens. He would tell us that this was what he and Mom had decided.

Dad would work on the Cohens' house now, redoing the floors and ceilings, the staircase and chimney, the gutters and the porch, repainting, reroofing, adding on two bedrooms, a laundry room, and a garden patio out back, *re-creating*—not *restoring,* there was no chance the Cohens' house had ever been so fine.

Four months later, my mother would send me away to boarding school—"handling" me would be too much for her, she would say. I would be sitting on the floor of my room, painting my toenails blue, chewing Bazooka, listening to *Sgt. Pepper,* when Mom would come in carrying her blue cup filled with gin and she would tell me that it was time for me to be off on my own.

"You'll learn Shakespeare and whatnot. It'll be fun. You'll like it." I would be thirteen years old then and my mother would call me Trouble. She'd say I needed some discipline. My mother would drink all the time now and by the end of the day, before passing out, she would be ranting about Dad and Rachel Cohen or weeping uncontrollably over Cat. Sometimes she'd dial the Cohens' number and yell and sputter swears into the receiver and hang up. Once, she wouldn't even hang up—she'd rip the cord from the wall and hurl the phone out her bedroom window. Lots of nights she'd sleep in the comfy chair in the kitchen or on the couch in the living room or wherever she happened to be when her body'd had enough.

Sometimes she'd sleep on Cat's bed and I'd hear her weeping until she passed out. I'd get a blanket and pull it over her and turn out all the lights.

In the morning, my mother would stagger into the kitchen and pour liquor into her blue cup. At first, she would send me from the room as if that would mean I wouldn't know she was drinking but soon she stopped caring if I saw. My mother didn't have drinks anymore; she had liquor. It wasn't measured; it was poured. Sometimes, it wasn't even poured into a glass, it just went directly from the bottle into my mother. Sometimes, she'd run into the bathroom first and throw up and then drink. Sometimes, she'd drink first, then throw up. Her skin would seem shiny and pale now and the lines on her face would have become creases. I would feel sad for my mother and I would think I understood why she drank so much: the only feelings my mother would seem to have left anymore would be anger and sorrow and they would seem to be eating her alive. At least the liquor made her numb. I would keep thinking that if I were only different, kinder, more cheerful, my mother would feel better and she wouldn't need to drink like that. Alone. All day. Soon, she would quit working at Old Stuff and she would avoid all her old new friends—Tilly and Janie and Jack Masterson—because they would tell her she had a drinking problem. That summer, the toilet in the powder room in the back hall would stop working and Mom would just close the door and tell me we weren't using it anymore. A shutter would be blown from the side of the house before I left for school and Mom would let it stay were it fell. Soon, she'd give away the chickens and begin making arrangements to sell Misty. Just after school started, she would write me a note telling me she'd had Maggie put to sleep.

I really don't think my mother sent me away because I was becoming Trouble; I don't think it had anything to do with what I was becoming. I think my mother sent me away because she didn't want me seeing what was happening to *her*.

Then it would be winter and I would be sitting on my bed alone in the dark in my dorm room at school, two hours away. I might be reading with a flashlight; I might just be sitting, thinking. My mother would have sold our house right after Thanksgiving and she would have already moved into a Cape Cod downtown. There wouldn't be much room, she would say, explaining why she threw out most of my things. What she saved, she would pack up in a liquor box and set aside for me in her attic. When I would call her collect, my mother would accept the charges and say "Uh-huh" as I'd tell her about school. Then she would tell me about the trouble my father was causing: for example, he wouldn't let her date anyone. Every time she would start seeing somebody, my father would find out and beat the guy up or slash his tires or threaten him in some other way and my mother would never hear from the guy again. She wouldn't be able to understand it—Dad had left *her*; he was remarried now; what did he care what she did? Before she would even really start, my mother would give up dating and, aside from drinking, she would come to focus all her attention on Bettina Nealy, of all people, someone more lonely and more needy than she herself. Suddenly, my mother would be talking about Bettina Nealy all the time, Bettina Nealy who was sick and housebound and whom my mother would be visiting every day. She would tell me about Bettina Nealy's medical conditions—she had a thousand of them, all ending with the letter *a:* edema, angina, asthma, glaucoma. My mother would be very lonely without her children or Dad or Gramma Hattie. Bettina Nealy needed someone and Mom would need someone to need her, so I guess they would be perfectly matched.

I would never go back to Salem to live. Suki and I would exchange letters until it was clear we'd left behind our common ground: Suki would be on the pep squad, chairing the junior prom committee, dating a nice boy on the chess team, but there wouldn't be any of that kind of high school for me. All these things we'd thought we'd share together—proms and parties and dates—Suki would have alone. At my school, there would be no proms; parties would be mainly in the afternoon, mainly with tea; and there would be nowhere to have dates, since we wouldn't be allowed to leave campus without a reason and going on a date wouldn't count. Those years, I would spend reading Shakespeare and Milton, writing thirty-page term papers, starting to learn about calculus, studying Gide and Hugo, alone in my room or in a remote carrel in the stacks on the fourth floor of the library. One day, I would receive a letter from Suki on pink floral stationery, sealed with a smiley face sticker, signed "I miss you so bad," and all her *i*'s would be dotted with hearts and I would cry and hold the letter to my lips and slip it in the back of my desk drawer. After that, I would never write her again. At night, I would dream about Cat.

I wouldn't see my father until my graduation and then, I would never see anybody so changed in so brief a time—in only four years, my father's hair would have turned completely white, his face would be soft and bloated, and he would walk with an old man's stoop. And I wouldn't be able to imagine that I'd ever been afraid of *him*. Franny would arrive with my father, holding his hand until she saw me waiting with my mother on the front lawn of my dorm and she would run to us, all long and lean and knobby-kneed, looking a lot like Cat. She would be hollering my name. Franny and I would laugh and jump around and I would give her a piggyback to my dorm. I would see her every holiday, but only briefly and it would never be enough, so that each time I saw Franny, it would feel like the first time I'd seen her since she left with Dad for the Co-hens' house. After my graduation that day, Franny would tell me how miserable she was. She would tell me how she hated Lydia and Perry and how Rachel Cohen had grown sour and yelled a lot, told everyone what to do and smacked Franny in the face now when Dad wasn't around. She would say Dad was drinking a lot. Most nights he would fall asleep with a book in his lap in a chair in the Cohens' living room. Franny would say she used to wake him, urge him to go up to his bed, until one night, Rachel Cohen would tell her to let him be, he deserved a stiff neck.

But this night, after I'd leave Gallows Hill, I would find my mother and father and Franny quietly sitting in the kitchen. This night, we would still be together; this night, we would still be a family. Franny would sleep in my bed this night and I would hold her, rock her, stroke her hair, and whisper, "It's okay, Franny," as she cried. My parents would sleep in the same room this night and when the house would finally be still, I would think that maybe it was possible, maybe it wasn't *impossible* that we would wake tomorrow morning and find my parents at the kitchen table, together, sipping coffee, sitting close, smiling.

As this day became night, the fire in my mind burned itself out and the sky became dark but clear and filled with stars, some bright and glittery, others so faint my eyes watered as I tried to pick them out, and I saw that the world was like that, filled with tiny bright points—people, places, events—a net of stars, each somehow connected to every other one. Infinitely many connections, impossible to trace.

Suddenly, I felt myself falling, nothing to catch me, nothing to stop me. I felt myself cut loose, launched, hurtling through space. I made myself a star, small from here, but radiant, burning. I would make my own path, be my own light. This was in my power and maybe this was all. I would burn it into the sky.